IVY SMOAK

This book is a work of fiction. Names, characters, places, and incidents are fictitious. Any resemblance to actual persons, living or dead, events, or locales is purely coincidental.

Copyright © 2015 by Ivy Smoak
All rights reserved

ISBN: 1523491337
ISBN-13: 978-1523491339

Cover art copyright © 2018 by Ivy Smoak

Cover photo by Kiselev Andrey Valerevich/Shutterstock.com

2020 Edition

To M.B.
Without you, M & B would not exist.

Prologue
Bee

I put my pencil down and read through my essay to look for any mistakes. When my eyes got to the bottom of the page, I smiled. I had just finished my last final. *Ever.* I couldn't believe I was really done. Four long years of late night study sessions and early morning cramming had finally paid off. Although, I still needed to actually pay those years off. *Why am I thinking about student loans right now?*

I grabbed my test booklet and walked to the front of the classroom. My Intro to Psych class was in a huge lecture hall. I had saved one easy class for my last semester and this was it. But now I almost wished that I was handing in my paper to a professor that I knew well. A professor that could tell me how proud he was of me and how he thought I was going to do great things. Instead, I handed my test to Professor Thornton who I had only ever spoken to when handing in assignments. She wouldn't know me from the other 200 students in the class.

"Have a good summer," Professor Thornton said and smiled.

"Thank you. You too."

She immediately looked back down at the book she was reading.

That was unceremonious. It didn't really matter. In just a few days, the dean would hand me my diploma and it would really feel like the end. I glanced over my shoulder at the other students still finishing up their exams. *Goodbye, college.* I opened up the door and walked out into the bright sunshine. Normally I hated endings. But this seemed more like a beginning than an end. Patrick was supposed to hear back about his internship today. I hadn't had any luck landing a job yet, but it was for the best. If Patrick got the internship, he'd be moving to New York City. And I didn't want to have to choose between an entry level job in Delaware and Patrick. Not that it would be much of a choice. Patrick would always win. Besides, he always encouraged me to go after my dreams. And I really wanted to hold out until I landed a job in advertising. Maybe I'd have more luck in New York.

Patrick and I had talked about moving in together after graduation. I pictured a cute little place in the middle of the city. It seemed romantic and perfect. Before Patrick, I never in a million years would have thought I'd wind up in New York. I liked the suburbs. There was something exciting about moving, though. Mostly just because Patrick would be there with me. The two of us suburban kids facing the big city together. I really hoped he'd get the internship. Otherwise we might not be able to afford to live together yet. Moving back in with my mom didn't seem nearly as exciting.

I looked around at the few students walking around campus. There were still two more days of exams. Most students were doing last minute studying, holed up in their dorms and the library. I had been lucky that all of my finals were early. Now I could spend my last few days here relaxing, something that I hadn't done that much of since I started. I pressed the button for the crosswalk. I was going to miss it here. I hadn't expected to feel so sentimental. This campus had become my home away from home, though. My life had changed for the better here. Mostly because I had met Patrick. I smiled to myself.

When the light changed, I crossed the street. In a few minutes I was outside of the Sigma Pi frat house. I walked up the steps and knocked on the door. *Please, please have gotten it.* Patrick opened the door. He had a huge smile on his face.

I took a deep breath. "Did you hear from MAC International?"

"Mhm." He closed the door and walked past me down the steps.

"Patrick?" I chased after him. He looked happy when he had opened the door. Was he actually upset?

He stopped and turned back around. He was still smiling.

"So..."

"So?"

"Patrick, you're killing me. Did you get the job?" I held my breath.

He flashed me the smile that I had fallen in love with.

"You got it?!"

"I got it, Bee."

I wasn't sure I had ever seen him look so happy. "Ah!" I threw my arms around him.

He laughed as he picked me up and spun me around. When he set me back down, he put his hand on my cheek.

"I can't believe I actually got it. I thought it was a long shot..."

"I knew you'd get it."

He leaned down and kissed me.

I would never get tired of the way he kissed me. He had this way of making me feel like I was the only thing that mattered to him.

"What do you think? Should we go look at apartments tomorrow?"

"Tomorrow? Yes!" I felt so giddy. I couldn't believe this was really happening. It felt like everything I had ever wanted was coming true.

"Did you know that this is the very spot where we met freshman year?"

"I know. I remember." I smiled up at him. "You were drunk. And you made some stupid vulgar comment. And I told you off."

"Yeah." He tucked a loose strand of hair behind my ear. "I'm pretty sure I said you had a nice ass."

I laughed. "Yup, that was it."

"I still don't know why you were ever upset about that. It's just true."

I laughed again. "Because it was rude."

He shrugged. "All I know is that as soon as you called me a drunk asshole, all I wanted to do was win you over."

"Well, you did."

"So this kind of seems like the perfect place, right?"

"The perfect place for what?"

Patrick got down on one knee.

"Oh my God." I put my hands over my mouth.

"Bee, you're the best thing that's ever happened to me. Meeting you right here, it changed me. I want to go to New York. And I want to know that you'll be by my side. I need you to always tell me when I'm being a drunk asshole." He laughed.

"Patrick, I..."

"I know, okay? I know your parents are divorced. And I know that you're scared to get married. But I'm not your dad, Bee. I'm not going to run off. I'm so in love with you. I love you with everything that I am. I'm never going to leave you. Marry me, Bee."

I didn't think he was going to propose, not yet. But it felt so right. I never wanted to live a day without him. "Okay."

"Okay? Does that mean yes?" He smiled up at me.

"Yes that means yes. Of course, yes!"

He slid the ring onto my finger.

"Oh my God, Patrick." I could feel tears start to stream down my cheeks. I looked down at the ring on my finger.

"Why are you crying?" He wrapped his arms around me. "You're so cute."

I pressed the side of my face against his chest. "I just never thought I'd be this happy."

Chapter 1
Bee

18 Months Later

The subway car screeched as it came to a stop. I quickly stood up and squeezed my way past the people boarding. It seemed like common sense to let people off the subway before getting on. But that philosophy somehow got lost when people were underground. Maybe it was similar to how I was somehow now immune to the smell of pee in the subway terminal and the loud sounds of the city. If I left the city now, it would probably be hard to fall asleep to the silence of the suburbs. Cars honking always put me right to sleep.

I slowly climbed the stairs. Luckily the office was only a block away from the subway station. The cold wind nipped my cheeks as soon as I emerged above ground. I pulled my jacket tighter around myself as I avoided tripping over a pile of trash on the curb.

In the distance, I noticed a homeless person sitting on the sidewalk outside my office building. *Just don't look at him.* I grabbed the handle of the door. *Damn it.* I didn't know why I couldn't walk past him. It just wasn't in me. And it was so cold this morning. I hadn't realized how harsh the winters were going to be in New York. I backtracked and handed the man a few dollars out of my purse. If I kept doing this, I'd be the next one on the street. I was barely scraping by as it was. Giving money to every homeless person I walked by really added up.

"Thank you, miss."

I smiled at him and retreated into the building. I kept my coat on as I walked toward the elevator. My teeth were still chattering.

"Bridget, I'm glad I caught you."

I turned around and looked up at my boss. He was at least ten years old than me, but that didn't seem to stop him from flirting with me constantly. "Oh, hi, Mr. Ellington."

"I told you to call me Joe." He smiled at me and put his hand on my shoulder.

Nope. "What can I do for you?"

"Coffee. Please."

"Sure. As soon as I get upstairs, I'll get you a cup."

"No, the good stuff down the street. Thanks, Bridget. See you in a few." He let go of my shoulder and stepped onto the elevator.

I wanted to tell him that it was 15 degrees outside. And that there was perfectly good coffee in our office. Instead, I bit my tongue and went back out into the cold. The place my boss was referring to wasn't exactly nearby either. It was three blocks away. I folded my arms across my chest and walked as quickly as I could.

When I finally arrived at the coffee shop, I could barely feel my nose. I got into the back of the line and rubbed my hands together. A woman walked up behind me. She was talking really loudly into her phone. I rolled my eyes to myself.

"What can I get for you?" the barista said with a big smile when I reached the front of the line.

"Could I have a 12 ounce cappuccino with soy milk and extra foam to go please?" I hated how pretentious Mr. Ellington's order sounded. I felt my cheeks blush.

"Sure thing. That will be $3.99."

I handed the barista the company card.

"Sorry, our register is being weird this morning. It's not scanning cards. Cash only."

"Oh, okay." I opened up my purse and rifled around. I had handed the homeless person my last dollar bills. But there was tons of change at the bottom of my purse. "I'm so sorry." I started pulling out quarters and placing them on the counter. I could feel my face turning even more red. This was mortifying.

"God. Don't you see that someone who's actually ready is waiting behind you?"

I turned around and looked at the woman behind me. "I'm really sorry. It'll just be a second." If she thought I was rude, she shouldn't be yelling into her phone in a small coffee shop.

"This is ridiculous," she snapped. "I'll have a latte. Whatever your biggest size is. With coconut milk and no foam."

Of course her order is as pretentious as Mr. Ellington's.

"Umm..." the barista looked at me.

"It's fine. I need another minute anyway."

"Okay," the barista said. "That will be $4.75."

"Here," the woman said and handed him a ten dollar bill. He pulled her change out of the register and handed it to her.

"And if you think you're getting a tip for not making me wait, think again." She grabbed her change and walked toward the other end of the counter where the pickup line was.

"What a bitch," the barista said under his breath.

I laughed. "I'm sorry I took so long." I slid the quarters toward him. I had ended up finding a few extra quarters. "Keep the change."

"Thanks." His big smile returned from earlier as he dumped the extra change into the tip jar. "I hope you have a great day."

"You too."

***

"It's cold." Mr. Ellington looked up at me.

"What?" I had walked back as quickly as I could. There was no way his coffee was cold. I bit my lip. *Maybe it's cold.* It was freezing outside.

"Well, room temperature."

"I'm so sorry, I..."

He held up his hand. "It's fine, Bridget. Please just warm it up for me." He handed it back to me and looked down at the papers on his desk.

I grabbed the cup out of his hand and went to the break room.

"Hey, Bee. You're running late today," Kendra said. She was pouring herself a cup of coffee out of the communal pot like a normal person. "Please tell me it's because you went out last night and had a good time?"

I laughed. "No, I was just picking up coffee for Mr. Ellington. Cold coffee, apparently." I poured the cappuccino into a normal coffee mug and put it in the microwave.

"He still has you fetching coffee for him? You're not an intern. You need to stand up for yourself."

I sighed and leaned against the counter. "I'm not sure there's any difference between an intern and a secretary in his mind."

"Well, except for how much he hits on his secretaries."

"Uh." I put my face in my hands. "Kendra, what am I doing here?"

"Warming up coffee?"

"You know what I mean." I looked up at her. This was supposed to be a stepping stone. I felt stuck. He's never going to look at me as anything more than someone to fetch coffee." And if I had to edit another one of his documents, I felt like I would scream. I hadn't spent four years busting my ass in school to be a secretary. This job was supposed to open doors, but I wasn't sure how much more I could take. And no matter how hard I worked, every door always seemed to be closed.

"Have you pitched him any of your ideas?"

"I've tried. He always interrupts me."

"Maybe do it in the meeting tomorrow? And then everyone will be listening, not just him. It'll almost force him into hearing you out."

"I'm supposed to be taking notes, not participating."

"Right, said no one ever." Kendra took a sip of her coffee. "But back to my other point. What did you do last night?"

"I watched T.V. And went to bed. Like a normal person."

"Normal people don't sit in their apartments alone every night. Come out with me tonight. It will be fun, I promise."

"I don't want to go out."

"Bee."

"Kendra."

She laughed. "There's a new bar opening up around the corner from here. And there are so many eligible bachelors who work around here. I'm sure the bar will be packed."

"If you must know, I already have plans tonight."

"With your T.V.?"

"No. I'm going over to Marie and Carter's for dinner."

"Hanging out with a married couple doesn't exactly count as plans."

"Of course it does. You're being ridiculous."

"Maybe tomorrow night, then? I don't want to go alone."

"Maybe."

"Which means no."

The microwave beeped and I pulled out the coffee mug. "Maybe means maybe."

"Sure. At least think about speaking up during the meeting tomorrow. You can't be afraid to show them what you got. See you at lunch, Bee."

I felt cold despite the fact that I was still wearing my winter coat in the office. *Am I afraid?*

Chapter 2
Bee

I pressed the buzzer outside of Marie and Carter's apartment building. "Marie, it's me. Let me in." I pulled my jacket tightly around myself. No answer came through the speaker system. I pressed the button again. "Marie, please, it's freezing!"

A second later the door buzzed. *Yes.* I grabbed the handle and almost ran inside. Marie was the first friend I had made in New York. She used to work at Kruger Advertising with Kendra and me. She had gotten a promotion a few months ago and then used her new position as leverage for a better pay grade at another ad agency, Blue Media. She had her dream job and Carter worked for the same company as her. They were the nicest power couple I had ever met. And Marie hadn't started as a secretary. I couldn't help but think I was on the wrong path. If I wanted to be where she was in a few years, I really needed to make a change. Maybe Kendra was right. I was just worried Mr. Ellington would be mad if I spoke up during the meeting. And I was so tired of feeling afraid.

I knocked on Marie's door and she immediately opened it.

"Hey, Bee!" She gave me a big hug. "Geez, I feel like it's been forever since we've gotten to hang out."

"I know. I guess Carter's keeping you busy?"

She laughed. "No, my new job has been keeping me busy." She released me from her embrace. "How is everyone at Kruger doing?"

"Great."

"Even you?"

"Yeah. I'm good."

"So Mr. Ellington isn't driving you crazy anymore?"

I laughed. "No, he still is."

"Hopefully you won't have to deal with him for too much longer. And as soon as you get a promotion and get some experience, I think I can land you an even better job with me."

I smiled. *If I ever get a promotion.* I didn't want to think about that right now.

"Hey, Bee," Carter said as he emerged from their bedroom.

Oh my God. That's why they hadn't let me in right away. They had been having sex. Carter's hair was all mussed up in the back. *Awkward.* "Hey, Carter."

"I'm starving," he said and sat down at the table. "What's for dinner?"

Marie laughed. "Pizza. I already ordered it."

"Perfect. Were you guys talking about Mason?"

"Carter! I haven't even brought that up yet."

"Oh, sorry, babe."

Marie laughed.

"Who's Mason?" I sat down on the opposite side of the table as Carter.

"Well, I was waiting for a good segue, but this will have to do." She sat down next to Carter. "He's this guy that we work with at Blue Media."

"Okay?"

"Bee, he's a really nice guy. And super charming."

"That's nice." Is that really why they had asked me to come over for dinner? To set me up on a date? I folded my arms across my chest.

"And he's really handsome."

"Really handsome?" Carter said. "I mean...I wouldn't say really handsome."

Marie laughed."Not as handsome as you, babe."

Carter smiled at her.

"Yeah...no," I said.

"No? We didn't even ask you a question yet," Marie said.

"The answer is no. I'm not going on a date with your weird coworker."

"He's not weird," Marie said. "He's really cool."

"He sounds awful."

Marie laughed. "He's actually super awesome. And I told him all about you. He can't wait to meet you. You have a date tomorrow night at 8."

"Wait, what?"

"It's already set."

"I'm not going on a date tomorrow night. I have plans."

"Plans to watch T.V. alone in your apartment?"

"Why does everyone think that's all I do?"

"Because you do it a lot."

"Okay, fine. I like binge watching awesome T.V. shows. Is that so wrong? And I do have plans. I'm going to go to a bar with Kendra tomorrow night." *Maybe.*

"No, you're going on a super awesome date with Mason tomorrow night. Which you won't regret because he's great."

"Great? I doubt that. What's wrong with him? Why would he agree to go on a blind date? No one does that. That's like the most awkward thing ever. He's probably a serial killer."

"People do it all the time. He's not a serial killer. He's a successful, handsome, businessman."

"Yeah, well I don't like successful, handsome, businessmen. You know that." I bit my lip. I didn't want to think about Patrick. *Stop thinking about Patrick!*

A buzzing noise sounded in the apartment.

"That would be the pizza," Marie said and stood up. "Just think about it, okay, Bee?"

No. "Okay."

Carter got up and answered the door as Marie grabbed some plates.

"What do you want to drink?" Marie asked. "White or red?" She held up two bottles of wine.

"White's good."

***

I was on my second glass of wine. The more I drank, the more I started to think about Patrick. I always tried to be good around Carter. It was awkward that he was still friends with Patrick. I knew they hung out. I ran my thumb along the spot where my engagement ring used to be. I just needed to know something. Anything. "Have you seen Patrick recently?" I looked up at Carter.

He glanced at Marie and then back at me. "Yeah, we usually catch the Giants games together. I saw him last weekend."

"Oh. Cool. How is he doing?" I tried to hide the eagerness in my voice. I hadn't heard from Patrick in months. I just wanted to know if he was still hurting too. Time was supposed to heal you. But I still felt broken. I was worried that I always would. Just thinking about him made me want to cry. I took a huge sip of my wine.

"He's good, Bee."

"Good. That's really great. I'm glad he's good."

We were all quiet for a minute.

"So when you say good..." I let my voice trail off. "Is he seeing anyone right now?" That's what I really wanted to know. I wanted to know if he had moved on.

"What does seeing someone even mean these days? Am I right?" Marie laughed awkwardly.

"Does that mean he is?"

"Bee. It's been six months," Marie said. "You need to move on too."

He's seeing someone else? My chest hurt. I took another sip of wine. I wasn't sure why I was surprised. He had moved on while he was still engaged to me. But the more time passed, the more I thought about the good things and not the bad. I missed him. I missed what we used to be. He had promised me that he'd never leave me.

"So, what is this Mason guy like?" My voice sounded small. I wanted to move on too. I wanted to be able to heal.

"He's super handsome," Carter said and laughed.

Marie rolled her eyes. "He's fun. I think he's exactly the kind of guy you should be dating right now."

"So he's gross?"

"No. He just knows how to have a good time. He's always the life of the party. Like I said before, he's charming."

"Is he friends with Patrick too?"

"Not that I know of." Marie looked at Carter.

"I don't think they've ever met," Carter said.

"Okay. I'll do it."

Chapter 3
Bee

I jumped onto my bed and pulled the covers up to my chin. My apartment was cold. Everything was cold. I was homesick. The only reason I had come here was Patrick. And now that he was gone, I wasn't sure what I was doing. I couldn't afford to continue living here on a secretary's salary. The apartment had seemed warm and full of life when Patrick had been here with me. But now it was easy to see it for what it really was. It was rundown and the heater was on the fritz.

I didn't want to pitch my ideas during the staff meeting tomorrow. And I didn't want to go on a blind date with some random guy. I was so sick of this city. Nothing good had happened to me here. New York had taken everything from me. All I wanted to do was go home.

Before I could change my mind, I picked up my cell phone, scrolled through my contact list, and pressed the call button. The phone rang.

"Hi, sweetie! How's the big city treating you?"

"Hi, Mom." My voice caught slightly.

"Sweetie, what's wrong?"

"I just want to come home." I pulled my knees to my chest.

"Oh, Bee." Her voice was soothing.

I couldn't help it. I started to cry. It was so nice to hear her voice. "Mom. I hate it here. What am I doing?"

"What happened? I thought you liked your new job? And what about all the new friends you said you made? You seemed so happy last time we talked."

"No." I always tried to pretend everything was okay around my mother. I didn't want her to have to worry about me. But I needed her right now. "I'm stuck. I don't think I'll ever move up in the company."

"Sweetie, you've never been scared of hard work. What's really wrong?"

"Everything. I don't belong here. I never wanted to come to this city in the first place. I followed Patrick here blindly. I lost myself in him. What the hell was I thinking?"

"You were in love. You weren't thinking."

I laughed and wiped away the tears under my eyes. "God, I feel like such an idiot."

"You know you can always come home. But don't let Patrick be the reason that you're running away from the city."

"I just feel so defeated. I don't know why it still hurts so much."

"I know. You remind me so much of myself, Bee. We both love so hard that we forget to take care of our own hearts."

My father had cheated on her. When she found out, it had completely broken her. I grew up faster watching the pain in her eyes. And I told myself I would never let it happen to me. Patrick had seemed like such a nice guy, though. The perfect guy. I felt like we were two parts of a whole. The city had gotten in our way. Or maybe he had expected me to change somehow. But I thought that he loved me the way I was. *The way I am.*

I didn't want to fall apart because of him. He didn't deserve that. If he didn't need me than I certainly didn't need him. My mom was right. If I left the city now it would be because of him. I ran my thumb along the spot where my engagement ring used to be. I wouldn't give Patrick the satisfaction.

"Does it get easier?" I asked.

"It does. It just takes time."

"More than six months I guess?"

"Maybe a little more than six months. I know I said you were a lot like me, Bee. But you're different in a lot of ways too. You're stronger than me."

"Mom..."

"You are. You're going to do everything you set out to do in New York. And one day you're going to stop thinking about Patrick. And you'll find the person that you're really meant to be with."

"I doubt I'll find him here. Everyone is so unfriendly here. And rude. Everyone just seems grumpy and like they're on a deadline all the time. I think they could all use a few weeks off in the suburbs."

My mom laughed. "You're in the heart of corporate America. Maybe try to find your dream guy in a different part of town than Wall Street?"

"Yeah, that's probably a good idea. I actually have a date tomorrow."

"You do?"

"Yeah. Marie and Carter set me up on a blind date with a guy they work with."

"That's wonderful."

I sighed. "Maybe. I don't think a guy who works in advertising is a great fit for me."

"But you work in advertising."

"No, I work as a secretary at an ad agency. And all the guys I work with are total pigs."

My mom laughed. "Well, either way, I'm glad to hear you're getting back out there. Wait, doesn't Carter work for an ad agency?"

"Yeah, but he's different. He's Carter. Marie and him are perfect together."

"Maybe this guy tomorrow could be your Carter. They work together and they're friends."

"And Carter is also friends with Patrick. I think I still might come home."

"I'm not stopping you, Bee. Just don't make any rash decisions while you're not thinking straight again."

"I'll try." I pulled my blanket up to my chin again. "Is it really cold there too?"

My mom laughed. "I'm only two and a half hours away from where you are. Of course it's cold here."

"It feels like I'm on another continent."

"Maybe I should come up for a visit. I've never gotten to see your place."

I looked around the empty room. Patrick had taken all the furniture except for the mattress and the small table set in the kitchen. I didn't want my mom to see where I lived. She worried about me enough without seeing my living conditions. "Soon. I've been slammed at work recently."

"Okay. Well, keep me updated if things change. I'd love to come up for the weekend. Just us girls. I can crash on your couch. It'll be fun."

I don't have a couch. "Mhm. That sounds great. I'll keep you posted. I should probably get some sleep. I have a long day tomorrow."

"And a sexy date at night."

I laughed. "Of course."

"Call me to tell me all about it. And text me when you get in tomorrow night. I just want to make sure you're safe."

"Marie and Carter already promised me that he wasn't a serial killer."

"Most serial killers don't go around telling people they're serial killers."

"I know. I'll text you."

"Goodnight, sweetie."

"Night, Mom."

Chapter 4
Bee

I pulled on a pencil skirt and my nicest blouse. Kendra was right. I needed to pitch my ideas at the meeting today if I ever wanted Mr. Ellington to really listen to me. Looking nice gave me a boost of confidence. I slid on a pair of stilettos. Normally I'd wear flats to work. Especially when it was so cold outside. But today I almost wanted the extra height. As if being taller somehow made what I had to say in the meeting more believable.

I looked down at the dress on my bed that I had picked out for my date later. It was sophisticated. When I met Patrick in college, I had been wearing cutoff jean shorts and a tank top. I didn't want to attract another guy like him. Sophisticated was good. I bit my lip. Or maybe I just didn't even want Mason to like me. I was sabotaging myself.

I tried to dismiss the thought as I grabbed my winter jacket and pulled it on. My date wasn't until eight. I'd have time to come back and pick out another outfit if I wanted. I rushed out of my apartment and down the stairs. The elevator had been broken for months. I wasn't sure if it was ever going to be fixed. But I had tackled these stairs in heels before.

The rush of cold air when I opened the door chilled me to the bone. It didn't matter what my mom said. Delaware never seemed this cold. Maybe the wind was stronger, pushing through all the sky rise buildings. I stared at the ground as I made my way to the subway. If I couldn't see any homeless people, I couldn't give them the rest of my money. My mom wouldn't just abandoned the idea of visiting me soon. And if she wanted to visit, I needed to save up to buy a couch. I would have tried to get a roommate, but that didn't exactly work in a studio apartment. Besides, the idea of getting a roommate I didn't know freaked me out too much. And the idea of moving into a different apartment freaked me out even more. My small apartment was the closest thing I had to a home right now. Even without Patrick in it.

I got onto the A train. I thought it would be fun to people watch on the subway. But it wasn't. There was no one as depressing as someone on the subway going to work. Everyone looked so sad and tired. It was like everyone in the city was depressed and in serious need of uppers. I couldn't judge them though. I had become one of them. I'm sure anyone who looked at me could see the sadness in my eyes. I wasn't even sure who I was anymore. But whoever I had become was the kind of person who would pitch her ideas unasked at a meeting. And I was going to finally get noticed. I just wanted one stupid thing in this stupid city to go my way for once.

The subway screeched to a stop and I squeezed past the people pushing their way on. I walked up the stairs back into the cold wind and looked back down at the ground. If I got a promotion and a raise, I could start giving money to homeless people again. Out of the corner of my eye I saw a man sitting on the curb outside of my office building. He was wearing tethered clothes, hugging his knees to his chest, shivering. *I can't.* I grabbed a few dollars out of my purse and placed it into his hand.

"Thank you." He looked up at me.

"You're welcome." I smiled and walked into the warmth of my office. Maybe being able to give money to homeless people and not feeling like I was going to starve if I did, was a good motivator for the meeting today. I stepped onto the elevator. Right before the doors closed, Kendra walked in.

"Hey, Bee. Has your maybe turned into a yes yet?"

"Actually, I can't tonight."

"No." She grabbed my elbow. "Come on. Hanging out with me is so much more fun than watching T.V. and you know it."

I laughed. "Yes, it is. But I actually have a date tonight." I smiled and looked away from her.

"Shut up."

I looked back at her and shrugged.

"Are you serious?"

"Why do you seem so surprised?"

"I don't know. It just seemed like you had kind of given up. You were one cat away from becoming a crazy cat lady."

"Psh. Crazy cat ladies have like a whole bunch of cats. I have none. And I'm not crazy."

Kendra shrugged. "Okay, give me all the details. What's his name? Where did you meet? Is he sexy? He must be sexy if he's getting your mind off Patrick."

I stepped off the elevator without answering her.

"Bee! You have to tell me."

"His name is Mason."

"That's a really sexy name."

"It is kind of sexy I guess."

"So...is he sexy?"

"I don't know."

"Why aren't you telling me?"

"Because I really don't know."

"What do you mean? Were you at one of those weird new places where they turn off all the lights and you just talk to people?"

"What are you talking about? No. I've just never met him. It's a blind date."

"A blind date? You never told me you were ready to date again. I have like a million guys to set you up with."

"I don't want to date your rejects, Kendra."

"Well, whose reject is this?"

"No ones. He works with Marie and Carter."

"Did he date Marie?"

"No. I don't think so anyway. I feel like she would have mentioned that. No actually. Definitely not. He's friends with Carter. I feel like they wouldn't be friends if Mason had dated his wife."

"Fair enough. What else did they tell you about him?"

"That he's a successful businessman. And that he's handsome. That's really all I know."

"A successful businessman, huh? I thought you swore off all the suits in this city."

"I didn't really mean that." I had meant that. The men here sucked. Or maybe it was just men in general. Maybe I should have just sworn off all men.

"So what made you suddenly decide that you're ready to get back out there again?" Kendra asked.

I pulled off my jacket and draped it over the back of my chair. "Nothing in particular."

She stared at me skeptically.

"Patrick's dating someone else." I looked down at my desk.

"I'm sorry, Bee."

"There's nothing to be sorry for. We're broken up. Of course he's dating someone else."

"Still. Are you okay?"

"Yeah, I'm fine. I think I needed to hear that he had completely moved on. I just needed a push. I'm done thinking about that asshole. And I should be dating someone else too."

"Absolutely." Kendra patted my shoulder. "Fuck him."

I smiled at her. That wasn't the first time she had said that. Probably closer to the hundredth. "And I'm taking your advice. I'm going to pitch one of my ideas at the meeting today."

"What happened to you overnight? I like this new kick ass Bee. I better get to my cubicle before Mr. Ellington gets mad at you before you've even done anything wrong. I'll see you in the meeting."

I turned my computer on as Kendra walked away. Kick Ass Bee. I'm not sure anyone had ever described me that way ever. But I liked it. Today was going to be the day that I turned everything around.

City of Sin

***

"Jenkins, work on getting that into effect. I'll contact the V.P. of Sword Body Wash. But I'm sure this will be a go," Mr. Ellington said.

I jotted the decision down in my notebook, even though it wasn't a good idea. Any company could sponsor a segment on a news station. And this one wasn't even local. Layla's Predictions was only broadcast in Miami. Yes, it had tons of viewers because Layla was hot and they made her do all sorts of random stuff. But Miami wasn't even half the size of New York.

"Great work this week team. This account is our focus for the first quarter of the year. And we'll need some more ideas for the campaign just in case the V.P. wants to go in a different direction. We can't afford to lose this account. We'll have another meeting next Wednesday. I'll want to hear more than one pitch."

"Mr. Ellington?" I said. My heart was beating out of my chest.

"Did you need Jenkins to repeat the pitch, Bridget?"

"No. I um..." I let me voice trail off. *You can do this.* "I actually have an idea on how to promote Sword Body Wash."

"We're going with Jenkins' idea." He looked away from me.

"Which isn't a good idea. No offense, Jenkins."

Jenkins lowered his eyebrows slightly.

"Layla's Predictions is only aired in Miami. And Sword Body Wash specifically said they wanted to grow their brand in New York. That's why they came to us. Because they knew we can do local guerilla style campaigns. The Knicks cheerleaders always perform in Central Park before game nights to help sell tickets. What if we joined up with them? Have an actor spray himself with Sword Body Spray and get the cheerleaders to chase him through Central Park? Everyone would see it. No one would know if it was real or not. News stations would inadvertently pick it up. It would be huge. And ridiculously cheap. That's the kind of thing that gets people's attention these days."

Jenkins laughed. "What would you know about what gets a man's attention?"

"Excuse me?" He didn't know about Patrick cheating on me. Had someone told him? Had someone told the whole office? I could feel my face turning red.

"Because you're not a man. Men want to look at a hot girl on T.V. doing silly stuff. Layla's Predictions is the perfect platform for a sponsorship by Sword."

Oh. I was flustered by his previous comment. I took a deep breath. "But it's not what they asked for. They want something in New York."

"And do you have connections to the Knicks?" Mr. Ellington said. "To get all of this set up?"

"No, but I..."

"Or maybe you know one of the cheerleaders?" Jenkins said.

"No. But we can easily..."

"This meeting is over. Let's talk in my office, Bridget." Mr. Ellington walked out of the conference room. He looked pissed.

Shit. I had thought it was a really good idea. I looked over at Kendra.

"I'm sorry," she mouthed silently.

I suddenly felt nauseous. What if I had just lost my job? What was I going to do? *Damn it.* I quickly walked out of the conference room and over to Mr. Ellington's office. The door was open. I walked in and stood in front of his desk. He didn't look up at me.

"Mr. Ellington?"

He finally looked up. "Close the door, Bridget."

God, this is going to be bad. I closed the door and walked back up to his desk.

"Sit down," he said. He didn't sound mad. I thought he'd be yelling at me by now.

I sat down. "Mr. Ellington, I'm sorry, I know that was out of line. But I think my idea..."

He held up his hand to silence me. "What do you think Sword Body Wash cares about?"

"Their brand. About being sexy."

"There's only one thing that any company cares about. Making money."

That wasn't true. Sword Body Wash cared about their brand. Their brand was everything to them. It's what made them money. I stayed silent. Anything else I said would just make it worse.

"And you have to spend money in order to make money. They gave us a budget of five million dollars. They don't want a cheap guerilla marketing ploy in the park. Especially when the Knicks cheerleaders aren't even wearing those short skirts because it's freaking ten degrees outside. That's not sexy. That's not going to make them money."

"Mr. Ellington, if you could just hear me out..."

"I did hear you out. And why the hell are you pitching ideas in the middle of my meeting? You're my secretary. You don't know the first thing about advertising."

"I majored in marketing with a minor in advertising. I do know..."

"You have no experience. A minor in advertising means nothing. I hired you to answer my phone and fetch me coffee. And whatever else I want. You need to have thick skin to be in advertising. Just do your job and don't worry your pretty little head about anything else."

What the hell? I stood up. "I don't want to just be your secretary forever."

"And you won't always just be my secretary. You're due for a promotion very soon. But I need to know that I can trust you. I don't need anyone working beneath me that I can't trust." His eyes wandered down my body.

"I should probably get back to my work, Mr. Ellington."

"Joe. Please call me Joe."

No. I turned around and retreated out of his office. Had I imagined that? He hit on me all the time. But had he seriously just implied that I was being promoted to sucking his cock? I must have imagined it. Even if I had, I still felt belittled. It didn't seem like Mr. Ellington thought I had what it took to work in advertising. And I didn't understand why, because my idea was good. It was so much better than Jenkins' stupid pitch.

I walked into the break room and got a cup of coffee. Ever since Mr. Ellington had hired me, he had flirted with me. Even when I had my engagement ring on. Had he really just hired me with the thought that I'd eventually have sex with him? That was preposterous. And disgusting. I started to wonder what had happened to his last secretary.

When I walked back to my desk there was a huge stack of papers and a note.

Bridget,
All these files need to be input into the computer. Type them up and email me before you leave today.
-Joe

Seriously? This was like a million pieces of paper. I sighed and turned on my computer. I guess I'd have to cancel my date tonight.

Chapter 5
Bee

"I'm so, so sorry," Kendra said. "For what it's worth, your idea was a lot better than Jenkins'."

"Thanks." I took a bite of my peanut butter and jelly sandwich. "Can I run something by you real quick?"

"Of course."

"I think if I'm ever going to make it in advertising I need to get some experience. There's probably a better shot of me getting something in one of the small agencies back home. Even if it's unpaid or something. Don't you think?"

"Back home?"

"Yeah. I'm thinking I might move back to Wilmington for awhile. Just until I figure some stuff out."

"Wait, what?" Kendra put her sandwich down on her desk. "You're not serious? Just because of the meeting? Whatever, people will forget about it tomorrow. And like I said, it was a good idea. Mr. Ellington will notice you eventually. You just need to give it more time."

I sighed. "I'm pretty sure Mr. Ellington has already noticed me. The only promotion I'll ever get here is becoming one of Mr. Ellington's mistresses."

"Ew." Kendra frowned. "I'm sure that's not true."

"Yeah, well I told him I didn't want to be his secretary forever. And he said I was due for a promotion. And then he looked at me in a really creepy way."

"He always looks creepy. You probably imagined it."

"But right before that he said that my skin wasn't thick enough to be in advertising. So what else could the promotion he suggested be? He definitely wasn't referring to an advertising gig."

Kendra took a sip of her diet coke. "If that really is what he meant, you can sue him you know. That's sexual harassment."

"I'm not going to sue my boss."

"And why not? He's a complete pig. If anyone ever filed a lawsuit, every girl in this office would sign off on it."

"Would you lower your voice?" We were eating lunch in Kendra's cubicle, which wasn't that far away from Mr. Ellington's office. "I tried. I gave it my best shot. I'm not cut out for this city. Mr. Ellington's right. I don't have thick skin. My skin is thin." I looked down at my arm. "Translucent, really. I'm so pale, I look sickly."

Kendra laughed. "You know what, fuck Mr. Ellington. You do have thick skin. You're finally moving on from Patrick. Don't let this set you back. You have that date tonight. Things are looking up. You're Kick Ass Bee."

"Yeah, I can't go on that date. Mr. Ellington is punishing me by having me transfer tons of useless documents into digital form. It's going to take forever. There's no way I'll have time to go back to my apartment and change before my date. I'm just going to cancel."

"You're not canceling."

"So you think I should just go like this? It will look like I didn't try at all. That's a terrible first impression."

"Bee, you always look great. Don't give me that shit. And being a dedicated employee is nothing to be ashamed about. But I agree, you have to look amaze-balls for a first date. And I have the perfect solution."

"I can't afford to go shopping. My rent is due in a few weeks and I..."

"It doesn't involve going shopping. I have a sexy dress here that you can borrow." She stood up and grabbed a dry cleaning bag that was hanging from the side of her cubicle.

"We don't wear the same size."

"Yes we do."

"Fine. But we don't have the same style."

"You mean you like to dress conservatively? I know. Which is why it's probably for the best that you have to borrow something from me." She pushed back the plastic that was covering it.

It was a short, low-cut black dress. Which actually wasn't what I was expecting at all. I thought there'd be more straps. And less fabric.

"So? What do you think?"

"It's great. Are you sure it's okay if I borrow it?"

"Absolutely."

"Why do you have this here?"

"I picked it up from the drycleaners before lunch. I was going to wear it to that bar that just opened up."

"Oh. Kendra, I can't borrow this if you're going to wear it tonight."

Kendra laughed. "Yeah, I'm fine going to that bar wearing what I'm wearing. I'm sure everyone's just going straight there after work anyway."

"Are you sure?"

"Absolutely. This dress is going to look amazing on you."

"I feel like going on this date a different night would be better though. I haven't exactly been having a stellar day."

"Which is why you should go. A great date will turn your whole day around. Besides, if you really want to get over Patrick you need to get under someone else."

"Ew. Seriously? That's terrible advice. I'm not doing that."

"Actually, it's great advice. And you know it. How did you get over the guy you dated before Patrick?"

"I didn't. I mean, Patrick was my only boyfriend. I never dated anyone before him."

"Wait, are you telling me you've only ever had sex with Patrick?"

"Jesus, Kendra, please lower your voice."

She laughed. "I'm sorry, but that's ridiculous. No wonder you were so upset about the break up."

"I was upset because we dated for five years and were engaged. And he was cheating on me. And I don't even know for how long."

"I know. I'm sorry. But you don't even know what else is out there. Dating is fun, Bee. There's someone out there that is so much better than Patrick. And probably a better lay too. You should really be more adventurous." She took a bite of her sandwich.

"Maybe."

"Let's stalk Mason. What's his last name?"

"I don't know. Marie didn't say."

"Damn. There's probably thousands of Mason's in New York."

"And isn't that cheating anyway? We're both supposed to go into the date blind."

"You don't think he already looked you up?"

"Wait, you think he did?"

"Maybe. Let's see what he could have found." She typed my name into Google and clicked on my Facebook profile. "Why the hell is there a picture of you and Patrick as your profile picture?"

"I haven't been on it in awhile."

"Bee, it still says you're engaged to him! What is wrong with you?!"

"I know. It's just...he never changed it either. I thought maybe it meant he was still holding on somehow. Won't he get a notification if I change it? It's almost like that makes it officially over."

"It was officially over when you gave him back the ring."

I ran my thumb along the spot where my ring had once been.

Kendra clicked on Patrick's name. "See." She turned her screen to me. There was a picture of Patrick with his arms wrapped around some brunette girl with huge breasts.

"Okay. I'll change my relationship status to single. I'm going to go get my work done."

"Bee." Kendra put her hand on my wrist. "I'm sorry. I wasn't trying to make you upset. I'm just trying to help."

"No, it's fine. You're right. If he really wanted me, he would have tried to make it work. I'll change it." I walked back to my desk and sat down.

I had thought Patrick and I were okay. We were both working long hours. When I had found out about him cheating, he had said it was my fault. That I wasn't giving him what he needed. Because I came back from work tired and ready for bed. So for a long time after I found out he was cheating I had blamed myself. As if him being a dick was somehow my fault. It wasn't. He was just an asshole. And I did need to move on. He wasn't the same person that he was when he had proposed. When he had proposed he had meant what he said. But the city had changed him. His new life wasn't something that I fit into. And now it seemed more like it was because I never belonged in New York in the first place.

***

"Hey, are you almost done?" Kendra was standing by my desk holding the dress in her hands. There were only a few people in the office still. It was past 5 o'clock on a Friday. Most people had left exactly at five.

"No. But I should be done in a few hours."

"Is it something I could help with?"

"You're already letting me borrow your dress. You should go have fun at that bar."

"Look, Bee, I'm sorry about earlier. I shouldn't have looked at Patrick's Facebook page. I wasn't trying to rub it in your face..."

"I know. You're just trying to help. And I am ready to get over him. But what if I don't know how? I don't even remember how to go on a date."

Kendra laughed and pulled up a chair to my desk. "Of course you know how to date. It's like riding a bike."

"A bike doesn't try to have a conversation with you."

"But you ride both a date and a bike."

"Oh, God." I rolled my eyes.

"Just be yourself, Bee. Any guy would be lucky to have you. You should try that thing where you say yes to everything."

"So, like if he says let's go have sex in my car I should say yes without even thinking about it?"

"Absolutely."

"I thought you told me to be myself."

Kendra laughed. "Well be a sexy, flirtatious version of yourself. How about I call you at nine? That way if you need an escape you can pretend there's some emergency you need to attend to."

"Now you're talking."

"Okay. I'll call at nine. But if you're already home in bed alone, I'm never speaking to you again. Our friendship is over." Kendra stood up.

"That's a little harsh."

"Tough love, Bee. And don't you dare start talking about Patrick on your date. There's nothing less sexy than talking about an ex on a date."

"Okay. I didn't realize how many rules there were to blind dates."

"You'll be fine. I'll call you at nine. Have fun." She gave me a huge smile.

"When you smile like that you look like a psychopath."

"Thanks. Bye, Bee."

"Bye, Kendra."

Chapter 6
Bee

I quickly slid off my pencil skirt and unbuttoned my blouse. My elbow hit the wall of the bathroom stall and I cursed under my breath. If I knew that this was going to be how my evening would start, I never would have agreed to go. I stepped into the black cocktail dress and held my breath as I zippered up the back. It was a little tight, but it would work. And it was definitely better than my work clothes, which I would have had to wear if Kendra hadn't just picked this dress up from the drycleaners during her lunch break. I'd have to text her to thank her again for letting me borrow it. She was a life saver.

Luckily I had worn heels to work today because of the meeting. The flats I tended to wear on a daily basis would have looked comical with the fancy dress. I stepped back into my high heels and smoothed the dress down. I took a deep breath. A black dress and black heels were perfect for a first date. He probably wouldn't even be able to guess that I had gotten ready at the office.

My nerves were starting to get the better of me. I had never been on a blind date before and I hadn't been on a first date in over five years. And of course Mr. Ellington had made me stay late tonight of all nights so that I wouldn't have time to go home and get ready. I didn't know anyone else who had to stay late on a Friday.

I folded my work clothes and unlocked the stall door. As soon as I saw myself in the mirror, I stopped. *Oh God, I look like a hooker.* The tightness of the dress pushed my breasts up. They were basically pouring out. I lifted the neckline as I walked over to the sink. Better. But not great.

I leaned over the sink and applied my favorite red lipstick. I smacked my lips together and stared at my reflection. The dark circles under my eyes were all I seemed to see. I grabbed some foundation out of my purse and blotted a bit under my eyes. These long hours were going to kill me. I ran my fingers through my hair. That would have to do. I needed to be across town and I was running late.

I stopped by my desk to drop off my work clothes and grab my jacket. I felt a hand on my shoulder and I screamed at the top of my lungs.

"Bridget, it's just me."

"Oh God." I placed my hand on my chest. "You scared me half to death, Mr. Ellington."

"Please, call me Joe." His hand lingered on my shoulder. "How many times do I have to remind you?"

I nodded my head. It didn't matter how many times he told me to call him by his first name. I would never find it appropriate.

"You're here late," he said.

"I know. I was finishing the documents you sent me. You should have gotten them. I emailed them to you a few minutes ago. I'm sorry, I didn't realize anyone else was still here." My heart was still beating fast. I looked around the room at the empty cubicles. It was just the two of us.

"I appreciate you staying so late. How about I treat you to a drink to show my appreciation? There's a new bar that just opened up down the street." He was hovering close to me. He always had a way of making me feel uncomfortable. I hadn't kept track of how many inappropriate passes he had made at me since I started here, but it was definitely more than I could count on two hands. And after the comments he made today in his office, I had never felt so uncomfortable around him.

I leaned away from him. "I can't tonight." *Or any night!*

"Oh. How is your boyfriend doing?"

"My fiancé. And we're not...I mean, he isn't..." I sighed. I felt my face flushing. "We broke up."

"So how about that drink? To help take your mind off things?"

"I can't, I have plans. If you'll excuse me, Mr. Ellington. I'm already running late."

His lips grew taught. "Maybe next time then. I hope you have a good evening, Bridget."

"You too, sir." I grabbed my jacket and hurried off. My heels clicked on the floor as I made my way to the elevator. I hated that sound. I always felt like it drew attention to me. Even though my flats would have looked ridiculous with the dress, I found myself wishing I had worn them today.

When I reached the tinted glass elevator doors, I looked at my reflection again. *Oh crap.* I turned to the side. The lines of my thong showed clearly though the tight fabric. The elevator dinged and I quickly stepped in. I had about a minute. As soon as the door closed, I dropped my jacket and purse to the floor and kicked off my heels. I slid my nylons and thong down my legs and shoved both into my purse.

I was just putting my feet back into my heels when the doors opened. I got off the elevator and looked at my reflection again in the tinted glass. *Much better.* I pulled on my jacket and rushed through the lush lobby. A wave of cold air hit me as I stepped outside. I was so sick of winter.

The street was relatively empty. Taxis didn't usually come by as often once the offices were closed, especially this late on a Friday. I began to walk toward the subway. The wind bit my cheeks and I pulled my jacket tighter around myself. I rounded the corner and saw a taxi speeding down the road. I stepped onto the curb and held my hand out for him.

The taxi slowed down and pulled to a stopped in front of me. I stepped into the street and reached for the door. But before I could, a man grabbed the handle.

"Hey! This is my taxi."

"Sugar, don't get your panties in a bunch. You'll get the next one."

"Excuse me?" *What the hell is his problem?*

"You heard me, baby."

I turned to him. He was a handsome pretentious bastard, just like every other suit in this city. I wanted to slap his beautiful, smug face. Instead I balled my hands into fists. "Where do you get off?"

"I'm running late," he said calmly.

"So am I."

"Then we should stop wasting each other's time." He climbed into the car.

"Hey!" I yelled as he closed the door. I slammed my palm against the window as the taxi sped off.

I wasn't just sick of the cold. I was so sick of this city.

Chapter 7
Mason

I loosened my tie and leaned back in the seat. It had been a long, hellish day, and I probably had a dreadful night ahead of me. The taxi raced through the streets. I glanced down at my watch. She'd probably already be there, early and eager. Every girl in this city seemed the same. It had been ages since I had gotten deep inside a tight pussy. I was getting a hard-on just thinking about it.

The only reason I had agreed to this stupid date was because I was getting two Knicks tickets out of it. Drinks, dinner, and dessert. The three Ds and I'd have held my side of the bargain. If I was lucky, she'd have two more Ds for me too. And if not, I could be in and out in just a few hours. Then maybe I'd hit the bar across the street from the restaurant and find myself some suitable entertainment for the rest of the evening.

I closed my eyes for a minute as the taxi sped on. I had come so close to punching my arrogant boss right in the face today. I desperately needed to unwind. This wasn't exactly the night I needed after such a shitty week. The taxi came to a stop. I pulled some money out of my wallet and tossed it on the seat in front of me.

"Keep the change." I stepped out into the cold night. Carter's wife had even made the reservations for the restaurant. There had to be something seriously wrong with this girl I was meeting if they were going to such lengths to set us up. The Knicks seats were courtside, after all. I walked into the restaurant. "Hi, I have a reservation for two, under Mason Caldwell." The hostess scanned the list.

"Yes of course. Right this way, sir." She scooted between the tables and I watched her ass. I'd always thought that hostesses should be required to wear yoga pants, but her tight black dress pants weren't half bad. She brought me to an empty table in the middle of the restaurant. I looked down at my watch. I was ten minutes late, and my date wasn't even here yet.

"Please just let me know if there's anything you need," the hostess said. She tucked a loose strand of hair behind her ear.

"I may take you up on that offer a little later." I flashed her a smile. I knew what my smile did to women. And it had the same effect on her as any other.

Her face turned crimson. I could definitely see myself bending her over this table. She turned away and walked back to her podium. She glanced over her shoulder once and blushed again when she made eye contact with me. Maybe I wouldn't need that bar after all.

"Good evening, my name is Ethan, and I will be your waiter this evening. Is there anything I can get for you while you're waiting?"

"Scotch. On the rocks."

"Great, I'll be right back."

I downed my drink, and then a second. I wasn't a patient man. This girl had better have a good reason for making me wait. I opened up the menu and scanned through the selections. Damn, this was going to cost me.

"I'm sorry I'm late, this jerk stole..." she stopped mid-sentence.

I looked up at the woman standing by my table. She was staring at me loathingly, but hell if I knew her. The curves on her body were delicious and her breasts were almost spilling out of her dress. I wasn't sure when the last time I had seen a natural blonde was, but she was definitely one. Her cheeks were flushed and she was biting her red lips. If I had been with her, I think I would have remembered.

"You've got to be kidding me," she said slowly.

"Are you Bee?"

The woman sat down across from me in a huff.

"It's Bridget, thank you. Only my friends call me Bee."

Chapter 8
Bee

"I'm Mason, it's nice to meet you." He extended his hand to me. I just stared at him.

"You seriously don't recognize me?"

"Have we met before? I think I would remember a face like yours." He gave me a seductive smile.

Oh, please. I wasn't going to play his games, no matter how handsome he was. "Well, it was about half an hour ago, so I don't expect you to remember."

Mason's lips curled into a smile. He did remember. "The taxi?"

"Yes, you stole my taxi. And acted like a complete asshole."

"I didn't steal your taxi, baby. I got there first."

"Like that! Don't call me that." My face flushed.

"What? Baby?"

"Yes, stop it," I hissed. "You don't even know me. And I take back what I said earlier. I'm not sorry that I'm late. If anything you owe me an apology."

"Is that so?"

"Yes, I spent the last thirty minutes hopping subway cars to get here as fast as I could. And for no reason at all."

"No reason at all?" His mouth was set in a straight line as he stared at me. His jaw line was sharp and he had small dimples in his cheeks.

Damn it, why am I staring at him? He was infuriating.

"Well, I'm sorry about the taxi. And for acting like an asshole."

"You're quite the gentleman," I said sarcastically.

"I am anything but gentle."

Everything below my waistline clenched. *What did he just say?* I gulped. My throat made a weird squeaking noise. "I should probably just go." I stood up, but he reached his hand out and grabbed mine. It felt like a spark of electricity went through my body.

"Don't." He locked eyes with me.

He was still holding my hand. I pulled away but sat back down. I was confused by my own reaction to him. He was a conceited asshole. But he was so handsome. I wanted to slap him and kiss him at the same time.

"How about we pretend the taxi thing never happened?" he said.

I took a deep breath. "Okay."

He put out his hand again. "I'm Mason, it's a pleasure to meet you."

I shyly shook his hand. "Bridget, but you can call me Bee."

"I'm honored." He flashed me another smile.

The waiter came over. "Good evening, Miss, my name is Ethan. Are you two ready to order?"

Crap. I hadn't even looked at the menu. I picked it up and scanned through the options. *I should pick something simple that won't get stuck in my teeth.*

"Two rib-eyes, medium. And a bottle of cabernet," Mason said. He snapped his menu shut and handed it to the waiter.

"Very well." The waiter grabbed the menu and also picked up mine before hustling off.

"You don't even know me. What if I'm a vegetarian?"

"I think you like meat in your mouth."

I gulped. "Excuse me?" God his words were suggestive. The restaurant suddenly felt stifling. I shifted uncomfortably in my chair.

"You heard me, Bee."

A shiver went down my spine. I just gaped at him.

"Well are you?"

"What?" I had no idea what he was talking about. I was too distracted by his comment.

"Are you a vegetarian?" he asked.

"No."

"That's what I thought."

CHAPTER 9
Mason

Her mouth was in an O shape. She was completely shocked by what I had said. I needed those red lips around my cock. This woman was refreshing. I was the one that should have been giving Carter Knicks tickets for hooking me up with this girl, not the other way around.

She looked up at me from under her long lashes. She seemed so innocent, but I could tell she had a wild side. If she didn't, she wouldn't still be sitting there. And I wanted to explore that side of her. Actually, I wanted to explore every inch of her.

"What brought you here?" I asked.

"Marie and Carter told me you were a nice guy. I should have known they were lying."

"I mean to New York."

"Oh." She pulled her lips into a stubborn line. "Why do you assume that I haven't lived here my whole life?"

She was challenging. I liked that. "Because you're soft."

"I don't know what you mean by that." She looked down at her hands.

"Honey, you don't even know how to properly hail a taxi."

"I do too!" she hissed. She leaned forward slightly, giving me a better view of her tits. "I'm just not used to everyone being so rude."

"Exactly. So when did you move here?"

She sighed. "About a year and a half ago. After graduation."

So she was young and inexperienced. This night had just taken an unexpected turn. "So why here?"

Her face flushed slightly. "Honestly, my college boyfriend and I moved here together. He got a job here, so I came with him."

"Boyfriend?" I raised my eyebrow. "He is not going to be pleased with the things I'm going to do to you."

Her slightly pink face turned crimson. "Don't be ridiculous. I wouldn't be here if we were still together. I'm not that kind of girl."

I smiled at her. So that's why they had set her up with me. She needed a rebound. And I was the perfect man for the job. Bee sat there, twisting her fingers in knots. She hadn't acknowledge my comment. She wanted this just as badly as I did. I bet she was wet just thinking about my rock hard cock.

"And what kind of girl do you think you are?"

"Just normal. I don't know. I certainly wouldn't cheat on someone."

She was getting more intriguing by the second.

"So what happened between you and your ex?"

Bee shrugged her shoulders. "New York, I guess."

"You mean he came here and started fucking every woman in the city?"

"Yes, you know the type?"

I'm the type. "Welcome to the city of sin, baby."

"The city of sin? Isn't that Las Vegas?"

"Las Vegas has nothing on New York. Trust me, you'll see."

"I think I already have."

"Right. Your ex certainly sounds like an asshole."

Bee smiled at me for the first time. Her eyes looked bright and eager. This was too easy.

"He's such an asshole," she said and laughed. She looked at me skeptically. Maybe she didn't believe that I wasn't the same type. "So what brought you to New York?"

"Born and bred."

"So I guess you're not very soft then?"

She was turning my own game against me. I tensed in my chair. "Baby, I'm rock hard. If you don't believe me, I'd be happy to show you."

I saw her gulp. Soon it would be my cock in her throat. She was staring at me. Her gaze would have been unsettling to other men, but I just stared back at her.

The waiter walked over, uncorked the bottle of cabernet, and poured us each a glass. "Your dinner will be out shortly."

CHAPTER 10
Bee

I crossed my legs under the table. His words had such an effect on me. I was getting damp between my thighs just listening to him. I felt like I could hear my heart beating. And his gaze was making me melt. I took a sip of the wine. It was crisp and refreshing. Hopefully it would calm me down. I couldn't seem to take my eyes away from his chiseled jaw and the five o'clock shadow that was starting to appear there. It had just been a long time since I had been on a date. Or since a man had looked at me the way that Mason was looking at me.

"So what did Marie and Carter tell you about me?" he asked.

"That you're in advertising." *God is he sexy.* "And that you're unbelievably sexy." *Shit did I say that out loud?!*

"Carter called me sexy? That's quite the compliment."

"No."

"Marie then?" He was smiling at me.

"Yes. I mean no." I didn't want to throw Marie under the bus. Marie had said he was handsome, not sexy. "I may have added that part in myself. Accidentally."

"So you don't think it's true? You don't find me sexy?" He loosened his tie a bit around his throat. I watched his Adam's apple rise and then fall as he studied me.

I needed to change the subject immediately. "What did they tell you about me?"

"They told me you were a secretary. Waiting on someone hand and foot all day? I could get used to that." His leg brushed against mine, and I felt that same electricity shoot through me as I had earlier.

"That's not what a secretary does."

"What do you do then?"

"I edit memos and make phone calls. And...fetch coffee." I sighed. He was exactly right. My job was ridiculous.

"I see. That is quite different than what I said. I do apologize." His seductive smile sent shivers down my spine.

Get a grip. I took a deep breath. "I don't really see why Marie and Carter thought we'd be a good fit." I ran my finger along the rim of my glass. Patrick was the only guy I had ever really dated. The dirty way Mason talked made it seem like he was way out of my league. At least sexually.

"Well they did tell me one other thing about you," he said.

"And what was that?"

"That you're kinky as hell."

"What?" *Is this some kind of joke?*

"That you like being tied up and fucked hard for hours. That nothing gets you off more than being on your hands and knees with a cock deep in your throat. And that your virgin ass is just waiting to be claimed."

What the fuck? Why would Marie say that? She had no idea what I liked behind closed doors. And I certainly wasn't kinky. Did Carter say it as a joke? "I don't know why they would have said that." I was completely mortified.

"Oh. Sorry, I may have added that part in myself. Accidentally, of course."

Desire flooded through my body. He wanted me. I couldn't seem to get Kendra's advice out of my head. Maybe I did need to get under someone else in order to officially get over Patrick.

"Well, if you don't like your job, you must have some hobbies that you enjoy?" he said.

The way he changed subjects in a flash was so unsettling. For the life of me, I couldn't think of a single thing I enjoyed doing. I was just imagining being tied up in my bed, with him on top of me. I bit my lip.

"No hobbies, Bee?" He put his hand on my knee to get my attention.

Oh God. The feeling of his hand on me made my whole body alert. "I like to read."

"That sounds relaxing." He let his foot glide against my shin. *What is he trying to do to me?*

"And what about you, Mason? What's your hobby?"

He slid his hand up my thigh, to the hem of my dress. "I like to fuck."

I choked on a sip of the cabernet. "Excuse me. I need to use the restroom." I stood up quickly and wound my way through the tables toward the bathroom.

I pushed through the bathroom door and exhaled. My heart was beating out of my chest. God I wished I had kept my panties on. I was practically dripping with desire. I ran into a bathroom stall and locked the door behind me.

What was it about Mason that was so exciting? *His handsome features. His naughty words.* I stood there trying to catch my breath. I didn't need to use the bathroom, I just needed to clear my head. He was wearing me down. But he was a pretentious asshole. I took a few more deep breaths. This was ridiculous. What had Marie been thinking? Mason wasn't the kind of guy I could date. Did Marie actually think we'd be a good fit? Or was Marie thinking along the same lines as Kendra?

I exited the bathroom stall and walked over to the sinks. I grabbed a paper towel, ran some cool water over it, and blotted it on my neck. This restaurant had the heat on too high. I kept my eyes on the mirror as someone else entered the restroom. The click of the lock made me turn my head.

"Hot and bothered?"

I pulled the damp cloth from my breasts. "Mason, this is the women's room. You can't be in here." I looked around, but we were alone. I gulped.

"Don't you ever break the rules?"

CHAPTER 11
Mason

Her face flushed as I walked over to her. When I reached her, I put my hands on the counter on either side of her and pressed my hips into hers. She didn't even flinch. I leaned over her, pressing my body more firmly against hers, and switched the water off. I put my hand on her thigh and slowly trailed it underneath the hem of her dress. She leaned back slightly, pressing her perfectly round ass against the sink.

"What, no one's ever made you come in a public bathroom, Bee?"

"No...I've never. We can't do this here, Mason." She put her hand on my chest. Her hesitance made me want her even more.

She said we couldn't do this *here*. But she wanted me. I pushed myself more firmly against her. I knew she could feel my hard cock pressed against her thigh. She looked down. *Yeah, she can feel it all right.* She looked back up at me from under her long lashes. The want was written all over her face.

I pulled away from her. "Baby, I know exactly what you want. Take off your panties."

"I..."

"Take them off, then turn around and put your hands on the sink."

She seemed to sway at my command. I was right. She wanted it rough and dirty. "Take them off, or I'll take them off for you."

She gulped. "I'm not wearing any."

"Fuck." I grabbed the back of her neck and brought her lips to mine. I pushed against her, pressing her ass back against the sink. She tilted her hips into me. I grabbed her ass and lifted her so that she was now sitting on the sink. She moaned into my mouth as I spread her thighs.

"I don't even know your last name," she panted.

"Is that really what you're worried about right now?" I slid my hand the rest of the way up her thigh and brushed my fingers against her wet pussy. "Because you're dripping wet for me, baby. I think we both know that all you want is my cock deep inside of you." I pressed my thumb down on her clit.

She tilted her head back and moaned softly. I put the tip of my index finger inside her wetness, circling her, teasing her relentlessly. "Mason," she whispered.

The way she said my name made me even harder. She reached down and grabbed my cock through my pants. My dick was straining against the fabric, wanting to burst out. Her eyes bulged slightly. *That's right, baby, you've never been with a man like me before.* Her lips parted slightly. I wanted to thrust my dick deep into that wet mouth of hers. But not yet. I was going to make her wait. She slid her hand up and down, stroking me hard. I grabbed her hand. Damn if she wasn't kinky, just like I said.

"Baby, I promise you'll get a taste. But we haven't even had dinner yet. It's not time for the main event." I kneeled down in front of her and pushed her legs farther apart.

"What are you doing?" She tried to move, but I was gripping her thighs tightly. The nervousness in her voice made my cock swell. She was so innocent. She wouldn't be after the night I had planned, though.

"I'm giving you what you want." I leaned down and sucked hard on her clit. Her body shuddered. I sucked again and then let my tongue swirl around inside of her. *Fuck she tastes good.* Her hand found the back of my head and tried to push me deeper. She didn't have anything to worry about. I was going to give her exactly what she wanted. I plunged my tongue deep inside of her.

"Yes!" She arched her back.

I placed another long stroke against her and moved back to her clit. She tried to move again, but I was holding her firmly in place. If she wanted more, though, I'd give her more. I slid one hand up her inner thigh and plunged two fingers deep inside of her. I began to fuck her with my fingers while still sucking on her clit. She withered under my touch. She was close now.

A knock sounded on the door. "Occupied!" I roared. Her tight pussy clenched around my fingers. She was worried about getting caught. *She's kinky as hell but doesn't want anyone to know. Just me.* I pumped my hand between her thighs, matching the rhythm with my tongue around her clit. She grabbed my biceps, her fingers digging into my skin.

"Mason!"

She clenched around my fingers again and I continued to plunge them inside of her, riding out her orgasm. Her breathing was ragged and her face flushed. She had that just-fucked look that I loved so much.

I pulled my fingers out of her and slid them into my mouth. She swallowed hard as she watched me, complete bliss on her face. I had her exactly where I wanted her.

Chapter 12
Bee

Mason was kneeling in front of me, staring into my eyes. No one had ever gone down on me before. Fuck that was hot. I had never experienced something so intense in my life.

Mason stood up and placed his hands on the sink on either side of me. He leaned in close. I thought he was going to kiss me, but instead he said, "You should clean up. Our dinner's probably getting cold." He leaned back and tightened his tie. He looked in the mirror over my shoulder and ran his hand through his hair.

I just sat there, staring at him. *How had he possessed me like that?* He pulled me off the sink and slid my dress back down my thighs. My knees felt weak. He slapped my ass hard and I let out a tiny yelp.

He smiled and strolled over to the door. He unlocked it and exited without looking back. The shame of what I had just done washed over me as soon as he exited the restroom. *What the hell did I just do?* I barely even knew him. I quickly turned to the mirror and smoothed out my dress. No, Kendra's dress, which she had loaned me. I flushed. I'd get it dry cleaned again before giving it back to her. If she found out what I had done in it, I would be completely mortified.

I wiped away some of the lipstick that had smudged on the side of my mouth, and smoothed down my hair. How could I go back and face him? He had just done something so intimate with me. But he was a stranger. I squeezed my legs together. I'd just go back to the table and excuse myself before I did anything else crazy. It had just been a long time since I had sex. *That's not an excuse.* I felt like such a slut.

Mason raised one eyebrow at me as I wandered back to the table.

"I should probably go."

His eyes were ablaze. "What?"

"I..." I stopped talking when I looked down at him. His cock was still bulging against his pants. I really wanted to taste him. He was so big. I wasn't even sure if he'd fit inside of me. *What am I talking about?!*

"Bee, sit down."

I shook my head. "I need to go."

"Sit down," he said more firmly.

I quickly scooted into my seat. God he was domineering. *And sexy.*

"I know that you enjoyed what we just did. That's only a taste. I've got so much planned for you."

My face flushed. "I think I've given you the wrong impression of me."

"Caldwell."

"What?"

"My last name is Caldwell. Do you feel better now?"

That name sounded so familiar. But I couldn't put my finger on it. "No, not really. I still don't know anything about you."

"I think it makes it a little better." He smiled at me. "Are you really telling me you've never hooked up with a stranger before?"

"No."

His lips curled into a smile.

"I'm glad you find me humorous."

The waiter came over and placed our steaks on the table. "Is there anything else I can get for you?"

It felt like he was staring at me. *Shit, does he know?* I had to be imagining it. No one had seen us; the door was locked.

"We're fine, thank you, Ethan," Mason said.

The waiter smiled and walked away. Dinner smelled amazing. I hadn't realized how famished I was. I quickly cut into the steak and took a bite.

"Mmm," I sighed.

"You do like meat in your mouth."

I swallowed. "I like steak."

"We'll see what else you like."

I grabbed my wine glass and took a long sip. I didn't have any resolve left. Even though my mind was telling me no, my body was telling me yes. I wanted him and I couldn't seem to control myself. I had never been so instantly attracted to someone in my life.

"I guess we will see." I gave him a challenging look.

"How many men have you been with?"

I shifted in my seat. There was never a segue between any of his questions. He was brash and didn't seem to give a fuck about what came out of his mouth. "That's an inappropriate question."

"We're on a date. All we're supposed to be doing is asking each other inappropriate, invasive questions."

"Fine. One."

"I don't mean how many boyfriends you've had. I mean how many men have you fucked, Bee?"

He was so condescending. "One."

He swallowed a bite of his steak. "You're serious?"

"Yes."

"I didn't know I was working with someone so inexperienced. I don't mind teaching. But I am surprised. Looking at you, I never would have guessed."

"What does that even mean?"

"You're sexy as hell."

"That doesn't necessarily mean that I'm easy."

"Baby, I just made you come in the bathroom with my tongue."

I leaned forward. "Yeah, which I've never done before."

"Wait, what have you never done before?"

"You know..."

"In the bathroom, you mean?"

"And your tongue."

He was staring at me. His Adam's apple rose and fell. Was my telling him this turning him on even more? He actually liked that I was inexperienced?

"And you know. The other thing too." I bit my lip.

Mason laughed.

I stared back at him.

"Fuck, Bee." He grabbed my knee under the table. "You've never had an orgasm before that? Are you serious?"

I blushed scarlet.

There was a hunger in his eyes. "Then you're about to have the best night of your life." A random waiter passed by our table. "Check please!" Mason yelled.

Chapter 13

Mason

"I'm not going to sleep with you, Mason."

She was still playing hard to get even though I had already proven that she was anything but. "Yes you are."

"You're awfully cocky."

I grinned. "Yes...I am." I looked down at my lap and then back up at her.

"That's not what cocky means." She looked around the restaurant to see if anyone heard us. She was so hot when she was flustered. " We've barely talked. I still don't know you."

"All you need to know is that I'm going to fuck your brains out tonight."

"Who talks like that?" She bit her lip.

"Apparently guys that you're into. Finish eating, you're going to need the energy." She looked down at her half eaten steak, but instead of taking a bite, she took another sip of wine. *Even better.*

Ethan came over with the check. "Is there anything else I can get for you this evening?"

"No, that'll be all," I said.

"Actually, I would like some dessert." Bee looked at me innocently.

"What? No, you don't need that."

Ethan got a shocked look on his face.

"Did you just say that I don't need that?" Bee had a shocked look on her face too. But it didn't look real. She had to be messing with me.

"That's not what I meant." She needed to stop playing games with me. Once I had her tied down she'd know her place.

"Then what did you mean, Mason?"

She was driving me crazy. I turned to Ethan. "Just the check please. She forgot that I already have dessert planned for her." I turned back to Bee. "Something better."

"Very well, sir." He put the bill down on the table. "I hope you both have a good evening."

As soon as Ethan walked away, Bee laughed.

"What is wrong with you? You made him think I was calling you fat. Which clearly you aren't."

"I'm sorry. You're so tightly wound." She put her elbows on the table and rested her chin in her hands.

How was she this sexy? I needed to get a grip. "Where do you live?"

"Yeah...I'm not going to tell you that. You might be a stalker or something." She took another sip of wine.

"You're being impossible."

She sighed. "The upper west side."

"My place is closer." I peeled a few hundred dollar bills from my wallet and put them on top of the bill. "Okay, let's go." I quickly downed my glass of cabernet.

"I'm not done."

"I already told you that I'm going to give you something better to eat." I stood up and reached for her hand.

The fight she was having within was visible on her face. She wanted to be a good girl. But she wanted to know what it felt like to be with a real man. And I needed my cock deep inside her tight pussy.

I leaned down and whispered in her ear. "You won't regret this. Baby, you don't even know what living is yet."

Her eyes shone with lust. I put my hand back out for her. Bee looked at me again. *She can't resist me.* She hesitantly put out her hand. I grabbed it and pulled her to her feet.

"Come with me." I intertwined my fingers with hers and led her to the front of the restaurant. This was going to be the longest cab ride of my life.

"I checked my coat. Hold on a second."

I reluctantly let go of her hand. I folded my arms across my chest and leaned against the wall. The hostess was staring at me, but I only had one girl on my mind. *Bee.* I shook my head. She had crawled under my skin. *What is this girl doing to me?* I was losing control. I walked over to the hostess and put my arm down on the podium.

"How was your meal?" she asked.

"Excellent. But you told me to ask you if there was anything that I needed. And I don't know about need..." I leaned in slightly and whispered, "but there is definitely something that I want."

Her face flushed. "And what might that be?"

"Your number."

The girl glanced to the left toward the coat check. "What about your girlfriend?"

"Baby, I don't do the whole girlfriend thing."

She leaned in slightly. "So what makes you think that I don't do the whole boyfriend thing?"

I laughed. "A girl like you? You're probably a serial monogamist."

"I'm not..."

"And that's why you could use a night with me." I cut her off. "To show you what you've been missing. One night with me and..." I pulled away from the podium when I saw Bee come back around the corner. I was just getting my composure back, but when I saw Bee I completely lost my train of thought.

"And what?" The hostess tried to catch my attention.

I patted the podium. "You missed your chance, sweetheart. Stick to the boyfriend thing." I walked over to Bee as she was putting her jacket on. As soon as she was done, I grabbed her hand again and steered her to the exit.

"Geez, slow down. There's no rush," she said.

"My erection would beg to differ," I said as I pushed through the doors and stepped onto the city street.

She pulled her hand out of mine. "Don't you know that you're supposed to woo a girl? What happened to chivalry?"

"The things I'm going to do to you tonight are going to be anything but chivalrous. And you're going to love every second of it." I grabbed both sides of her face and kissed her hard. Instead of pulling back like I thought she would, she leaned in, pressing her hips against my erection. I forced her mouth open wider with my tongue. *Maybe I should just fuck her in the alleyway.*

Chapter 14
Bee

I felt slightly dizzy when he finally released me from his grip. I was in way over my head. This wasn't me. I didn't have sex with strangers. A few people passed by us on the sidewalk. *Are they staring?*

I looked up at Mason, but realized his eyes were on my cleavage. I glanced down. *Shit*. My dress had slid down during out kiss. My lace bra was peeking out above the neckline. No wonder people were staring. I quickly grabbed the top of my dress and lifted the neckline back in place.

"I was considering our options," Mason said, as his eyes wandered over the rest of me. I had never felt so self-conscious in my life.

"Options?"

"Well, I could either wait to take you back to my place, or I could give you your dessert right now. It seems like the thought of getting caught excites you."

"What?" I looked around us again. It was late, but there were dozens of people around us. *The city that never sleeps.*

"Take your pick, Bee."

I stared back at him. Where did he even mean? We couldn't do it here. My heart was racing. He was right, I did get turned on by the thought of getting caught. Or maybe I was just so turned on because of the way he was looking at me. *What is happening to me?*

"Can't decide, huh? I'll give you five seconds, or I'll decide for you."

"I..."

"How about both?" He grabbed my hand and led me down the street.

"Where are we going?" I almost had to jog to keep up with him. He didn't answer me. He just walked silently, looking to the left and right.

"This will do," he finally said. He stepped left, pulling me with him toward a back alley.

I stood my ground. "I'm not going down there. Are you trying to get mugged?"

"No one would try to mug me. I'm going to fuck you, right here, right now." He lightly brushed my cheek with his fingertips.

His words were naughty but his touch was gentle. A chill ran down my spine.

"Let's go. Now."

When I didn't respond, he slapped my ass hard. I yelped in surprise. *Oh my God!* Any passerby could have seen that. My heart was beating so fast. I stood there staring at him.

"Bee, you do not want to make me wait."

"Maybe I do." I was more aroused than ever. I liked the feeling of the sting from his palm.

He slapped my ass again.

"I like when you do that."

I watched his Adam's apple rise and fall. He exhaled slowly as he looked down at me. "I told you not to make me wait." He bent down and lifted me over his shoulder.

"Mason, put me down," I hissed. But I didn't really want him to. His hand gently caressed the spot where he had slapped me. I couldn't control the moan that escaped from my lips. With each step into the darkness of the alley, I wanted him more and more.

He stopped and slowly set me back down on my feet by a dumpster. The alley was anything but sexy, but Mason made up for it. His face was shadowed, but I could still see his chiseled jaw.

"Do you think anyone can see us?" I asked.

I watched as Mason unbuttoned and unzipped his pants. He pushed them and his boxers down slightly, releasing his massive cock.

"Do you really care?

I gulped. He wasn't lying. He was huge. His cock didn't even compare to Patrick's. There was no way that I could fit the whole thing in my mouth.

"That's what I thought," he said. "Don't be shy, baby. You know you want to know what a real man feels like."

I was mesmerized. I reached out my hand and wrapped it around him. He groaned in response and stiffened even more. My hand barely fit around him. I ran it up and down his length and he groaned again. His cock felt strong and muscular. *Is that even possible?* It didn't matter. I knew exactly what I wanted and I didn't care if it was wrong. I needed to know what it felt like for him to be inside of me.

I continued to stroke him as I stood on my tiptoes and kissed him. He pushed my back against the brick wall and lifted both my hands above my head, holding me firmly in place. He pressed his erection against me and I met it with my hips. *Even this feels good.*

"I promised you dessert. Get on your knees." He released my hands.

I wasn't good at giving head. Patrick had even told me that. But I had never wanted a cock as much as I wanted Mason's. Just the thought of him in my mouth made me breathless. I wanted to taste him. I pressed my finger against my lower lip.

"Turn around."

"What?" I was just about to kneel. I wanted him.

"You need to learn to obey me."

Obey. Everything below my waist clenched.

"Put your hands on the wall."

I gulped and quickly turned around. Whatever he was about to do, I wanted it. I wanted his massive cock so deep inside of me that I screamed.

As soon as my hands touched the cold wall, Mason was pushing up my coat and dress. My ass was completely exposed, the cold nipping at my cheeks.

"Spread your legs."

I followed his instructions. He was about to give me exactly what I wanted. But instead of his hard cock thrusting inside of me, I felt his fingertips brush the back of my knee. *Oh.* He ran his fingers up the back of my thigh. I arched my back, shoving my ass higher into the air. I needed him.

He answered with a hard slap on my bare ass. The sound echoing in the alleyway was worse than the feeling. Actually, it felt good. He caressed my cheek where his hand had landed. The contrast was unsettling. He slapped me again. I felt my ass jiggle under his hand. *Why do I like this?*

I could hear his breathing getting heavy behind me. *Is he getting off to this?* I wanted him to get off inside of me, not like this. He slapped me again, harder, and I let out a yelp of pain.

He grabbed the sides of my dress and pulled it down. He smoothed the cloth back in place and gently cupped my searing cheek. I whimpered under his touch.

"Now get on your knees."

I didn't hesitate this time. I turned around, got down on my knees, and stared up at him, waiting for whatever was next. He was stroking himself as he looked down at me. If it was possible, his erection had gotten even thicker.

"Is this what you want, Bee?" He continued to stroke himself.

I nodded. I did, I wanted him. "Yes."

"Tell me exactly what you want."

"I want you in my mouth. I want all of you, Mason. Every inch."

"Fuck, Bee." He grabbed a fistful of my hair and shoved his cock into the back of my throat.

Chapter 15
Mason

Her mouth wasn't big enough for me, but she was taking it all. She said she wanted every inch and I was going to deliver. I gripped her hair and pushed myself deeper into her throat. She still had lust in her eyes. She liked the taste of me. *Just wait until I cum right in that sweet mouth. You'll drink down every ounce and beg me for more.*

Bee moaned and tightened her lips around my shaft. *Fuck.* I released her hair. I wanted to see what those red lips could do. She locked eyes with me as her mouth slid to my tip. Her tongue swirled around me.

She reached up and gripped my balls in her hand as she slid her lips down. I felt the familiar pull deep in my gut. This girl was good. I wanted to fuck her warm mouth, but I waited. She was enjoying this as much as me, and I wanted her to get a good taste of what I was going to do to her later. I groaned when my tip hit the back of my throat. I felt the resistance, but I wanted to enter that tightness and claim her mouth.

I reached my hand to the back of her head. But I didn't have to push her deeper. Instead, she grabbed my ass and took my cock all the fucking way down.

CITY OF SIN

Her lips trembled around me as a moan escaped from her lips. This girl wasn't innocent at all. She was a fucking animal.

Bee pulled back and her tongue swirled around my tip again, teasing me. She leaned forward and grabbed the base of my shaft. She slid her hand and mouth up and down in perfect rhythm, faster and faster. Her throat must be sore, but I wasn't done with it yet.

She moaned again. *I bet she's dripping wet now, just wishing I was pounding that tight pussy.*

I unwound her hand from my length. "Touch yourself."

I watched as she slid her hand up her thigh. *Shit.* I wanted that to be me. I wanted to taste her again.

She hesitated at the top of her thigh.

"Pretend it's my tongue, deep inside of you, making you come all over again."

She slid her hand between her thighs. She moaned as she touched herself, her lips vibrating against my shaft. She had the perfect amount of suction. I groaned as I watched her head bobbing up and down. She pumped her hand between her thighs as she sucked me hard. A girl getting herself off made me hard as a rock.

I grabbed a fist full of her hair and pounded myself inside her mouth. She locked eyes with me again. "Time for dessert, sweetheart." I grabbed her hair harder and thrust myself deep inside her wet mouth, pounding against the back of her throat. After several more thrusts I felt me cock throb against her lips. My hot cum shot into her mouth, again and again. Her eyes glazed over as she drank me down hungrily. She moaned against my shaft, sending a chill down my spine.

When she pulled away, she wiped the side of her mouth and put her finger in her mouth. Fuck was she sexy. I wanted those red lips around me all over again. Her other hand was still between her thighs, swirling around that tight pussy. She watched me as I zipped my pants. I knew exactly what she wanted.

"Bee," I said softly and rubbed my thumb against her bottom lip. Her skillful mouth had earned her a reward. "It's your turn."

She bit her lip where my thumb had just been. I reached down, grabbed both her hands, and pulled her off her knees. I pushed her back against the brick wall, reached down, and slid my hand between her hot thighs. She needed to know the way that she had made me feel. I plunged my finger deep inside of her.

She tilted her head back against the wall. "Mason," she moaned breathlessly.

I pumped my hand relentlessly, watching her breathing hitch with every pump. She was so wet for me, and I wanted her sweet juices again. I pushed her thighs apart and bent down in front of her, shoving my tongue inside that delicious cunt.

She moaned again. "Oh God!"

I trailed my free hand up her stomach until I found her luscious breasts. I squeezed her breast hard as I licked up and down her slit. Her body writhed against my hand. She was so responsive to my tongue and my touch. I felt my dick swell against my pants, imagining how she'd react with me deep inside her.

I slid my fingers back inside her tightness and placed my lips around her clit.

"Mason!"

I sucked hard and felt her clench around my fingers. I squeezed her breast again as she came. *Fuck.* She had come again for me in less than a minute. *Where has this girl been hiding?*

Chapter 16
Bee

My knees felt weak. If he wasn't still holding me against the wall I would have melted to the ground. He kissed the inside of my thigh before pulling my dress back down. I bit my lip. Everything he did and said was dirty. It was scary how much he affected me.

He stood up and put his hands on the brick wall on either side of my head. I gulped. He already had another erection. I could feel it pressed against my thigh, right next to where he had just kissed me. He leaned in so that our lips were less than an inch apart. His breath was warm. The cold wind was picking up around us. I shivered as I stared back at him.

This was unbearable. The intensity I felt with him seemed unreal. He was irresistible. I tilted my head back so that he'd kiss me. When his kiss didn't come, I wrapped my arms around the back of his neck and made the move. His kiss was soft and gentle. His tongue tasted like sex. I needed him now, all of him.

"You promised me something," I whispered as seductively as I could.

"I'm true to my word, Bee." He let his hands fall from the wall and he intertwined his fingers with mine. He led me out of the alley.

Once we were back on the sidewalk, he let go of my hand and stared at me.

"It's freezing." My teeth were chattering. "Can we go?" What, was he going to make me beg to take me back to his place?

"Show me what you got."

"What do you mean?"

"Get us a taxi."

"Isn't that the man's job?"

"Yeah, but I'm no gentleman. Don't start getting the wrong idea about me now. Besides, you need to learn how not to be a pushover."

"I'm not a pushover," I said. His words stung because they were true. I thought about how I was always the last one at the office. And how I let my boss hit on me without standing up for myself. I was a pushover for coming to New York in the first place. I hated it here. This was the first good night I'd had in months.

"Show me what you got," Mason repeated.

I turned to the street. A taxi was coming by. I waved my hand and stepped out onto the curb. The taxi sped by.

I sighed. "They usually stop."

"Watch and learn, sugar." Mason cracked his knuckles.

I rolled my eyes at him.

He stepped onto the curb. As the next cab came into view, he put his fingers to his mouth and whistled while sticking his other hand out to signal the driver. The taxi pulled up in front of us.

"Well that's great if you can whistle."

"You can't whistle?"

I shook my head.

"I'm surprised." He leaned in close. "Your lips are very talented, Bee."

I blushed. I had never liked giving head before, but with Mason it was different. Everything was different with him. And he still had more to show me.

"After you," he said. I reached for the handle, but he quickly grabbed it before me.

"Déjà vu."

"You have to stand right by where the door opens. Or else you can easily be swooped."

"Swooped? Is that was assholes call that move?"

Mason opened up the door. "Get in."

I slid into the seat. He slammed the door and quickly walked around the taxi. He got in beside me. *This is it.* I was becoming one of those girls. The kind that sleep around. I had never slept with anyone but Patrick. And everything I had already done with Mason seemed better. *What if I don't want this to be a one night stand?* He wasn't the commitment type. There was absolutely no way.

He moved to the middle seat so that my left side brushed against him. That feeling of electricity shooting through me would never get old. He leaned over and grabbed my seatbelt. He pulled the strap across my torso and buckled it in place. His eyes locked with mine. He liked me strapped down. Was he really going to tie me up back at his place? I was more excited than nervous at the prospect.

He turned to face the driver. "Trump International." Mason quickly buckled his own seatbelt and leaned back. "And we're in a hurry."

"Of course, sir." The driver turned off the curb and sped off into the night.

"I thought you said we were going to your place?" I asked.

"That's where I live."

"Isn't that an office building?"

"No, Bee, it's a hotel."

"You live in a hotel?" Was he loaded? Marie and Carter hadn't mentioned anything about that.

"It has apartments too. Well, condos, technically."

"Where?"

"I'm not sure I want to tell you that. You could be a stalker after all."

Chapter 17

Mason

She was staring at me innocently from under her long lashes again. I'd need to call Carter and thank him in the morning. I owed him for this one.

I leaned back in my seat. Trump International was the only good thing I still had. Just telling girls I lived there made their panties drop. It would be hard to walk away from that. But enough was enough. It was time to go off on my own. Besides, I'd completely crush dickweed Darren when I started a competing advertising agency. I'd be back in Trump International in no time, maybe in the penthouse.

I put my hand on Bee's leg. I didn't want to think of my fucked up boss or my shitty job. All I wanted was to lose myself inside of her.

She crossed her legs, pushing my hand away.

She was losing her nerve. I needed to get her attention back. I put my hand on the back of her neck and gently rubbed my thumb up and down the top of her spine. She shivered under my touch. *That's right, baby.* "Nervous for the main event, are you?"

"Should I be? What are you planning on doing to me?" Her voice was wispy with desire.

"What do you want me to do to you? What's your wildest fantasy?"

She bit her lip in thought. Her wildest fantasy was me. It was written all over her face. Soon it would be my cum dripping down that pretty face.

"Tell me more about yourself, Mason."

I scowled at her.

"We have a few more minutes to get to know each other."

"What do you want to know?"

"Do you have any siblings?"

"I don't see why that's important. But yes, I have a younger brother."

"Does he live here too?"

"You mean in the city?"

She nodded.

"Yes."

"What about your parents?"

"What about them?" *What's with the rapid fire questioning?*

"Do they live near you?"

"They live closer to you, actually. On the upper west side."

"Are you close with your family?"

"Close enough."

"You don't like answering questions do you? So mysterious."

"There won't be many secrets between us soon. By the end of the night I'm going to know every curve of your body and everything that makes you tick. And that's all I need to keep you crawling back for more."

"That's all superficial. Maybe I'm ugly on the inside."

"I don't think so. You're quite charitable with those lips, Bee." I smiled as her face turned crimson.

"You know what I mean," she continued.

Damn it, what is taking so long? This had to be the slowest taxi I'd ever been in. I glanced in the rearview mirror. The cabby was staring at Bee's tits. I gave him a fuck off look and put my arm across her shoulders.

I leaned over to whisper in her ear. "You worry too much, Bee. Maybe I can make you relax." I lightly bit her earlobe. A soft moan escaped from her lips. I licked the inside of her ear, caressing her softly.

She grabbed my knee.

"You liked my fingers, driving you insane."

"Yes," she whispered.

"Better than any dick that's been inside of you."

"Yes."

"And my tongue, driving you over the edge."

"Mmm." Her whole body seemed to quiver.

I moved my tongue behind her ear and she tilted her head to the side.

"Are you wet for me, Bee? Ready for my cock to spread you wide?"

She moaned.

"I'm going to claim every inch of you. You'll never want anything but my cock inside of you."

Her fingers dug into my skin.

"I'll show you how close the line is between pleasure and pain. You have no idea what you've been missing all these years." I bit her earlobe once more and leaned back in my seat.

She looked up at me with pleading eyes.

"We're almost there, Bee." I pointed out the window.

Bee's jaw dropped as soon as my place came in view. *That's right, I'll be fucking you with views of Central Park.*

"That's where the mysterious Mason Caldwell lives?" She smiled, but her smile vanished almost as quickly as it had appeared. She turned away from me and looked out the window.

"Wait till you see inside, Bee." *Wait until you see what I'm going to do to you inside.*

CHAPTER 18
Bee

It felt like my heart sunk in my chest. *Caldwell*. I knew I had recognized that name. I stared at the towering building as the cab came to a stop outside. *Why me?*

"The wait is over. I'm going to fuck you so hard you won't be able to walk for days," he whispered in my ear.

I pushed my thighs together. My heart was beating so fast. *Shit.*

He slid over to the side and stepped out of the taxi. He closed the door and began to walk around the cab. *Mason fucking Caldwell.*

I pushed the lock down on my door. "West 96th Street!"

The driver just looked back at me.

"Go, now."

"Ma'am are you sure..."

"Please! Just go!"

Mason reached for the door handle just as the taxi driver stepped on the gas. Mason slapped the window with his palm.

"Bee!" he yelled at the top of his lungs.

As soon as the taxi pulled away from the curb, I regretted it. I was still wet from Mason's naughty words. Was he really as good as he said he was? I turned around and looked out the back window. Mason was standing in the middle of the street, staring at the taxi as I drove away.

CHAPTER 19
Bee

My phone was buzzing in my pocket. Marie was calling me. I let it go to voicemail. I was so mad at her. If I talked to her now, I'd just say something I regretted. There was already one missed call from Kendra. My rescue call. I should have taken it. I felt so dirty. Of all the guys in New York, why had Marie set me up with Mason Caldwell?

The taxi pulled to a stop outside my apartment building. I paid the driver and stepped onto the sidewalk. I ran into my building, up the stairs, and into my apartment.

I began to pull my clothes out of my closet and throw them into a box. Fuck New York. Fuck Mr. Ellington. Fuck Patrick. And fuck Mason Caldwell. Enough was enough. I had given it my best shot. Now I just needed to get out of New York. There was nothing left for me here.

When I got to the back of my closet I stopped. My wedding dress was hanging there. I pulled it out and placed it on top of the box. Patrick and I were supposed to get married in the fall. The bridal store had called a few weeks after Patrick and I had split up. The alterations were already done, and they wouldn't take it back. I should have been married right now. To the boy that I fell in love with freshman year.

Instead, I was alone in a dingy apartment and I had just sucked Mason Caldwell's dirty cock. I sat down in front of the box and started to cry. How could this have happened? Where had I gone wrong?

***

I slowly opened my eyes. Someone was knocking on my door. I had fallen asleep on the floor. *Ow.* My whole body ached. It looked like I had blown my nose on the train of my wedding dress. *Great.* I yawned and got up.

Whoever was outside my door knocked again. I looked out the peephole. It was Kendra. She looked really upset. *Shit.* I never called her back. She probably thought I had been abducted. I opened up the door.

"Oh my God, you're alive." She threw her arms around me.

"Hi, Kendra."

"You're alive." Now she sounded mad. She let go of me and pushed my shoulder. "Do you know how worried I was? I've only called you a million times! I thought you were dead in a ditch." She stared at me.

I was still wearing her dress. I looked down. It was wrinkled and slightly stretched out.

She looked past me at the box of clothes on the floor. "We'll talk about my dress later. What are you doing?" She gestured toward the box.

"I'm moving, Kendra. I'm done."

"The date was that bad?"

I sat down on the edge of my bed. I felt my face blush. "I actually had a really good time. Until I figured out who he was."

"What do you mean?" She sat down next to me.

"It was something that Patrick said to me."

"What? I thought you were done thinking about Patrick? Please don't revert back just because of one bad date."

"I'm not. I..." I let my voice trail off. "There's more to the story of Patrick cheating on me. I didn't tell you everything."

"Okay?"

I swallowed hard. This was so embarrassing. I hadn't told anyone that Patrick had cheated on me with more than one woman. I still wasn't even sure how many other women he had slept with while we were together. And I really didn't want to know. "When I confronted Patrick, he told me that he was just doing what was expected of him. That women were like an employee perk or something."

"That's a pretty lame excuse. Men are disgusting."

"He used to go to these, like, underground clubs or something? I don't know. I don't really want to talk about that part. But he said that it was the boss' son that had taken him to all those sleazy places. Almost like an introduction to the city or something ridiculous like that. Patrick said that his boss' son could get you anything you wanted." I scrunched up my face. "Like any weird sexual fantasy you had, he could find the person to help make it happen."

"I don't understand why this has anything to do with Mason."

"The founder of MAC International is Max Caldwell. I think Mason is his son."

"Wait, seriously?" Kendra laughed. "That's a pretty far leap."

"Mason seemed...I don't know. It was him. You should have heard the way he talked. He said his hobby was fucking women. He was a tool. And it's his fault that Patrick cheated on me."

"Bee, that's ridiculous. I bet he isn't even Max Caldwell's son. Caldwell is a common name. And so is Mason." She pulled out her phone and opened up Google. A few seconds later she frowned. "Okay, well maybe he does have a son named Mason. Is this him?" She put her phone in my face.

"Yeah, that's him."

"Wow, he's so sexy. Damn. Why doesn't Marie ever set me up with anyone?"

"Kendra, he's a dick."

"Well Max Caldwell has another son. Matthew. Maybe he's the one that helped entertain Max's new hires?" She showed me a picture of Matthew. He didn't look much like his brother. He was handsome, but in a more sophisticated way. I couldn't really explain it, but he looked tight-laced. He didn't look like he frequented underground clubs and had connections with all sorts of weird loose women.

"No. It's Mason. It's definitely Mason. He talked like he had sex all the time. And he was...experienced."

"Shit, did you have sex with him?"

"No. Not exactly."

"What does that mean?"

"It doesn't matter. He's a man whore. And I'm moving."

"Come on. Let's go talk to Marie. I'm sure she can clear this up for you. Besides, if he is Max Caldwell's son, then he's loaded. And you shouldn't write him off so easily. You could use a few nice things."

"Kendra! Don't be gross. I don't want his money. I don't want anything to do with a guy like that. He's worse than Patrick."

She looked around my apartment. "Why is it again that you won't move in with me? We could split the rent and my apartment is a lot nicer than this."

She had asked me a few times to move in with her. It was another step that I wasn't quite ready to make. My last good memories of Patrick were in this apartment. It was like changing my relationship status on Facebook. It just seemed so final. I didn't want to have a conversation about moving right now. Besides, if I was moving anywhere, it was back to Wilmington.

"I'm not ready."

"But you're ready to move back to Wilmington? Come on, let's go. And change out of my dress." She picked up a pair of jeans and tossed them at me.

Chapter 20
Bee

Kendra held down the button on the call box. "Marie, it's Kendra and Bee!" When no answer came through the speaker system, she pressed the button again. "You have a lot of explaining to do, Marie! Wake up!"

"I doubt she knew." I said. "She even told me that Mason and Patrick didn't know each other."

"Still. She set you up with the guy that taught Patrick how to be a cheating piece of shit. And thought he was a good match for you. If you ask me, that's pretty fucked up."

Marie was probably asleep. This was ridiculous. All I really wanted was to be curled up in bed, pretending last night had never happened. I shook my head. *How will I ever forget his touch?* The way Mason had possessed me had made me feel so alive, so amped up. I needed to calm down and get some more sleep. *I need to dream of him.* I shook my head. He was disgusting.

The door buzzed. Kendra ran over, grabbed the handle, and held the door open for me. As soon as we stepped onto the elevator, Kendra crossed her arms in front of her chest.

"You know, I could have set you up with someone," she said. "Someone who isn't worse than Patrick."

"Maybe next time."

She sighed as we got off the elevator. We stopped in front of Marie and Carter's door and Kendra knocked loudly. A second later Marie opened it.

"Bee, Kendra, what are you guys doing here?" Marie asked groggily. Her hair was matted on one side and she was wearing a silk robe. But I was too agitated to care that I had woken her. Seeing her made me upset all over again.

"You didn't tell me that you were setting me up with Mason Caldwell!"

"What are you talking about? I did. I told you his name, Bee. What are you doing here?" Marie repeated and rubbed her eyes.

"Mason Caldwell?! How could you, Marie?" I walked past her and into her apartment. I sat down on the couch and put my face in my hands.

"Oh my God, he stood you up? Carter! Carter get out of bed right this instant! I can't believe Mason would do this, Bee. I told him how important you were to me. Carter promised this wouldn't happen." She tilted her head toward her bedroom. "Damn it, Carter! Get out of bed!"

"No, Marie, that's not it," Kendra said and sat down next to me.

Carter stumbled out of their bedroom, yawning. "Oh, hey, Bee. Hey, Kendra. Geez, it's a little early, isn't it?"

"Bee, what happened? What did he do?" Marie said.

"It's not what he did. We actually had an okay time." I felt myself blushing. This was ridiculous. "He's an asshole, Marie."

I heard a buzzing noise and Carter pulled his cell phone out of his robe pocket. "Geez, I have a ton of missed calls." He put the phone to his ear. "Hey, man, what's up?" He paused. "Oh, no need. Bee's actually right here."

I glared at him. Marie started to shake her head back and forth and wave her arms.

Carter put the phone down and held his hand over the receiver. "I already told him you were here. Sorry, Bee."

"I don't want to talk to him," I said.

Carter looked over at Marie, but she just glared back at him. He lifted the phone back up to his ear. "Mason, she doesn't want to talk to you right now."

"Damn it, Carter! You weren't supposed to tell him that!" I shrieked.

"What was I supposed to say? You are here, and you don't want to talk to him. Don't look at me that way, Marie."

"It's fine, I'll talk to him."

Carter walked over and handed me the phone. "I'm going back to bed."

I looked down at Carter's phone in my hand.

"Were going to give you some privacy," Marie said and grabbed Kendra's arm. Kendra followed her into the kitchen. It wasn't that much privacy. The kitchen was open to the family room.

I sighed and put the phone to my ear. "Hello, Mason."

"Bee, what the hell?"

"What the hell yourself, Mason."

"Stay where you are. I'm coming to get you."

"Don't you dare." *Who does this guy think he is?*

"I do dare."

"Mason, I can't see you again."

"And why not?"

"Because you're Mason Caldwell. Which means that your father is Max Caldwell."

"What does this have to do with my father?"

I swallowed hard. "My ex-fiancé worked for him."

"Stay where you are."

"Just tell me, Mason. Did you introduce my fiancé to a bunch of sleazy women?"

"You don't understand. Just let me explain..."

"Go to hell, Mason."

"Bee, if you would..."

"Bridget. Only my friends call me Bee." I hung up the phone.

Chapter 21
Mason

What the fuck? No one ever hung up on me. I shoved my phone back into my pocket. *This isn't good.* If her ex-fiancé worked for my dad, then I had definitely met him. *Shit.*

I put my hand in the air to signal a nearby taxi. The cab pulled to a stop in front of me. I climbed in and gave him Carter's address. No girl had ever blue balled me. I had already made up my mind to have her, and have her I would. Bee was mine. I'd have her today and anything I had done wouldn't matter. She wouldn't care after I gave her the best night of her life. I was getting hard all over again just thinking about her tight ass and those luscious red lips.

I closed my eyes and let my head fall back against the seat. *Who the hell is her ex?* I tried to go through all the men that reported to my father. None of them seemed like Bee's type. They all acted like a bunch of pussies. A girl like that shouldn't have been with one of them anyway. As far as I was concerned, I had done her a favor. She should be thanking me.

But she knew. She knew who I was. Whoever that little shit was had told her all about me. And she probably thought it was my fault that he had cheated on her.

I punched the back of the passenger's seat.

"Watch it!" the cabbie yelled at me.

I leaned back in my seat. *What am I going to tell her?* Temptation and opportunity were different than action. But she didn't want to hear that. It depended on what she already knew about me. I could skirt around the truth. It was one of my specialties. I stared out my window at the passing buildings. We were getting close.

Chapter 22
Bee

Marie and Kendra were staring at me.

I turned away from them and looked down at Carter's phone. He had eight missed calls from Mason. I put the phone down on the coffee table. Why did Mason even care about clearing the air with me? He was a rich, eligible, sexy bachelor. He could have any woman that he wanted. Just not me. I tried to think about what Patrick had said. Company perks he had called them. *Disgusting.*

"Bee, I had no idea." Marie sat down across from me. "If I had known, I obviously wouldn't have set you up with him."

"I know." I looked down at my lap. "He said he was coming over. I can't see him."

"I'll take care of him," Kendra said.

"You never really told me that much about what happened with Patrick. I didn't even know that his boss' son was taking him to strip clubs," Marie said.

"Well it's awkward to talk about. And it wasn't really strip clubs. Patrick made it seem like his boss' son was showing him around the city with the other new hires. And that he had all these weird connections. I didn't realize he was going to underground clubs and stuff. I thought he was seeing the top of the empire state building. But when I eventually realized, Patrick made it seem like you could just tell Mason your fantasy and he'd figure out a way to make it happen. Like he knew every person with weird fetishes in the whole city."

"Gross."

"Yeah."

"I don't get it though. Mason seems like such a nice guy at work. And he makes a decent salary. I don't know why he'd be doing that. It doesn't make any sense. Maybe his father is just a bad guy? Or maybe it's Max's other son?"

"It's definitely Mason. And I don't know why he did it, but he did. They're both disgusting."

"You can't really blame him for the things that Patrick did though. Just because he introduced Patrick to other women doesn't mean he made him cheat on you."

"That's a fine line."

"Maybe you should hear him out."

"I don't want anything to do with guys like him."

Kendra cleared her throat.

Marie glanced at Kendra and that back at me. "I need to tell you something, but you have to promise you won't get mad at me."

"What?"

"You promise you won't be mad?"

"I'm not going to get mad at you. Just tell me."

"Mason is known as a bit of a playboy. I just thought he might help you get over Patrick and I didn't think..."

"You knew what kind of guy he was?"

"I didn't know about the underground clubs or any of that. I didn't even know he knew Patrick."

"But you knew he was a womanizing asshole?"

"He always seems so nice at work. I thought maybe they were just rumors. And you did have a good time. You blushed when you were talking about him."

"How could you, Marie?"

"I was just trying to help you get over Patrick. You need to move on. You've been moping around for months. It's not healthy."

"But you picked the worst possible guy."

"I picked a handsome, successful..."

"Oh, come on, Marie," Kendra cut in. "Give it a rest. You screwed up."

"I know." Marie turned back to me and grabbed my hand. "I just wanted you to know where I was coming from. But I'm so, so sorry, Bee."

The buzzer sounded through the apartment.

"I can't see him again," I said. "Kendra, can you..."

"Yup. I've got you." She left the apartment.

Chapter 23
Mason

A tall woman with skin the color of hot chocolate came out of the building. She stared at me with her deep brown eyes. I instantly felt a little less cold. I turned back to the speaker system and pressed the number for Carter's apartment again. Bee had crawled under my skin. And right now, she was the only girl I could think about. I wasn't used to feeling like this. She liked making me wait. I never waited for anyone. I needed to fuck her and move on.

The woman tapped me on the shoulder.

Fuck, not right now. "What can I do for you, sugar?"

"Sugar? Wow. Innovative."

I laughed. "Can I help you? I'm kind of in the middle of something right now."

"The pictures don't do you justice. I'm Kendra."

"Pictures?"

"You're Max Caldwell's son right? The infamous Mason Caldwell? I've heard a lot about you."

I looked down at her. I didn't have time to play games right now. "What exactly are you referring to?"

"Your side business? See, I have certain needs. And I was hoping you could help me out?"

I didn't want to talk business right now. "My services aren't free, sugar." I pressed the button on the call box again. "Fuck, is this thing even working?"

"God, it's true? You're disgusting."

"What?" I turned around and looked at the woman again. "Oh, fuck, are you friends with Bee or something? Did she send you down here to talk to me? Just let me up to see her."

"It killed her when she found out her fiancé was cheating on her. And you helped that happen." She poked me in the middle of my chest.

"I don't even know who her ex-fiancé is. All I know is that I need to talk to Bee. In private. So what do I need to do to make that happen? I can get you whatever you want. Just name it."

"What is wrong with you? She's been through enough. She doesn't need someone like you in her life right now. Just leave her alone."

I can't leave her alone. I can't stop thinking about her. I ran my hand through my hair. "This whole thing is just a misunderstanding."

"Do you or do you not give your father's new employees certain perks for signing with MAC International?"

I laughed. That was an interesting spin on it. "I don't work for my father. I work for an ad agency across town. Finance isn't really my thing. Come on, sugar, just let me up to see Bee."

"That doesn't answer my question."

"Look, I like her, okay? We had an amazing date until she just ran off in a taxi without any explanation. I'm not trying to mess with her life. I just want to talk to her."

She stared at me for a second. "She doesn't want to see you. I'm sorry."

"Okay. I respect that." I stood there, staring at her.

"If you respect that, then why aren't you walking away?"

Because I'm going to follow you back into the building. This woman was infuriating. "Do you work at Blue Media too? You look familiar."

"No. I work at Kruger Advertising with Bee."

"Oh. Never mind." I turned away and smiled. That's all I needed to know. I pulled out my phone and scrolled through my contact list. I pressed the call button and held my phone to my ear as I hailed down a taxi.

"Vargas."

"Hey, Vargas. It's Mason. I'm calling about that favor you owe me."

"Whatever you need, man."

"I need you to find out the last name of an employee at Kruger Advertising. Her first name is Bridget and she works as a secretary there."

"That's all you need?"

"Run her name through the system too. I want to know everything about her. And the name of her ex-fiancé. He works at MAC International but that's all I know about him."

"He works for your father?"

"Yeah."

"What's this all about? Something juicy I hope?"

"Just run the name, Vargas." I hung up the phone. If Bee wanted chivalrous, I'd give her chivalrous. No one ever refused to talk to me. I was used to getting what I wanted. And right now, all I wanted was Bee.

Chapter 24
Bee

I poured myself a cup of coffee and leaned against the counter in the break room. It was a new week, so it was time for a fresh start. I just needed to stop dwelling on the past so much. One stupid date and one very bad day at work wasn't enough to make me give up on the life I had made for myself here. I had stuck it out after Patrick had left me. And that was the worst thing that was going to happen. It could only get better from here.

Just because Mr. Ellington said I didn't have thick skin and Mason Caldwell said I was soft, didn't mean those things were true. I was going to make it in advertising. And I was going to find a guy that was worthy of my time. I wanted to prove everyone wrong.

Thinking about Mason made me so angry but at the same time it made my skin tingle. I walked back toward my desk and froze. There was a huge bouquet of roses on the middle of my desk. I pulled out the card that was attached to them.

Bee,

I hope you don't mind, but I'm going to keep calling you that. I had an amazing time with you on Friday. I can't stop thinking about you. And I don't want to stop. I'm

sorry about what happened with you and your fiancé. Let me help you get your mind off him. I'm taking you to dinner tonight.
-Mason

What? He couldn't come here! How did he even know where I worked? God, my mom was right. *He's a serial killer.* I pushed the vase to the side and sat down in my chair.

"Wow, nice flowers," Kendra said and perched herself on the side of my desk. "Who are they from?" She arched her eyebrow.

"They're from Mason."

"How romantic."

"No. He's not romantic."

"I know I already told you this after I talked to him, but I think he really likes you. He was pretty persistent about talking to you. What kind of guy goes through all this trouble for a hook up?"

"A lunatic."

Kendra laughed. "Those roses are beautiful."

"They're okay."

"So, what did you mean when you said you didn't exactly have sex with him?"

"I meant I didn't have sex with him. Don't you have work to do?"

"Well, maybe whatever weird non-sex thing you did is what has him hooked? You'll have to tell me sometime. Because I never get roses. And you're welcome. While I was talking to him, I may have let it slip that you work at Kruger Advertising." She smiled at me.

"Kendra!"

She walked back to her desk without responding.

***

Each minute that passed made me more and more nervous. *He isn't seriously coming here, is he?* He can't just show up at my work. I tried to focus on the document I was editing, but my mind was scattered. I couldn't stop thinking about the spark I felt when he touched me. I wasn't sure if I could control myself around him.

It was almost 5 o'clock. As soon as it was time to go, I was going to race out of here as quickly as possible. Maybe I'd miss him.

"Jenkins! Good to see you, man."

Oh my God, it's him. And of course he knows Jenkins. He probably set up all the men here with prostitutes too.

"You too, Caldwell. What are you doing here? Trying to spy on the competition?"

"At Kruger? I don't think so."

They both laughed.

"I'm actually here for pleasure, not business. If you'll excuse me," Mason said.

Pleasure? Gross. Who talks like that? There was no way I was going to dinner with him. I ducked down behind my desk. *What the hell am I doing?* But it was too late. I could already hear footsteps approaching my desk. Maybe he'd think I had left for the day. *Shit.* My coat was still on my chair. The footsteps stopped right in front of me. I leaned down farther to peer under the desk. He had really big feet. *Feet really must be a sign of endowment.* I had always thought that was a rumor.

I could smell his cologne from where I was. Just the smell of him made me slightly aroused. *What is happening to me?*

Mason began to walk around my desk. I closed my eyes, hoping that if I couldn't see him, he couldn't see me.

"As much as I like you on your knees, how about we have dinner first?" Mason said.

I slowly opened my eyes. His hand was in front of my face.

"Oh, yeah, I was just looking for a pen I dropped. I can't find the darn thing anywhere. Slippery devil." *What did I just say?*

He laughed.

It was deep and sexy. *God.* I got to my feet without taking his hand.

"You look beautiful tonight, Bee."

"Thanks. I'm sorry, though, I'm really busy. I don't have time to go to dinner. I have to stay late. I would have called you, but I didn't have your number."

"Are you asking for my number?" He flashed me his jaw dropping smile.

"Nope."

"Mhm. After dinner I promise that you'll want it."

"I just said I can't. So if you'll excuse me." I tried to walk past him, but he sidestepped, blocking my path, so that I ended up just a few inches in front of him. He smelled amazing.

"Are you saying no to me?"

Am I? "Yes."

"So, it's a yes?" he said.

"What? No."

"Bee," he said and picked up my jacket. "You have a lot to learn. For one, you should never say no to me." He grabbed my hand.

I felt the same electricity shoot through my body. I quickly pulled my hand out of his. "I'm sorry, Mason. But I'm not interested in pursuing whatever this is."

He bent down so that his lips were by my ear. "I promise you that tonight will be worth your time, Bee."

I pressed my thighs together.

"Bridget, do you have those papers I asked for?" Mr. Ellington came out of his office. He frowned when he saw Mason.

Maybe this was exactly what I needed to get Mr. Ellington to stop hitting on me.

"Stop, Mason, not at the office." I giggled and pushed on his chest. I internally rolled my eyes at myself.

Mr. Ellington's frown deepened.

"Yes, Mr. Ellington." I smoothed down my skirt even thought it didn't need it. I picked up a folder off my desk and handed it to him. "Is there anything else I can do for you tonight?"

"Not tonight, no."

"Okay, great. Let's get going, baby," I said and put my arm through Mason's. I tried not to look at either him or Mr. Ellington. What was I doing? Getting away from one snake and into bed with another.

Mr. Ellington turned and walked back into this office.

Thank God. I sighed and tried to take a step away from Mason, but he held me in place.

"I'd like to know what that was about," he said. He kept his hand on my arm. "I think you owe me an explanation."

"I owe *you* an explanation? You're the one that owes me an explanation."

"Let's discuss it over dinner then. My treat."

What if Kendra was right? Maybe I should hear him out. Guys like him didn't need to do stuff like this. Maybe Patrick had made the whole thing up. All he did the last few months of our relationship was lie to me. I grabbed my jacket out of Mason's hand and walked past him. "We'll split the cost," I said over my shoulder.

Chapter 25
Mason

I watched her ass sway back and forth. Being chivalrous was not going to be easy. I quickly caught up to her. She didn't look at me until we both got onto the elevator. She leaned against the side of the elevator and crossed her arms over her chest. It pressed her tits together. I had to force myself to look up at her face. She was pouting slightly, her lips full and sultry. All I wanted to do was fuck her pretty little face again.

"Just so we're both clear, this is not a date. I'm going to dinner with you to hear you out. That's it."

"It seems like a date to me. I sent you flowers. And picked you up at work. And you're already calling me baby. It's all moving a little fast, but I think I'm okay with that."

Bee laughed. "You didn't pick me up. You just walked over here from Blue Media."

"Hmm." The doors opened and I held my hand out, motioning for her to go first. I saw it, but only for a second. She looked surprised that I was letting her exit the elevator first. I wasn't even trying to be chivalrous. That's just what men did. Clearly her ex hadn't been a man. Vargas was still working on getting me his name. But I had already found out a lot about Bee. I opened up the door to her office building for her.

"Thanks," she said, and walked through.

"You're quite welcome." I put my arm around her shoulders as we walked down the sidewalk.

She immediately dropped her shoulder. "Please don't touch me, Mason." Her face was flushed.

She still wants me. She was stubborn. And I liked the fight in her. Everything about her was refreshing.

"You just looked cold."

"Yeah, well, I'm fine, thank you," she said and pulled her coat tighter around her slim frame.

"I don't know what you think you know, but I promise that it isn't everything you need to know about me," I said.

"It is." She had a cute scowl on her face. I wanted to rip all her clothes off right in the middle of the sidewalk. And I bet she'd let me. But I didn't want to just fuck her. I wanted her to beg me for it.

"It's not. How about you tell me exactly why you're so upset?"

"I know what kind of perks your father's business has."

"Perks?" I raised my eyebrow. It was the same thing her friend had said to me. Apparently her ex was just at good at spinning a web of lies as I was. Handing out perks didn't pay the bills.

"Yes, perks. Don't act so innocent. I know all about you, Mason Caldwell. And I don't want to know anything else."

"Like I told your friend, I don't work for my father. Finance is not my forte. I work at Blue Media with Carter. You know that."

She looked flustered. "That's not what Patrick said."

I couldn't help but laugh. Patrick was an ass. A complete suck up. "Patrick? Patrick is you ex-fiancé?"

"Why are you laughing?"

"I'm sorry. He just doesn't seem like your type."

"Yeah, well he's not *now*. You taught him how to cheat on me. And how to not care. You turned him into a monster."

"I just unleashed what was already there. Patrick is a dick."

"He didn't used to be. Not before we moved here. Not before he met you."

"Honey..."

"Don't call me that!" she yelled.

I smiled at her. "You're welcome, by the way."

"What are you talking about?" She looked so mad. I wish all that passion was being used in a better way.

"If he couldn't make you orgasm, then you shouldn't have been with him anyway."

"Seriously? You think I should be thanking you?"

"Yes. And I can think of one way you can thank me right now."

Her eyes shone with lust for a second. She shook her head back and forth. "What, so your dad asks you to show all his new hires the city? So instead of showing them normal things like the Chrysler Building, you show them all the underground clubs where they can fuck whoever they want? And set them up with prostitutes? You tell them there's no consequences? Well there are. He hurt me."

I could see that hurt in her eyes. She was broken. I wanted to be the one that fixed her. I was pretty sure I was exactly what she needed. And right now, she was exactly what I needed. "I show people that are new to the city how to have a good time. It's not like I forced him to do the things he did."

"So you admit it?"

"Admit what?"

"That you're...that you..." She bit her lip. She didn't have the guts to say what was on her mind. It was that unspeakable and wrong. And she loved it. She loved what I was. "Did you even care that he was seeing someone?"

"Bee, he never mentioned you." I never asked questions. Some of the men even had wedding rings, but it was none of my business. None of them ever mentioned if they were with someone. I had assumed it, but I never knew it. Bee didn't need to know that. Finance jobs were as rough as advertising. Every man in a high level gig in this city needed to let off steam. Women had a hard time understanding that.

I'd tell her whatever she wanted to hear, though. I needed my cock deep inside of her. I was done messing around. She didn't need to know anything about my second business. I'd fuck her and be done with her, just like all the rest of them.

She looked down at her feet. I let my eyes wander down her curves.

Chapter 26
Bee

"So you didn't know he was cheating on someone?" Maybe I was overreacting. Patrick was a cheater. Which meant he was also a liar. He had made it seem like no one was faithful. Like his new friend Mason had told him that women were expendable. He made it seem like Mason was basically a pimp. Which was ridiculous. Mason had a job as an ad executive. He was sophisticated and well off. He wasn't a pimp.

"No, I didn't."

I took a deep breath. "Why do you even know where places like that are?"

"Places like what?"

"I don't know what they're called. Sex bars?"

Mason laughed. "I told you what my hobby was."

I gulped. "I thought you were joking."

"We need to cross here." He lightly touched my elbow.

This time I didn't flinch. I still wasn't sure what kind of man he was. But I did know that I wanted him. I wanted him in a way that I had never wanted anyone else. I wasn't sure what it was about him. But I just wanted to kiss his beautiful face.

He leaned toward me as we crossed the street. "I don't joke when it comes to sex."

"No?" I could hear how breathless my voice was. I hated how it sounded.

"No." He leaned down and nipped my earlobe.

Holy shit.

"And I promised you the best night of your life. I still need to deliver."

I gulped. Friday night had been one of the best nights of my life. What we had done should have been embarrassing. But it wasn't. Mason made me feel so sexy. No one had ever wanted me like this before. He made me feel desired.

"Here we are," he said.

I stopped in my tracks. We were standing outside La Masseria dei Vini. "This is my favorite restaurant." I smiled up at him. What a weird coincidence. Maybe we had more in common than I thought.

"Is it? I love it here too. They have the best gnocchi in the whole city."

"I know. That's what I always order here."

He smiled and opened up the door for me.

I was completely torn. Tonight he was acting like such a gentleman. On Friday he had acted like a sex god. And from what Patrick had said, he was a complete douche bag. How was I supposed to know which one he really was? I bit my lip and walked into the restaurant.

Mason walked up to the hostess stand. "We have a reservation under Mason Caldwell."

The hostess looked up at him. I noticed her face blush. No matter what kind of guy Mason was, he definitely had a reputation.

"Of course. Right this way, Mr. Caldwell."

Mason put his hand on the small of my back and led me to our table. He pulled my chair out for me. Patrick had never done that. I quickly sat down.

"So tell me," he said as he looked at his menu. "Why do you want your boss to think that we're together?"

"I don't."

He lowered his eyebrows slightly. "I know when a girl is flirting with me. You were pretending to. Tell me why."

He didn't really ask it as a question. More as a command. It sent a chill down my spine. I was relieved when the waiter walked over.

"Good evening, and welcome to La Masseria dei Vini. I'm Franco and I'll be your waiter tonight. Can I start you off with something to drink? We have a featured..."

"We'll have a bottle of Chateau Bordeaux. And we'd both like Gnocchi Verdi for our entrees. Thank you, Franco." Mason kept his eyes on me. Everything he did was so unnerving.

"Yes, sir. I'll put your order in right away." Franco left the table.

"You should have let him finish," I said. "It's kind of rude to cut the waiter off when..."

"Tell me why, Bee."

I sighed. He clearly didn't mind cutting people off. "My boss hits on me sometimes. He's inappropriate. I thought maybe he'd stop if he thought we were together. I don't know why I did it. He flirted with me when I was wearing an engagement ring too. It's not going to stop him."

"You shouldn't let your boss walk all over you."

"You don't know me."

"I'd like to."

I swallowed hard.

"Why are you working for a guy like that anyway?"

"I can take care of him. I just thought him seeing us together might help for a few days."

"That doesn't answer my question. I'm sure there are other secretary jobs around."

"Because I don't want to be a secretary. I'm trying to get my first job in advertising. This is my way in."

"You want to be in advertising?"

"Yes. And don't even say it. I know you think I'm soft. And you probably think I'm not cut out for advertising because I don't have thick skin. I wasn't born in the city and therefore don't belong here. Yadda yadda. That's not going to stop me. You'll see."

He just stared at me for a second. "All I was going to say is that women who work at ad agencies don't usually start out as secretaries for dicks."

"Well I can't just get any job I want because my father has connections all over the city. I have to work my way up."

"You don't know me either, Bee."

Chapter 27
Mason

She thought she had me all figured out. But she didn't know me. And she didn't really want to. Because I wasn't a good guy. I certainly wasn't any different than her ex. All I wanted was for my cock to be deep inside of her. Maybe then I could stop thinking about her.

"I'm sorry. I didn't mean to suggest..."

"Yes you did," I said.

Her face flushed slightly. I liked embarrassing her. When her cheeks were red it reminded me of how she looked after she came. I shifted in my seat. Screw chivalry. I was taking her back to my apartment tonight.

"Then tell me about yourself," she said. "Tell me what I'm missing."

"What do you want to know?"

"Where did you go to school?"

"Harvard."

"Harvard?"

"That's what I said, baby."

She frowned. "So if you didn't work as a secretary at Blue Media, how'd you get a job there?"

"I have my own connections. I don't need my father's. And I'm very good at networking. I can be incredibly persuasive."

"I know."

I smiled at her. She barely even seemed upset that I had introduced her fiancé to a bunch of sluts. I bet she was thinking about my cock right now. She wanted this just as badly as me. If I had to answer a few stupid questions first, then fine. Game on.

Our waiter came over and poured us each a glass of wine.

"To an adventurous evening," I said and lifted up my glass.

She raised her glass. "I guess we'll see." She clinked it against mine.

That's a yes.

"So how did you pay for Harvard? That's a very prestigious school."

"You mean expensive?"

"Well, yes." She put her elbows on the table and leaned forward slightly.

"My parents paid for it."

"You're very fortunate. I went to the University of New Castle, with instate tuition, and I'm still paying off student loans. I probably will be forever."

"The University of New Castle? One of my friends used to work there."

"Really? What did he do?"

"He was a professor. He didn't teach there for very long though."

"What was his name? Maybe I had him."

"James Hunter."

"Oh, Professor Hunter?"

"So you did have him?"

"No, I never had a class with him. I definitely heard about him, though. Didn't he get fired for sleeping with a student?"

"Yeah, her name's Penny. And James didn't technically get fired, he resigned. They're actually living in the city now."

"That's really sweet."

"I guess."

"That's a pretty crazy coincidence. Two sexy, rich, bachelors dating young women from the University of New Castle? Not that we're dating. Obviously." Her face blushed.

"Mhm." I took a sip of wine. *She really doesn't know anything about me.* She thought I had everything in my life handed to me. In a lot of ways I did. But not anymore. I didn't want to talk about my family. I didn't want to talk at all. I just wanted to fuck her. I leaned forward slightly. Maybe what she wanted to hear was that we were dating? Security would get her to come back to my place. "I mean, technically this is our second date in less than a week. So we're kind of dating."

"We're not dating, Mason." Her face was turning even more red. "I said I'd split the bill with you."

"That's not happening. I really like you, Bee."

She locked eyes with me. "You don't like me. You don't even know me."

"I know quite a bit about you, really. First of all, you're exquisite. And you're kinky as hell but you're embarrassed about it. You're a secretary for a dick. This is your favorite restaurant. I assume you're indifferent to roses since you didn't thank me. You like being bossed around because you're indecisive."

"I'm not..."

"You're definitely indecisive, because you seemed to have written me off, yet here we are. You grew up in Delaware and followed your asshole of an ex here even though you never pictured yourself in New York. And you're wondering why you're still here if the only reason you came was to be with him. You're torn about what to do because you're stuck in a job you hate in a city you don't fit in."

Chapter 28
Bee

Part of me wanted to tell him to go screw himself. But a bigger part of me knew that what he said was true. Was I really that transparent? I had made a life for myself here. I had an apartment that I called home and new friends that I considered family. But I was struggling. Just the other day I had said I was ready to move back to Wilmington. I thought I could leave a small town and never look back. I was so wrong. And I was indecisive. Which is why I felt stuck. I just wanted to be back in my apartment, alone. The Bachelor was on tonight, and that's all I really needed.

"Dinner is served," Franco said as he walked up to our table with two plates in his hands. Franco smiled at me as he set down our entrees.

The only people that were actually nice in New York were the ones that were trying to get a good tip.

"Is there anything else I can get for you?" Franco asked.

"I think we have everything we need," Mason said. "Thank you, Franco."

I looked down at my dinner. I wasn't even hungry anymore. And I couldn't afford to be eating at a place like this. I lifted up my purse and pulled out a few twenty dollar bills. I wasn't sure that was enough to cover my half, but it's all I had. I set it on the table.

"I said I'd pay," Mason said.

"I'm actually not feeling very well. I'm just going to go."

"I didn't mean..."

"You did mean it. And you were right about me. I don't belong here. We're wasting each other's time, Mason. I'm not the type of girl you're looking for." He had me all figured out. And I was embarrassed of who I had become. I was confident while I was in college. I thought I could do anything I set my mind to. Being an adult sucked. I was completely lost. And I needed to work on finding myself again. Alone. Not with Mason Caldwell.

"You're exactly the type of girl I'm looking for." His words made me cold.

"I don't do one night stands."

Mason frowned. "I never said that's what this is."

"Isn't it, though? You said sex was your hobby. It's not a hobby for me. It's more than that. I don't know, I'm just..." I let my voice trail off. "I'm sorry about the other night. I don't know what I was thinking. Actually, I wasn't thinking."

He just stared at me. His silence was unnerving.

"I gave you the wrong impression of me."

"When I made you come in the bathroom? Or when you sucked my dick in the alley?"

"Both." I still couldn't believe I had done those things. "I'm just going to go, okay?" I stood up.

"Don't."

"What's the point, Mason?"

"You didn't let me finish before, Bee. I want to give you a reason to stay in New York. I want to be the reason why you stay."

The way he was looking at me made me tremble. He was starting to get a 5 o'clock shadow along his chiseled jaw line. His brown eyes seemed to pierce into my soul. He may not be as bad as Patrick made him out to be, but he still wasn't a good guy. Why was he saying these things to me? Just so he could fuck me? He couldn't possibly be serious.

"I can't stop thinking about you," he said. "Please just sit back down. We can do this your way, okay? Let's just take things slow."

Chapter 29
Mason

What the fuck did I just say? I downed the rest of my wine.

"You want to take things slow?"

No, I want to fuck you on this table. "Yes."

She puckered her lips slightly as she thought about what I had just said. I wanted to stand up and kiss her. I needed to taste her lips again. I was completely out of my element here. Why the hell had I just agreed to take things slow? I never took things slow. I always took what I wanted. And I wanted her badly. It was just in my head. I wanted what I couldn't have. It was stupid and immature, but it was there. A primal want. She was teasing me. I wasn't sure if she was doing it on purpose. But when I finally did have her, I was going to punish her for it. I couldn't wait to spank her bare ass again. I could feel myself starting to get an erection. *Fuck.*

She sat back down across from me. "I'm not sure I believe you."

"You sat back down."

"That's because I'm indecisive and soft."

"Trust me, baby, I'm hard enough for both of us."

She laughed and then stared at me with her big brown eyes.

Her laugh was enticing. I tried to shake away the thought. Taking it slow was just a means to an end. The goal was still getting her to scream my name with my cock deep inside of her. It was just going to take more time than I originally thought. And I wasn't one to back away from a challenge. Especially when a girl like Bee was the prize.

"I'm bad at reading people," she finally said.

"I can tell. You dated Patrick."

She frowned. "I'm talking about you. The first time we met, you stole a taxi from me. But I gave you the benefit of the doubt. And then we did all those...things." She blushed. "You even admitted to knowing all about those disgusting underground clubs. But then the flowers, and saying you want to take things slow?" She stared into my eyes. "I don't understand. What do you want from me?"

"I just want to get to know you."

"Okay."

"So, Bee, what is it exactly that you wanted to talk about?"

"This really is amazing," she said after taking a bite of her food. She was ignoring me on purpose. She had to be intentionally driving me crazy.

I tried the gnocchi. It was okay. "It is really good." I had never been to this restaurant before. I was just using what Vargas had found out to win her over. She wanted to ask me something, but she looked embarrassed. "I can tell you have a question for me. So spill it."

"How many women have you slept with?"

"I don't know," I shrugged. *She did not want the answer to that question.*

"Well, I mean, you must have a guess."

Oh God. "Dozens?" I tried to say vaguely.

"Dozens with an s? So like 24?"

"I'd say several dozen."

She scrunched up her face. "That's...dirty."

"Well you're the one with the dirty mind."

"Me?" She laughed. "Yeah right."

"You're asking about my number. So you must be picturing yourself beneath me, or maybe you prefer to be on top. Are you like a sex addict or something?"

She laughed. "You think *I'm* a sex addict?"

"You accosted me in a bathroom and an alley."

"Okay, hold on. It was the woman's bathroom, which you shouldn't have been in. And you literally carried me into that alley."

"Minor details." I winked at her.

She responded by rolling her eyes.

"You know, I'm clean, if that's what you're worried about." I gestured toward my lap.

"No, I'm not." She bit her lip. "But that is good to know."

"And what about you, Miss Sex Addict?"

"I'm not going to respond to that name. I'm not a sex addict."

"Right, you're actually a serial monogamist. Of course you're clean."

She shrugged. "At least I'm not a whore."

"Did you just call me a whore?"

"It depends. How many of the dozens of women that you slept with were your girlfriends?"

"I don't really do the whole girlfriend thing."

"I knew it. Just one night stands."

"I didn't say that either. I date. But I'm not one to settle down."

"Have you ever had a girlfriend?"

"Not in a long time."

"You're being impossible."

"Impossible?" I smiled at her.

"Your answers are so vague. How on earth am I supposed to get to know you?"

"You're the one that's being impossible."

"I'm not."

"And stubborn."

"I..." she scowled. "I'll answer whatever questions you have."

"Why are you really still here?"

"Because I want to prove everyone wrong. I do have what it takes to be in advertising. I have great ideas, I just need to make people listen. I refuse to move back to Delaware just because my fiancé cheated on me. It would just be a copout. I need to be here. I need to do this for myself."

"That's very inspirational, Bee. But I don't mean in New York. Everyone comes here to prove that they have what it takes. I mean why are you with me, right now? Why didn't you walk out a minute ago?"

"I'm attracted to you."

"That's good to know." I leaned forward slightly. "I think you're sexy as hell, Bee."

"I've never really felt so..." her voice trailed off. "I like the way you look at me. Like I'm the only girl in the room. No one's ever made me feel desired like that before. I know we don't have that much in common. But I can't stop thinking about you either."

I have you right where I want you. "It's called sexual chemistry, baby."

She shifted in her seat as she crossed her legs together. It was obvious that she wanted me. But tonight I was going to play the game like she wanted me to. I wasn't going to touch her at all. Not even a kiss goodnight. She'd be begging me in no time at all. I'd have to add the taking it slow route to my playbook.

"I just have to ask. That thing you do for your father's employees. What is it exactly?"

"It's nothing important. I'm trying to start my own ad agency. So I need the extra money. It's not a big deal."

"That's ambitious."

"Does that surprise you?"

"Not at all, actually. And I get it. I could use some extra money myself."

"Would you rather this be an audition?"

She gulped. "An audition for what?"

"Well, I could always use someone like you on my roster."

"What?"

"Bee...I'm joking." Men would pay a lot for her. But I wanted her for myself.

"Oh," she laughed.

"Now I have to ask. What exactly did Patrick tell you?"

"He made it seem like you were kind of...I don't know, like a pimp."

Fitting. "Do I look like a pimp to you? Am I wearing a purple fur coat with a cane?"

"No."

"There you go."

Chapter 30
Bee

Tonight had been much more like a first date than our actual first date. I couldn't help but be a little suspicious of his complete 180. Every now and then he would say something entirely inappropriate. And I couldn't deny that I liked when he did. I liked both sides of him. I almost wished he was being a little more like he had been on our first date. I crossed my legs under the table.

"I should probably get you home," he said.

"Yes, you probably should." There was no invitation back to his place. Or any suggestion that he wanted tonight to continue. I bit my lip. I wanted him more now than I had the first night, now that he wasn't offering. I didn't want his hands on me to become a distant memory.

Our check had come and he had paid for the whole meal despite my protests. And now he was just staring at me. Did he want me to make the first move? I was so out of my element. I had only ever really dated Patrick. My experience was close to zero. I swallowed hard. "Unless you want to do something else?"

A small smile crossed his handsome face. "Not tonight. I have an early morning tomorrow."

"Right, me too."

"Okay then." He pulled on his wool jacket and stood up.

I didn't want him to put on more clothes, I wanted him to be taking them off. I stood up and grabbed my jacket off the back of my chair.

"Allow me." He grabbed my jacket and held it up for me.

He was a gentleman. Despite what he had said on our first date, he seemed to be the most respectful man I had ever met. And un-respectful at the same time. I slid my arms into my jacket as he pulled it up onto my shoulders. His fingers brushed across the back of my neck as he pushed my hair over the collar of my jacket. My skin tingled where he had touched me. It was the first time he had touched me since we had started our dinner. I quickly turned around and looked up at him. His face was just a few inches from mine. I saw his Adam's apple rise and fall as he stared down at me.

But he quickly turned away from me, placing his hand on the small of my back for a second, directing me toward the exit.

He said we could do things my way. But I wasn't sure taking things slowly was my way. I had fallen for Patrick so quickly. And Mason Caldwell was more captivating than Patrick. I was in way over my head. Maybe Mason knew that. Maybe that was why he had said we could take things slowly. Because he was respectful. *No. He's not respectful.* I had never been so confused in my life.

He opened up the door for me and I walked out into the cold night. It was well past 8 o'clock and now that The Bachelor was over, I really had nothing to do back at my apartment. I wanted him to come with me. Maybe he would make it feel warm and full of life again.

I watched him hail down a taxi. I thought he might grab my hand again or drape his arm across my shoulders with an excuse to keep me warm. But he didn't touch me at all.

A taxi stopped right in front of him and he opened up the door for me. I walked up to him and placed my hand on his forearm. I could feel his muscles beneath his wool coat and suit jacket. "Thank you for a wonderful evening. I'm sorry that I thought you...well, that I suggested that you were..."

He pulled out his wallet, ignoring me. "I believe you said you wanted my number." He handed me his business card.

I looked down at the card. His cell phone number was listed at the bottom. "I didn't actually, but thank you." I leaned forward slightly. His cologne was making me slightly dizzy. I wanted him to kiss me goodnight.

He smiled down at me. "Get in the taxi, Bee."

I looked up at him. *Why isn't he kissing me?* I batted my eyelashes in what I hoped was a seductive way.

"You do realize how hard you're making it for me to take things slow?" he asked.

"Maybe I don't want you to take things slow with me."

"Trust me, baby, you do."

His words made me cold. "Goodnight, Mason."

"Goodnight, Bee."

I was sure my facial expression didn't hide my disappointment. I guess I needed to step up my game. Hopefully Kendra could give me a few dating tips. I climbed into the taxi and Mason closed the door behind me.

He tapped on the front passenger's window and the cabbie rolled the window down. "West 96th Street," Mason said as he slipped the taxi driver some money.

How does he know my address?

I turned to look at him as the taxi sped off. He was standing on the sidewalk staring at me. He waved before shoving his hands into his pockets. He had a smug grin on his face.

Is he stalking me?

CHAPTER 31
Bee

I looked down at Mason's number in my phone. I didn't want to play games with him. Waiting around to hear from him was awful. So why wasn't I texting him?

"Are you going to call him or not?" Kendra said and sat down on the edge of my desk.

"I think I am." I bit the inside of my lip. Why did he have to be so hard to read? I thought I wanted to date a nice, normal guy after Patrick. Mason wasn't either of those things. But I couldn't stop thinking about him.

"So do it. It's been a day and a half. You've made him wait the proper amount of time. Any longer and he'll think you're not interested."

I turned my chair toward Kendra. "I'm just not sure if he's what I'm looking for."

"It's not like you have to marry him. Geez, Bee, you need to live a little."

"But what's the point of starting something if you don't see a future?"

"Um...to have fun? What is wrong with you?"

"I don't want to get hurt again." That's what I was worried about. Mason didn't do relationships. What if I fell for him? What if I ended up wanting more than whatever it was he was offering?

"Can I see something real quick?" Kendra gestured to my phone.

"Sure." I handed it to her and looked at the roses on my desk. They really were beautiful. I should at least text him and thank him for sending them. That was innocent enough.

"Okay, sent," she said and smiled at me.

"Wait, what? What did you just do?" I grabbed my phone out of her hand and looked down at the message she had just sent Mason: "What are your thoughts on having sex in the office?"

"Kendra!" I slapped her arm. "What is wrong with you?!"

She laughed. "I'm trying to get you laid."

"I was going to text him and thank him for the flowers."

"Which would not have gotten you laid."

"But I..." I stopped talking when my phone buzzed. *Oh no.* I clicked on the message that Mason had just sent me.

"I was wondering when you'd text me, Bee. Sex in the office? It depends on the partner. If you're suggesting the two of us, I think our sexual chemistry might just be perfect for that. I'm about ready for my lunch break, if that's an invitation."

I could feel my face flushing.

"What did he say?" Kendra asked.

"Nothing really."

She grabbed my phone again.

"Give it back, Kendra." She held it out of my reach and began typing again.

Damn it. Now that I knew what having a sibling would be like, I was glad I never had one. If she wasn't so much taller than me I'd be able to get it back. "Seriously, Kendra. He can't come here."

"Too late." She dropped my phone on my desk.

"What did you say to him?"

"Nothing really." She winked at me.

"I really hate you sometimes." I picked up my phone and read the text that she had sent Mason: "I think I know the perfect spot. See you soon."

"So where were you thinking?" Kendra asked.

"I wasn't thinking anywhere. You're the one that sent him the message. I'm just going to tell him I..." I couldn't even think of an excuse. I couldn't say I sent it to the wrong person. And I had no idea what I could say I meant to say instead. I was screwed. I gulped, thinking of Mason screwing me.

"How about the mailroom?"

"I'm not going to have sex with him in the office."

"But you are going to have sex with him outside the office?"

"I don't even know yet. He said he wanted to take things slow."

"Well apparently he doesn't really want that." She nodded to my phone.

"Maybe he does. He didn't even respond to you. You probably freaked him out."

"Or he's too busy running over here to respond. Or maybe he's buying condoms. You should unbutton the top few buttons of your blouse."

"No." I put my hand over my chest. "And when he gets here, I'm just going to tell him you sent those messages."

"What is so bad about having sex with a super hot guy in the mailroom?"

"Everything. We could get caught. And I could get fired."

"So...no protests to the actual sex part? I knew it. You totally want him."

"That doesn't mean I can't wait until we're alone. In a bed. I'm not a sex addict." Mason had jokingly called me a sex addict. *Shit. Am I one?* Kendra was right. I did want him. And I was kind of excited that he was coming here.

"I can't believe you want to have sex with him. I'm so excited for you."

"You're being weird."

"I'm not. Please unbutton the top two..."

"No."

"Bee, you should flaunt what you have." She reached toward my shirt again.

"Stop trying to touch my breasts."

Kendra laughed. "Then move your hand."

Chapter 32
Mason

She was just fucking with me. Besides, asking and begging were two very different things. Jumping the gun too early was counterproductive. Especially if I wanted to have her more than once. And after putting in all the work, it was definitely looking like I'd want to reap the reward for awhile. At least until I found something better.

"Number 69."

That's appropriate. "Thanks," I said and grabbed the bag off the counter. I tossed some money in the tip jar and walked out into the cold. There was a gala at the end of the week that I was going to invite Bee to. That would be the night that I'd finally have her. Until then, it was teasing only. If she wasn't begging me by Saturday, I'd just have to give in. Besides, one night with me and she'd be hooked. I would be able to have her whenever I wanted. That was worth a week of hell.

I opened up the door to the building that Kruger Advertising was located in. Compared to Blue Media, it was a small organization. I used to scoff at them. But now that I wanted to start my own agency, I saw it in a different light. It would be competition to me. And I'd need to crush them. I got onto the elevator and pressed the button for the 14th floor. Bee would lose her job once I ran them out of business. There were other ad agencies in the city, though. She'd be able to find a new job. Besides, I'd be long done with her by then. She wouldn't be my problem anymore.

Or I could just hire her to work beneath me. I shook away the thought. That was a lawsuit waiting to happen. I stepped off the elevator and turned the corner.

Kendra, the woman I had talked to outside of Carter's apartment had her hand on top of Bee's breasts.

Maybe Bee was even kinkier than I had realized. I wasn't opposed to fucking both of them. Just the thought made me start to get hard.

"Stop it, Kendra," Bee hissed. "You're going to give him the wrong idea."

Too late.

"You asked him here to have sex with you. Stop being so prude," Kendra said.

"I did not. You did."

It was a good thing I had brought lunch without the thought of actually fucking her. Otherwise this would have really hurt my plan. I should have known Bee hadn't invited me here to fuck her in a storage closet. That wasn't exactly her style. At least, it wasn't how she wanted people to think of her. I'm sure I could have her coming in just a few minutes if we were alone somewhere on this floor. And now that it wasn't on the table, it made me want it even more. She was good. As much as I liked looking at Kendra fondling Bee's tits, my lunch break was only so long. "Hello, ladies."

When they turned toward me, Kendra pulled on Bee's shirt, undoing the top few buttons. I could see the top of

Bee's perky breasts, just begging to come out. I quickly looked back up at her face, which was bright red. She put her hand on top of her chest.

"Oh, hi, Mason," she said.

I lifted up the bag in my hand. "As much as I loved your proposal, I only have thirty minutes until I need to be back at Blue Media. And thirty minutes isn't quite enough time." I winked at Kendra. Her face flushed too. *This is too easy.*

"Oh, shucks," Bee said. If possible, her face turned even redder. She was ridiculously cute when she was embarrassed.

I needed to focus. "I hope you're hungry. I picked up sandwiches from that little bistro down the street."

"Wait, Quest Bistro?"

"Mhm. Have you heard of it?" I already knew she had. Apparently it was her favorite lunch spot.

"It's my favorite. I always order grilled cheese and..."

"Tomato soup? You're kidding." I handed her the bag. "That's exactly what I always order." Not really. But Vargas was a genius. And I needed this angle.

"I'm pretty sure our taste buds are soul mates." She smiled shyly up at me.

"Well, I'm going to leave you two lovebirds alone. But I have heard that quite a few people have hooked up in the copy room," Kendra said before walking away.

"I'm so sorry about her," said Bee.

"I guess I'm supposed to assume you're not thinking about having sex with me right now?" I took my sandwich out of the bag and unwrapped the paper from it.

"Kendra actually sent that text."

"Oh, yeah I got that," I said and took a bite. I pushed the takeout bag back toward her. "But that doesn't really answer my question, Bee."

"What can I say? I'm a sex addict remember?"

I laughed. "I thought you were denying that?"

"I can't believe you like Quest Bistro too," she said, ignoring my comment. I watched her open up the lid on the soup. There was a faint tan line where her engagement ring once was. For a second I felt slightly guilty. But just slightly, and only for a second. I had done her a favor. And I was going to show her why settling for Patrick would have been a mistake. She needed a man. What she needed was me.

"I go there for lunch all the time," I lied. But the sandwich was fantastic. Maybe our taste buds were soul mates. *Soul mates.* There was no such thing as a soul mate.

"It's weird that we never ran into each other before our blind date."

"Well, technically we did. You hailed me a taxi."

"So you admit it?"

"Of course I admit it. Although, you kind of gave it to me."

"You're the worst." She took a bite of the sandwich. "Or the best. This is just what I wanted today. So much better than peanut butter and jelly."

I laughed.

She just looked up at me.

"Oh, you're serious?" I asked. "What are you, five?"

"It's actually pretty good. And cheap." She looked embarrassed again.

I knew she was low on cash. I had looked up her address. It was a rundown apartment in a not so great area. And she was working as a secretary for a dick. She had to be desperate for a job. Asking her to the gala would be perfect. It would be the best night of her life. She'd fall for the wealth and charm, right on top of me. I wondered if she'd be offended if I paid her afterward. She needed the money. And I wanted to help her out. *What am I thinking?*

"Maybe you should pack yourself a peanut butter and jelly sandwich sometime and reminisce about when you were young."

"I'm not sure that would help me reminisce," I said. "I've never even had one."

"You've never had a peanut butter and jelly sandwich?"

"Can't say I have."

"What kind of kid goes through childhood without trying peanut butter and jelly?"

"I don't know, it was never in my lunch. Maybe our chef wasn't fond of it." Now I was just rubbing my money in her face. She wasn't going to accept my invitation if I acted like a complete ass.

She bit her lip. "We have to fix that immediately." She pulled a paper bag out of her purse. "Here."

"I'm not eating that."

"I'm a good cook."

"I'm not sure cooking has anything to do with making that."

"Which is probably for the best. Because I'm not really a good cook."

I laughed. "If I try this contraption, do I get anything in return?"

"The delicious taste?"

"How about you owe me a favor?" I took a big bite.

"Wait! I didn't agree to that."

"Too late," I said, with my mouth still full. Hell, it was actually pretty good. Sweet and savory at the same time. Just like her.

"I don't owe you a favor."

"Actually you do, baby."

"God." She rolled her eyes at me. "You're incredibly immature."

"Said the girl who just rolled her eyes at me."

She sighed. "Touché. Did you like it?"

"It's actually really good."

"See!" She smiled at me. "There's a break room around the corner if you want to go sit down and eat."

I was perched on the side of her desk, staring down at her. "This is good. I have to get a feel for your desk anyway."

"Why?"

"Well, I'm sure we'll eventually break in here at night and make love on it. Since you're into office hookups and all."

"Make love?" She lowered her eyebrows slightly. "Have you ever used those two words together?"

"What, you don't think I'm capable of making sweet, sweet love?"

She laughed. "You said you were anything but gentle."

"When I'm fucking."

"So you don't want to fuck me anymore?" Her face instantly turned red and she glanced behind her to see if anyone had overheard her. They hadn't. Just me. And she looked disappointed. Like the only thing keeping her in the city was the idea of me fucking her.

Perfect. I couldn't help but smile. "So you do want me to fuck you?"

"I didn't say that."

"You implied it."

"I told you that I was attracted to you."

I was getting excited by how much she wanted me. I really could take her to the copy room right now. And I wouldn't mind having a printout of that ass. "What happened to taking things slow? Are you making it hard for me on purpose?"

She glanced down at my lap for just a second. She was trying to see if I was hard. I liked how much she seemed to fight with herself. When she finally unwound it was going to be intense. And I couldn't wait to be on the other side of all that passion. But that had to wait until Saturday night. Not right this second, despite how much the want was written on her face.

"So am I the worst or the best?" I asked.

"What?"

"You called me both earlier. So which is it?"

"A combination?"

"Well, is the urge to kiss me or spank me greater?"

Her lips parted slightly.

"Or maybe you're the one that likes being spanked?"

"I don't…"

"Don't you though?" I leaned down so that my lips were beside her ear. "Do you want me to spank you in the copy room? Or maybe you want to skip the foreplay and go right to the main event?"

Her throat made a small squeaking sound.

"Rain check. I have to get back." I placed a kiss on her flushed cheek. It was warm against my lips. And soft. I had to resist the urge to do it again. I wasn't even supposed to be touching her, let alone kissing her.

Chapter 33

Mason

"What about that one?" I pointed to a red dress on a mannequin. The mannequin wasn't nearly as curvy as Bee. She would look absolutely amazing in it. And it was perfect for the gala. It wouldn't look too bad on the floor of my bedroom either.

"Why the hell are we here again?" asked my brother, Matt, leaning against one of the display cases.

"I told you."

"You don't usually do this to get laid. What does she have on you?"

"Nothing."

"If you ask me, you like her," he said.

"I don't like her. I just want her."

Matt crossed his arms in front of his chest. "You're right. You don't like her. You like her like her."

"What the hell is that supposed to mean?"

"It's the step between like and love."

I laughed. I didn't fall in love. And Bee certainly wasn't going to be the girl that made me change my ways. "I have no idea why I asked for your help. She'll look good in anything. This dress is perfect."

"Do you know her size?" Matt asked.

"Yeah. I pulled a dress off the rack."

He frowned at me. "Why exactly do you know her size?"

"I had Vargas get some information on her."

"You do realize how creepy that is, right?"

I shrugged my shoulders. It wasn't creepy. It was efficient. And it was what was winning her over.

"So what else did you find out about this girl that you almost love?"

I lightly punched his shoulder and tried to ignore him. He was right though. I never tried this hard. Hell, I never really had to try at all. Women heard my name and flocked toward me. It was one of the only benefits of being a Caldwell.

"Do you at least have a picture? I want to see the girl that stole my brother's small, shriveled up heart."

"She didn't steal my perfectly normal sized heart. But I do have a picture." I pulled out my phone and clicked on my open tabs. I wasn't sure where Vargas had gotten this picture. But it had been on the front page of the report he had given me. And I found myself constantly looking at it. Just because she was nice to look at.

"Damn, she's hot."

"That she is."

"So what does she do?"

"That's a weird question coming from a guy who doesn't do anything."

"Hey, someone had to take over the family business. And Dad doesn't need my help yet. He's made that perfectly clear. He hates all my suggestions. I'm pretty sure he's still holding out hope on you taking it over."

"Yeah, that's not going to happen."

"How are you doing anyway? I can't imagine being cut off."

"I'm doing fine. Because I have a good job." And I still had some of the money left that my dad had given me. Once I ran out, that might be a different story. I knew the clock was ticking. I needed to land my first account before I lost my apartment.

"Still. Thousands is different than millions. I do not want to know what living is like without being able to take a bath in 100 dollar bills whenever I want."

He was right. I wasn't used to having to watch my cash flow. I probably shouldn't have been buying this dress for Bee. But I wanted to. *Not because I like her.* "I said I'm doing fine."

"How is the new venture going?"

I didn't want to talk about it. I never failed at anything. But I wasn't even close to having enough cash to start my own ad agency. And without my father's name backing me, no one was willing to give me a loan. My side business helped. It was currently the only cash coming into my new business. What I needed was more clients. Pilfering my father's new hires was easy. I needed more access to high-level employees. But I didn't want to spend my time growing that. I wanted to be starting my own company, not introducing men to sluts. After spilling the news to my dad that I had other plans for my future, he had basically said he was done with me. That was a year ago. I thought I would have started the agency by now. It was still a while off at this rate, though. "It's going slower than I'd hope."

"Well, when I'm in charge of MAC International, I'll reinstate your allowance."

"I don't need it," I said. "I'm going to do it without Dad's money."

"Eh. It'll kind of be my money then."

"Still." I didn't want handouts. Especially not from my little brother who hadn't really worked a day in his life. I was sure he was capable of running MAC. He had majored in finance at Harvard to appease my father. But the money was his only motivation. He didn't really want to run a finance company either. I didn't want to live like that. I wanted to prove that I had what it took to make it on my own. My dad would see.

"You didn't answer my question. What does this girl do?"

"She's a secretary at Kruger Advertising."

"Really? Mom and Dad will be thrilled about that," he laughed.

"I don't really care what they think."

"Clearly. Maybe that's why you're falling for her. Because she's the complete opposite of who our parents expect you to wind up with."

"Maybe."

"I knew it! You are falling for her."

"I didn't say that..."

"You kind of did. How much access do you think she has to files at Kruger?"

"I'm assuming she has clearance for everything."

"So, there's your answer."

"What?"

"You're not going to want to take your clients with you from Blue Media. They're a huge conglomerate. Burning your bridges with them wouldn't be helping you. But taking Kruger's clients? That's a different story."

"You want me to use Bee to get access to Kruger Advertising's client list?"

He shrugged. "You said you didn't love her. So I don't really see what the problem is."

I looked down at the dress I was holding. Matt was right. I was already getting Bee to trust me. It would be easy to convince her to get me access to the documents. Or at least I could steal the information from her computer without her knowing. If I had a list of clients, I'd be able to get a loan even without my dad cosigning. I might not even need a loan if I could get one of Kruger's large accounts to sign with me right away. I shook my head. That seemed dirty. Even for me.

"Unless you do love her..."

"No. I don't even like her." But I did. I couldn't stop thinking about her. That's why I was at the store buying her a dress.

"If you say so."

"And that's actually a really good idea. I'm not sure why I didn't think of it." Because I was distracted. Bee had thrown me off my game. And I didn't want to risk losing her over something stupid like that. Matt had no idea how to start a business. His advice wasn't exactly something I was looking for.

"You were blinded by love."

"Stop saying stupid shit."

"When do I get to meet her? I haven't met any of your girlfriends since you were still living at home. Have you even had a girlfriend since high school?"

"No. And you don't get to meet her. Because she's not my girlfriend."

"You do realize that I have tickets to the gala on Saturday, right?"

I cleared my throat. "That's not where we're going."

"Isn't it, though? Every important person in the city is going. Which includes me. And you. And apparently a lowly secretary from Kruger Advertising with a pretty face. It's a genius move actually. Showing her the riches and glam and then wooing her into bed with you. Well played."

Shit. I did not want him to talk to Bee. He'd ruin all my plans. I didn't want it to be just a one night. I wanted to be able to have her whenever I felt like it. "We're actually going to that winter festival thing."

"I've never heard of it. Which means you probably made it up. So I guess I'll see you at the gala. Can we please go get something to eat now? I'm starving."

Damn it.

Chapter 34
Bee

"Do you have plans with your new boyfriend tonight?" Kendra asked. She already had her jacket on and was most likely heading to a new club or bar since it was Friday. I couldn't think of one Friday night she had stayed in since I met her.

"He's not my boyfriend. And no, we don't have plans." I actually hadn't heard from Mason since he had stopped by with lunch on Wednesday.

"Want to go out with me then?"

"Not especially."

"You do realize that you're being rude, right? Come on, we're going. No more excuses. Besides, if you want Mason to want you, you have to appear unavailable."

I did want Mason to want me. I had waited for him to text me all day today and yesterday. After lunch on Wednesday, I had texted him and thanked him for the sandwich and soup. But he had never responded. For some reason it made me want him even more. I knew he was probably doing it on purpose. Which meant maybe I should appear unavailable on purpose. I could use some advice from Kendra. I was so out of the dating game that I didn't know what I was supposed to be doing.

"Okay," I said and switched off my computer.

She looked surprise. "Wait, really?"

"Yeah. Let's go." I stood up and grabbed my coat.

"Okay..."

"I thought you'd be happy, not suspicious."

"But you always say no."

"Well I think I need some guidance."

"That sounds about right. Let me text Marie real quick to see if she can come too. Girls night!" She pulled out her phone and typed out a message to Marie.

I popped my head into Mr. Ellington's office. "Is there anything else you need tonight, Mr. Ellington?"

"Not tonight, Bridget. There are a few important changes I want to discuss with you next week, though." He was looking at me in that creepy way again.

"About my position?"

"More than just your position. I have high hopes for you, Bridget."

My back got slightly straighter. He looked creepy, but maybe he was talking about an actual promotion. *High hopes.* I couldn't help but smile. Kendra was right, he just always looked creepy.

"Have a good weekend. And please close the door."

"You too, Mr. Ellington." I closed the door. I didn't want to say anything to Kendra yet. I knew better than to get my hopes up. But I couldn't help but think I may have finally landed my first advertising job. Maybe Sword Body Wash hadn't liked Jenkins' idea after all.

"Good news," Kendra said. "Marie's meeting us there." She linked her arm in mine and we walked together toward the elevator.

City of Sin

***

I was on my second cosmopolitan. Whenever the three of us went out together, we liked to pretend we were straight out of Sex and the City. Although it was anything but the truth. I was a homebody. Marie was married and barely had time for us. Kendra though...Kendra probably was close to being a Samantha. She was good at living in New York. She encompassed the confidence I wished I had.

"Bee," Marie said and waved her hand in front of my face.

I tended to space out when I had too much to drink. "Sorry, what did you say?"

"Have you slept with him yet?"

"No. Not really."

"Right, and Kendra and I are dying to know what exactly that means. Spill it."

"We did other stuff."

"Like what?"

"He was so forward. I excused myself to go to the bathroom while we were at dinner and he followed me. Into the ladies' room."

"And..."

"He went down on me." *Did I just say that out loud?* I needed to stop drinking. My filter was disappearing fast.

"After knowing you for 30 minutes? I guess the rumors were true."

"What rumors exactly have you heard again?"

"Basically that he's a sex god."

"That's not a thing."

"Well, did you like it?"

I could feel my face flushing. It was the most amazing thing I had ever experienced in my life. "It was good, yeah."

"Mhm. Does that mean it was better than Patrick?"

"Patrick and I never really did anything like that." I felt overheated just thinking about Mason. And now my stomach seemed to flop over at the mention of Patrick. I took another sip of my drink.

"Patrick never went down on you?" Kendra asked. "Why were you with him again?"

"Because we loved each other."

"Back to Mason," Marie said. "Did you two do anything else?"

"We may have done more stuff like that in an alleyway."

"See," Kendra said. "Kick Ass Bee. She appears more once she's had a few drinks."

I liked that nickname.

"What has Kick Ass Bee been doing with Mason since your first date?"

"Nothing really. He hasn't even kissed me again. He said he was willing to take things slow."

"Because that's what you want?" Marie asked.

"He thinks that's what I want. But I kind of just want him. And him not texting me back is driving me crazy."

"Well, what did you say to him last?"

"I thanked him for lunch."

"I think you need to let me borrow your phone again," Kendra said and put her hand out.

"No, I got this." I pulled my phone out of my purse and looked to see if he had texted me. He hadn't. I started typing: "If the silent treatment is a new dating game, it's brilliant. Because I've never wanted you more than I do right now. More than I wanted you in the bathroom. And the alley. More than I've ever wanted anyone before." I pressed send.

"What did you say?" Marie asked.

"Here." I slid my phone toward Marie and Kendra.

"Oh my God," Kendra said. "Did you seriously send this?"

"Yup." I took another sip of my cosmo.

"Way to just throw it all out there. What happened to pretending to be unavailable?"

"Oh, crap. You're right." I grabbed the phone back and typed: "But Kendra said I'm supposed to be unavailable. So ignore that last text. And thank you for the roses. I actually love roses." I pressed send again. "All fixed."

Kendra grabbed the phone out of my hand and looked down. She started laughing. "Bee! No more drunk texting for you."

"Let me see," Marie said and grabbed my phone. She started laughing too. My phone started buzzing in her hand. "He responded."

"What did he say?" I asked.

"He asked if you were drunk." She smiled at me.

"Was it that obvious?" I grabbed my phone back.

Sure enough, his text said: "Bee, are you drunk?" I bit my lip. I couldn't hide from the truth now.

"Maybe a little," I wrote back.

A second later my phone buzzed again. "Where are you?"

"At a bar with Kendra and Marie. Girls night!"

"Which bar?"

"He's being weird," I said and put my phone back in the middle of the table. "I think he's stalking me."

Marie laughed. In just a few seconds, my phone started ringing. "Aren't you going to answer that?" she asked.

"Is it him?"

"Yeah."

"I don't want him to hear drunk me. I'm rambling too much."

Kendra grabbed my phone. "Hello, Mason." Her eyes flicked toward me. "She's absolutely wasted."

Silence. I rolled my eyes at her.

"I think a ride home would be good."

"Kendra!" I said.

Ignoring me, she continued. "We're at the Tiki Lounge."

Silence.

"Okay, great. See you soon." She hung up.

"What did you say to him?"

She laughed. "You literally just heard the whole conversation. I told him you were plastered and that you could use a lift. He was still at work, so he's just down the street."

"I don't want him to take me home. He's going to try to seduce me."

"I think you should let him," Marie said.

"You are both terrible people. We're taking things slow. He's going to think I'm an alcoholic."

"Then I'll tell him all you do is sit at home at night and watch T.V. That should clear everything right up."

"Don't tell him that! Crap, do I look okay?"

"You look great," Marie said. "Besides, the lights are probably going to be off anyway."

I grabbed my phone off the table. "I'm just going to leave before he gets here. Tell him I got sick or something."

I hopped off the bar stool before either one of them could stop me and walked as quickly as I could toward the exit. I didn't want Mason to see me like this. I grabbed the door handle and almost ran outside. As soon as I turned the corner I ran straight into someone.

I instantly smelled his cologne. Which made my knees feel slightly weak. His hands were securely on my hips. I looked up at Mason Caldwell's handsome face. All I wanted was for him to lean down and kiss me.

"What are you doing here?" I said without moving. I didn't want him to take his hands off me.

His lips curled into a smile. "I'm taking you home."

"Your home or my home?"

His eyebrows lowered slightly. "Your home."

"I think I'd rather see your home." Apparently cosmos made me ridiculously forward.

"You're drunk."

"And you're handsome."

"Let's get you home." He let go of my waist and draped his arm across my shoulders.

I felt safe next to him. I liked how tall and muscular he was. I let my head rest against his shoulder.

We stopped on the curb and he put his hand out for a taxi.

"We can just take the subway," I said. "It's a block away."

"I don't ride the subway."

"Why?"

He shrugged. "I just haven't in a long time."

"Do rich people not ride the subway or something?"

"I guess you could say that." His arm tightened around me.

I wasn't sure if I had felt this warm since winter had started in this stupid city. "Why did you come?"

"Because you're drunk."

"Marie and Kendra would have taken me home."

"I just wanted to make sure you were safe."

"Safe? Hmm. I assumed you didn't actually like me. You never texted me back." I breathed in his scent.

"I'm here, aren't I?"

I looked up at him. He had told me he wanted to be the reason why I stayed in New York. I was beginning to think his dirty words and cool demeanor were all just an act. He did like me. If he didn't, he wouldn't have come here to take care of me. Patrick had never really taken care of me. Even when I was sick, he just avoided me. Mason wasn't the same as him. Mason was so much better.

A taxi stopped in front of us. He opened up the door for me and held my hand as I stepped inside. I didn't want him to take me home. I wanted this to be the start of the night, not the end. I slid into the middle seat to ensure that he'd be right next to me.

He smiled as he climbed in next to me. "West 96th Street," he said to the taxi driver.

The car immediately pulled off the curb.

"Are you sure you don't want to go back to your place?" I put my hand on his knee.

"You have no idea how much I want that. I want all of you, Bee. But not like this. You've had too much to drink." He tucked a loose strand of hair behind my ear before wrapping his arm around my shoulders. "You're not even going to remember this tomorrow morning."

Is that why he's being so sweet? Because he doesn't think I'll remember? He really was a good guy. He just didn't want anyone to know.

"Maybe," I said and rested my head against his shoulder. "Can you text me back now?"

"From now on, I'll always text you back."

"You know, you don't always have to act all macho. I like this side of you too. I like everything about you." God he smelled good. *Who smells this good?* "Except for the fact that you go to tons of strip clubs. You shouldn't do that. It's gross."

"Oh, they're much better than strip clubs. But I haven't been to anything like that since we've met."

"Really?"

"Really."

"Why?"

"We're here." He unwound his arm from around my shoulder.

I instantly missed the warm feeling. He got out of the taxi and held his hand out for me. I grabbed it and he pulled me to my feet. His fingers stayed intertwined with mine as he leaned down and told the cabbie to wait.

He walked me to the front door of my apartment building. I looked up into his eyes. He hadn't frequented any underground clubs recently because he liked me. He didn't have to say it. I wasn't sure why he wouldn't say it, but he didn't need to. I could tell by the way he was looking at me. The same way he always did. Like he desired me. I desired him too.

I grabbed his collar, pulling his face toward mine. When our lips touched I felt that spark go through me again. My whole body seemed to tingle as his tongue collided against mine. He pushed my back against the brick wall and deepened the kiss. He pressed his whole body against mine, pinning me against the wall.

And then suddenly he stepped back, leaving me completely breathless. It felt like I had waited forever for him to kiss me again. I didn't want it to be over so soon. "Mason, I..."

"Your super has a package for you," he said, cutting me off. He looked down at me as he ran his hand through his hair.

"What?"

His Adam's apple rose and fell. "Goodnight, Bee."

He turned away before I could say goodbye.

Chapter 35
Bee

I woke up with a pounding headache. Last night came flooding back to me. My apartment was freezing. I missed Mason's warm arms wrapped around me. I pulled my comforter up to my chin, but I was still shivering. And it definitely didn't help my head at all. I climbed out of bed, pulled on another pair of pajama bottoms, and downed some aspirin.

My apartment was a mess. I had put away the clothes I had ripped out of my closet but my apartment still looked dirty and old. And sad. I had decided to stay. So it was time to transform my apartment into what I wanted it to be. Not just remnants of what it used to be with Patrick.

I opened up the cabinet under the sink and pulled out a bunch of cleaning supplies. I was finally ready to move on. The first step was to rid my apartment of all things Patrick.

***

I rested the broom against the wall and leaned down to pick up a slip of paper that was on the floor. I unfolded it and let my eyes dart across the words.

I'm holding a package for you because it wouldn't fit in your mailbox. Stop by anytime after 8.
-Naomi

Mason's words from last night came back to me. He had said that the super had a package for me. *He sent me something?* I opened up my door and quickly walked downstairs. I wished I had seen the note earlier. Naomi was usually more agreeable earlier in the day. And I still needed to bug her about fixing my heater. I knocked on her door.

After a minute she opened it, keeping the chain lock on. "You look a mess," she said through the small gap in the door.

"Oh." I touched the side of my head. My hair was in a ponytail and my face was probably greasy. Or maybe she was just referring to the fact that I was wearing two pairs of pajama bottoms.

"Tsk. And you wonder why you can't keep a man. Tsk."

I hated that noise she always made. I took a deep breath so I wouldn't snap at her. "I was cleaning and found the note you left." I held up the piece of paper. "You said there was a package for me?"

She closed the door.

"Naomi?" *What the hell?* I knocked on the door again.

"You can add patience to the list," she said as she opened up the door again. "I had to unlock the door. Tsk."

Growing up in the suburbs meant no chain locks. When someone stopped by, we welcomed them in and offered them tea and crumpets. Well, maybe not exactly, but we were friendlier than this. "Sorry, Naomi."

"Your rent is due soon. Are you going to be late again?"

"No. I won't be. Actually, there was something else I wanted to talk to you about. The heater in my apartment seems to shut off every night and..."

"It's already on my list."

I bit the inside of my lip. "I know, Naomi, but it's been on your list since November. The winter will be over before..."

"Your problem isn't any more important than anyone else's."

"But it's freezing up there."

"It's a New York winter. You'll get used to it." She grabbed a package off the floor and shoved it into my arms.

"Maybe my rent can be a little less then, since I'm saving money on heat?"

She squinted her eyes as if she was just really seeing me for the first time. "I'll think about it," she said and slammed the door in my face.

I'd take her thinking about it. If I was going to freeze to death, at least I could save a little bit of money in the process. I looked down at the box in my hands. It was wrapped in brown paper and there was a silky green ribbon around it. There was no address anywhere on the package. My name was just scrawled on the side. And it looked like Naomi's handwriting.

Had Mason hand delivered this? That would mean that he had seen my apartment building and met Naomi. I knew I was financially beneath him. But he hadn't written me off after seeing where I lived. He had still left the package. Maybe he didn't care about stuff like that. I still felt a little embarrassed though. He lived in a freaking hotel. And I lived *here*.

I opened up the door to my apartment. At least it was clean now. I put the package down on my bed and stared at it. What on earth was in there? Mason and I still barely knew each other. Maybe it was a hangover kit or something.

No. He had sent me this before I had even drunk texted him. Which meant he had been thinking about me since our lunch date. And not just thinking about me, but buying me something. I had wanted him to come up last night. I had been pretty surprised that he hadn't said yes. But it made me like him even more. He was respectful. He thought I was too drunk to make that decision. But I wasn't. And I remembered every part of our conversation last night.

I sat down on my bed and untied the green ribbon. I pushed it out of the way and ripped the brown paper. There was a white box with a small envelope on top of it. I opened up the envelope and pulled out the card.

Bee,
    I'll be picking you up at 7. I can't wait to see you again.
-Mason
P.S. I ate a peanut butter and jelly sandwich for lunch today. You're rubbing off on me.

I ran my finger across his words. I liked that he never asked. There was no uncertainty on his part. He wanted to see me, so he was going to see me. Every time we talked I liked him more and more. I couldn't deny the fact that I had a huge crush on him. That was the best way to put it, because for some reason it felt like I could never really have him. He was out of my league. But it made me want him even more.

I looked back down at the package. Had he sent me a peanut butter and jelly sandwich? Or maybe something for our date? I slowly lifted off the lid and pushed aside the tissue paper.

Oh my God. I picked up the dress and stood up so that I could see the whole thing. It was a deep red, mermaid style dress with a plunging neckline. It was simple but elegant at the same time. *So elegant.* He hadn't just been thinking about me, he had been buying me the most beautiful dress I had ever seen. It was like something one of the contestants from Miss America would wear. There was something different about the fabric of this dress. I wanted to say it was almost heavy, but that didn't explain it right. It wasn't like other dresses I had. It was well made. The fabric was luxurious. And somehow it looked like it might fit me. Mason was a good guesser.

7 o'clock. I grabbed my phone and looked down at the time. I still had a few hours. But I somehow needed to look worthy of this dress. I laid it down on my bed and ran into the bathroom.

***

I took the last of the hot curlers out of my hair and ran my fingers through the curls to loosen them. My makeup and hair were done. Now I just needed to see if the dress fit me.

I put on my nicest bra and pulled the dress over my head. It was the perfect fit. I never would have chosen something that accented my breasts so much, but it was beautiful. I took a step back from the mirror. It hugged my curves like it was made for my body. I didn't really want anyone to stare at my cleavage all night though. Maybe I had something that would draw attention toward my face. I pulled out my box of earrings and picked up a pair of dangling earrings with diamonds. Patrick had bought them for me a few months before I found out that he was cheating. It was probably because he felt guilty. I hadn't worn them since our breakup. But when I looked at them now, I didn't want to cry. They were the nicest jewelry I had aside from the engagement ring I once wore. And I wanted to look nice for Mason.

Marie was right. Mason was a perfect choice to help me get over Patrick. It was already working. And maybe I was what he needed to. If I wasn't, why would he have bought me this dress? This was too elaborate of a scheme for a one night stand. He liked me. The thought gave me butterflies in my stomach. This was more than a rebound for me. Maybe this was why I had wound up in New York. Mason had said he wanted to be the reason I stayed in the city. And I didn't realize it before, but he already was. I was actually happy. I was happier than I had been in months. I put on the earrings and looked at my reflection in the mirror. It was like they were made for this dress.

I picked up my phone to look at the time. There was a message from Marie: "Kendra and I are dying to know how the sex was. Text me back."

I laughed. "Still don't know that yet," I texted back. But maybe I would soon. I looked at my reflection in the mirror again. Tonight could be the night. If he could resist me in this dress, maybe he was gay or something. The thought made me laugh again. If there was anything I was sure about regarding Mason Caldwell, it was that he was straight. And right now, for some reason, he wanted me.

There were still a few minutes before he was supposed to be here. I grabbed my notebook and flipped to a blank page. It was like I was living in a fairytale. This was how every girl desired to feel at some point in their lives. Something that captured this would make a great advertisement. For what I wasn't sure. But it was a good idea. Hopefully it wouldn't be an idea that just sat there forever without anyone hearing it.

A buzzing noise sounded through my apartment. Mason was downstairs, waiting to come up. But I didn't want him to see my place. It was bad enough that he had seen the inside of the building. I set my notebook down on my nightstand and grabbed my nicest jacket out of the closet.

I locked my door behind me and walked down the stairs as quickly as I could in my heels.

Chapter 36
Mason

I pressed the button again. *I should have called her.* She was drunk last night. She probably didn't even remember that I told her she had a package.

I leaned against the wall next to the call box. She had wanted me to come up last night. And for some reason I hadn't. I kept telling myself it was because she hadn't begged me yet. But that wasn't it. I wanted her to remember our first time. I wanted her to dream about. I wanted her to crave me as much as I was craving her.

My phone buzzed in my pocket. There was a text from my friend, James: "Please tell me you're coming to this thing. I'm pretty sure Penny and I are the youngest ones here right now."

I was excited to show Bee off. "My date and I will be arriving shortly. We'll help spice things up, don't worry." I pressed send.

"Spice things up? Like the Caldwell Christmas party 2012 spicy? This will be an interesting evening."

I laughed. I had brought a prostitute to my family's annual Christmas party that year. It did not end well. Well, actually, she did give me a happy ending. But my family wasn't happy. "Nope, I have an actual date this time. And I think Penny and her are going to hit it off." *If Bee's actually coming.* I pressed the button on the call box again.

James' response came right away. "I'm not even sure what you mean by an actual date."

"Don't embarrass me, asshole." I shoved my phone into my pocket as I heard the click of the front door opening. Bee emerged from her apartment building.

I had never seen her look more beautiful. Her cheeks were flushed from the sudden burst of cold. And her lips were the same color as the dress. The dress looked like it was made for her. Her long coat hid her round ass but her tits looked amazing. "Bee." My voice sounded weird. I quickly cleared my throat. "You're breathtaking."

She smiled shyly. "Mason. No one has ever...you didn't need to..." her voice trailed off. "Thank you for the dress. I love it."

I wanted to walk over to her and kiss her. But I had already planned out how this evening was going to go. And it definitely didn't start with a kiss. I wouldn't get her to the gala if I gave in to that urge. We'd end up in her bed in just a few minutes. I wanted to show her everything I had to offer.

"You look beautiful in it. We better go. We're already late."

"Where are we going?"

I walked over to the town car I had rented for the evening. The driver hopped out and immediately opened the door.

Bee walked over to me and looked up at me expectantly.

"You'll see. Get in the car." I nodded to the open door.

She climbed in and I walked around to the other side. When I got in, she was already in the middle seat. She wanted our bodies to be pressed together. I certainly wasn't going to complain.

"You're in a tux," Bee said.

"I am."

"You look very handsome."

I smiled down at her. "Where do you think we're going?"

"I have no idea. Somewhere fancy?"

I laughed. She didn't even know about the most anticipated event of the winter. Women would die for tickets to the Silver Gala. All the city's most prestigious young professionals were going to be there. I had gotten laid every night of the Silver Gala since I graduated from college. Tonight wouldn't be any different. "We're going to the Silver Gala."

"Oh, of course." She pressed her lips together and turned to look out the window as the car started.

"Do you even know what that is?" I put my arm around her back. Touching her wasn't on the list of things I couldn't do. Actually, I was going to be touching her a lot. I could see what it did to her. She'd be begging me before the night was even half over.

"No." She looked embarrassed. "But it does sound fancy, so I was kind of right."

"Mhm." I shifted slightly so that our thighs would be touching. "The Silver Gala is held every year to raise money for St. Sabela's Children's Hospital."

"I knew you were a good guy."

"I never said I wasn't." There was a fine line between her wanting me and wanting more from me. I needed to make sure I didn't cross that line. But it was just too easy to tell her whatever she wanted to hear.

"You implied it."

"I'd be happy to remind you about all the bad things I'm into. I'm no saint, Bee."

"I know."

I could see it in her eyes. She liked that I wasn't a good guy. She liked that I was forward and brash. It took all my willpower to not kiss her.

"I'm happy to remind you tonight," I said.

"Maybe you should."

"Baby, I'm planning on it."

"Don't call me that," she said. But for the first time, it didn't sound like she meant it.

"We're here," the driver said as he pulled to a stop in front of The Plaza Hotel.

Chapter 37
Bee

It really did feel like I was dreaming. I stared up at the grand old building through the car window. I had admired it from a distance whenever I walked through Central Park. The door opened and Mason put his hand out for me. I hadn't even noticed he had gotten out of the car.

He looked so handsome. When I was trying to convince myself to stay away from him, I had tried to ignore his good looks. But he was one of the most handsome men I had ever met. And with his wool jacket unbuttoned and his tux showing, he looked like he was straight out of a magazine. He could have been advertising anything. I'd want to buy whatever it was. How had I wound up here? I felt like the luckiest girl in the world.

"Are you planning on driving off without me again?" He raised his left eyebrow.

I put my hand in his and stepped out of the car. "Not in a million years. Are you trying to get rid of me?"

He laughed and intertwined his fingers with mine. "Not in a million years, Bee."

I looked down at our hands. I felt like my hand fit well in his. It really seemed like I was exactly where I was supposed to be. Everything leading up to this point had been worth it if Mason was actually the guy he seemed to be.

The guy who wanted to be the reason why I stayed in New York. I was falling for that guy.

We walked up the red carpet on the front steps. The lights on top of the canopy above us lit up the entrance beautifully. It looked like something out of an old movie. Mason pulled two tickets out of his front coat pocket and handed them to the man who had just opened up the door for us.

The man looked down at the tickets. "Mr. Caldwell, the gala is being held in the ballroom." He handed the tickets back to Mason. "Down the hall to the left. I hope you both have a wonderful evening."

"You too," Mason said.

I gripped Mason's hand a little tighter when we walked into the hotel. The marble floor led to the most ornate staircase I had ever seen. The Plaza Hotel's emblem was emblazoned on the floor in gold. And the chandeliers completed the royal look of the entranceway.

Mason pulled me in the direction of the ballroom.

"It's beautiful," I said and looked back over my shoulder.

"Not as beautiful as you."

"Usually your pickup lines aren't so cliché." I smiled up at him.

"I'm not trying to pick you up. I already have you." He squeezed my hand.

The way he said it made my body feel warm. Is that what he thought? That I was his? It had been a long time since I had felt connected to someone. That's what I wanted. To be a part of a "we" again.

"Have you ever been here before?" I asked.

"I come every year."

"How many years have you been coming?"

"Six, I believe."

"So you've been donating to the hospital since you graduated? You're a bad boy with a good heart, Mason Caldwell."

"It's a good cause."

"Who do you usually bring to these events?"

"No one important in a long time." He smiled down at me. "Have you ever been to this hotel?"

"What purpose would I ever have for going to The Plaza Hotel?"

"Something fancy?"

I laughed. "I haven't done anything fancy in a long time."

"I heard the mattresses are exceptionally comfortable here."

I swallowed hard. I loved when he talked like that. I wanted to be witty back. "We're pretty good without a mattress."

"You don't have to remind me." He stopped outside the coat check. "Turn around, Bee."

I turned away from him. He slowly pulled my coat off of me, tracing his fingers down my arms. The electricity shot through me even stronger than before. He pushed my hair to the side and kissed the back of my neck. "Truly breathtaking," he whispered. The heat of his breath on the back of my neck made my skin tingle.

I turned around and watched him grab the tickets out of his pocket before handing both our jackets over to the attendant.

"The hospital thanks you for your very generous donation, Mr. Caldwell. I hope you and your lovely guest enjoy the evening. You will both be at table three."

"Thank you."

The man opened up the door to the ballroom for us.

I followed Mason inside. Whether or not I was breathtaking was questionable, but there was no question about this room. It was absolutely beautiful. All the decorations were adorned with gold. And the chandeliers were even more extravagant than the ones in the entranceway. There was a dance floor in the middle of the room, surrounded by ornately decorated round tables. It was like a room for a wedding reception, only way fancier than any wedding I had ever been to.

"Come with me. I want to introduce you to someone," Mason said.

I held on to his hand. I was suddenly incredibly nervous. All the people here were rich like him. If he hadn't bought me this dress, I definitely would have stuck out in the crowd. And not in a good way.

"James," Mason said and stopped in front of a man I instantly recognized. He was that professor who had gotten fired from the University of New Castle. Although, I guess Mason said he had actually resigned. He hadn't changed at all. I never had a class with him, but I had seen him around campus. He was hard not to notice. He was ridiculously good looking. And he had this air of authority around him. It almost transported me right back to school.

The two men briefly hugged and slapped each other's backs. It was funny when guys did that. They just had to make hugging masculine too. I couldn't help but laugh.

Someone else laughing made me look away. It was the girl standing right next to James. She was really pretty. Her long red hair looked beautiful against the green fabric of her dress. She seemed to be tickled by the fact that they had slapped each other's backs too. She was staring up at James in the most loving way. I wasn't sure I had ever looked at anyone like that.

I looked back at James as Mason and him ended their hug. There was so much warmth in the smile James gave her as he wrapped his arm back around her shoulders. I had heard rumors about their relationship at school. But the horrible rumors couldn't have been true. They definitely seemed to be in love. Not that I had much to compare it to. My parents got divorced when I was really young. And my relationship with Patrick had ended in disaster. Marie and Carter were the only real couple I knew. And they seemed perfect for each other. But even they didn't look at each other like that.

"Bee," Mason said and turned back to me. He wrapped his arm around my back so that his hand was resting on my hip. "Bee, this is James and Penny."

"Hi," I said, and nervously shook James' hand and then Penny's. I liked that Mason kept his arm around me. It was like I was his and he was excited to introduce me to his friends. I always got nervous at things like this. But I felt comfortable next to him.

"Bee actually went to the University of New Castle," Mason said.

"I thought you looked familiar. What year did you graduate?" Penny asked.

"A few years ago. In 2015."

"Oh." Penny smiled up at James. "We had some overlap, then. We moved here in 2015. Maybe we had a class together?"

"I don't know," I said. "I spent most of my time at the Sigma Pi frat house. My ex lived there. Maybe I saw you there?"

"That must be it! One of my best friends lived there too. Tyler Stevens."

"I knew Tyler!"

"Wait who was your boyfriend?" asked Penny.

"Patrick Huff."

"I don't recognize it. But I'm sure I ran into him. Although, I didn't spend that much time there. James took up most of my time." She smiled up at him again.

"Maybe we shouldn't talk so much about our exes, Penny," James said.

Penny laughed. "Sorry." She looked up at Mason. "Sorry, Mason, I didn't mean to remind your girlfriend of her ex."

"Very funny, Penny," Mason said.

I wasn't sure what was so funny. But I didn't want to dwell on it.

"What did you major in, Bee?" James asked.

"Marketing. And I had a minor in advertising."

"I'm surprised I never had you in one of my classes."

"Yeah, I always tried to get in, but your classes filled up so fast. I heard you were a great teacher."

He laughed. "I wasn't that great. You didn't miss out on anything."

"You were great," Penny said. "He was definitely the best professor I ever had."

"That's just because you were sleeping with him," Mason said.

Oh my God. I was about to apologize for what Mason had said when Penny started laughing again.

"You're probably right," Penny said. "James was definitely the highlight of my time at the University of New Castle. And everything after that too." She looked a little embarrassed when she said it. But her embarrassment seemed to evaporate when James leaned down and placed a kiss on her cheek.

"I still have to do the rounds," James said. "Want to come with me and we can spare our dates the boredom?"

"Sound like a plan," Mason said. "I'll be right back, baby." His hand slid down my hip and he lightly squeezed my ass before walking off with James.

Oh my God. Did he seriously just goose me in front of all these people? I hoped my face wasn't as red as my dress.

Penny turned to me. "I can't believe you're from Delaware too. I never meet anyone who grew up where I did."

"Me either," I said. "It's quite the transition moving here."

"Yeah it is. But Central Park is really nice."

"That's what I always say to everyone whenever I miss having a lawn."

Penny laughed. "Me too."

"Do you ever miss it?"

"Home? Or having a lawn?"

I laughed. "Both, I guess."

"Sometimes." Penny looked over at James again. "I've found that the company is more important than the location."

"I just have to say that you and James are the most adorable couple I've ever seen."

She laughed.

"What?"

"He does not like being called adorable. You know, I don't think I've ever seen Mason like this."

"Like what?" I asked.

"The way he looks at you. I've never seen him look at anyone that way. I think he really likes you."

"Why did Mason say 'very funny' when you apologized for reminding me about my ex?"

"Oh. Nothing really."

"Come on. Us Delaware girls have to stick together."

She smiled "I don't know. His reaction to what I said was more so about the fact that I called you his girlfriend I think. It's just that Mason doesn't really date. I've known him for almost two years and I've never seen him with the same woman twice."

"Really?" I looked over at him and James. I had never seen him like this before. He looked like he was in his element, making small talk with these people. Maybe I didn't know him as well as I had thought.

"But you shouldn't let that bother you. Like I said, I've never seen him like this before. He seems different."

"I feel like every time I'm with him he's different."

"Every time?"

"We've been on a few dates already."

"See. You have nothing to worry about. You two are already dating."

"We haven't really discussed that yet."

"Sometimes you just know."

"Like with you and James?"

"It wasn't easy with us either. I mean, he was still married when we met."

So that part was true. "I guess. I feel like there's still so much I don't know about him. It's hard to let myself fall when there are so many uncertainties."

"I still learn new things about James every day."

"Really?"

"Yeah. I mean, I haven't even met his parents yet."

"But you've been dating for a really long time."

"Mhm. Every time we make plans, they cancel at the last minute. I guess I'm just not exactly their first choice for their son."

"I'm sure that's not true."

Penny laughed. "No, it is. James is way out of my league."

"I'm completely out of my league with Mason too!"

She laughed again. "I am so glad that you are with Mason. Now we can finally go on double dates. Whenever he comes over, I feel like I end up being the third wheel."

"They are kind of cute together," I said and looked over at them again.

"Do you know what I miss most about Delaware?" Penny asked.

"What?"

"Grottos Pizza."

I laughed. "That is my favorite pizza ever. There's so many on the boardwalk that whenever I eat it, it just tastes like summer."

"I know! Pizza here is great, but it doesn't taste like summer."

Mason and James both shook someone's hand and then started walking back over to us.

"Can I ask you something real quick?" I asked.

"Of course."

"Do you think Mason knows how to be in a relationship?"

Penny hesitated for a second. "Yes. Mason is a really good guy. It just takes some time to get to know the real him."

"Tell me about it."

"Please don't worry about what I said before. I think you're perfect for him. I mean, look at how he's looking at you."

Mason was staring at me. Maybe I was imagining it, but it wasn't that different from the way James was looking at Penny. Maybe this really could be more.

"And you're lucky," Penny said. "You don't have to worry about meeting Mason's parents anytime soon."

"What do you mean?"

"After everything that's happened between them? They're not even speaking. It's been good for him, though. He seems more grounded now."

Wait, what? He hadn't mentioned any of that to me. An ad executive made good money, but not great money. How were we here? How did he afford the dress I was wearing? Or the fact that he lived in a hotel? All that money couldn't be from his side business. Could it? I looked down at the dress I was wearing. Was it possible that Patrick had actually paid for this dress? The thought made me nauseous.

"I'm going to steal her away now," Mason said and wrapped his arm around my back again.

I almost jumped when he touched me.

"It's always a pleasure," Mason said to Penny.

"Always," Penny said. "It was really nice to meet you, Bee. And get Mason to give you my number." She looked back over at Mason. "Next time you come over, you're bringing her."

"I think I can arrange that," Mason said.

"It was nice to meet you, Bee," James said and stuck his hand out to me. "Like Penny said, you're welcome to our home anytime."

I shook it. *How does Mason have such nice friends?* James and Penny seemed so normal. Everything I knew about Mason was anything but normal.

Chapter 38
Mason

I steered Bee away from James and Penny. "You seemed to hit it off with Penny. Were you reminiscing about the University of New Castle?"

"A little. Are you not speaking to your parents?"

I pulled away from her slightly, but kept my hand on her hip. *Damn it, Penny.* "We had different opinions on how my future was going to play out."

"How are we here, Mason? How do you afford all these nice things?"

I pulled her onto the dance floor and grabbed her waist. "What do you mean? I have a good job."

"I know you have a good job. But all this?" She looked around the room. "And you're saving up to start your own ad agency on top of everything else."

"Yeah. I am. So what?"

"What money did you buy this dress with?"

"My money?" What the hell was she getting at? I grabbed her hand, spun her, and then pulled her in even closer than before.

"Could you only afford this because of people who paid you for...services?"

I laughed. She had to be kidding. Of course that's how I bought her that dress. And I wasn't sure why she was upset about it. She looked fucking fantastic. But I'd tell her what she needed to hear.

"Okay," I said. "No, I'm not talking to my parents. But they're the only reason why we're here right now. They gave me the tickets." It was true. My parents donated money every year under Matt and my names. That's the only reason I had tickets. I didn't originally tell her that because she seemed to be eating up this good guy nonsense. It was a good charity. And I was glad it was under my name. I needed the good karma. "What, are you only with me for my inheritance?"

Her face blushed. "No. Of course not. I just wanted to make sure Patrick didn't buy me this dress."

Oh. So that's what she was upset about. She knew I took money from her ex. But Patrick hadn't given me nearly enough money to pay for what she was wearing. And that was an awfully pessimistic way of looking at it in the first place. "Would it make you feel better if I told you I still got money from my old man?" I didn't. But she didn't need to know that. What little money I did have left from him was dwindling fast.

"No. I don't know. Yes?" She looked so flustered. But she kept her hands clasped behind my neck. She wasn't trying to run out on me again.

"Bee." I touched the side of her face. "I bought you this dress. Because I really like you. And I wanted to come here tonight with you. I don't want to talk about my parents or Patrick. I want to focus on us. Because I'm really loving *us*."

"I'm really loving us too."

Of course you are. "And since you're a gold digger, you'll be happy to know that one day I will inherit millions from my parents." As of right now, I wouldn't. I was sure they'd come around once I started my own successful company though. "But at that point, I'll already have millions of my own." At least that was the truth. Because I'd do anything to make it happen. Except for following Matt's advice. I wouldn't use Bee for information. That was where I had to draw the line.

"I'm not a gold digger, Mason."

"I know. At least, I hope you like me for more than my money." I tucked a loose strand of hair behind her ear.

"I like you for a lot of reasons," she said.

"You do, huh?"

"I'm here, aren't I?"

Shit. She remembered last night perfectly. What else had I said?

"Ladies and gentleman." There was a stage off to the right of the dance floor and the president of St. Sabela's Children's Hospital had just taken the microphone. "As you all know, without all of your generous donations, we would not be able to continue the groundbreaking research that gives children the chance to be children. The gift that you have endowed is impossible to put into words. So I'm not going to bore you with a long speech."

Everyone laughed.

"Without further ado, it is with great pleasure that I announce that dinner is served. Here's to a fun night."

There was a loud smattering of applause.

"Shall we?" I said. "Or are you planning on sprinting out the door?"

"I think I'd rather stay."

"I was hoping that would be your answer." I reluctantly let go of Bee's waist. I liked the feeling of her hips beneath my hands.

She looked up at me with her beautiful brown eyes as she unwound her hands from the back of my neck. I grabbed her hand and lead her over to table three. Matt was already sitting there, staring at us. I knew he was about to embarrass me, but I was still excited to introduce Bee to him. It had been a long time since I had introduced a girl to someone in my family.

"By the way, you're about to meet my brother."

She smiled. "Which one is he?"

"The one that's almost as handsome as me."

"I call you handsome one time, and now you're all conceited about it."

I laughed and stopped next to Matt's seat. "Bee, this is my brother, Matt."

"It's nice to finally meet the girl that my brother is so infatuated with."

I would have been pissed at him, but Bee seemed to be pleased by what he said. Maybe Matt wouldn't try to ruin this for me.

"You're just as pretty as the pictures," Matt said and put his hand out for Bee.

"Pictures?" Bee glanced at me.

"Yeah. You do realize that my brother is stalking you, right?"

What the fuck, Matt?

Bee laughed.

Apparently she thought Matt was joking. Which was good. Because I was borderline stalking her.

"Is he a serial killer too?" Bee asked. "He kinda has that serial killer vibe to him."

"What is that supposed to mean?" I said.

"Nope, he's not a serial killer. Just a stalker," Matt said. "That dress looks amazing on you by the way. Much better than on the mannequin."

"Thanks." Bee's cheeks looked rosy as she glanced up at me again. "You two go shopping together? That's cute."

"Cute? I wouldn't classify us as cute." This girl was getting the wrong impression of me. I needed to turn this thing around. I pulled her seat out for her and put my hand on the small of her back.

"Thank you," she said and sat down. I pushed her chair in and sat down in between her and Matt.

"So you work at Kruger Advertising?" Matt said. "Tell us all about that."

Shut the fuck up. He was fishing for information that I didn't want. He was going to ruin this whole thing for me. And I was so close. I was hours away from claiming her pussy. Matt was not going to screw this up for me.

"There isn't much to tell," she said. "I'm trying to work my way up, but right now I'm just a secretary. It's not exactly exciting work."

"I'm sure that's not true. Secretaries are the heart of the company. What account is your team currently working on?"

"Oh. Um." She frowned slightly, but then smiled, dismissing whatever reservations she had. "It's this body wash account. The marketing idea Kruger Advertising came up with is actually really dumb. They're partnering up with some news segment in Florida. I mean, don't tell anyone I said that." Her face turned slightly red again.

"What news segment?" Matt asked.

I kicked him under the table.

"Fuck," Matt said, and grabbed his shin under the table. He shot me a nasty look.

"Are you okay?" Bee asked.

"Yeah." Matt let go of his leg. "I'm just super hungry. Where the hell is that food they promised?"

Bee picked up the glass of wine in front of her and took a sip. She looked uncomfortable. I had this whole night planned out. Wine her, dine her, and then make her get on her knees and beg for my cock. Nothing was going to distract me from the end game. I put my hand on her knee and slowly traced my palm up her thigh. I heard her gulp. I was starting to wish I had bought her a shorter dress.

Chapter 39
Bee

Mason had kept his hand on my thigh the whole time I was eating. And it was very distracting. The food was delicious, but all I could think about was his hand. I wanted to be alone with him. But I didn't know how to bring it up. When I had tried to invite him up to my place last night, he had rejected me. Maybe the dress and the makeup would make him say yes. I couldn't stop thinking about our first date. I wanted to pick up where we had left off. And every day it didn't happen, I wanted it more and more.

He was starting to get a 5 o'clock shadow. He had loosened his tie slightly so that he looked a little more casual despite his tux. I ran my thumb across my ring finger. I was definitely ready to move on. And despite all the things I didn't know, I found myself falling for Mason. Penny was right. Sometimes you just knew. And I knew I wanted Mason. I just hoped he wanted more than just sex. Tonight was kind of the reassurance I needed. He had introduced me to his brother and one of his best friends. If he just wanted a one night stand, I wouldn't be here right now.

Mason stood up and put his hand out for me. "May I have this dance?"

I smiled up at him. "Of course." I put my hand in his and he pulled me to my feet.

It was a fast paced song. I laughed as he crossed one of his feet over the other and spun around.

"Are you laughing at my sweet dance moves?"

I laughed again as he did another move that had to be straight out of the handbook for dorky dancing. "I didn't realize you were a terrible dancer."

He laughed and grabbed my hand. "Luckily I'm with you so no one even notices me."

"I'm sure that isn't true."

The song switched to a slow paced one. He pulled me to his chest and placed his hands right above my ass.

"It's definitely true. You're the most beautiful girl here, Bee."

The way he was looking at me made my heart beat quicken. *Kiss me!* Instead of answering my silent plea, he just stared down at me. I was very aware of his hands on my back. They seemed to slide a fraction of an inch lower. He slowly raised his left eyebrow.

I swallowed hard. Did he want me to ask him? It seemed like he said he wanted to take things slow out of respect for me. He was just being nice. But I didn't want him to be nice anymore. I wanted him to be like how he was that first night. I wanted him to say what was on his mind.

"What do you want, Bee?" He ran the tip of his nose down the length of mine. But his lips avoided mine again. "Tell me what you want."

I wanted unspeakable things. And I was too embarrassed to ask him. "What do you want?"

"Isn't it obvious? I want you." He leaned down and placed a soft kiss against my lips.

I grabbed the back of his head and immediately deepened the kiss. I had missed the taste of him. And the tingly feeling he gave my body. I loved the way he kissed me. It made me feel like I was floating. I was vaguely aware of the fact that his hands had slid down onto my ass. But I didn't care. I loved his hands as much as his tongue. I ran my fingers through his hair and made out with him in the middle of the dance floor. Just like I had always dreamed about doing during high school dances when no one even asked me as their date. And I didn't care that people could see us.

He seemed to pull back far too soon. "It's impossible to control myself around you." He squeezed my ass before moving his hands back up.

"I don't want you to control yourself around me anymore."

He seemed to study my face for a second. "How about I give you that tour of my place?"

"Okay." Showing me his place was just a nice way of asking for sex, right? I hoped so. I wasn't sure how much longer I could wait. I was done taking things slow. It was time to move into the fast lane and press my foot down on the gas.

He grabbed my hand and led me off the dance floor. "I'm going to go get our coats. I'll be right back." He dropped my hand and walked toward the doors. God was he sexy. I folded my arms across my chest as I watched him walk away.

"You always looked beautiful in those earrings."

The blood in my body seemed to freeze. I'd recognize his voice anywhere. *Patrick.* I turned around. I hadn't seen him in person in a few months. His hair was different. He looked good. He certainly seemed to be handling the breakup better than me, at least before I met Mason. But then again, Patrick wasn't the one whose heart had been broken. He had done the breaking.

I blinked hard. For some reason, seeing him made me want to cry. All those memories of us seemed to flood back. It was like ripping off a Band-Aid too soon. Maybe my wound wasn't healed yet. But he wasn't the same person that I loved. I didn't even know him anymore. It was like looking at someone I loved and looking at a complete stranger at the same time. And I didn't know what to say to him. I wasn't going to thank him for a compliment, that was for sure. I didn't want to speak to him at all.

"You look amazing, Bee."

"Thanks." *Damn it! He doesn't deserve my thanks!*

"Do you want to dance?"

"No. I'm here with someone."

"Oh."

"What about you?" I didn't really want to know the answer. But at the same time I did.

"Yeah." He looked over his shoulder. "My girlfriend just went to the restroom."

Girlfriend? "That's great. I'm happy for you." I wasn't happy for him. Is that why he had come over here? To tell me he was dating someone else? My chest was starting to hurt. This dress was too tight. It was growing hard to breathe. I wanted to walk away but my feet seemed stuck in place. There were so many things I still wanted to say to him.

He gave me a small smile. "I still miss you. I think I always will."

"Don't, Patrick." *Why is he doing this to me?*

"I'm just telling you the truth."

"I didn't realize you were capable of telling the truth."

"Bee..."

"You don't get to say that you miss me, Patrick. That's not fair. You're the one that messed this up. You don't get to miss me now. Not when you didn't like being with me when we were together."

He stared at me. "You know that's not true. I loved you. You know that."

Loved. Past tense. "You should probably get back to your girlfriend. Or are you just talking to me because you're hoping you can cheat on her too?"

Patrick laughed. "I just wanted to see how you were doing."

"I'm good. No, I'm great. I've never been happier." I was having trouble holding back my tears now. I blinked faster.

"I'm glad that you're happy."

"Are you?"

"Of course I am. I still care about you."

Fuck you! "If you cared about me, you wouldn't have betrayed me."

"I didn't betray you. I made a mistake."

"A mistake is something you make once, Patrick. It's not something you make dozens of times."

"I told you I was sorry. I don't understand why you won't forgive me."

"Because I loved you. Your betrayal hurt so much because I loved you so much."

"I know. But I'm not doing that anymore. I just don't understand why you wouldn't give me a second chance."

"Because it was more than one time. You had a million chances to tell me the truth. We were engaged, Patrick. If I hadn't found out, you would still be doing it. And we'd be married."

"That's not..." He sighed. "I would have stopped. I have stopped."

"That's great. I'm happy for you and your new girlfriend. Hopefully that'll work out better for you."

He ran his hand through his hair. "We're not even serious. It's not like she's you."

"Well, sorry." I hated him. I hated him for saying he missed me and pretending he cared about how I was doing.

"I miss you," he said again. "I miss what we had."

I wiped underneath my eye where a tear had finally escaped. "What we had wasn't real."

"That's not true. You know that's not true."

"You really should get back to your girlfriend."

"Let's get out of here," he said, ignoring my comment. "Maybe we can walk through Central Park and talk? I know how much you love that."

I wanted to slap him. He never offered to go to Central Park with me when we were actually together. "No. I told you, I'm here with someone. We've already talked about all of this. It is what it is. We don't have anything else to talk about."

"I think we do. You don't seem fine, Bee. And I'm not fine either. You're all that I think about. You're my other half."

"Give me a break. You're so full of shit."

He grabbed my wrist. "Let's just go somewhere quiet to talk. You can see my new place..."

"You have a girlfriend. What is wrong with you?" I pulled my wrist out of his grip.

"Fine, I'll go break up with her first. Would that make you feel better?"

"No. It would make me feel better if you stopped talking to me. I don't want to be having this conversation. I don't want anything to do with you."

"Come on, Bee. I still think we can work this out."

"We can't."

"You keep saying that. But you're not really telling me why."

"Do you remember when we first moved here? And how nervous I was? It was so different from what I was used to."

"Yeah. I do."

"And remember what you said to me? You said that when you were with me, you felt like you were home. That meant the world to me. And then you promised me that the city wouldn't get in our way. You promised."

"And I said I was sorry. I'm different now."

"I know. I'm very aware of that. Because the guy I fell in love with promised me he wasn't going to run off. He said he loved me with everything that he was. And he said he'd never leave me." I was crying now. I hated remembering how sweet he was. Because I didn't understand how that person had disappeared. It felt good to finally get that off my chest. It wasn't just about the cheating. It was about breaking his promises. That almost stung more. I might have been able to forgive the cheating. But I couldn't forget his broken promises.

"I didn't leave you, Bee. You kicked me out."

"Because you cheated on me. And when I found out, I realized that your promises were all empty. And I don't trust you. I'll never trust you again."

"Bee?" I felt Mason's hand touch the small of my back. "Is everything okay over here?"

I rubbed my eyes with my palms to remove my tears. "Yes. Patrick was just leaving."

"You've got to be kidding me," Patrick said as he glared at Mason.

"Nice to see you again," Mason said and nodded at Patrick.

Patrick turned back to me. "You're seriously not giving me a second chance, but you're sleeping with a guy like him?"

"That's none of your business," I said.

"You think I'm bad? Do you have any idea who this guy is? What he does?"

"I know that he's nice to me. And that he likes spending time with me. Which is a lot more than I can say about you."

"You're so gullible, Bee. This guy is a piece of shit. He's just using you. And if you're okay with that, then you've changed too."

Using me? Using me for what? Sex? I looked up at Mason. He looked so mad. Was he hiding something else from me?

"You're mad at me for what I did. But that's all he does," Patrick said. "He's the one you should be mad at. Not me. Don't you see that? He's the one that ruined us."

"How about you step back, man," Mason said.

"Make me." Patrick grabbed my wrist again. "Let me take you home."

"Don't touch me, Patrick." I pulled my arm away from him. "I'm not going anywhere with you. You can't blame what happened between us on Mason."

"Come on." Patrick grabbed my wrist again. "You have to trust me on this."

Mason shoved his chest. "She asked you not to touch her."

"Mason." I put my hand on his arm. I didn't want them to fight. God, this whole thing was ridiculous. People were starting to stare at us.

"What, like she's yours to touch?" Patrick said.

"Yeah. She is mine. So fuck off." Mason sounded so mad.

"You think that guys like him date girls like you?" Patrick laughed. "He doesn't even date. He's a womanizing asshole. Don't you see that?"

Girls like me? The only person that could make me feel worse about myself than I could was Patrick. His insults had always hurt me the most. I thought maybe it would be easier to hear now that I wasn't in love with him. But it still hurt. Lots of people were staring at us now. Mason had invited me to this extravagant thing. And Patrick was right.

I didn't belong here. I was embarrassing Mason and myself.

I opened my mouth to say something, but there was nothing left to say. I just needed to get out of there. I turned around and ran toward the exit.

Chapter 40
Mason

Shit. I ran after Bee.

"This isn't over!" Patrick yelled.

Yeah it is, asshole. I threw open the doors and spotted her down the hallway. "Bee."

She kept running.

"Bee!" I quickly caught up to her. "Stop."

She ignored me.

"Just stop." I got in front of her and grabbed both her arms. There were tears streaming down her cheeks. I had a strange tightness in my chest as she looked up at me. I didn't want to see her cry. It hurt me to see her like this. "Bee." I wiped away her tears with my thumb. "Hey, it's okay."

"Mason, I'm so sorry." She looked embarrassed. But she didn't have anything to be embarrassed about. Patrick was a dick. And now everyone else knew he was too.

"There's nothing to be sorry about." I wiped her tears away again. "Please don't cry." I pulled her against my chest. It was strange holding her like this. I let my fingers run through her hair. "It's okay." I said. It may have been strange, but I liked it. I liked how small she felt in my arms. And I liked that she wanted me when she was upset.

I wanted to be the one she turned to. I wanted to protect her.

I looked down at the top of her head. "My place is only a few minutes away."

She lifted her head and looked up at me.

God she was beautiful. Even when she cried she was beautiful. I wiped away her tears again with my thumb.

"Can you take me home?"

I felt the night I had planned slipping away. But I'd give her whatever she wanted to get her to stop crying. I hated seeing her like this. "Of course." I pulled my phone out of my pocket and called my driver. Bee let me wrap my arm around her as we made our way outside. The car was already waiting out front. I wrapped Bee's coat around her shoulders. If I had any idea that Patrick was going to be at the gala, I would have planned something else.

But I didn't dislike the position I was in. Having Bee cling to me like I was her lifeline was something I had never experienced before. When I sat down in the car, she put her head on my shoulder.

Maybe this was more than I was letting myself believe. Maybe this was what I really wanted. And not just the tight feeling in my chest. Her. I wanted her. And I didn't want to just sleep with her. I wanted this.

She lifted her head and looked up at me. She had stopped crying. "I'm so sorry, Mason. Before Patrick showed up, tonight was so...perfect."

I smiled.

She sat up. "I'm sorry that you had to see that. I'm so embarrassed. And I embarrassed you in front of all your friends..."

"You didn't embarrass me. I don't think you could embarrass me if you tried. You were the most beautiful girl there. Everyone else was envious of me."

"Yeah, right."

"I'm usually right."

She laughed. "I just hope I didn't ruin your whole evening."

"All I cared about doing tonight was hanging out with you. Besides, the night isn't over yet."

She looked down at her lap.

Maybe this could still end the way I wanted. Same plan, different location. The car pulled up outside her apartment. "Let me walk you up." I got out of the car before she could protest. I opened up the door and held my hand out for her.

She took it and I pulled her to her feet. I kept my hand in hers as I walked her to her door.

"Thank you, Mason. Tonight was..." she laughed. "Actually, it was like a fairytale."

I leaned down and kissed her. I had won the whole chivalrous game. I had made her think that I was her knight in shining armor. And now I wanted my prize. When I pulled back, she was panting.

CHAPTER 41
Bee

Mason was amazing. I had only known him for a little over a week, but he didn't run away when I cried. He held me. This wasn't a one night stand kind of guy, despite everything I had heard. He was sweet. He was the nicest guy I had met in New York. Actually, he was the only nice guy I had met in New York.

"If it's a fairytale, I believe that I'm the prince you won over. So what do you want to do with me now that you've won me?"

"Say goodnight and go out again when I haven't been crying for half an hour?"

Mason laughed and looked down at his watch. "It's only 11 o'clock. It seems a shame to cut the evening short."

"What did you have in mind?"

"I think you should let me come up."

I couldn't help it. I was embarrassed of where I lived. He had basically just taken me to a ball. We weren't supposed to wind up in a rundown old apartment after that. I didn't need him to feel any more sorry for me. I was such a mess.

But at the same time, I could feel my body caving in. I wanted him. I wanted to know what he'd feel like inside of me.

He was staring into my eyes.

The way he was looking at me made me tremble. He was starting to get a 5 o'clock shadow along his chiseled jaw line. His brown eyes seemed to pierce into my soul. He was a better guy than Patrick. But that didn't mean he was a good guy. If I invited him up, I might never hear from him again. Could I live with that? I wasn't sure if I would be able to let him go. But he might not even be asking to come up for sex. Maybe he just wanted a cup of tea.

"Let me show you how good it can be." His breath was warm against my skin.

He was talking about sex. And I must have looked a mess. I didn't want our first time to be like this. Or possibly our first and last. "I think maybe we should call it a night." I pressed my thighs together.

"Your body doesn't agree with you."

I gulped.

"You look overheated despite the fact that it's fifteen degrees outside."

"I...I had too much to drink."

"Your pupils are dilated."

"It's dark."

"You're pressing your thighs together."

I didn't have a good excuse for that. "So?"

"It's because you want me. You're dripping wet, and you're trying to hide it from me."

"I'll let you up if you want to talk." *Shit. Why'd I say that?* I wouldn't be able to resist him if he came up. I was inviting him into my bed and he knew it.

Mason's lips curled into a smile. "You just want to talk to me?"

"Yes."

"That's a waste of a good evening."

"Did you want to come up or not?"

Mason pulled away from me. "Show me the way."

I took a deep breath and punched in the code to unlock the doors. It made a beeping sound and I grabbed the handle. I walked into my building and started up the stairs. I could feel his eyes on my ass. It gave me a warm feeling in the pit of my stomach. I had already crossed the line. A public bathroom. An alleyway. Why not finish what we had started?

On the third floor I walked over to my door. I fumbled with the key in the lock. When I stepped in, I turned on the light. I hadn't expected to be bringing him back with me. I was so glad I had spent the afternoon cleaning.

"Did you live here with Patrick?"

I turned to look at Mason. He was looking around the apartment. I was so embarrassed. He lived in Trump International. He wasn't used to seeing apartments like this. He was tall, broad shouldered, and muscular, and he made the apartment look even smaller. "Yes."

"It's...nice."

I laughed. "It's horrible, I know. And I can't even really afford it. A secretary's salary isn't exactly great money." I leaned against the kitchen counter.

He walked over to me and ran his hand down the side of my neck. "Is that really what you want to talk about right now?"

"No." I wanted him to kiss me, but he didn't.

"So, when that incompetent ex of yours fucked you...did he do it here?" He ran his hand along the edge of the counter.

I swallowed hard. "No."

He walked over to the kitchen table. "What about here?" He put his palm down on the table.

Chapter 42
Mason

I watched her look down at the kitchen table and then back up at me. She shook her head.

"There's something sexy about hard surfaces, don't you think? Most people like a little bit of give. But I like to fuck. Hard."

I smiled as I saw her glance down at the bulge in my pants. I pulled off my suit jacket and draped it across the back of the chair. I undid my tie and put it on top of my jacket.

"What are you doing?" Bee asked.

"We both know that you didn't invite me up here to talk." I unbuttoned my shirt as I walked over to her.

She stared at my six pack. She couldn't resist me. But she stayed plastered to the kitchen counter.

"You want this just as much as I do." I ran my hands up the sides of her thighs and over her hips. "No, more. Because you've never had a real man inside of you. After I'm done with you, you'll never be able to scream another man's name."

"I..."

"I won't tell anyone what kind of girl you are. Your secret is safe with me." I ran my hands up the silky fabric and tugged on the zipper.

"Mason?" The tremble in her voice made me smile.

"You know, the best way to get over someone is to get under someone else."

Her breathing was accelerating. Her face was flushed. She wanted this just as badly as me. Her dress fell off her shoulders. When I finished un-zippering it, the dress slid down even more, exposing her bra. I ran my hand down her back to her bra strap. Her skin was still cold from the frigid air outside.

"I thought eating lots of ice cream was the best fix," she said with a laugh and grabbed my arms. She kept her hands on my biceps, stopping me from going farther. But it seemed liked she just liked the feeling of my muscles underneath her palms. Because she had "fuck me" written all over her face.

"No, having lots of sex is the only way."

"Lots of sex?"

I moved my hands to the counter, but she kept her hands on me. I leaned in close so that our lips were only a few inches away. "Tons of sex."

She gulped.

"So what kind of stuff are you into? Because you are not as innocent as you're pretending to be."

"I don't..." She took a deep breath. "I'm not..."

"That kinky, huh? You like unspeakable things? You know, I'm still trying to decide what I'm going to do with you."

She gulped again. I had already won her over. Now I wanted her to beg me. I wanted her naked and on her knees, begging for my cock.

"I was starting to think that you were a good guy."

"I'm not." I raised my eyebrow. "And I don't think you want me to be."

A small groan escaped from her lips.

"Here's what's going to happen, Bee. First you're going to finish getting out of that dress. Keep the heels on. Then you're going to lie down in the middle of your bed and raise your arms above your head. I'm going to tie your hands to your bed post. And then I'm going to fuck you harder than you've ever been fucked." My erection was tugging at my pants just thinking about it.

Bee bit her lip as she looked up at me. She shook her head.

What? Girls never said no to me. "Do you need me to repeat myself?"

"No, I heard you. Do you want some tea?" She ducked under my arm.

"What? No." I didn't like this dancing around game. I had put in the necessary time. I had come up here so I could finally fuck her and that's what I was going to do.

Chapter 43
Bee

I zipped my dress back up and opened the fridge. My whole body felt overheated. I leaned in to let the cool air hit my face as I tried to stop panting. I had almost lost all my resolve. God, he was so sexy. I looked over my shoulder at him and then quickly turned back to the fridge. The way his shirt was unbuttoned, revealing his perfectly sculpted torso, made it hard for me to focus.

I wanted to sleep with him. Badly. How could I not? He was handsome, and quick tongued, and said all the right things to make me feel alive down there. But he had just admitted that he wasn't a good guy. I wasn't sure if the past week had just been a lie or a game to him, but I didn't want us to become a one night thing. It wasn't just crazy attraction. I was really starting to like him. I just needed more time. I wanted to get to know him. I wasn't ready to say goodbye yet.

I shook my head and grabbed two beers from the fridge. "How about a beer then?

He eyed me suspiciously. I popped the tops off and handed him one.

"Okay, we'll do it your way then." He took a long, slow sip of the beer while he walked over to my bed. He kicked his shoes off and slid under the covers.

"What are you doing?" I wasn't sure how many times I was going to have to ask him that question.

"You wanted to talk. Let's talk." He patted the bed beside him. He took another sip of his beer and put his arm behind his head.

I looked back at the kitchen chairs. It would look ridiculous if I pulled one up next to him. I could control myself. *Couldn't I?* Besides, the apartment was cold. It would be nice to have the warmth of the covers. *Or his arms. Damn it, get a grip!* I took a deep breath and walked around to the other side of the bed. I quickly took off my heels and climbed into the bed, keeping my distance.

"So, Bee, what is it exactly that you wanted to talk about?"

I sat cross legged and took a sip of beer. I tried to keep my eyes on his face, because his six pack was too distracting. He looked so comfortable in my bed. "I just feel like I still don't know you."

He frowned slightly. "You're shivering, Bee."

"What?" The apartment was cold. But I was also excited and nervous. The way he was looking at me made goose bumps rise on my skin.

"Here." He moved right next to me and put his arms around my shoulders. "Better?" He raised his eyebrow at me.

"Yes." My voice sounded small. He ran his hand up and down my arm. I took a deep breath, smelling his cologne. He smelled like one of those cologne sample from a magazine. I let my head rest on his shoulder. Even though we were in bed together, it didn't seem like he was being forward. He was actually being a gentleman. Something that he swore to me he wasn't. He was so sexy, but he was also funny and easy to talk to.

"I can't read you at all. This whole week you were such a gentleman, despite the fact that you like to deny that you are. I just don't understand you."

"It's easy to be a gentleman around you. I think you bring out the best in me." He frowned again. He clearly wasn't used to saying things like that. He almost looked pissed at himself for admitting it out loud.

"You're different than other guys in this city."

"And why is that?"

"You're actually nice. I don't know anyone else who would have comforted me while I was crying after only knowing me a few days."

"I didn't like seeing you cry."

"I really like you." I shifted so that I could look up at him again. "I just want to know that it's more than just physical attraction."

"It's more than just physical. I promise you, it's more than that for me." He leaned down and kissed me.

CHAPTER 44

Mason

I looked down at the girl's head on my chest. *Bee. Shit.* I rarely ever spent the night. And I definitely never spent the night after not even having sex. We had made out a lot. But mostly, we had just talked all night. And laughed. She was so down to earth. So much different than the other women I had been meeting in the city. I ran my fingers through her long hair. I thought I was lying when I said it was more than just physical. But I wasn't. I was falling for this girl. She stirred and sighed against my chest. *Shit.*

I unwound her arms from around me and pulled my hand free from underneath of her. I tried not to make the bed move as I climbed off it. I stared down at her as I buttoned up my shirt. We must have fallen asleep talking. *What the hell is wrong with me?* This girl had crawled under my skin.

I needed to get out of there. I grabbed my suit coat and tie and headed to the door. My hand lingered on the knob. I turned back around. She was sleeping so peacefully. I couldn't just leave. She'd wonder where I had gone.

She rolled over in bed and reached out her arm where I had once been. She moaned softly, but didn't open her eyes. I didn't want her to think I was just going to abandon her once I was done with her. But isn't that the plan? I shook away the thought and walked back over to her bed. There was a notebook and a pen on her nightstand. I'd leave her a note, inviting her over to my place tonight.

The past week didn't matter and neither did the future. All that mattered was tonight. Finally claiming her. And if I could focus on that, and not the tightness in my chest, maybe I could get a grip. I was just messed up from not having sex in a week. The last time I had cum was in her mouth in that alleyway.

I lifted up the notebook and flipped to a random page. There were a few notes scribbled on the page.

Jenkins' pitch - Layla's Predictions - guessing penis size. Win a sample if she guesses wrong.

I laughed. That sounded like something Jenkins would pitch. I had heard of Layla's Predictions. Layla Torrez was a sexy weather girl from Miami. Was that what Kruger was currently working on? It didn't say what account it was for. But having Layla predict penis size was a pretty wild idea. How was she even supposed to do that on T.V.? There were scribbles over the words on the rest of the page. But I was able to make them out.

Idea - Local, guerilla style campaign. Knicks cheerleaders Central Park performance for selling tickets. Team up - have an actor spray himself with body spray and have the cheerleaders chase him through Central Park. Everyone would see it. No one would know if it was real or not. News stations would inadvertently pick it up. Attention grabbing and cheap.

That was a really good idea. Had she come up with that? I looked down at her sleeping. Clearly her boss hadn't liked it, or it wouldn't have been crossed out. I suddenly felt dirty. I shouldn't be reading this stuff. I flipped through the pages of notes until I came to an empty one. On the left side were a few more notes. I couldn't help but let my eyes wander over them.

Idea - Fairytale. Get a box in the mail with a dress and a note. Get dressed up and picked up for a romantic evening. Everyone loves a fairytale and the idea of finding your prince.

I smiled to myself and picked up the pen. She must have written that last night. I was no Prince Charming. But it didn't matter. After one night with me she'd be hooked. Maybe she already was. Which meant tonight would just seal the deal.

Bee,
Thanks for an amazing night. You looked absolutely stunning in that dress. I'm making you dinner tonight at my place. And I believe you said I didn't need to control myself anymore. So don't worry about what to wear, because you won't be wearing it for very long. I'll see you at 8.
-Mason

I put down the pen and turned toward the door. The apartment was dreary. I didn't want her to be in a place like this. It didn't even feel like her heat was working. I wanted her in my bed, ready for me whenever I wanted. I picked up the pen again.

P.S. The sleepover is at my place tonight. I can take you to work in the morning.

I put the pen back down and looked over at her. She looked so beautiful. She was still wearing the red dress, and it hugged every curve. I had the urge to kiss her cheek.
What the fuck is wrong with me?! I ripped the sheet of paper out of the notebook and placed it on top of it. Without looking back at her, I went over to the door and quickly left before I did anything else stupid.

Chapter 45
Bee

I yawned and stretched my hand out, but all I felt were empty sheets. I slowly opened my eyes. Mason was gone. I looked around the small, empty room. *I can't believe he saw my place. I can't believe I cried in front of him.*

I put my hands over my face. *God.* I had made such a mess of last night. Mason had been so fun and flirtatious and I had just fallen apart when Patrick had shown up. But I was over him. He had asked me for a second chance. And I didn't agree to it. I didn't want him back. I wanted Mason.

My apartment was embarrassing. But Mason had acted like he was at home. He knew I was upset and instead of trying to sleep with me, he had comforted me. We had talked all night. Technically he had tried to sleep with me right when I had let him in. But he respected my decision. We just snuggled. I liked the way his arms felt around me. And now that he was gone it was freezing.

I climbed out of bed. Luckily whatever fancy, expensive material the dress was made out of somehow resisted wrinkles, because it still looked amazing.

My phone buzzed on my nightstand. I went to grab it when I saw a note with Mason's handwriting. I quickly picked it up.

Bee,

Thanks for an amazing night. You looked absolutely stunning in that dress. I'm making you dinner tonight at my place. And I believe you said I didn't need to control myself anymore. So don't worry about what to wear, because you won't be wearing it for very long. I'll see you at 8.

-Mason

P.S. The sleepover is at my place tonight. I can take you to work in the morning.

If that wasn't an invitation for sex, I didn't know what was. My heart starting beating faster. *I'm going to have sex with Mason Caldwell.*

I took a deep breath. Was I really going to go have sex with someone that I only knew for several days? *Yes!*

I bit my lip. When had I become one of *those* girls? I sat down on the edge of my bed. Mason made it seem like it wasn't just about sex. If sex was all that he was after, then he would have just slept with a hooker or something. This was more. Last night was more. He seemed to care about me.

I looked down at my phone. Marie had texted me.

"I heard you scored tickets to the Silver Gala! Tell me everything!"

I smiled and wrote back. "Yes, Mason had tickets. It was really amazing."

My phone started buzzing in my hand. I slid my finger across the screen. "Hi, Marie."

"You are so lucky," she said. "I would give my left arm to go to that event. Everyone who's everyone goes to that thing."

"It wasn't that big of a deal. I didn't even recognize anyone besides Mason."

"Bee, it's a huge deal. Do you even know how much tickets cost for that thing?"

"I don't know. A lot? It was really fancy."

"It's $3,000 a plate. And not just anyone can attend. It's crazy exclusive. Mason must have it bad for you."

$3000 dollars a plate? The food was good, but it wasn't that good. "Why would it be exclusive? It's a charity thing. Wouldn't anyone who donated be allowed to go?"

"Well, right. But it's anyone who donates a ton of money. And I mean a ton. Way more than just the cost of the dinner."

"Wow." I looked down at the dress I was wearing. How much did it cost?

"So, did you meet anyone?" Marie asked.

"I met a few of Mason's friends. And his brother."

"Meeting the family already? That's a big step."

"Mhm." My mind was wandering back to Mason's parents. They weren't speaking. My mom always used to tell me to find a boy who treated his mother right. That was how you could tell if they'd treat you well. If Mason wasn't speaking to his mom, that probably wasn't a great sign.

"Is everything okay with you?" Marie asked.

"Yeah, I just..." my voice trailed off as I looked down at his note again. What would Marie think of this invitation? I wasn't going to ask. Because I had already decided to go. It felt like this was an opportunity of a lifetime. Even if it wasn't going to be a lasting thing, I'd regret not going.

"You just what?" Marie said.

"It was weird. At the gala, I ran into Patrick."

"How the hell did he get tickets? Did everyone have tickets to this thing except for me?"

I laughed. "I don't know. I'm sure he didn't buy them himself if they cost $3000."

"Probably not. So what happened?"

"He was asking why I wasn't willing to give him a second chance. And I got to say a lot of stuff that I wished I had said before. I think he might have been trying to get back together with me. But I said no. A few weeks ago, I probably would have said yes. It was different seeing him this time though. It was like I was actually seeing him for what he was."

"Does that maybe have anything to do with the guy you were there with?"

I couldn't help but smile. "Yes. Mason even comforted me afterward. He came back here and we talked and laughed all night." *And kissed a lot.* "He's such a sweet guy."

"Really?"

"You sound surprised."

"Oh, no. I mean, I don't know. I can't really picture Mason doing that. He seems so...macho. I feel like panties drop whenever he enters a room. I never would have thought someone would describe him as sweet."

I laughed. "Macho? Well, I think maybe he's softer than he lets on. Not that he isn't sexy. Because he is...really, really sexy." I was rambling just thinking about his abs. My words were greeted by silence. I pulled my phone down to see if the call was still connected. The seconds were still ticking by. I put the phone back to my ear. "Marie? Are you still there?"

"Bee, are you falling for him?"

Was I falling for a guy who knew every secret underground strip club in the city? Was I falling for a guy with a reputation for one night stands? Was I falling for a guy who had inadvertently ended my engagement? "I think I am."

Marie squealed into the phone. "Kendra can suck it! I knew setting you up with him was a good idea."

I laughed. "Yeah, I really owe you one."

"Maybe I should quit my job at Blue and start a matchmaking service."

"Maybe you should."

"I'm sure Carter would love that. You should call Kendra and tell her that you're in love with Mason and that she was completely wrong."

"I'm not going to do that. You just love being right about stuff. I'm sure you're going to call her as soon as we hang up anyway."

"You're right. I am."

"And I never said I was in love with him." I was falling for Mason Caldwell. But I wasn't in love with him. I couldn't be in love with him. I wasn't ready to be in love again.

"Right again. You didn't. But Kendra doesn't need to know all the details. I'm going to call her now. Bye, Bee!"

"Bye, Marie." I was pretty sure Marie had hung up before I had even said goodbye. I looked down at the note

Mason had left me. I couldn't be in love again. Because I wasn't ready to be hurt again. And Mason was the type of guy who didn't stick around for long. I needed to remind myself of that. If I allowed my head to catch up with my heart, then I'd be back at square one, alone in this horrible city. That was what love always led to. I just wished I was better at compartmentalizing.

***

My mind had flitted back and forth all day. But here I was, standing in front of the veranda with Trump International Hotel And Tower written in huge gold lettering. I felt like I had been standing still ever since I had given the ring back to Patrick. Mason made me feel like moving again. And if tonight was going to be the last time I saw him, I was going to take advantage of it. I was going to spend the night in a hotel that I would never be able to afford to come back to, with a man that was way out of my league. And I was going to sleep with him. Because I was an adult. And that's what adults did.

Sleep with rich men for one night? Slut! I shook the thought away. I refused to stand still anymore. I wanted to live again. I walked up the stone steps.

"Good evening, ma'am." The doorman said as he opened it.

I had spent so much time standing still that I had become a ma'am instead of a miss. "Good evening," I said and walked into the building. The entrance was breathtaking. The floor was marble. And all the walls were adorned with mirrors with gold accents. I instantly felt out of place in my worn wool coat and boots that were knock offs of Steve Madden. And where was I supposed to go? I pulled out my phone.

"Can I help you, ma'am?" The man at the front desk asked.

I should have called Mason while I was still outside. This was awkward. I put my phone back in my pocket and walked up to the front desk. "Hi, sorry, yes. I have plans with Mason Caldwell. Dinner plans. Nothing weird. He lives here somewhere. In the building. Not the hotel part. The condo part I think? I just don't know what room his is." *What the hell was that? Does he know I'm here for sex?*

"You're here for Mr. Caldwell?"

"Yes?" *Why did I just say that as a question?* "Yes, I'm here for Mr. Caldwell."

The man frowned. "One moment please." He lifted up the phone and pressed a few numbers. "Mr. Caldwell, there is a young woman at the front desk who is here to see you." There was a pause before he continued. "She doesn't seem like the normal..." He had clearly been cut off. "Oh." He cleared his throat. "Sorry. Very well, sir. Have a good evening."

I didn't seem like the normal what? Women he usually dated? I probably wasn't. Mason was rich and I was just me.

"Sorry for the confusion, ma'am. I will need to see your I.D., though."

I wanted to ask why. But I didn't want to seem out of place. Maybe visitors always had to show their I.D.'s at fancy places. I pulled my driver's license out of my purse. It still said I lived in Delaware. I hadn't taken the time to switch everything over yet.

"Bridget Cowan?"

"Yes, that's me."

"Very well." He hit a bell on the front desk and a bellboy magically appeared. Magically because I hadn't seen him before and there didn't seem to be any doors nearby. "Adam will take you up to Mr. Caldwell." He handed me my driver's license back. "Sorry again about the confusion."

"What exactly was the confusion?"

"Nothing, ma'am. Have a good evening." He looked away from me, even though I was standing right there. *Oh my God, did he think I was a prostitute?*

I quickly walked over to Adam who was waiting by the elevator. When we stepped on there was actually elevator music. Like in all the old movies I used to watch with my mom. But I wasn't really focused on the ornate details. I turned toward Adam. "What kind of women does Mr. Caldwell usually entertain?"

Adam turned away from me. "Mr. Caldwell doesn't usually entertain."

I laughed.

Adam looked uncomfortable. He probably hadn't lied. The women that came to Mason probably entertained him, not the other way around.

"How often does he have visitors?" I asked.

"I don't know, ma'am. I'm only part-time."

"I see. Who was the last visitor that you escorted up to see him?"

Adam seemed relieved. "His brother came over a week or so ago."

"Oh." Mason had told me he hadn't gone to any of those clubs or anything since we had met. So maybe that meant no late night visitors too. Maybe the guy at the front desk just thought I didn't look like a normal guest at Trump International. It really seemed like he thought I didn't look like one of Mason's normal hookers though.

But it didn't matter either way. I wasn't going to get in my own head tonight. It was time I enjoyed myself. This was what single people did. Especially single girls who really wanted to start dating the man they were about to see. *Stop it.*

Chapter 46
Mason

I opened up the lid to one of the pans on the stove and oil splashed onto my t-shirt. "Shit." I quickly pulled off my shirt and tossed it onto the floor. I didn't know why I had offered to cook. I had no idea what the hell I was doing. Dinner didn't really matter, though. Tonight was only about one thing. And we both knew it. But it was more than just sex to me. I needed to hold out until she begged me. If I could stick to the game plan, I could have her for as long as I wanted. Which meant she most likely had to eat this meal before I fucked her. Hopefully it was edible.

I opened up the oven door and looked at the casserole dish. It looked like it was cooking nicely. The broth was bubbling and it smelled good. I closed the door and leaned against the kitchen counter.

Bee was refreshing, but she was also torturing me. Ever since I had started attending the gala I had always gotten laid afterwards. Bee had ruined my perfect record. And I was mad at her. I had talked with her all night. *Talked.* And tonight wasn't just about finally having her. It was about punishing her for all the hell she had been putting me through. The waiting was unbearable. I could feel my erection pressing against my jeans. Even thinking about her made me hard. Or maybe it was just because I hadn't cum in over a week.

A knock sounded on the door. I took a deep breath. I just needed to stick to the plan. And hopefully she didn't catch on that the front desk thought she was a prostitute. That would not be a good start to our evening. I ran my hand through my hair and opened up the door.

I don't know what it was, but she seemed to look even sexier every time I saw her. She didn't say anything, she was just staring at my abs. It was a good thing I was a messy chef. This was a pretty good start to the night. I had the urge to kiss her. But we weren't in a relationship. I didn't need to kiss her hello. *Stick to the plan.*

"You're not wearing a shirt," she said, without looking up at me. Her eyes seemed to be stuck on my abs. She was horny. Maybe even as horny as me. It was written all over her face.

"I got oil on it while I was cooking. I can go put on another one if you want."

"No, that's okay." She finally looked up at my face. "Maybe I should just take mine off so we're even?" She laughed and then looked away from me, clearly embarrassed. "I was actually debating whether or not I should wear any clothes at all. You know, the whole naked under the trench coat thing?" Her face was bright red. "But I'm not, see." She took off her jacket. "Fully clothed." She closed the door and her eyes gravitated back toward my six pack.

She was so innocent, yet somehow kinky as hell. There was no debate about what was on her mind. She looked nervous and excited at the same time. Wasn't that enough?

CITY OF SIN

She clearly wanted me. *Screw dinner. Screw the plan. I needed her now.* I pressed myself against her, pinning her against the door. I grabbed her arms and lifted them over her head. She didn't resist my touch at all.

"Keep your arms up," I said. I pushed her sweater up her waist, over her breasts, and up her arms. I threw her sweater down on the floor.

She kept her arms raised and blinked her long lashes at me.

I had never been tempted to abandon a plan before. What was this girl trying to do to me? I moved my hand to her back and unstrapped her bra. I tried not to think about the fact that I was the one caving in as I pulled her bra slowly down her arms, exposing her ripe breasts. Her nipples were hard, making her arousal even more evident. She looked embarrassed, standing in the middle of my foyer without her top. She moved her hands to cover herself, but I grabbed them.

"Turn around." I couldn't wait to tie her up and have my way with her. I could still make this happen under my terms.

She shook her hands free and placed them on my six pack. I lowered my eyebrows. No one ever defied me. She was pushing all my buttons. She lowered her hands down my stomach and touched my belt. I looked down at her as she unhinged the clip and pulled my belt out of the loops. Her fingers were shaking as she unbuttoned and unzipped my pants. Everything she did was so sexy and it had me on edge.

"Turn around," I repeated.

She bit her lip as she looked up at me.

Fuck it. I grabbed the back of her neck and brought her lips to mine. If she wasn't going to listen to me, I'd just fuck her until she screamed my name. I was done playing games. I needed to be deep inside her tight pussy. I grabbed her ass and lifted her legs around me.

Chapter 47
Bee

I wrapped my legs around him and grabbed the back of his neck, deepening the kiss. My resolve had started to disappear when I saw his perfectly sculpted body. And any resolve that may have remained had evaporated as soon as he removed my bra. I didn't know what I expected to happen tonight. But this was what I had wanted. My plan was to be sexy and I'm pretty sure I had failed. But it didn't seem to matter. We had barely said five words to each other before he had started undressing me. I had never felt so wanted in my life. And I had never wanted something so badly in my life.

Mason held me against him and set me down on the edge of the kitchen counter.

"We'll do it your way then," Mason said. His voice sounded tight. He was so wound up. He grabbed one of my boots and pulled it off, quickly followed by the next.

"My way?" I panted. I couldn't help it. I was so aroused. He was so sexy and domineering. And his words were so dirty. I wanted his tongue back in my mouth. *No.* I wanted his tongue *down there*. I swallowed hard.

"Vanilla." He undid the button of my jeans and quickly unzipped them.

I had no idea what he was talking about, but I no longer cared. Everything he did was so sexy. I wanted to do whatever he wanted. But I was nervous, because I had no idea what that entailed.

"Mason." My voice sounded breathless. I put my hand on his chest.

He pulled back and looked at me.

"You promised me a tour." I was chickening out. I had only ever had sex with Patrick. And he cheated on me. I wasn't good at this. I wasn't experienced like Mason was. I couldn't make him feel the way he was making me feel.

"You're killing me, Bee." It seemed like he was undressing me with his eyes. It was unnerving and exciting.

"I'm not very experienced," I blurted out.

"Is that what this is about?" He smiled at me seductively. "I know that." He kissed the side of my neck. "Baby, I was the first person to ever make you come." He kissed the side of my neck again.

"Mmm." *God.* I put my hand on his chest again. "I just think that maybe this is not going to be as good as you're thinking." I was so embarrassed.

He sighed and placed his hands on the counter on either side of me. "I like that you're inexperienced. Trust me, you're not going to disappoint me. You couldn't possibly disappoint me."

I wasn't sure if that was true. He said he was going to do it my way instead of the way he wanted. Wasn't that disappointing? I didn't want that. I wanted all the dirty things he talked about. I wanted him to do unspeakable things to me. "I don't want to do this my way. I want to do it your way."

He lowered his eyebrows slightly.

"I want you to do whatever you want with me." I put my hands out in front of me. He had talked about handcuffs before. I think I wanted that. "Whatever you want." *God, I'm such a slut.*

"Fuck, Bee." He grabbed my waist and lifted me up over his shoulder.

"Mason!"

He slapped my ass hard.

Oh God. I liked how that felt. His palm stayed pressed against the back pocket of my jeans. He was carrying me somewhere, but instead of paying attention, I was looking at his ass. I had unzipped his jeans, so they were hanging slightly lower than the waistband of his boxers. His ass looked good in jeans. Even better than it did in his suit pants. I ran my hand down the muscles on his back and traced the waistline of his boxers. I could get used to this view.

As soon as I thought it, he threw me down onto his bed. When I looked up at him, he had an unfamiliar glint in his eyes. He looked like he had me right where he wanted me, like I was finally giving him what he needed. I swallowed hard. The sheets smelled like his cologne and it was arousing me even more. I wasn't sure how many other girls had lain just like this in his bed before, but he was looking at me like I was the only thing in the world that he wanted.

"Get in the middle of the bed," he said as he stared down at me.

I didn't want to move. I wanted to revel in this moment.

He grabbed my wrist and pulled me to my feet. His grip was tight. "If we're doing this my way, it means you have to listen to me."

"Okay."

He put his hand on the side of my face. "Trust me, baby, you're going to like this."

"And why do you think that?"

"Because you're tired of making decisions. You want someone to take control for you. That's why you're here. You want me to show you everything that you've been missing. You want to surrender to me."

"And that's what you want? You want to take control of my body?" I never wanted him to stop looking at me the way that he was right now. He was right. I was so sick of making decisions. I wanted him to make them for me.

He smiled down at me. "I just want you."

"Okay." It seemed like he always knew exactly what to say. Maybe he'd still like me even if I wasn't good at this. I wanted to surrender to him. And maybe I could learn how. "Show me."

"Turn around." His voice was more authoritative than before. It was like how he got me to stay on our first date. I liked how demanding he was.

This time, I turned away from him. He pushed my hair to one side and ran his fingers down my spine. The feeling of his fingers on my skin made my heart race. Something glimmering caught my eye. I looked over at his headboard and spotted two sets of handcuffs. He hadn't been joking. And I couldn't wait to feel the metal around my wrists.

When his fingers reached the waistline of my jeans, he ran his hands around my hips. His fingers brushed against the top of my thong. I could feel his erection pressed against my ass. Every inch of me felt aroused, and he had barely touched me. I wanted him so badly.

"Mason." I arched my back slightly and pressed my ass against him.

"Don't move," he said and pulled back slightly.

I couldn't wait. It felt like he was torturing me on purpose. I reached down to pull my pants off, but he grabbed my hands.

"Bee, you asked me to show you."

His warm breath on the back my neck made me ache between my thighs. "But I..."

He grabbed my arm and turned me around so that I was facing him. "You need to do exactly what I tell you." The smell of his cologne made me even wetter.

I let my eyes wander down his six pack.

He grabbed my chin and titled my face back up to his. "Do you trust me, Bee?"

Do I? "Yes."

He frowned for a fraction of a second, but then the intensity returned to his features. "Then close your eyes."

I wanted to protest. I didn't want to not be able to see him. But I had asked him to show me. I closed my eyes.

His hands immediately fell from my arms. I was suddenly very aware of the fact that I was topless in the middle of his bedroom. I tried to listen to what he was doing. It sounded like a drawer may have opened. A second later, I felt something silky fall against my face. I opened my eyes, but I couldn't see anything. He tied the blindfold tightly around my head.

"But I want to see you." I reached out and my hand landed on his chiseled abs. I loved the feeling of his muscles.

"You need to learn how to give up control."

My hand slid upwards as he kneeled down in front of me. He hooked his fingers in my belt loops and slowly pulled my jeans down over my hips. As he pulled my pants down my thighs, he left a trail of kisses down my right thigh.

"Mason," my voice trembled. I wanted anything that he would give me, his fingers, his tongue, his cock.

He kissed the inside of my thigh. "Don't speak." He placed my hands on his shoulders as he helped me step out of my jeans.

I had been so focused on his abs that I hadn't even noticed how muscular the rest of him was. I let my hand wander down his shoulders to his biceps.

A second later I felt his warm breath through my lacy thong. *Fuck.* He was right. A blindfold made it better. All I could focus on was what he was doing to me. *Or not doing to me.*

"Now turn around," he said. His voice was firm and demanding.

I was so wet. *Why is he torturing me?* And I didn't want to let go of his biceps.

"Turn around, Bee."

I reluctantly turned around. I was bad at being told what to do. But I wanted to experience his world. And I just wanted him inside of me.

"I love how eager you are, Bee. But the buildup is half the fun." He pushed the center of my back, making my fall forwards. I immediately put my hands out to catch myself. My palms landed on his soft comforter. He pressed down on the small of my back, making my ass jut into the air. He grabbed my waist and pressed his hard cock against my ass. It felt huge, even through his jeans. He moved one hand to my stomach and slowly let it dip beneath my thong. He lightly stroked my wetness.

God, yes. I pushed my ass against his boner.

"Fuck, you're so wet." He lightly brushed his fingers against me, teasing me.

"Please," I moaned and gyrated my hips.

He sunk his finger inside of me.

Yes!

"You're so tight." He slowly moved his finger in and out of me.

"Faster," I groaned.

Mason pulled his finger out. "Patience, Bee." He turned me around and put my hands on his six pack.

I let my fingers trail down his abs. *Had he taken off his pants?* My heart skipped a beat as my fingers ran down his happy trail. *He's naked.* I wrapped my hand around his massive cock. I wished I could take this stupid blindfold off. I so badly wanted to see his naked body.

"Tonight is not about you asking for what you want," Mason said. "It's about giving you what you need."

Was giving him head what I needed? Maybe it was. I wanted to please him. I liked giving him head. And I liked the taste of him. I was about to kneel in front of him when he pushed me back onto the bed.

"Get in the middle of the bed. And put your hands above your head."

I moved backward to what I thought was the center of the bed and put my hands above my head. The bed sagged slightly and I felt the cool metal of the handcuffs against my skin. They sent shivers through my body as he secured them to one of my wrists and then the other.

"The safe word is vanilla," he said.

"What?"

"The safe word."

I had heard the phrase safe word before, but I didn't know that people actually used it. *What is he going to do to me?*

I heard the bed squeak as he got off of it. I felt so exposed, handcuffed to his bed wearing nothing but my thong. I heard him open a drawer. *What is he doing?* Not knowing was making me even more wet. I tried to pull my arms down, but the metal dug into my wrists. If I had known he was going to do this, I would have touched him more when I had the chance

A moment later I felt the bed sag slightly as he climbed back onto it. He sat between my legs, leaned over me, and put his lips around one of my nipples. He sucked on it hard and his fingers squeezed my other nipple. I could feel them getting hard.

"Mason," I moaned.

"You needed to be restrained for this." He rubbed something delicate across my stomach. It almost felt like feathers. He squeezed my nipple hard as he rubbed the feathers along my other breast. The feathers tickled my breast and then I felt a cold object encircle my nipple. I suddenly felt a sharp pain where his mouth had been a moment before, as the cold object clamped down on my nipple. I tried to move my arms, but I couldn't. He pressed his thumb against my clit.

"Oh." It was painful, but the pain was overcome with pleasure as he massaged my clit. He pushed my thong to one side and brushed his fingers against my wetness. I groaned. I wanted him inside of me again. But he quickly moved his hand away.

"Fuck you taste good. I've been craving you all week."

Did he just lick his fingers? The pressure was growing on my nipple. He squeezed my other breast hard and attached another clamp to my other nipple.

"Mason," I whimpered. The clamps bit at my skin. I tried to move my arms again, but I was completely immobile. The more my nipples swelled, the more I could feel the pressure. It hurt but for some reason I kept getting more aroused. Maybe it was because I knew he was naked between my thighs.

He pressed his palm against my groin. "You're so wet for me, baby."

I groaned as he pulled my thong off my hips and down my legs. "Mason?" I wanted to see him. I wanted to watch what he was doing to me.

He kissed the inside of my thigh. "Yes?"

"I need you inside of me."

He answered me by putting his lips around my clit. He sucked on it hard. *Oh my God.* My hips rose to meet him. He pushed them back down, holding me firmly to the mattress. He sucked on my clit again and then stroked his tongue against my aching pussy. He spread my thighs wide and thrust his tongue deep inside of me.

"Yes," I moaned as his tongue explored my walls. I pulled on my restraints. I wanted to run my hands through his hair and push his tongue even deeper. The metal handcuffs dug into my skin. The sensation of my swollen nipples and his tongue deep inside of me was too much. I tilted my head back and let myself surrender to him. "Mason!" He lapped up my juices as I orgasmed around his tongue. He sucked once more on my clit, and then released my thighs. Even though I had just come, I still craved his cock.

I felt something silky being bound to my ankle. "What are you doing?"

"Your body is very responsive. You're going to need to be completely restrained."

"I already am restrained."

"Are you still nervous around me even though I just made you come?" He attached the same thing to my other ankle.

"Yes."

"Good." He lifted one of my legs and tied it to the bottom of his bedpost, and then did the same with the other. I tried to move my legs, but I couldn't. My legs were spread and my arms bound. I was completely at his mercy. And it was so hot. I heard the sound of Velcro. He put something cool against my lips. "Suck on this."

I opened up my mouth and felt the cold metal object. It was small, about the size of my pinky. He removed it from my mouth. And trailed it down my chest and stomach. "I'm going to fuck your mouth now, Bee." He pressed the object against my clit.

I shuddered. "With that?"

"No, not this. This is for your pleasure." He pushed the metal object inside my aching pussy. The coolness made me shiver. It was small. I could barely feel it. I wanted his cock, not that. The bed sagged slightly as he straddled me. He put the tip of his cock on my neck and slowly brought it up to my chin. He pressed his tip against my lips. I parted them and he thrust his cock into my mouth.

I could taste his salty pre cum. I tightened my lips around him. I so badly wanted to see him and touch him. He pumped his length in and out of me and then pushed it deep into the back of my throat. He was so deep that my nose pressed against his happy trail. But I didn't choke. I wanted him in my mouth. I wanted to taste him again. He began to slide his cock in and out of my mouth faster and faster. He was going to cum in my mouth. I swirled my tongue around his shaft and then he pulled out.

"No." I wanted to reach out and grab his cock. "Mason, I want to taste you."

"I know." He leaned back and slid his finger inside of me, next to the metal object. My breathing hitched. He pushed down on the metal object and it started to vibrate. I pulled on all my restraints, ignoring the metal cutting into my wrists. The vibrations seem to echo through my whole body.

"Oh my God, that feels amaz..." My word were cut off when he slammed his cock back into my mouth. I wrapped my lips tighter around his shaft. I wanted him to know how good this felt. I took him all the way to the back of my throat, swirling my tongue around his base.

It was getting hard to concentrate with the small vibrator inside of me. I squirmed. He grabbed a fistful of my hair and guided his cock in and out of my mouth. He thrust his hips faster and faster. I could barely focus.

His cum exploded into the back of my throat. I could picture his abs tightening as he found his release. He continued to pump his cock in and out of my mouth, shooting more cum into my mouth. I drank him down hungrily as my own orgasm washed through me.

The vibrations continued. The intensity was becoming unbearable. He slipped his finger inside of me, turned off the vibrator, and pulled it out.

I had gotten to taste him, but now I would never know what it felt like to have him inside of me. I was so wet I felt like I was dripping down my thighs.

"Is something wrong?" He wiped my bottom lip with his finger. I must have been making a pouty face.

"I thought we were going to have sex."

"Baby, I'm not done with you yet."

"Oh." I gulped. He had already made me orgasm twice and he had cum in my mouth. *Is he really ready to go again already?* I pulled on my restraints.

"Always so eager."

"Please let me see you."

"Hmm." Mason twisted my nipple clamp slightly.

"Ow!"

"You've never done anything like this, have you?" He pulled off the clamp and swirled his tongue around my nipple. It was so sensitive, but his tongue was soothing. He sucked on it softly.

"No."

He removed the other clamp and lightly sucked on my aching nipple. The sensation was even more arousing than the clamps themselves.

"Please, Mason. Take off my blindfold."

Mason kissed the inside of one of my ankles and untied the restraint, and then did the same with the other ankle. "You're bad at giving up control."

"I'm not," I lied. I was. I was really, really bad. But no one had ever pleasured me this much before. And somehow all I wanted was more. I'd do whatever he wanted. Even if it meant not getting to see his beautiful face. Now that I could move my legs again, I spread my thighs wide, hoping he'd get the hint at the invite.

I heard the clink of metal and my hand fell out of the handcuff. My other hand was released a second later. I tried to reach out to him, but he quickly flipped my body, so that my stomach was now pressed against the mattress. He grabbed my hips and hoisted them in the air so I was on all fours.

"Don't worry. You'll learn."

I felt a sharp pain as he slapped my ass. I cried out.

He gently ran his fingers along the spot where he had just struck me, cradling my ass check in his hand.

Why do I like that? It hurt, but I also felt aroused.

"That was for talking back." He slapped my ass again in the same spot.

"But I..."

"That was for moving when I asked you to stay still." He slapped me again.

"Mason!" *Damn it, what is the safe word? Do I even want to say it?*

He reached around me and rubbed my clit. I moaned under his skilled hands.

"That was for making me wait till right now to have you naked on your knees in my bedroom." He struck me again, even harder. "You've been teasing me. Do you have any idea how much you've been torturing me?"

I couldn't take it anymore. I knew, because he was doing it to me right now. "Fuck me, Mason. Please fuck me." I immediately heard the rip of foil.

He rubbed his palm against my ass and then moved his hands to my waist. "Baby, I'm going to fuck you. Hard." He immediately thrust himself deep inside of me.

I gasped. He moved slowly, stretching me wide. He was being gentle as I adjusted to the thickness of his cock.

I arched my back as he thrust himself even deeper, filling me with every inch of him. He grabbed my hips and pumped his length in and out of me. I moved my hands to his headboard and pushed back, matching his thrusts. His fingernails dug into my hips as he moved faster. He tilted his cock up against my g-spot and my whole body shuddered. I pushed against the headboard and forced him even deeper. He grabbed my hair and pulled, tilting my head back and making me arch my back even more.

I wasn't sure why, but him being rough with me was arousing me even more. "I'm going to come again."

"Not yet." He spanked me again and pulled out of me.

"Mason." My voice sounded so needy. *God, what is he doing to me?*

He grabbed my hips and flipped my body over so that my back was pressed against the mattress. "You're mine."

He put his hand on the side of my face." Do you understand me? I'm not sharing you with anyone."

"Yes." There wasn't anyone else I wanted. Just him.

He pulled my blindfold down so that I could finally see him. There was an intensity in his eyes that I had never seen before. But there was something else there. He looked almost bewildered.

I reached up to touch his face, but he grabbed my hand, pinning it down against the mattress.

"I didn't say you could move." He leaned into me, thrusting his massive cock back inside of me.

"Mason!" I moaned. I ran my other hand down the muscles of his back and to his ass. I wanted to explore every inch of him. If possible, his ass felt as muscular as the rest of him. Before my hand could wander anymore, Mason grabbed it and pinned it down to the mattress too.

He began to move his hips even faster. "Come for me, Bee."

As if his words were a command, I felt myself begin to clench around him. "Oh God, Mason!" My orgasm crashed down on me. All the buildup had somehow made it even more intense. Every time he made me come was better and better.

His fingers tightened around mine as he found his own release. He stared down into my eyes as he thrust back inside of me one more time. I was pretty sure the expression on his face matched my own...pure bliss.

He pulled out of me and collapsed next to me on the bed. "Fuck, Bee." He ran his hands down his face.

"Does that mean I wasn't disappointing?" I wasn't sure why, but I felt like I needed his approval. I wanted him to have liked that as much as I did. He had been with so many women. How could I possibly compare to all of them?

Before he could respond, a loud beeping sounded through the apartment. I hadn't noticed it before, but it smelled like something was burning.

"Oh, shit, the food." Mason got up and sprinted out of the room naked, grabbing his boxers off the floor on the way.

Chapter 48
Bee

I grabbed a collared shirt that was lying on the back of a chair in his bedroom and put it on. It smelled strongly of his cologne, which was now becoming my favorite smell. Women in T.V. shows and movies wore men's dress shirts all the time and it always looked sexy. Hopefully I could pull it off. I ran my fingers through my hair and made my way out of his bedroom.

I had been so caught up in Mason earlier that I hadn't even realized how amazing his apartment was. Everything was so clean and new looking. Basically the opposite of where I lived. I stopped at the end of the hallway and stared into his living room. I don't know how my eyes hadn't gravitated to the view before. I walked toward the far side of the living room. Instead of a wall, there was just a sheet of glass that looked out on Central Park and the city skyline around and behind it. The city was so bright. It almost looked like it was still decorated for Christmas. This Christmas was the first one I hadn't gone home to celebrate. I had been so afraid that if I went, I'd never come back. I felt so small looking out at the city below. Any problems I had suddenly seemed insignificant. But maybe it wasn't because I was looking out at the expanse of the city. Maybe it was because of the guy that I was with.

Mason wrapped his arms around me. "You look so much better in that than I do."

I laughed and turned around. I clasped my hands behind his neck and looked up into his eyes. "Your view is amazing. I don't think I've ever seen something so beautiful."

"I prefer looking at you."

"Then you don't know what you're missing." I looked back over my shoulder.

He grabbed my chin and turned my face back up to his. "In answer to your earlier question, you were definitely not disappointing." He leaned down and placed a soft kiss against my lips. "And you made me burn dinner."

"*I* made you burn dinner?"

"Mhm. I happen to find you incredibly distracting."

I laughed and peered over his shoulder. The living room was open to the kitchen. It had marble countertops and shiny stainless steel appliances. It would have looked like it was out of the pages of a magazine if whatever Mason had been cooking wasn't sitting on the stove, completely black.

"Actually, all I'm really craving right now is ice cream," I said.

"You want ice cream for dinner? What are you, five?"

"It just so happens that I crave chocolate after really good sex." I unwound his arms from around me.

"So, this is probably the first time you've ever craved chocolate after sex then?"

Was he really looking for my stamp of approval too? He had to be kidding. Obviously that was the best sex I had ever had. If I was lucky, Patrick lasted five minutes.

Mason and Patrick weren't even on the same sex scale. I innocently shrugged my shoulders.

He leaned down and lifted me over his shoulder.

I laughed. "Mason, I'm capable of walking to the kitchen." I reached down and slapped his ass.

"Yeah, we're not going to the kitchen." He pushed the bottom of my shirt up and kissed my bare ass as he carried me back toward the bedroom.

Chapter 49
Mason

It hadn't snowed since New Years, but it was so cold that there was still a white blanket of snow all over Central Park. Except for the path that I was currently running on. You couldn't find perfectly white snow anywhere else in the city.

I ran across the small bridge where I would usually turn around and picked up my pace. I needed the fresh air and the extra exercise. I hadn't felt quite right this morning. That tightness in my chest had returned. It was probably the fact that I had ice cream for dinner. I rounded a corner and sprinted up a set of steps.

Who was I kidding? It wasn't the ice cream. It was her. We had fallen asleep on the couch watching this stupid old black and white movie. We had turned it on halfway through and Bee had tried to explain what was going on to me the whole time instead of just letting me watch it. We had spent the majority of the time laughing instead of paying attention. And it was perfect. It was better than the gala. And it was better than any fancy restaurant.

"Shit." I stopped at the top of the steps and put my hands on my knees. The cold air felt like ice in my lungs. It didn't matter how far I ran away from her. I couldn't shake that feeling in my chest. I stood up and ran my hands through my hair. I had run to one of the corners of Central Park. Cars honking and speeding by somehow relaxed me. Normally on my runs I would think about work. Not women. I was normally good at compartmentalizing. It was different with Bee, though. I couldn't stop thinking about her. I'd have to start listening to music on my runs.

***

My heart rate was still decelerating as I leaned against the side of the elevator. I thought a run would make me feel better. It hadn't. And now that I was almost back to my apartment, all I wanted to do was fuck her again.

I stepped off the elevator and walked down the hallway. I had left Bee alone and naked in my bed. The thought made my cock start to press against my athletic shorts. *What the fuck is wrong with me?* I was never like this. I put my key in the lock. Fucking her again this morning would make this feeling go away. *Right?*

I heard the shower running as I closed the door behind me. Fuck, that was even better. I pulled off my shirt as I made my way to my bedroom and tossed it on the floor. I kicked off my shoes, pushed off my short and boxers, and opened up the bathroom door. The room was covered in a layer of steam. I could just make out the silhouette of Bee through the glass. It didn't seem like she had heard me come in. I stood there for a second, staring at her. I couldn't believe I had waited over a week to fuck her. But my patience had paid off. Now I'd never have to wait again.

I opened up the shower door.

Bee immediately tried to cover herself. "Oh, God." She laughed but kept her hands on her body. "Mason, you scared me."

The beads of water running down her naked body had to be the sexiest thing I had ever seen.

"Mason? Are you okay?"

I stepped into the shower and pulled her face to mine.

She immediately wrapped her arms behind my neck.

It wasn't just me. She couldn't get enough of me either. The water falling down on top of us made it hard to breathe while I was kissing her. But right now, she was the only sustenance I needed. I grabbed her legs and lifted her thighs around me.

She moaned as my cock pressed against her clit.

That's right, baby. You need me too. "Are you on birth control?"

"What?" She was panting as she looked up at me.

"Are you on the pill?"

"Yes."

"Are you clean?"

"I was halfway through my shower..." She paused and stared at me. "I mean, if you're talking about...um, yeah, I'm clean."

Fuck yes. I hated wearing condoms. I grabbed her ass and shoved my cock deep inside her tight pussy.

"Mason!" Her head dipped back and her nails dug into my shoulders.

I knew she was sore. I knew she wasn't used to a cock as big as mine or getting fucked three times in less than 24 hours. But she had no idea what her body could take. How much she could give me. I shoved her back against the cold tiles. I had a lot to teach her.

I thrust myself deep inside of her. *Fuck.* It was like her pussy was made for my cock. And I knew I was the only one she wanted inside of her.

Her hands moved to the back of my head. She wanted me to kiss her again. But I didn't have time to go slow right now. I had to get to work. I grabbed both her hands and pressed them against the tiles, pinning her in place. I began to thrust faster, harder, pushing her to her limits. I wanted her to scream my name.

Last night was about her, showing her that she needed me. There was no way she wasn't addicted now. So today was about me and my needs. And I needed to fucking cum or I was going to end up jerking off in a bathroom stall at work just thinking about her. I moved my hips faster, enjoying the sound her ass made as it bounced against the sleek tile wall.

"Mason," she moaned.

"That's right, baby. Say my name when you come."

She immediately started to clench around me. *Damn she was responsive.* She might not always listen to me, but she always came when I told her to. That was one demand she couldn't seem to resist.

"Mason!"

I bit my lip. I didn't want to come in her. Not right now.

As soon as her orgasm subsided, I pulled out of her and set her back down on her feet. I pushed down on her shoulders so that her back slowly slid down the wall. She stared up at me with her innocent doe eyes. But she wasn't innocent at all. She knew exactly what I was about to do, and she fucking loved it. I wanted her to know she was mine. I needed her to know that she belonged to me now. I ran my hand up and down my length and aimed down at her.

My first shot of cum landed on her chin.

She didn't even flinch.

My second and third shots landed between her breasts.

I stepped under the water and quickly rinsed off. She was looking up at me like I was her fucking God. *That's right*. She would worship me on her knees whenever I asked. Because I owned her now.

Chapter 50
Bee

"You look different," Kendra said as I sat down in her cubicle to eat lunch with her.

"I don't know what you mean by that." I unwrapped the granola bar I had bought from the vending machine and avoided her gaze. I had been distracted all morning. The more time that passed, the more it seemed like Mason was a dream.

"You look all happy."

"I think I look normal."

"Not to burst your bubble, Bee, but you usually don't look this happy at work."

I shrugged my shoulders. "I had a good weekend."

"Oh my God, you had sex with him, didn't you?"

"Kendra, can you please keep your voice down?"

"You did. Bee!" She put her hand on my arm. "Give me all the details. Was he big? God, I bet he was big. Where did you do it? Please tell me you got to see where he lives. I've always wanted to stay at Trump International."

"Why do you know where he lives?"

"Oh." Kendra laughed. "Just a guess." She took a huge bite of her sandwich.

"Did you look him up?"

"Eh. Marie told me that you went to the Silver Gala this weekend. And I knew Mason was rich, but I didn't know he was *that* rich."

"That doesn't really answer my question."

"Fine, okay? I did some very light snooping. It's not a big deal." She smiled at me and shifted in her seat slightly. "Do you want to know what I found out?"

"No." *Yes?*

"Are you sure?"

"What, is it weird? It's probably weird, right?"

She laughed. "No."

I bit my lip. "Okay, tell me."

"First tell me how good he was in bed."

I shoved the rest of the granola bar into my mouth.

"So good you can't even talk about it? I'm so jealous."

"I think my body is addicted to him."

"And your head?"

"My head is wondering why he's with me if he's that good at sex. He could have any girl that he wanted. Why me?"

"Because you're Kick Ass Bee."

"Seriously, Kendra."

"Why are you always so hard on yourself. You're fucking gorgeous. And you're broke. Guys like the whole damsel in distress thing. He probably thinks he's saving you. Maybe he has some weird complex or something."

"Is that what you found out when you were stalking him?"

"No. But did you know that his parents are billionaires? Not just rich, Bee. Freaking billionaires. Him and his brother are going to inherit so much money."

"I know he's wealthy."

"And he graduated from Harvard with honors."

"I know he went to Harvard."

"Okay, fine. So you know all that stuff. But did you know that he hasn't had a girlfriend since high school?"

"How could you possibly know that?"

"Deep, deep Facebook stalking."

"And you said I don't have a life? Is that what you were doing all weekend?"

"I was looking out for you."

"I know." I bit the inside of my lip. "He told me on our first date that he didn't do the whole relationship thing."

"You never told me that."

"I didn't think I was ever going to see him again."

"And what about now? Are you okay with that *now*?"

"I don't know. I mean, he's not acting like he wants to stop seeing me. He's picking me up after work."

"Is he seeing anyone else?"

"I don't think so." He had said he hadn't been to any of those clubs since he had met me. But that didn't meant he wasn't dating anyone else. Or that we were in fact dating. He had said he wasn't going to share me. *That I was his.* "I think that maybe he's changed."

"Overnight? I don't think so, Bee. He's a playboy."

"A playboy? I don't think he's actually like that. He's a really nice guy."

"You should Google image search him. He's with a different woman in every picture. I think you need to be realistic about what you're getting yourself into."

"I'm really just trying to enjoy the present for once."

"So you really don't care at all that you're just one of many?"

It didn't feel that way when I was with him. When we were together it seemed like he couldn't get enough of me. *He only wants me, right?*

"He's a rich, intelligent bachelor with commitment issues. Just be careful, okay?"

A pit in my stomach was forming. Mason had said that I was his. But he had never said that he was mine.

Chapter 51
Mason

I pulled my phone out and looked at it under the table. I had gotten into a routine the past two weeks. In the morning, I woke up and fucked Bee. I went to work all day and tried not to think about her. And then I came home at night and fucked her again. It had been the best two weeks of my life. She had somehow transported me back to high school where I had no control over my erections. And my dick knew it was time. But instead of being with her, I was at a bar with James and his little brother. That would normally be fun, but tonight I just wanted to fuck Bee and then curl up on the couch with her and watch whatever was on T.V.

My cell phone screen was blank. She still hadn't texted me. Who worked this late on a Friday night? I slid my phone back into my pocket.

"Dude, you've got it bad." James' little brother, Rob, was visiting from out of town. And he had a tendency to tell it like it was. He had liked pushing my buttons ever since we were kids. But now that we were adults, I couldn't just beat him up whenever he pissed me off.

I laughed. "Yeah, right." I took a sip of my beer and looked away from him.

"Please don't tell me you're going to turn into my brother," Rob said.

"Penny's hot, but she's a little young for me."

James cleared his throat. "Have either of you been following the government shutdown? It really seems like it's going to happen. Without the FCC..."

"No one wants to talk about that," Rob said. "Stop being boring. Back to you." He pointed at me. "This girl has got a hold on you."

"No she doesn't. Give me a break."

"You haven't stopped looking at your phone since you've gotten here."

"Hey!" Matt said and clapped Rob on the back. "It's been forever, man." He sat down next to me and pulled off his jacket. "What did I miss?"

"We were just talking about how Mason is whipped," Rob said.

Matt laughed.

"You're just jealous that I'm getting laid every night," I said.

"I'm fucking rich and I live in a college town," Rob said. "Plus, have you seen me? I get laid all the time." He took a sip of his beer.

I laughed. "Living there was a brilliant idea. I can't even argue with your logic. Do you ever miss it, James?"

"No. I was a professor. I wasn't going out partying, screwing students."

"Just the one student?"

"Yup, just Penny. How many times are you guys going to ask me that?"

"I just don't get it," Matt said. "If you didn't care about keeping your job, you should have nailed as many girls as you could. College girls? Fuck. You really let the ball drop."

"You guys have seen Penny," Rob said. "I get it. I mean...damn."

James laughed. "Yeah, I got the best girl there. Rob can have all my leftovers. Penny is all I need."

Rob frowned. "They're not leftover if you never tapped them."

James shrugged. "I'm going to go get another drink. Anyone else want another beer?"

"No, I'm good," I said. "I can't stay that much longer anyway."

James laughed. "It's too late, Rob. He's already like me."

"Mason, I just got here," Matt said. "Come on, you have to be my wingman. There is a blonde at 9 o'clock that I have to nail."

"I told Bee I'd pick her up once she's done with work."

"Wow, you really are whipped." Matt made the sound of a whip cracking to emphasize his point.

"See!" Rob said. "And he keeps checking his phone. He's like a teenage girl in love."

"I'm just checking the score of the Knicks game," I said. But I wasn't. I wanted Bee to text me. I had been thinking about her all day.

"Every screen in this bar has the Knicks game on," Rob said. "Seriously, what is wrong with you?"

"He's in love," James said and sat down.

"I'm not in love. And what do you even know about it? You're divorced and dating a girl that's barely legal."

"Just because you're in denial doesn't mean you have to be a dick."

"Fine. You're in love. Great. I'm not."

"Yeah you are," Matt said. "You haven't stopped talking about Bee ever since you met her. You're completely infatuated. Rob's right. You're acting like a high school girl with a crush."

"Jesus, why not a high school boy with a crush? You're all crazy." I took a sip of my beer. I wasn't going to turn into some whipped dick. I just needed to stop thinking about Bee for two seconds.

"Oh," James said. "Speaking of Bee, I need her number."

"I thought you already got the girl you wanted from the University of New Castle?"

"Yeah, I did. It's not for me. Penny wants it."

"I don't think them hanging out is a good idea."

"Why?"

I shrugged. "Why does Penny even want to?"

"Because her only other friend from Delaware that's here is a guy. And I'd rather her hang out with your new girlfriend."

"She's not my girlfriend. And it's going to be weird if they're friends if we stop seeing each other."

"*If?* There you go. Point made," James said.

"That doesn't mean anything."

"You said if, not when. I think it's great, Mason. You don't have to act so defensive."

"I don't," Rob said. "I think it's terrible."

Matt laughed. "I'm just happy she's a poor secretary. Because Mom and Dad are going to be pissed. Not that they aren't already pissed at you."

"She's not going to meet them," I said. "We're just fucking."

"Whatever you say," James said. "I still need her number."

"Yeah, I'm not giving you her number. Tell Penny I'm sorry."

"What is she doing tonight anyway?" Matt asked.

"Studying," James said.

"Has she gotten close to any of her new professors?"

James frowned. "No."

Rob laughed. "I don't know why, but Penny is completely obsessed with this guy." He put his hand on James' shoulder. "Trust me, I've made tons of passes at her, and she always says no."

James pushed Rob's hand off his shoulder.

Matt laughed. "Maybe I should come visit you," he said to Rob. "I feel like I'm the only one who hasn't been with a marketing major from a party school. I must be missing out on something."

"Yes! You should wait till the spring, though. When the skirts come back out. Right now it's all North Face jackets and Uggs."

"Sold."

My phone buzzed in my pocket. I quickly pulled it out and slid my finger across the screen. Bee had finally texted me: "Are you sure you don't want to just meet up tomorrow? I'm so sorry this is taking so long."

I didn't want to wait to see her until tomorrow. I wanted her now. And I refused to let her go back to that dingy little apartment. She didn't belong there. She belonged with me.

"Did she finally text you?" Rob asked.

"I told you, I was just checking the score."

Matt whistled. "Whipped."

I grabbed my coat and stood up. "Whatever. Fuck you guys. I'm gonna go get laid."

James laughed. "Yeah, I'm gonna get going too. The joys of not being single."

Rob groaned. "Lame. I'll be your wingman, Matt. Come on."

"Sounds good to me," Matt said. "Have fun with your girlfriends."

I didn't bother protesting. It didn't matter what they said. I knew it wasn't true. The wind hit me hard on the way out the bar. I was slightly buzzed and overheated inside, but there had to be a wind chill of below zero out here. "Shit it's cold," I said and buttoned up my jacket.

"Let me give you a ride," James said. His car was already waiting for him outside and the driver had just opened his door.

"No, it's fine. I'm just going to take a taxi."

"Her office is on my way. Come on."

"I thought you were going home?" I asked.

"I need to make a stop first."

I shrugged. There weren't any taxis driving by at the moment and it was too cold to stand on the curb waiting. "Yeah, that'll be great." I walked around the side of the car and got in. I used to have a driver. I used to have a lot of things. "So, where are you going?"

"I'm going to go see my parents."

"Are they still refusing to meet Penny?"

James sighed. "I don't even know why she wants to meet them. But I want to give her what she wants. And the fact that I can't is driving me crazy."

"They'll come around."

"Like your parents?"

"My dad will get over it," I said.

"How is the new venture going?"

"Okay. Slower than I wanted."

"I know you always say no, but if you just need some seed money..."

"Thanks, but no thanks." I didn't want his handouts. He had more money than he knew what to do with. And I was going to get there too. Without anyone's help. "I'm more just waiting for the right account. It needs to be something big if I'm going to quit my job." But it wasn't just the account. I was used to living a certain way. And the money I had from my parents was running out. Just thinking about it made me feel like I was drowning. I didn't want to have to crawl back to my parents. Time was running out and all I was doing recently was hanging out with Bee. *What is wrong with me?*

"Remember that time you convinced that kid at camp that chocolate was poisonous and he threw it all out?"

I laughed. "Yeah. We got to have s'mores every night for the rest of camp."

"You can convince anyone to do anything. You've got this."

"Yeah." But my mind wasn't on my business. It was on Bee. I was starting to think I wanted her more than I wanted to start my own company.

James pulled an envelope out of his coat pocket. "Here."

"I don't want your money."

"It's not a check."

I took the envelope and opened it up. It was a list of companies with contact info for their C.E.O.'s or lead marketing executives. I looked up at him.

"Some companies I work with that could use fresh ad ideas," James said.

"I can't..."

"Honestly, it would help me too. I own stake in some of them. Use me as a reference when you call them."

For some reason this handout didn't make me feel like shit. He was doing it because he knew I could help. And we had been friends our whole lives. This was better than a check. With one big client, I wouldn't need my side business anymore. I already felt less stressed.

"Thanks, man."

"You're doing me the favor." He smiled and looked out the window of the car.

I wasn't really. But I was glad he was making me feel that way. "I'm glad you're back."

James laughed. "Don't get all sentimental on me."

"Seriously. The city wasn't the same without you." James and I had lost touch after college. He had gotten married to that bitchy ex-wife of his and completely cut me out. Or maybe I just hadn't tried hard enough to stay friends. James had been different when he was with Isabella. Like he was in some weird trance. Maybe he had just been depressed. If I had known more maybe I would have tried to help him. I had heard rumors about him falling off the wagon. But those were just rumors. Besides, now that he had found Penny, it was like we were kids again. He was back to his old self. And I liked Penny. She could hang out with all of us and hold her own. And she was the best at bringing out James' fun side. Mr. and Mrs. Hunter were the ones missing out, not Penny.

James shrugged. "I was always going to come back. I just needed a break."

"Yeah. Look, I don't actually want Penny to be mad at me. I'll text her Bee's number."

"I was hoping you'd say that. So, if you want to do a double date..."

"Don't push it."

James laughed. "I told her I'd try."

"How did you know with Penny?"

"How did I know what?"

"That it was more than just sex? That you wanted more?"

"I couldn't stop thinking about her. Even before we had sex. She suddenly became all that mattered. It wasn't that I wanted more. I needed more."

I looked out the window. Bee was sweet and innocent and beautiful. And I was me. I wasn't the type of guy that a girl like Bee would date. No one would ever get serious with me. But I could feel myself being consumed by her. Wanting and needing seemed like a fine line. I couldn't cross that. I wasn't even sure I knew how.

"I think Bee's great," James said.

"I know." I leaned my head back against the seat. "She deserves someone a hell of a lot better than me. I don't even know what the fuck I'm doing. I like my life. I like being single. Maybe Rob is right. I'm losing my mind."

James laughed. "Trust me, Rob is rarely ever right."

The car pulled to a stop outside of Bee's office building.

"Thanks for the ride. Tell Mr. and Mrs. Hunter I said hi."

James laughed. "I will."

"And if they still don't want to meet Penny, tell them to go fuck themselves."

"I might do that too."

I laughed and stepped out of the car.

"Mason?" said James.

I leaned down before closing the door. "Yeah?"

"I think until life gives you something right, it's hard to realize how wrong you've been."

"I'm not you. And Bee isn't Penny."

"I know. You've got it easier than we did. You're not going through a divorce and she's not your student. Just think about it."

"Yeah." I tapped the top of the car. "Have fun at your parents'." I closed the door and walked up to Bee's office building. *Until life gives you something right, it's hard to realize how wrong you've been.* There was nothing wrong with my life. But Bee did make it better. It had been a long time since I had something to look forward to.

Chapter 52
Bee

I was the last one in the office tonight, as usual. I went through the document one last time. It was the final proposal for Sword Body Wash. Mr. Ellington had wanted an added clause in the pitch once he found out about the possible government shutdown. He wanted to make sure it was as provocative as possible, and the FCC disbanding would certainly let it be more provocative. The segment was airing on Tuesday. The government probably wouldn't shut down by then anyway, so this was a complete waste of my time. But it didn't matter, because I was done. I pressed send on the document.

I couldn't have been more excited to see Mason. I pulled out my phone. Earlier I had texted him, asking if he'd rather meet up tomorrow instead. He was out with his friends. And I had monopolized him for the past few weeks. But I was hoping he'd say he wanted to spend time with me instead. I couldn't get enough of him. It was hard to follow Kendra's advice about being careful when I was feeling like this. Mason said he wanted to be the reason why I stayed in New York. I think he already was. It was crazy to feel like this after just a few weeks. *Right?*

I looked down at my phone. He had never texted me back. I couldn't help but be a little disappointed. I had slept at his apartment every night for the past two weeks. He had a really nice place. But that wasn't the reason why I always agreed to spend the night. It was nice having someone to kiss goodnight and wake up next to. It was strange how familiar it seemed, yet different at the same time. Patrick had never looked at me the way Mason did. And it wasn't just that I wanted to stay, Mason usually insisted upon it. Like there was nothing he wanted more than to fall asleep with his arms wrapped around me. It didn't matter what he said. Or what Kendra liked to warn me about. Mason was a good guy. And I was falling for him.

Tonight, though, I would go home to my cold apartment alone. I didn't want to text him again. If he didn't want to see me, I could survive one night on my own. It was so strange how something could become normal so quickly. I liked when he met me outside of my office. I liked how he grabbed my hand and hailed down a taxi for us to share. And even though I had just seen him this morning, I missed him.

I switched my computer monitor off. I had definitely gotten used to having something to look forward to after work. I grabbed my jacket.

"Bee."

I smiled and turned around. Mason was standing there smiling back at me. His hair was a little mussed up and the tie around his neck was loosened. He looked more relaxed than he usually did. I wasn't sure if it was because he had been hanging out with his friends or if he had too much to drink. But he looked so handsome.

He closed the distance between us and leaned down and kissed me.

"I didn't think you were coming," I said.

He smiled and laid his jacket down on the back of my chair. "I wasn't going to stand you up. Is there anyone else here?"

"No. I'm the last one. But I'm done now, if you want to go..."

"I have a better idea." The way he was looking at me made my heart race. He kissed me again. I could taste the alcohol on his tongue. His hands drifted from my back to my ass.

"Mason." I put my hand on his chest. "Are you drunk?"

"No." He moved one of his hands to the side of my face. "I missed you. And I want you. God, I want you."

"I missed you too." I put my hands behind his neck. "But we should probably go home."

"Home?" He laughed and kissed the side of my neck.

"I mean, your place or my place. Either one of our homes. Wherever you want to go." *What is wrong with me?*

He kissed the side of my neck and unbuttoned the top button of my blouse. "I like that you're comfortable at my place. But I don't want to go home." He unbuttoned another of my buttons.

"Mason, we can't do this."

"You said you were the last one here." He lifted me up, pulling my thighs around his waist. "We can go home after I make you come." He pushed the papers on my desk out of the way. "A few times."

I laughed.

"Bee." He set me down on the edge of my desk. "You have two choices. Here or the cab." He put his hands on the desk on either side of me and raised his eyebrow.

I couldn't ever say no to him. I never wanted to. Especially when he looked at me like that. I grabbed his tie and pulled his face down to mine.

He quickly unbuttoned the rest of the buttons on my blouse, while his tongue collided with mine. He pushed up my skirt, tracing his hands along my bare skin. His fingers were cold, but the feeling of them against my skin made my whole body feel warm. I wanted him so badly. He slid his hand up the inside of my thigh.

I immediately put my hand on his erection, which was pressing through his dress pants.

He pulled back slightly. "In a hurry?"

"I don't want to get caught," I said breathlessly.

"Is that all?" He unhinged his belt and undid his pants.

I shook my head back and forth. "I've been thinking about you all day. Or maybe I can't think straight at all because I want you all the time. Either way." I looked down at his boxers. "There's only one thing I need right now." When I looked back up at him I gulped. His Adam's apple rose and fell as he stared down at me.

"Where have you been all my life?" He grabbed both sides of my face and kissed me hard.

Waiting for you. When his hands moved back down to my ass, I put my hands in his hair. Everything about him was hard except for his hair. I loved how soft his hair was.

His tip pressed against my wetness. He groaned into my mouth as he slowly entered me. I loved that I could make him feel that way. That I could please him like this.

He pulled my ass closer to the edge of the desk, thrusting himself even deeper inside of me.

"Mason!" I slammed my hand down on my desk, hitting my keyboard. A second later I heard the hum of my computer turning back on.

His fingers were digging into my ass cheeks. "I don't know what you like more. My cock deep inside of you, or the idea that someone might catch us with my cock deep inside of you."

I moaned as he spread my thighs even wider. I really didn't want to get caught. "Faster."

He leaned over me, moving his hips even faster.

"Harder!"

His lips moved back to my neck. "God, I love you."

What did he just say? Does he realize he just said that?

He tilted his hips, hitting that spot that only he could.

"Mason!" I grabbed his tie, pulling his lips back to my neck.

He pushed the center of my chest, making me fall back onto the desk. My forearm hit my stapler and it made a clicking noise, sending a staple into nothing.

Mason leaned over me, putting his hand on the opposite edge of the desk. He wrapped his other arm around my thigh, pressing it backward, thrusting himself deeper inside of me.

"Fuck," he murmured after something crashed to the ground.

I pulled his face back to mine. A second later, I felt the warmth of him spread up into my stomach. It was my new favorite feeling in the world. He groaned into my mouth as he found his release.

He didn't need to tell me when to come tonight. I was already at the tipping point, and him losing control was enough to tip me over the edge. I was panting when he placed one last kiss against my lips.

His chest slowly rose and fell as he stared down at me. I tried to search his face. But he didn't look like he had just confessed that he loved me. He looked like he had when he had first come into the office, except even more relaxed. Maybe he was a little drunk. Or maybe I had imagined him saying it.

***

I slowly opened my eyes. We were in Mason's bed and my head was on his chest. *God, I love you.* I knew he said it. I heard him say it. Maybe he hadn't meant to. But I liked it. I wanted him to say it again.

I lifted my head and stared down at him. *Do I feel the same way? Do I love him?*

I swallowed hard. He didn't do relationships. Kendra had warned me to be careful, but I had completely ignored her. It was like I had jumped onto a sled and the hill in front of me was icy. There was no way to stop. Mason had a way of pulling me into the present. He didn't seem to care about the past or the future. I wasn't worried when I was with him.

But I still didn't know him that well. I accidently called his apartment home and he accidentally said he loved me. We hadn't even talked about whether or not we were exclusive, let alone all of that. He could be seeing someone else. I tried to dismiss the thought. We had spent every night of the past couple weeks together. If he was seeing someone else, he wasn't seeing them very often. And he had said he loved me. *Mason Caldwell loves me.*

What am I doing? Patrick had used me. As a face for his work functions. As an idea maybe. I didn't even know anymore. But he had stopped loving me. I was worried that Mason was using me for a different reason. For the things that Patrick had paid someone for.

Mason and I did more than have sex, though. He made me laugh. Like, water coming out of my nose laughing. He made me happy. And that's why I was scared. I didn't want to lose him. But if he did think women were expendable, how much time could I possibly have left? I reached up and touched the side of his face. He had scruff on his face and I liked how it felt rough against my palm.

He shifted in his sleep and I immediately moved my hand away from his face.

He yawned and opened his eyes. He smiled when he saw me staring at him. "I like waking up to you." He grabbed my waist and pulled me on top of him.

I laughed and put my hands on either side of him on the mattress. I wanted to talk to him about how I was feeling, but I didn't want to scare him away.

"Hey," he said and put his hand on the side of my face. "Is everything okay?" He was so sweet. And it made my stomach churn even more.

"You don't do relationships."

He sighed and put his hands behind his head. He stared at me for a second before saying, "I haven't in a long time, no."

"So what does that make me?"

He smiled. "Mine."

I laughed. "Seriously, Mason, what are we doing?"

"Enjoying each other's company."

"Right." I smiled but I felt like crying. Right now we were enjoying each other's company. And when that changed, we were done. When he decided I wasn't fun anymore. I liked when he called me his. I liked the way that sounded way too much.

"Bee, I really like you."

"I really like you too."

He reached up and tucked a loose strand of hair behind my ear. "Then what's the problem?"

"Are you going to get bored with me?" As soon as I said it, I regretted it. I sounded so childish. Of course nothing lasted forever. I knew that better than anyone. I wasn't sure what I even meant with that question. He'd get bored with me eventually, just like Patrick. I wasn't enough.

"That's what you're worried about?"

"I've just never done anything like this before."

"Like this?" He raised his eyebrow at me. "What do you think we're doing?"

I laughed. "I don't know." I put my hand on his hard chest. I just needed to ask him. "Are you seeing anyone else?"

"No."

"So those clubs..."

"I already told you. I haven't been to one since I've met you. You give me everything that I need."

Do I give him everything he needs? How can I, if I don't know what those places are? Is it just sex? Is it shows? Is it more than that? "Can you take me to one?"

"What?" He lowered his eyebrows.

"To one of those places? So I can see it?"

"I'm done, okay? I don't need that anymore. I don't need the money. I've been approaching everything wrong. I just need a big client."

"For the ad agency? Or for the..."

"The ad agency."

"Please, Mason. I want to understand."

He frowned. "Do you trust me?"

I searched his face. *Do I?* "I mean...do you still send people to them? For money?"

"I'm going to stop. Bee, you have to understand..."

"I need to see it. I need to see what Patrick wanted instead of me. I need to see why you don't do relationships. I need to see what's so great about this thing that I know nothing about." *I need to know why I'm never enough.*

"You're not going to let this go, are you?"

I shook my head.

"Fine."

"You'll take me?"

"If that's what you want." He looked pissed. But the expression on his face was fleeting. His frown faded and he gave me a playful smile. "Now make me my breakfast, woman." He lightly slapped my ass.

I laughed and pushed on his chest. "You're the worst."

"A man can dream. How about I make you waffles then?" He kissed my cheek.

"Really? You know how to make waffles?"

"Don't sound so surprised." He rolled out of bed and pulled on a pair of pajama bottoms.

I propped my head up on my hand. "Well, after you burned dinner the other night..."

"If I recall, you distracted me. Honestly, though, don't get too excited. They're Eggo Waffles. I'm good at using the toaster."

"I knew it."

Chapter 53
Mason

"Fuck." I walked into the kitchen and opened up the freezer. I grabbed the box of waffles, pulled two out, and slammed the door. What the hell had I just agreed to? I placed the waffles in the toaster and pressed the button.

My friends had gotten in my head last night. Or maybe I just had too much to drink. But I told Bee that I loved her. And she didn't react. She pretended that she didn't hear. Or maybe she hadn't heard me.

Damn it. I sat down on one of the stools in the kitchen and ran my hand through my hair. She definitely heard me. She just didn't feel the same way. Which I already knew. Why would she love me? How could she?

I looked down at my hands. I was serious when I told her she was all I needed. But she didn't believe me. If she had, she wouldn't be insisting on seeing one of those places. And the way she said Patrick's name. It had looked like she was about to cry. She wanted to know why he was bored in their relationship. She wanted to see why she wasn't enough for him. And she had already seemed to have her mind made up that she'd never be enough for anyone. But that wasn't true. All I wanted was her.

And now I had to take her to one of those fucking clubs. That would be the icing on the cake. She was clearly looking for a reason to leave. And what did it matter? I didn't actually love her. I barely knew her. I said it by mistake. I didn't love anyone. My rationalization wasn't helping. Because what was really bothering me was that she didn't feel the same about me.

"Shit." My chest hurt again. This was why I didn't do relationships. I didn't like not having control. I rubbed my chest with my hand. She deserved better than me. She wasn't the one that didn't have enough to offer...I was.

I looked up as she walked into the kitchen. She was dressed in jeans and a tight, long sleeved shirt. Was she already leaving? I didn't really know what love was. But this might be the closest I'd ever been to it.

"I thought maybe you could take me after breakfast?" she said. She looked nervous.

"I'm not going to get bored with you." I wasn't ready for her to go yet. And after I took her, it would be over.

She pressed her lips together. "Please, Mason. I just want to see it."

I stood up when the waffles popped out of the toaster. *Which place was the least damning?*

Chapter 54
Bee

We were standing outside an unmarked building.

"I'm actually getting hungry for lunch," Mason said. "There's this place down the street that's really good. What do you say?"

"Is it really that bad?" I asked. He looked upset. *No.* He looked guilty.

"I don't know why we're here," Mason said. "I told you I was done with this. I wish you would just trust me."

"It's not really that." I folded my arms in front of my chest. "When Patrick broke up with me, he made it seem like it was my fault. Like I wasn't giving him what he needed."

"Do you still have feelings for him?"

"No." My voice sounded small, but I meant it. "I just need to know."

He looked a little relieved. "Patrick is a dick. That's all you need to know."

"Please, Mason."

He sighed and tapped three times on the door. There was a buzzing sound and a little box next to the door lit up. Mason pulled out his phone and looked down at something before pressing the button on the box. "Sunset," he said into the small speaker and then let go of the button. He put his phone back in his pocket.

A huge bald man in jeans and a black t-shirt appeared at the door.

"She's with me," said Mason.

"Did she sign the forms?"

Forms?

"I'll vouch for her," Mason said.

The bouncer looked me up and down. His eyes made my skin feel cold. "She doesn't work for the press?" he said.

"No." Mason sounded annoyed.

The bouncer stared at me for another minute. "Fine. If there's a leak, it's on you, Mason."

"She's not going to tell anyone." Mason looked at me. "Right?"

"I won't," I said. *Geez, what the hell is behind those doors?*

"Good to see you," the bouncer said and slapped Mason on the back. "It's been awhile."

"Yeah." Mason looked back at me again. "I've been busy." He lowered his eyebrows for a second but then looked away. He seemed sad.

Had he missed coming here? Or was he sad that I didn't trust him? Of course I couldn't trust him. I didn't know what weird stuff was behind those doors. And Mason had introduced Patrick to whatever it was. I wasn't trying to vilify Mason. But I felt nauseous standing there. I didn't care why Patrick had cheated on me anymore. I cared about why Mason was going to cheat on me. Because he would. Maybe not anytime soon, but he would. Maybe I could prevent that. I wanted to be able to give him what he wanted. Because I was falling for him. No matter what I told myself. I could see myself loving him. I could see a future with him. And it terrified me.

I wasn't backing down now. I was here. And I was determined to see what was behind those doors.

"Are we good to go then?" I asked.

The bouncer smiled. "She has a lot to learn." He winked at Mason.

"This isn't a training session," Mason said, and walked past the bouncer.

Training session? I felt even more nauseous. Did Mason bring women here to show them what men wanted? Did he practice with them? How many woman had he actually slept with? I took a deep breath and followed Mason as he opened up the second set of doors.

It wasn't what I expected at all. I stopped in my tracks and looked around. It was just a hallway, but it was beautiful. It reminded me a little of The Plaza Hotel. Everything was painted black but there were gold designs hung on the walls. Everything seemed to shimmer. I could hear music, but all I could see were doors. Tons of doors. And the hallways curved on both sides like it looped around in a circle.

"Mason, is that you?!"

I turned my head to the sound of a females' voice. A woman in a tight, silvery dress had just come out of one of the rooms.

Mason didn't say anything.

But the woman walked over as quickly as she could in her heels and wrapped her arms around him.

Mason kept his hands to the side, not touching her.

"Mason," she pulled back and put her hands on the collar of his jacket. "Thank you. I owe you." She leaned forward again and whispered something in his ear. Mason's body seemed to stiffen.

I wanted to punch her in her face.

Mason cleared his throat, but the girl didn't let go of his collar. "We need a private room," he said.

"Private?" The girl glanced over at me. "Are you sure?" She trailed her fingers down his abs and stopped at his belt. "I have something new to show you."

He grabbed her wrist so she couldn't unbuckle his belt. "We're just here to observe."

The girl frowned and turned away from him. She opened up a cabinet, but I wasn't interested in what she was doing. I was too busy staring at Mason. He wasn't looking at the girl, but he wasn't looking at me either. Maybe it was a mistake coming here. He seemed tense and upset. I just needed to know what was behind those doors.

The girl slipped a key into Mason's hand. "Room 16. You have my number if you change your mind." She looked at me and winked.

Fuck you.

Mason grabbed my hand and pulled me down the hallway, away from the strangers.

"Did you train her?" I whispered.

Mason didn't say anything. Instead, he stopped in front of a door and slid the key into the lock.

"Mason?"

He sighed. "Yes, I did."

"Did you have sex with her?"

"No." He didn't look like he was lying, but his face was strained. He opened up the door and I followed him in. The walls were the same as the ones in the hall, but the room was more dimly lit. There were leather seats and a coffee table where a bottle of champagne and glasses were sitting. I wanted it to be gross. But it seemed classy somehow. Like this was where rich men went to screw around on their wives. The only thing that gave away where we were was a stripper pole in the middle of the room.

I turned around. Mason was already sitting on the couch. I looked down at his lap. "Did you do other intimate things together?"

"Fuck, Bee. What do you want me to say? I let her suck my dick? Fine. I feel like I'm on trial here."

"Who is she? Where did you even meet?"

He sighed. "She's an ex cheerleader. I met her at a bar. She doesn't mean anything to me. She's just some girl."

Just some girl. Like me? "What did she whisper in your ear?"

"Nothing important."

Oh God, why did I come here? I turned away from him and stared at the opposite side of the room. There was a gold curtain. It must separate us from wherever the music was coming from. Maybe it was a naked band. Like a weird groupie thing?

I wanted to think this place was disgusting and horrible. But it made sense that Patrick had come here. It was fancy. It was better than our small, dingy apartment. It was better than anything I could give him. Better than me. I never wore short, sparkly dresses for him. Maybe I had stopped trying. Maybe Patrick had been right.

"Can we please just go now?" Mason said. "You've seen it."

"How do you get money doing this?"

Mason sighed and ran his hand down his face. "I get a finder's fee for new recruits. The better they are, the more money I get."

"Where do you find women to bring here?"

"Bars. One night stands. I don't know. Why does any of this matter? I haven't done it since we've met."

"And what about the guys you bring here to enjoy these girls you've trained? How do you make money doing that?"

Mason laughed. "My clients pay me to find them the hottest new places. And to make sure their identities are kept safe."

"And your father pays you to take out his new hires?"

"No. I use his new hires as a way to find new clients. My dad doesn't even know about it."

"He doesn't know about your sex ring?"

"It's not a sex ring."

"I don't understand." I sat down next to him, putting enough space between us so that we weren't touching. "Why do you do it?"

Mason opened his mouth, but then closed it again. He leaned back in his seat. "Because I'm good at it."

"Do you like it more than advertising?"

"It's a hobby, not a career."

"That's not what I asked."

"It's just a means to an end. You know I'm trying to start my own ad agency. I need the cash."

"Why, because you're not speaking to your parents?"

"I'm trying to make something of myself, Bee."

"Here?"

"What do you want me to say? That I'm good at fucking? That I know when a girl would be good at this job depending on how skilled she is in bed? That I can tell how loose a woman is by talking to her for less than a minute?" He ran his hand through his hair. "I'm trying. I really am. I haven't been here in weeks."

"I didn't ask you to not come."

"You're right. You didn't." He looked hurt.

"Are you mad at me?"

"Why are we here, Bee?"

"I told you. I wanted to see."

"You know what? Yes. I'm mad at you. We have a good thing. Why are you trying to ruin it?"

"A good thing? All you want me for is sex."

Mason laughed. "Is that really what you think? If I just wanted sex, I'd come here."

"That's what I'm afraid of."

"I'm not Patrick."

"Aren't you just like him though? Didn't he learn about all of this from you?"

"If you're still hung up on him, maybe you should be yelling at him instead of me, Bee."

"I'm over him."

"Clearly you aren't. You didn't want to come here for me. You came here for him."

"Mason, that's not..."

"I don't want to talk about your ex. If you want to see it, then see it." He pointed to the curtain.

"I'm sorry."

He stood up. "You came here to see. I'm not sure what you're waiting for." He walked over to the curtain and pulled it back.

There was a stage in the middle of the circular room. Women in much less than silver dresses were on the stage. Half of them were topless and there were some on stripper poles. And they all had necklaces which held medallions with numbers on them. Two girls were doing a little more than making out at the end of the stage. Chandeliers hung from the ceiling. Some curtains were open and others closed around the room.

I was pretty sure there weren't couples talking behind the closed curtains like Mason and I were. A girl wearing a silver dress like the one that had greeted Mason walked passed us with a tray in her hand. Maybe you just needed to give blowjobs to get a waitress gig here.

A different woman in a silver dress went up to the two girls making out. She said something to them and they stood up, holding hands and followed the silver dressed woman to one of the rooms with an open curtain. One of the girls straddled the man sitting on the couch before the curtain was closed.

I turned around and looked at Mason. I was surprised to see that he was staring at me instead of the naked woman that were only a few feet away from us.

"They're numbered?" I asked.

"So you can get the one you want."

"That's disgusting."

"They're all clean."

"That's not what I meant." I turned back to look at the stage, but before I did I noticed a box on the wall by the curtain. It looked like a call box outside of an apartment. I lifted my finger. "Is this how you..."

"You really don't want to touch that," Mason said, grabbing my hand before I could push one of the buttons.

I gulped. He immediately dropped my hand and folded his arms across his chest. He was right. Seeing this was enough. I knew what would happen if I selected one of those buttons. Dirty whore sex.

I looked back at the stage. "Which number would you choose?"

Mason sighed. He came over to the curtain and leaned against the wall, but he continued to stare at me. "I'm sick of standing still. I don't want this life anymore. I want you."

"I want you too."

Mason laughed. "No, you don't."

"If we really have a shot at whatever this is, I needed to see this."

"So that you'll resent me? Give me a break." Mason turned his head to the women on the stage. "We both know what you really want to ask me. So just ask it."

He was right. I had to know. "Who would Patrick choose?"

"Number twelve. That's his type."

I looked back at the stage. She had long dark hair. Her skin was perfectly tanned. I wanted her tits to be saggy and for her ass to have stretch marks, but that wasn't the case. She was perfect. And she didn't look anything like me. I ran my thumb along the spot where my engagement ring once was. I wasn't Patrick's type. He liked women like number twelve. Why was he ever even with me? That's why he never looked at me the way Mason did. He wasn't even attracted to me.

"Mason, I'm sorry."

He didn't respond.

I turned around but the room was empty, the door ajar. "Mason?" I ran out of the room and down the hallway. "Mason?!" I yelled as I pushed open the doors.

"I guess it didn't work out for you?" the bouncer said.

"What?"

"You know, if you need more practice..."

I felt like I couldn't breathe. "Excuse me," I said and walked past him and out the front door. Snow had started falling and there was already a coating on the ground. I pulled my jacket tightly around myself. I wasn't expecting to leave here alone. Mason and I had walked here together through Central Park. I had made a huge mistake. I shouldn't have come here. I should have trusted him.

I pulled my phone out of my purse and pressed on his name. I held my phone up to my ear but it went straight to voicemail. *Shit.* Maybe he had decided to walk home?

I ran across the street and down the steps into the park. The ground was getting sleek in spots, but I couldn't stop running. I needed to catch up to him. I needed to tell him I was sorry.

I didn't care about his past with ex cheerleaders and girls in sparkly dresses. None of that mattered. What mattered was us, right now. And I loved us. I needed to stop thinking the worst would happen when all Mason ever showed me was his best.

I turned the corner and saw him in the distance. "Mason!" I yelled at the top of my lungs.

He scrunched up his shoulders and picked up his pace.

I knew he had heard me. I picked up my pace and slid on the wet sidewalk, landing hard on my ass. "Damn it." My hand landed in a pile of snow. I looked at Mason and then back at the ground. "Hey, Mason!" I picked up a handful of snow, waded it up, and threw it as hard as I could.

It hit the back of Mason's jacket. He stopped and shook his head. When he turned around he was actually smiling. He started walking toward me. "You're going to regret that!" he said.

Crap. I turned around and tried to walk as fast as I could on the wet pavement. A second later, a snowball hit my ass. I heard Mason laughing in the distance. I grabbed another snowball, turned around and threw it at him. He easily dodged it, grabbed another handful of snow, and threw it at me.

I tried to run away but his snowball hit my ass again. I felt his hands grab my hips as he spun me around. He was smiling but it didn't quite reach his eyes.

"I don't like when you're mad at me," I said.

"Then don't make me mad."

I lightly pushed his chest.

He pretend to fall backwards and pulled me down on top of him into the snow.

"Mason!" I laughed.

"I don't like when you're mad at me either." He ran his fingers through my hair.

"I'm sorry. I do trust you. I just..."

"I know." He stared at me for a second. "Was that the closure you needed?"

I nodded. "Am I your type?"

He smiled. "Isn't it obvious?"

I put my hands on his chest. "I don't know how to be casual. If we're going to do this, I want to be exclusive. I know you don't do relationships but..."

"We already are, Bee."

He didn't say boyfriend and girlfriend, but he had agreed. I was his and he was mine. I wasn't sure if anything had ever felt so right before.

He dusted snow off the back of my jacket. "We better get home before we're buried alive."

I laughed and climbed off of him. As soon as he got up, he wrapped his arm around my shoulders.

Chapter 55
Mason

"It's so beautiful," Bee said as she looked out the window.

I plopped down on the couch beside her and pulled her feet onto my lap. "It's only pretty because we're not out there."

"No, it's still pretty."

We had both skipped work today and had pretended to be snowed in. It was perfect. *She* was perfect. I turned my attention away from her and toward the window. "The trash trucks can't get through the streets. There's trash all over the sidewalks. It's gross."

Bee laughed. "That's a pessimistic view. It's like a winter wonderland."

I ran my thumb along the inside of her ankle, clearly sending shivers through her whole body. I loved having that effect on her. She was looking at me in that way that made my chest feel tight. But I was getting used to the feeling. I was 80 percent sure it didn't mean I was having a heart attack.

"I can't even remember the last time I had a snow day," she said.

I smiled. "Building a snowman with your parents and neighborhood snowball fights? That's what the suburbs are all about, right?"

She pressed her lips together and looked back out the window. "No, not really. I mean, maybe." She folded her arms across her chest. "I don't know."

I had hit some kind of nerve. Normally I'd change the subject if a conversation went south. But it wasn't like that with Bee. I wanted to know these things about her. Hell, I wanted to know everything about her. "So what was it like for you, then?" I continued to rub my thumb along the inside of her ankle.

She smiled and turned back to me, but her smile looked forced. "I mean, it was pretty much like that." She shrugged. "What about you? I assume you were still talking to your parents back then? Plus you have a brother. I'm guessing all sorts of shenanigans?"

I lowered my eyebrows slightly. What was it that she didn't want me to know? "Well, Matt and I had a nanny that we used to love to torture. We had plenty of snowball fights with her. And hot chocolate. She made the best hot chocolate. And what about you, Bee?"

"Actually, I could go for some hot chocolate right now." She tried to move her foot off my lap but I grabbed her ankle.

Her brown eyes got wide. For a second it looked like she was going to cry. It made my chest feel even tighter. "I'd like to know whatever it is you don't want to tell me about your childhood. That is, if you'd like me to know. If not, I'll let you fix me some hot chocolate." I gave her a small smile.

She sighed and leaned back against the pillows. "It's not like it's anything interesting. My parents got divorced when I was really young. My dad basically disappeared overnight. And I didn't hear from him very much. My mom had to work two jobs to pay the bills, so she couldn't be around that much either. Not that she had a choice. And I was shy and nerdy. I didn't have that many friends. I think part of it was that I didn't want to get close to anyone, you know? I was afraid that they'd leave too. It was stupid." Bee laughed and looked down at her lap.

"It's not stupid."

She looked back up at me. Her cheeks were slightly rosy, like she was embarrassed that she had told me about her lame excuse of a dad. I felt protective of her. She might not admit it, but I could see that it still hurt her. If I ever met him, I'd have to remember to beat the shit out of him.

"I always loved the snow, though," she said. "Whenever my mom was home during a snowstorm we'd have a contest to see who could catch the most snowflakes on our tongues. She'd always make me say my number first and then claim that she had caught a few less than me."

"Hmmm." I ran my hand along the inside of her calf, massaging it gently. "Are you two still close?"

"You mean, does she call me all the time wondering if I've been mugged at gunpoint on the dangerous streets of New York City? And worry about me going on blind dates with serial killers?" She raised her eyebrow at me.

It was probably meant to look stern, but she looked adorable. I grabbed he hand and pulled her onto my lap.

She laughed as I ran my hands down to her hips.

"I hope you told her I wasn't a serial killer?"

"I'm still not completely sure that you aren't. But I did tell her all about you."

I laughed. "Good things?"

"There aren't any bad things to tell." She smiled and put her hands on my shoulders.

"Does that mean that you are no longer scared of getting close to someone?"

"I'm terrified."

I had expected her to laugh. Or deny it. But there was her answer. She was terrified of getting hurt again. I wasn't going to hurt her. She wasn't just some girl I was sleeping with. It didn't matter that I was drunk the other night. What I had said was true. I was falling in love with her. And it didn't even freak me out as much as I thought it would. It was just a fact. "I promise I'm not going anywhere."

"Isn't that what they all say?"

"Maybe. But I mean it." I moved one of my hands to the side of her face. "I can't even remember a time when I was this happy."

She searched my face for a second and then smiled. "And here I just thought you wanted me for my body."

"Well." I grabbed her waist and spun her so that her back was pressed against the mattress and my torso was pinned against her.

She laughed as I pushed her shirt up, revealing a strip of her smooth skin.

"I'd be lying if I said that wasn't a small part of it." Her nipples were hard, showing clearly through her t-shirt. She made me feel like a horny teenager again. As if I had no control of my hormones. I wanted her all the time. I ran my fingers up her stomach, but she grabbed my wrist before I could wrap my hand around one of her perky tits.

"Please don't break my heart, Mason." Her face was suddenly serious. It almost looked like she expected me to kick her out of my apartment right after she said it. Like this was the final out. After this second I'd be crossing that line, I'd be hurting her.

But I was already two feet in. Breaking her heart meant not seeing her anymore. And that wasn't something I was interested in. I liked waking up to her, and falling asleep with her head on my chest. The look she was giving me showed me that she was already in too. She was falling for me just as fast as I was falling for her. And maybe I was just as terrified as she was, not of the feeling, but of getting my heart broken.

I shifted my weight so that my face was right above hers. "Baby, I will never get enough of you."

Chapter 56
Bee

The office was abuzz this morning. Our first proposed advertisement for Sword Body Wash was going to be aired tonight and everyone was doing last minute preparations. And Mr. Ellington was beside himself with excitement. The FCC had disbanded yesterday with the announcement of the government shutdown. That had been the biggest worry with the sponsorship idea, that they'd cut the broadcast when Layla Torrez started measuring men's penis sizes live on T.V. Now that wasn't an issue. Apparently the C.E.O. of Sword Body Wash was just as excited. Hopefully they'd still blur everything out. The whole thing was ridiculous.

"I assume you're staying for the viewing party tonight?" Kendra said and sat down on the edge of my desk.

"Even though it's the stupidest marketing idea ever?"

Kendra laughed. "Don't be bitter that Mr. Ellington didn't go with your idea. We'll all have a good laugh. It'll be fun."

"Does Layla Torrez even know what she has to do? She'll probably walk off before they even tape the segment."

"Apparently they never tell her what she's guessing until she's on the air. That way she can't prepare."

"I feel so bad for her."

"Yeah, me too," Kendra said. "But do you know who I don't feel bad for?"

I peeled my eyes off the report I was writing and looked up at her face. She was smiling at me.

"Who?"

"Carter told Marie that Mason is going around the office talking to his buddies about his new girlfriend nonstop."

I smiled to myself. "Really?" He still hadn't said those words to me. But he had said that we were exclusive and that he wasn't going anywhere. We were a couple. I felt my cheeks blushing. Hearing that suddenly made the fact that my ad pitch had been rejected in favor of a pornographic ploy not matter quite as much.

"Yes, really," Kendra said. "So what Marie and I are both wondering is why you didn't tell us about this huge step?"

"We hadn't exactly discussed those labels yet. Did he really say that?" I couldn't help the smile that was now plastered to my face. Just thinking about Mason gave me this warm fuzzy feeling in my stomach.

"He did. I never thought you of all people would end up with Manhattan's hottest playboy."

I laughed. "I think that title is a little bold. He's not really like that."

"Not anymore. He's given up his life of sin. You really have a hold on him."

I felt my face blush again and looked at the beautiful roses on my desk. They had arrived this morning with a note from Mason, saying that he had noticed the other ones he had given me were wilting. Which he had noticed while he was banging me on the desk. I'm sure my face turned even redder.

"And you've also been playing hooky."

"It was such a mess out yesterday. Getting to work is hard in the snow."

"Mhm. So on a scale of one to pre Patrick cheating on you, how in love with Mason are you?"

I wanted to believe that I was just falling in love with Mason. That I hadn't actually crossed that line yet. I wasn't the type of girl that just fell head over heels for some guy. With Patrick, our relationship had progressed slowly. But with Mason? It was like I had sledded down the steepest slope imaginable right into his arms. It wasn't just that I wanted to be with him every second. I needed him. He made me feel happy and desired and whole. That was it. He made me feel whole again.

I looked up at Kendra. "I've never felt this way about someone before."

"Holy shit." She dragged out the 'o' and 'y' in holy. "You like him more than you liked Patrick?"

I tucked a loose strand of hair behind my ear. For some reason I felt like I wanted to cry. I liked him so much more than Patrick. And it scared the hell out of me. I didn't want to lose him. I couldn't lose him too.

"Hey." Kendra scooted off the edge of her desk. "Bee, what's wrong?"

I wiped the tears quickly off my cheeks. *What is wrong with me?*

Kendra wrapped her arms around me and squeezed me tightly. "Tell me, Bee."

"Nothing good lasts forever."

Kendra laughed and pulled away. "That's not true. Look at Marie and Carter. They're so happy."

"They're the only example of a happy couple that I know. They're the exception. I've just gotten used to the idea that I'm going to end up alone. Like you said, I'm meant to be a cat lady."

Kendra smiled. "Mason sounds a lot better than a clowder of cats. I know you were scared to get back out there. But you shouldn't be scared now. The hard part is finding someone worthy of your love. You've already found him. And from what it sounds like, he's completely smitten with you."

"Until he gets bored with me."

"Hon." Kendra put her hand on top of mine. "Stop selling yourself short. I know how Patrick made you feel. We've all been dumped. It sucks. But it doesn't mean you give up and buy cats."

I laughed. "I know." I was so scared, though. The thought of Mason leaving me too terrified me. Patrick had promised me that he'd never leave me either. A promise was only as sincere as the person giving it. I wanted to believe that Mason was sincere. He seemed so sincere. And that's why it was so scary. Because I believed him. And I loved him. I was so in love with him.

***

The conference room had been turned into a mini theater for the viewing party. Jenkins was sitting at the front next to Mr. Ellington. His left knee kept bouncing up and down, clearly jittery with the anticipation of how all this was going to turn out.

"It's on, it's on! Shhh!" Jenkins yelled as Layla Torrez appeared on the screen. They had dressed her in an outfit that was not at all appropriate for a weather girl to wear. Layla immediately asked what she was guessing today.

The voice of Brian Scott, the news anchor, came through with a touch of humor. "Penis sizes."

The whole conference room laughed at Layla's shocked reaction. But I just felt bad for her. The stupid men at Kruger advertising were making a joke at her expense. This could ruin her career. A few seconds later the segment went to commercial break.

Mr. Ellington stood up and faced all his employees. "Here's to another successful campaign. And to the FCC disbanding." He lifted up his glass of champagne.

It seemed a little early to celebrate the success of the campaign. Layla still had time to run away screaming. "This is so horrible," I whispered to Kendra.

"I thought it would be funny, but I feel really bad for her. Did you see her face?"

"What would you do if it was you?" I asked.

"Well, it's still going to be blurred out, right?"

"I think so?"

"Well, no harm then, I guess," said Kendra.

"They're in a public park in the center of Miami. It's after work. Tons of people are surely walking around."

Kendra shook her head. "That poor girl."

The news came back on but I tuned it out. "Jenkins is such an ass. Imagine if he were in her position."

Kendra laughed. "No one would watch the segment if Jenkins was the one guessing. Unless he was in that dress. Hell, I'd watch that."

"Gross." I looked up at the screen. Layla had just pulled out a ruler and was measuring some sweaty guy's junk. "Thank God they blurred it out."

"The FCC may not be censoring shit, but no respectable news station would show a flaccid dick to the general public. But considering how low cut her top is, he's probably erect."

"Do we really have to sit here and watch this?"

"It's kind of hilarious though. Oh my God." Kendra nudged my shoulder and pointed to the screen.

"What?" I turned my head toward the T.V. Layla Torrez was taking off her dress. "She barely ever guesses wrong."

"What a terrible day to lose."

"That whole park is seeing her in her underwear. Or not..." Layla had just turned away from the camera and unhooked her bra. "Isn't Sword going to get backlash from torturing a weather girl?"

"The body wash that gets Layla Torrez naked? It's not a terrible sales pitch."

The broadcast had cut to commercial again.

The phone in the conference room started ringing and Mr. Ellington immediately grabbed it. "Kruger Adver..." A smile curled onto his lips. "We'll send over our next pitch in a few days." Pause. "You too." Mr. Ellington hung up the phone and stood up again. "Everyone's talking about it. Sword Body Wash is trending on Twitter. And we just secured our biggest client ever." He raised his glass again.

"Great work, Jenkins. This is the kind of thing that makes partner."

I rolled my eyes. I wasn't going to sit here and watch this shit show. Maybe Mr. Ellington was right. Maybe I wasn't fit to be in advertising. I didn't want to do anything like this. Advertising was supposed to be clever and well thought out. Besides, all that was left to see was Layla do the weather nude, hopefully still censored. I could leave that to my imagination.

"I'm going to get going," I whispered to Kendra.

"Running off to Mason?" she asked.

"And to lick my wounds."

"Your idea really was better. This is the most ridiculous news segment I've ever seen."

"Yeah." When Mr. Ellington turned back to the screen, I quietly stood up and tiptoed to the door. When my hand wrapped around the handle I heard someone clear their throat. *Shit.*

"We could probably all use some coffee, Bridget," Mr. Ellington said.

"Actually, I was going to get going. It's almost six and..."

"And? I pay you to work the same hours as everyone else. And you took off yesterday. Which means you owe me more time."

Seriously? I worked longer hours than everyone else here. Especially him. And yesterday was the only day I had ever taken off. I was allowed to have two weeks vacation. Working longer hours after taking off wasn't part of that. What an asshole. I swallowed hard.

"If you want special treatment, maybe you should start dressing like that Layla girl."

Jenkins snickered.

Fuck you. "I'm just not feeling well," I said.

"You can take a seat after you get coffee. Decaf for me. What does everyone else want?"

"I think I'm going to throw up," I said.

"Ew. Get out of here. And don't throw up on the carpet. I'll just dock your pay."

I put my hand up to my mouth for good measure and grabbed the door handle. I ran out of the room and to my desk. I wish I did have to throw up. Because I knew just where I'd do it. All over that perverted, sexist's desk.

CHAPTER 57
Mason

My phone buzzed in my pocket. I quickly pulled it out and looked down at the screen. I had been hoping it would be Bee, but it was James. I swiped my finger across the screen. "Hey, man."

"Tell me you saw that broadcast?"

"What broadcast?"

"The one where the weather girl predicted penis sizes and then fucked some guy during the weather report."

I laughed. "What is that, some weird porno that you and Penny are into? Sounds weird."

"Just turn on the news, Mason."

I grabbed the remote and turned on the T.V. Owen Harris was reporting about some scandal. In the corner of the screen was an image of a blurred out couple in front of a Doppler map of Miami. "What the hell?"

"Sword Body Wash was sponsoring the segment, Layla's Predictions. Their marketing rep upped the stakes without their permission. They had her having sex live during the news segment. Sword Body Wash is in deep shit."

I laughed. "That's hilarious." As soon as I said it, I realized what this meant. Bee had said that Kruger was currently working on a body wash account. And in her notebook she had mentioned Jenkins' pitch...measuring penis sizes. "Wait, was the marketing rep from Kruger?"

"Bingo. Which means they need someone to help them clean up this mess. They need you."

I thought about Bee. "But what about Kruger?"

James laughed. "No one's going to want to hire them again. I'm friends with a guy on their board. Their investors bailed. They're going to go under, Mason. They'll be bankrupt in a matter of days. I'm sure I can get the rest of their client list. This is what you've been waiting for."

Bee was going to lose her job. I couldn't swoop in and steal all her company's clients. I stared at the T.V. "I don't know, James."

"This is a huge break. Why don't you sound excited?"

"Bee works for Kruger."

"Oh. Shit." James cleared his throat. "Mason you can't tell anyone about this, especially Bee. The company hasn't announced what's going on yet. If anyone from Kruger finds out it could lead to insider trading. My friend on the board would go to..."

"I won't tell anyone."

James sighed. "I'm sorry. I only told you because I knew you didn't have stock in Kruger. I had no idea that Bee worked there. I guess that's a conflict of interest for you?"

I stared at the screen. James had just handed me the biggest opportunity of my life. But it meant keeping a secret from Bee. She trusted me. I didn't want to mess up what we had. "What am I supposed to do?"

"This is your dream. These clients are basically being handed to you on a silver platter. You have to do this."

"Fuck." I put my elbows on my knees.

"Just hire her when you start your own agency. She doesn't have to be out of work for long."

"That's a lawsuit waiting to happen. Hiring my girlfriend to work beneath me? Jesus."

James laughed. "Wait. Girlfriend?"

I ran my hand down my face. "I don't know. I think so?"

James whistled. "Well, as your girlfriend, I think she'd want you to do this. Although you can't actually ask her because..."

"Yeah, I got it. Insider trading. You really think she'll understand after it's over?"

"Kruger is already dissolving. There's nothing that you can do to fix that. You don't even work for them."

"That doesn't really answer my question. What would Penny do if you two were in this situation?"

James laughed. "I tell Penny everything, so..."

"Not helping."

He sighed. "When we were first dating and I didn't have her trust yet? She probably would have done something stupid and rash."

"I can't fuck this up. I'm crazy about her. When we first met she was ready to move out of the city." The tightness in my chest returned. Maybe I was having heart problems. "She can't leave."

"If she loves you, she'll understand."

"I don't know if she loves me."

"Well, like I said the other day, you can convince anyone to do anything. The contact info for Sword Body Wash is on that list I already gave you. It's up to you. But you have to decide soon. Someone else is going to swoop in if you don't."

"Yeah." I stood up. This was what I always wanted. And if Bee did love me and if we became a permanent thing, I'd need to provide for her. Just the thought of finality in that made my stomach turn. Was I even ready to settle down? Would I ever be? "Thanks, James. I'm going to call them now."

"Good luck. Tell me how it goes."

"Mhm. Later." I hung up the phone and walked toward my office.

Matt had told me I could use Bee to get new clients. I hadn't done that. I hadn't done anything bad. She'd know about Kruger dissolving in a few days anyway. It would be fine. She'd understand. I grabbed the envelope James had given me and unfolded the piece of paper inside. It was alphabetical by company name. James was ridiculously organized.

Sword Body Wash was near the bottom. The chief marketing officer was John Landry. I typed in the number before I could change my mind. This is what I had always wanted. My own ad agency. If I landed this account, I could shove it in my dad's face. I had been unfocused the past few weeks. I had pushed my ambition aside for a good lay. That wasn't me. I was going to get this account. And every other account that Kruger had. I pressed the call button.

After a few rings someone on the other end answered. "John Landry, Sword Body Wash."

"Hi, John. This is Mason Caldwell. I heard you were in need of a new advertising agency."

John laughed. "Obviously. This is a fucking nightmare."

"You could definitely use a PR fix."

"Any ideas about that?"

"Well, my firm could help you through it. I have several years of experience cleaning up messes that other ad agencies have made for brands. And if you wanted to sit down and..."

"Look, you're not the first call we've gotten. And you won't be the last. If you have an idea, pitch it to me. I'm just going to go with the best one."

I hadn't prepared anything. So I just said the first thing that came to my mind. "I think you should go back to your roots."

"Our roots?"

"Your brand thrived with guerilla style campaigns. And I know you're trying to grow your brand here in New York, which is where we're located. How about you do something here to get everyone's mind off what just happened in Miami. Even make it seem like it just happened because your body wash is just that good, like you didn't put advertising dollars in it."

"Like what?"

"The Knicks cheerleaders perform in Central Park before games to sell tickets. Let's team up with them. We can have an actor spray himself with body spray and have the cheerleaders chase him through Central Park. The new slogan can be...we can't control what happens when women are around Sword. It takes care of the Layla's Prediction fiasco too. Don't take the blame. Blame the awesome product."

"Interesting spin."

"It heightens the brand. We can't hide from what happen. We have to own it. And get the buzz on something else as soon as possible."

There was silence on the other line. "What agency do you work for again?"

"We're actually new. So you'll have our undivided attention."

"I like what I've heard. We're expecting a few other calls, but how hard would it be to set this up with the cheerleaders?"

"I know a few of them. All I need is the go ahead and I'll make the calls."

"I'll be in touch, Mason." John hung up the phone.

I pulled the phone away from my ear. I was pretty sure I had him. I tried to think of who I knew on the Knicks squad. At least a third of them probably. I had even introduced a few of them to my other business. I'd call the girl that I ran into at the club the other day first. She was an ex Knicks cheerleader, and I knew she still had a pull with a bunch of the women on the squad. She owed me, so she'd be the perfect person to convince them to do it. This was such a great idea. It would definitely work.

I heard a knock on the front door. That must be Bee.

"Oh fuck." I stared down at the phone in my hand. I had just told John the first thing that had popped into my head. But it wasn't my idea. I had read it in Bee's notebook. I had stolen her fucking idea. "Shit." I slammed my phone down on my desk. She would have understood me stealing Kruger's clients. Hell, she probably would have been thrilled that I'd screwed over her boss. But she wasn't going to understand this. What the hell had I just done?

CHAPTER 58
Bee

I knocked on the door again. Maybe Mason wasn't home yet. We usually shared a taxi home from work, but he knew I was getting off late. He had probably gone out with friends or something.

Home. I smiled to myself. His place did feel like home to me, because he was there. On a scale of one to pre Patrick cheating on me? I laughed to myself. There was no comparison. I was in love with Mason Caldwell. And Kendra was right. I needed to give myself more credit. I knew that Mason felt the same. Living in fear wasn't living. I just needed to tell him how I felt. I needed to tell him I wanted the boyfriend and girlfriend labels.

But not right now. Because he wasn't home. I pulled my phone out of my purse and looked down at the screen to see if he had texted me. There were five missed calls from Kendra. *What the hell?* I quickly pressed on her name and put my phone to my ear.

She answered on the first ring. "Oh. My. God."

"What?"

"Please tell me you're in front of a T.V."

"No. What's going on?"

"Layla's Prediction's escalated a little quickly."

"What do you mean?"

"Their ratings skyrocketed when she started doing the weather nude. Mr. Ellington called and told them he wanted them to take it further."

"Further than what?"

"They had sex on live T.V. It was a freaking porno."

"Who had sex?"

"The random guy whose cock she measured wrong."

"And they kept filming? How could they air..."

"They can air whatever they want. The FCC wasn't going to stop them. There is no FCC."

"Holy shit. And Sword was happy with this?" Geez, I really didn't have any idea what companies wanted. Mr. Ellington was right.

"No. Sword is pissed. Mr. Ellington did it without their permission. You got out just in time. He's losing it over here. He hasn't said it, but I'm pretty sure we lost the account."

I didn't even know what to say.

"You were right, Bee. It was a stupid idea. Mr. Ellington realizes that now. He should have gone with yours. And I know he remembers. Bee, this could be the big break you've been looking for. He's probably going to fire Jenkins over this. You may have just landed an advertising gig!"

"Oh my God. Are you serious?"

"He hasn't said it, but it's sure looking that way."

I leaned against the wall outside of Mason's apartment. "I did it?" I felt like I was in shock.

"You did it! Bee!"

I laughed into the receiver. I had kicked New York's butt. I had found the most amazing guy and had finally landed my dream job. I didn't hate New York anymore. I loved it. "I need to call Mason."

"Yeah, yeah. Go call your boy. But tomorrow after you get your promotion, we're all going out to celebrate. Besides, Marie and I need to get to know your new boyfriend better."

"Deal." I couldn't stop smiling.

"Goodnight, Miss Ad Exec."

"I love the sound of that. Goodnight Miss Ad Exec yourself." I hung up the phone and immediately clicked on Mason's name. There was no one else I'd rather share this news with. I felt like this was everything I had worked so hard on coming to light. *Finally.* I thought all New York did was take. But it was giving. I did have what it took to be here.

The ring on my phone seemed to echo. I pulled my phone away from my ear. Mason's phone was ringing inside his apartment. I heard him curse inside. I knocked on the door again. "Mason?"

A second later the door opened. "Hey, baby. Sorry, I was taking a nap." His hair was mussed up. But it didn't look like it did in the morning after he slept on it. It looked like he had run his hands through it to make it look like he had just woken up.

"Are you feeling okay?"

"Yeah." He crossed his arms in front of his chest. "What's up?"

What's up? I had been spending every night at his place for the past few weeks. What did he think I was doing here? I tried to give him a heartwarming smile. "I heard you were telling people at your office that you had a new girlfriend."

He laughed. "Who told you that?"

"Carter told Marie."

"Yeah? Well, I didn't say that."

"Oh." I bit my lip. What the hell was his problem? I needed to change the subject. "I have really good news." The cheerfulness didn't reach my voice. It sounded more likely a desperate plea for him to invite me in.

"Look, I'm not feeling very well. You should probably just head home. I'll call you tomorrow if I'm feeling better."

Hadn't he just said he was feeling fine a second ago? All the jittery excitement I had while talking to Kendra on the phone had been squashed down. Now I just felt like I wanted to throw up. He was pushing me away. Why was he pushing me away? I shouldn't have brought up the girlfriend thing. Of course he hadn't said that. He hadn't even said that to me. I took a step back. I didn't want him to see how much his words effected me. How him rejecting me was more important than the fact that I was about to get my dream job. I was so pathetic.

"Yeah. Okay. Well, I hope you feel better. Sorry I disturbed you."

"Not a big deal. See ya." Mason put his hand on the door.

I turned around and walked away from his apartment. It felt like he had slapped me. I couldn't even control the stupid angry tears that started to fall down my cheeks. Apparently he was not the one I should be sharing good news with. I wiped my eyes with my palms and silently cursed myself for making a sniffling noise with my nose.

"Bee?"

I didn't turn around. I didn't need this right now. I should be out celebrating with my friends. But instead, there was a panicky feeling rising to my throat. The same feeling I had gotten when I thought Patrick might be cheating on me. The feeling that everything was slipping away. I didn't like someone else having control of my emotions. I pressed the button by the elevator.

"Bee." Mason grabbed my wrist.

I quickly wiped my tears away and pulled my wrist out of his grip. "It's fine, Mason," I said without turning to look at him. "You want me to go, so I'm going."

"Hey." He pulled me against his chest. "I'm sorry." He ran his fingers through my hair. "I get cranky after I wake up from naps. I'm sorry."

His heart was beating so fast and I could feel the heat radiating off of him through his clothes. Maybe he was sick. And there was something really comforting about his reaction to my getting upset. He just stood there with his arms around me and didn't say anything about the wet spot my tears were leaving on his dress shirt. I'm sure he would want me to leave as soon as he saw my scary red monster eyes.

"It's okay. I'm just being silly. Go get some rest." I pushed on his chest, but he didn't release me from his hug.

"I want you to stay."

"Mason..."

"Please don't go." There was something strange in his voice. It made it seem like if I left he was scared he'd lose me forever. I breathed in his heavenly scent. I never wanted to be anywhere except for next to him. How did he not realize that?

"Geez, I don't know why I'm so emotional. I just had a really bad day at work. We had to watch Jenkins' stupid idea for this sponsorship. And my disgusting boss doesn't take me seriously at all."

"I thought you had good news?" Mason pulled back and looked down at me.

"Yeah." I reluctantly let go of his biceps. "Well, maybe. Apparently Jenkins' idea went terribly wrong..."

"The sex on live T.V. thing? Sword Body Wash is really pissed."

"How do you know about that?"

He lowered his eyebrows for a second but then laughed. "It was all over the news. And I'm friends with Jenkins. He told me about the account."

"You're actually friends with him?"

Mason cleared his throat. "Acquaintances, really. Anyway, back to your news?" He ran his hand through his hair.

"Kendra just called me. She thinks my boss is going to fire Jenkins. Which means there will be an ad exec position open. I just need to remind my boss that I actually had a good idea for the Sword account. I think I'm going to get a promotion." My angry tears were replaced by an over the top excited smile.

"Oh."

"Oh? Mason this is huge. It's everything I've ever wanted."

He smiled. "I thought I was everything you ever wanted?"

"You know what I mean."

"Well, you shouldn't get your hopes up. You don't know for sure."

"I was kind of hoping you'd want to celebrate."

"Doesn't that seem premature? I mean, you never know..."

"Mason!" I put my hands on both sides of his face. "I'm getting a promotion! I won't have to be a secretary for an asshole anymore. I'll be able to give money to homeless people again!"

"Wait, what? You shouldn't be giving money to homeless people, Bee. They just buy drugs and booze. If you want to give them something you should just give them food."

"They're hungry and cold. They'll use the money I give them for food and warmer clothes."

Mason laughed. "You're so naive. You really don't belong in the city." There was a playful twinkle in his eyes.

"Yes I do." I poked him in the middle of his chest. "I'm going to have a good job, a good salary, and the man of my dreams. I'm killing it in this city. I'm owning New York."

"The man of your dreams?" His normally charming smile suddenly seemed wicked and seductive.

"Yeah. The man of my dreams."

"Well, maybe we should celebrate by making all your dreams come true." He raised his eyebrow at me.

"I was hoping you'd say that."

He leaned down and placed a soft kiss against my lips. His fingers ran down my back, stopping at the arch as he pulled me against him. And in an instant I knew that we were okay. All the tension seemed to evaporate when his tongue parted my lips and a low moan escaped from his. He really was the man of my dreams. My naughty, sinful dreams.

CHAPTER 59
Bee

As I stepped off the elevator, Jenkins stepped on with a box full of his personal belongings.

"Jenkins, I'm sor..."

"Save it, Bridget. You didn't like the idea anyway. Not that what happened was my fault. That piece of shit is throwing the blame on me. He was the one that made the call. He's the one that should get the can, not me. That old son of a bitch. I'll show him."

"I hope you do."

Jenkins laughed. "Later, Bridget." The elevator doors closed behind him.

I meant what I said. I didn't get along with Jenkins, but I was sorry that he had gotten fired. This whole mess was Mr. Ellington's fault. Jenkins shouldn't have been the one to take the blame. But at the same time, there was a little pep in my step. Because his job was going to be mine. And if I needed to remind Mr. Ellington I had what it took, I had a whole speech prepared.

I pulled my coat off and laid it across the back of my chair. I rubbed my hands together to help warm them. Mr. Ellington's office door was closed. I wasn't sure when the best time to talk to him would be. Maybe first thing. But he had just fired Jenkins. Maybe he was in a firing kind of mood.

My thought process was disturbed when something lightly touched my shoulder, making me jump.

Kendra laughed. "Geez, a little amped up, huh?"

"Yeah. I was just trying to decide if I should go talk to him. I saw Jenkins on the way out."

"You missed the show. He threw a stapler at Mr. Ellington's head. It was hilarious."

"Really? Wow, I can't picture Jenkins doing that at all."

"People do crazy stuff when they get fired."

"They do." I pulled my chair out and sat down.

"What are you doing? Aren't you going to go talk to him?"

"I think maybe I should wait till a little later. He might be in a bad mood if he just got hit with a stapler."

"He dodged it."

"Still." I shrugged my shoulders. I could feel myself wimping out.

"Don't give him more time to find a replacement for Jenkins. Show him it's you. No, tell him it's you. Bring back Kick Ass Bee for a few minutes."

"Okay." My heart was starting to beat really fast. I was so nervous. "You're right." I stood up from my chair. "I'll do it now."

"Attagirl."

I smoothed down my skirt before knocking on Mr. Ellington's door. *You got this, Bee.*

"Come in," Mr. Ellington's gruff voice sounded through the door.

I took a deep breath and opened up the door. "Can I speak to you for a second?"

He gestured for me to come into the room. "Close the door behind you, Bridget."

It always made me nervous when I was alone with him. I wasn't sure if it was because he was my boss or because of how his eyes always seemed to travel down my whole body.

"What can I do for you?" he asked, not looking up from his desk.

Crap. He was in a bad mood. I knew I should have waited. I cleared my throat. "Is this a good time, Mr. Ellington?"

He sighed and looked up at me. "It's Joe, Bridget. Please just call me Joe."

"Sorry. Joe," I said. His name sounded weird coming out of my mouth. But I'd rather start the meeting off on a good tone.

He smiled. "Take a seat."

As I sat down, he stood up. He walked over to the side of the desk I was on and sat down on it, so that he was staring down at me. It seemed like a friendly thing to do, but I couldn't shake the feeling that he had done it so he could stare down my shirt. I leaned back slightly.

"So, Bridget. What can I do for you?"

"Well, I heard that there was a new ad exec job opening."

Mr. Ellington laughed. "I'm pretty sure everyone heard that when Jenkins was yelling at me."

I smiled. "Right. Well, I've been thinking a lot about my position here..."

"Your position?" He raised his left eyebrow. "You mean, directly beneath me?"

"Umm...yes. About that..."

He held up his hand. "I know what this is about."

"You do?"

"I do. We had discussed you getting a promotion a few weeks ago. And you never came in for a follow up discussion."

When he had mentioned a promotion before he had made it seem dirty. Like he wanted me to start giving him hand jobs under his desk or something. That was why I had never followed up. But maybe I had it all wrong. Maybe he had been planning on giving me an advertising job the whole time. Maybe he actually liked my idea.

"Exactly," I said. "I was hoping we could discuss that a little more."

"What did you want your promotion to entail?"

"Well, do you remember my idea from a few weeks ago? For Sword Body Wash. Partnering with the Knicks cheerleaders..."

Mr. Ellington swiped his hand through the air. "Jenkins lost us that account. But your idea wasn't a good fit for the brand anyway. We've already discussed that."

I wasn't expecting him to say that. "Okay, well, I know that the only thing that a company cares about is making money." I regurgitated what he had said at our other meeting back to him. And it felt like I was regurgitating it for real, because it wasn't true. Sword Body Wash cared about their image and their brand. But that wasn't what Mr. Ellington wanted to hear. He wanted to hear that he was right. And I really wanted this promotion.

"Exactly, Bridget. Which means we always have to give our clients the very best. Experience means everything to our clients. Experience which you do not have."

Shit. "I have a lot of other ideas, though. Maybe we could go through them?"

"This wasn't exactly the direction I thought you'd want to go," he said.

"What direction did you see me going?"

"South. Definitely south." His eyes wandered down my body in that way that chilled me to the bone.

"Mr. Ellington..."

"Personal assistant."

"What?"

He laughed. "I want to promote you to my personal assistant."

"Oh." My heart was beating out of my chest. Maybe all of this was in my head. He was actually trying to give me a normal promotion. It was just one that I wasn't interested in.

"I was hoping you'd be a little more excited."

"No. I am. But, Mr. Ellington..."

"If you're going to be my personal assistant, I think we need to get on a more personal level, don't you?" He stood up, clearly not wanting me to respond. He put his hand on my shoulder. "First, you need to start calling me Joe."

I felt frozen in place. I wanted to push his hand off my shoulder. I wanted to tell him to stop looking at me in that disgusting way. But I couldn't seem to find the words. I just sat there staring at him.

"You're beautiful, Bridget. You do know that, right? That's why you've been teasing me for months?" His hand moved to my neck and his fingers grabbed the collar of my shirt, pulling it down slightly. He ran his thumb along my collarbone. His hands felt clammy against my skin. "So let's get a little more personal. How about you put those lips of yours to good use. I could really use a pick me up after the morning I've been having."

He unbuttoned the top button of his suit pants with his other hand. "And maybe you can work up to that ad exec position you so badly want. After I get what I want. Which is trying out every position with you." He unzipped his pants.

"Mr. Ellington..." My voice finally kicked in again. But it sounded so weak. It was more of a whisper.

"Joe. My name is Joe. It's okay, Bridget. I know you're nervous. I know how badly you want this promotion. How about you get on your knees and show me you have what it takes."

Oh, hell no. I finally willed my body to move and I elbowed him right in the groin. Luckily he still had his boxers on so I didn't have to feel his surely small dick against my arm.

"Fuck!" He yelled and took a step back, grabbing his crotch.

I stood up and pointed my finger at him. "I will never, ever get on my knees for a promotion. I am not a hooker." The thought of Mason working with those women popped into my head. But it was quickly squashed down when Mr. Ellington spoke.

"You bitch!" His eyes bulged slightly. They finally weren't looking at me in that creepy way. "You're fired," he spat out.

"What?"

"If I had known how prude you were, I wouldn't have hired you in the first place."

"I thought you hired me because of my degree? Because you thought I might have a place at this ad agency. That's what we talked about when you hired me. That's why I took this job in the first place."

He laughed. "Welcome to New York, honey. Now get the hell out of my office."

I wanted to say something clever, but the look on his face was enough. Elbowing his junk was more satisfying than anything I could say. I turned around and walked out of his office with my head held high.

As soon as I stepped out of the office, my confidence waivered. The people in the cubicles near Mr. Ellington's office were staring at me. They had probably heard us yelling at each other. Kendra would be over any second, wondering if I got the promotion.

I quickly pulled open my drawers and grabbed all their contents. I didn't have that much in my desk that was actually mine. Most of it belonged to Kruger Advertising. I pulled open the last drawer. There was a picture frame facing downward in it. I had completely forgotten that it was even there. I picked it up and turned it over. It was the first picture that Patrick and I had of us together. We were sitting on a couch in his frat house. His arm was wrapped around my shoulders. I looked so happy. If I closed my eyes I could picture this moment like it was yesterday. We had just had our first kiss. I looked happy in the picture because I was happy, happier than I had ever been. I was so in love with him. Looking at the picture a month ago would have made my chest tighten. But it didn't now. The city had changed him, but it had changed me too. I ran my finger across Patrick's smiling face. It seemed like a distant memory.

I put the picture back into the drawer and closed it. I didn't need it anymore. I had lost that feeling when I had lost him. It had just taken me a long time to realize it. I shoved my pens, notebook, and few pictures that still lined my desk into my purse. I had just lost my job, but I didn't have a whole box like Jenkins because I never belonged here in the first place. I grabbed the vase of flowers with the dozen roses that Mason had sent me.

I thought that all New York did was take. It took Patrick from me. It took my self confidence. It took all my money. But now I loved this stupid city, because if I hadn't moved here, I never would have met Mason. The city had taken a lot, but it had given me more. Mason was the reason that the picture of Patrick no longer bothered me. I wasn't in love with Patrick anymore. I was in love with Mason.

I'm in love with Mason Caldwell.

I pressed the elevator button. I needed to tell him.

"Bee!" Kendra was slightly out of breath as she ran up to me. She looked at the flowers in my arm and then back at my face. "What happened?"

"I got fired."

"Seriously? Why?"

"Because I wouldn't suck his dick."

Kendra laughed. "Wait." She grabbed my arm. "He didn't actually ask you to do that?"

"In those words? No. But he undid his pants and told me to get on my knees."

"Holy shit. Bee, you have to tell someone."

"Who? My boss?"

"I don't know. Someone on the board maybe? There's people above him. He didn't start this company. It's sexual harassment. You could win that lawsuit."

"I really just want to put it behind me. I'm going to find something better."

"Anything is better than that. But what are you going to do? You couldn't afford your rent as it was."

For the first time, I realized what losing my job actually meant. I didn't have any money. It was possible that my bank account was at zero. I had student loans. And my rent was past due. I hadn't been to my place in so long I had completely forgotten to pay Naomi. "I..." my voice trailed off. "I don't know. I just felt so good about elbowing him in the groin that I hadn't really processed what was happening. I just lost my job."

"You elbowed his dick?" Kendra started laughing.

"And now I'm going to be homeless."

"You're not homeless. You can come stay with me."

"But I can't afford half the..."

"I was paying it by myself anyway. Just until you get another job. Then you can pay half." She smiled at me. "You didn't think I was going to let you run back to Wilmington, did you? You belong here."

Several weeks ago I would have fought with her about that. But she was right. This is where I belonged. At least, this is where I needed to be right now. "Are you sure?"

"Of course I'm sure. I've been begging you to come live with me for months. Now you have no choice."

I laughed and gave her a big hug. "Thanks, Kendra. You're the best."

"I'm glad you're not pissed at me. I'm sorry if I got your hopes up. I really thought that position would be yours."

"Me too. It's not your fault. You're still the best."

She laughed. "I can't wait to shove that in Marie's face. She won't stop talking about how awesome she is since things have been going so well between you and Mason."

I released Kendra from my hug. "About that. When is it too soon to tell someone that you love them?"

Kendra smiled. "Wait for him to do that first."

"Okay. But what if..."

"Trust me, Bee. Let him say it first. If you're feeling that way, I'm sure he is too."

The elevator doors dinged open and I stepped on. Her words didn't really deter me. Mason had already told me he loved me. Right back there on my desk. I smiled to myself and stepped onto the elevator.

"Should I come over tonight to help you get your stuff?" Kendra asked.

"It's okay. I'm going to ask Mason to help me."

"Of course you are. See you later, roomie."

I smiled as the elevator doors closed.

***

I pulled out the last box that was in the corner of my closet. I lifted off the lid. It was filled with things that Patrick had left here. Including his worn University of New Castle t-shirt that I always used to sleep in. After I had kicked him out I had slept in it until his scent had completely disappeared. There was a scrapbook at the bottom of the box that I had made him, which led up to a photo that his friend had snapped of his proposal. I didn't open it. He had left a few CDs and movies here when he had moved out. Things that we had listened to or watched together. I was pretty sure he had done it to torture me. I had sat in that same shirt crying, watching Fight Club. Which was ridiculous.

I'd just throw the box away. I was done thinking about Patrick. I didn't even feel sad about leaving the apartment. Moving in with Kendra would be a fresh start. I could officially leave the past in the past. Coming back to this apartment while I was dating Mason had felt strange anyway. Like I was holding on to something. I was ready to let go. I put the lid back on top of the box.

Shit. Patrick still had a key. And I couldn't afford to pay the replacement fee. I pulled out my phone and quickly texted him.

"I'm moving out of our old place today. I need your key. And I have some stuff you left here. Could you stop by after work?" I pressed the send button.

I already knew what his response would be. He had to work late and wouldn't be able to come. That was always what he responded back to me when we were together. And he'd wait awhile to respond. He wouldn't want me to think he didn't have anything better to do than text me. Which was stupid. Because everyone always had their phones on them. I almost jumped when my phone vibrated right away.

"I'm on a lunch break. Can I come now?"

So maybe that was just the way he acted when I cared if I got a response. "Yeah. I'm packing now. See you soon." I put my phone back down on the floor.

The last time I had been alone with Patrick was right here in this apartment. I had thrown my engagement ring at him. I ran my thumb along the spot where the ring had once been. I had spent five years of my life loving him. It was weird for that to suddenly mean so little.

I stood up and grabbed the wedding dress from the closet. It was the last thing hanging there. Patrick had never seen it. And he never would. I opened up the lid of the box labeled "donate" and put the dress inside. I never even tried it on after I got it. I quickly put the lid back on the box.

I wasn't in love with Patrick anymore. But that dress still made me want to cry. A wedding dress is full of hope. This one should have been black and ragged. It only symbolized our end. And I couldn't wait to drop if off at Goodwill.

There was a scraping sound in the lock on my door. Patrick was just letting himself in without knocking, like he belonged here, like he still belonged in my life despite everything that had happened. The door opened and he looked down at me. He gave me a small smile and leaned against the door frame.

"Hey." I stood up and pointed down at the box filled with his stuff. "While I was packing I found some of your stuff if you want it. And I'll take that key."

"You got it," he said and tossed the key to me. I caught it in my hand. It was strange that I had never asked for it back. I kept hoping we'd be able to work it out. Asking for his key back seemed so final.

"I'm glad you still had it." I realized now that it was stupid for me to ask for it. It would have only cost a few dollars to get a copy made. Maybe a small part of me just wanted him to know that I was moving on too. That I was finally ready to let go.

"It was still on my keychain," he said.

"Why?"

He shrugged. "What made you decide to move?" He looked around the small room. "So many memories."

"It was just time to move on."

"Are you moving in with Mason?"

"It's none of your business."

"Bee." He said my name in that way that made me always confess all my worries to him. And what did it matter if he knew my reason for moving?

"I'm moving in with Kendra."

"Why?"

"I need to save money. I got fired today."

He stopped leaning against the door frame and walked into the room. He sat down on the end of the bed we used to share. "If you need money..."

"No. That's okay, Patrick."

He locked eyes with me. "I still care about you."

"I know." I wasn't angry anymore.

He put his elbows on his knees and leaned forward slightly. "So, what's in that box? I thought I got everything."

"You left some CDs and stuff like that."

"Right." He pulled the lid off the box and picked up the worn t-shirt. "I thought you loved this?" He smiled at me.

"I did."

"I want you to have it." He held it out to me.

"It's yours."

He brought it back down to his lap. "I'm not sure I ever remember you sleeping in anything else. Well, except when you didn't wear anything."

"I'm giving it back."

He looked down at the rest of the contents in the box, sifting through the DVDs and CDs. He pulled out the scrapbook I had made him and opened up to a random page. "I wanted you to have all this stuff. I left it here on purpose." He turned the page.

"It's yours. I made that for you. Everything in that box is yours. If you leave it here I'm just going to donate it."

"I'm not sure anyone's going to buy this scrapbook." He gave me a small smile.

"Especially if you don't even want it. I'll just throw it out."

"I want it." He closed it and tucked it under his arm. "And I want you to have this." He held the shirt out again."

I didn't want to fight with him. I reached out and grabbed it. Just having it on his lap for a second made it smell like him again.

"I'm sorry, Bee. I know you won't accept my apology, but I am. I'm so, so sorry."

I looked up at his face. He never looked so sincere. "I know. I'm sorry too."

He moved off the bed and sat next to me on the floor. "I wanted to call you after you gave the ring back. Every night. But I didn't know what to say. I knew that I broke your heart. That was the hardest part. Knowing that I hurt you. No excuse could fix that. But I am sorry. I fucked up."

"And what about you? Did us ending things break your heart?"

"You know it did. You were my first love, Bee. And I still love you. I think I always will."

I'd always love him too. But I wasn't in love with him anymore. That was the difference.

"Before moving here, I was terrified of losing you. It's funny that bringing you here was what tore us apart."

"You can't blame the city for that." I knew it was ironic. I had been blaming New York for everything that happened to me. But I knew how ridiculous that was. It was easy to put the blame on anything but myself.

He shrugged. "Yeah. I guess. Honestly, what it comes down to is that I thought I was ready to get married. I wasn't."

"You could have talked to me about it."

"I know. I just didn't want to lose you."

I didn't know what to say to him. So I just looked back down at the shirt in my hands.

"Are you still with him?"

I looked back up at Patrick. "Yes."

"He's bad news, Bee. I don't ever want you to feel what I made you feel again. And I know you're not willing to give me a second chance. I get that. I'm not trying to win you back here. But I care about you. You shouldn't be dating a guy like Mason."

"You don't really know him."

"No, I think you don't. He's a player and a cheat. He does whatever it takes to get ahead. He's not a good guy."

"You're wrong."

"He's cutthroat."

"Last time I saw you, you said that guys like him didn't date girls like me. Like I didn't deserve him."

"I meant that you're a good girl and he's a dick."

"I can take care of myself."

"I know you can. I'm just..."

"Worried that someone else will break my heart?"

He sighed and pulled out the DVD of Fight Club from the box. "You can donate all this stuff if you want. I can't watch this without thinking of you. You've ruined my favorite movie for me." He laughed and lifted the lid of the donation box before I could stop him.

My wedding dress was sitting on top. Patrick didn't say anything. Instead, he ran his hand down the lacy fabric and stared at it. I grabbed the lid to put it back on, but he pushed it away.

"You would have looked beautiful in this." He looked over at me. "I didn't know that you had bought a dress."

"What, did you expect me to wear, jean shorts and a tank top?"

He smiled. "I guess not." He moved his hand off the dress. "You're giving it away?"

"What else would I do with a wedding dress?"

"I'm sorry."

"You don't have to apologize anymore. You were right. I didn't pay enough attention to you. I was always beat from work. I blamed you, but it was my fault too. I never said I was sorry. But I am. I'm sorry too."

"I took you for granted."

"I let you."

He nodded and put his hand on my knee. "Whenever you walk down the aisle, make sure it's a guy that's worth it. Someone better than me. You deserve the best, Bee." He didn't say it, but he meant a guy that wasn't Mason.

"Thanks, Patrick."

He stood up and put his hand out for me. I grabbed it and he pulled me to my feet. He pulled my against his chest and wrapped his arms around me. I breathed in his familiar scent. His hug was comforting. I finally felt at peace with what had happened between us. I thought I had gotten all the closure I needed at the gala. But apologizing to him was what I had really needed.

"Losing you is the biggest regret of my life." He lightly kissed my forehead. "If you ever decide you're willing to give me a second chance, I still want it."

I took a deep breath, letting the scent of him linger around me for a second longer. I knew what he had just said, but I think we both knew this was the last time we were ever going to be together. I let go of his back and he released me from his hug.

"I still have your number." I smiled at him.

He grabbed the scrapbook off the bed and walked over to the door. I thought he was going to leave without looking back, but he turned around before closing the door. "And my shirt."

I hadn't realized it, but I was still holding it in my hand.

"Bye, Bee."

"Bye, Patrick."

Tears prickled my eyes when he closed the door. I took a deep breath. That was it. We were done. I tossed his shirt down on my bed. That was the only thing I'd keep. Because it was more than just a memory of him. It had been there for me when he hadn't been.

CHAPTER 60
Mason

I placed the last box in the truck I had rented and pulled down the door, locking it in place. I thought Bee would be devastated when she got fired. Especially since she thought she was going to get a promotion. And I had let her believe she was getting it when I knew the company she worked for was folding. It felt like our relationship was a ticking time bomb that was quickly approaching zero. Me stealing clients from her former company wasn't a big deal. I wasn't sure why I ever thought that it would be. She'd probably be happy to screw over her pervert of a boss. She hadn't told me exactly what happened today, but she hadn't mentioned anything about Kruger going bankrupt. It seemed like her boss had tried to pull something on her. And it made my blood boil. I wanted to beat the shit out of him.

I shook my head. Like I could protect her? I was the one that had screwed her over. I had stolen her advertising idea for Sword Body Wash. Which in itself didn't matter. Except that I got the account. John Landry had called me this afternoon and said that they liked my pitch the best. *Bee's pitch*. She had lost her job and I had just gotten enough money to keep my apartment without my dad's help. She was going to hate me.

It was like I could hear the clock ticking down to our demise. I should just tell her right away and apologize. It was an accident. I just said the first thing that popped in my head. But I had read her notebook without her permission. I ran my hand down my face. *Fuck.* I couldn't talk my way out of this one. I had already gone over every possibility in my head. Each choice ended up with her leaving. And she couldn't leave.

"Done!" she said.

I almost jumped. I hadn't seen her walk out of her apartment building. "You turned in the keys?"

"Yup. I'm officially homeless." She laughed. "Maybe I should make a sign and join all the homeless people who I gave tons of money to."

I laughed. "You're adorable." I wrapped my arms around her. I didn't want to let go. I wanted to hold her like this, with her smiling and happy, forever. *Forever.* I felt the tightness in my chest. We only had a little time left.

"I do have one more favor to ask," she said and pulled back. "On the way to Kendra's can we stop by Goodwill? I have some stuff to drop off."

"Sure." I reluctantly let go of her. I watched her climb to the passenger's side of the truck, leap onto the step, and slide into the seat.

I just needed to keep thinking. There had to be a way where she ended up with me. There had to be. I walked around the truck and climbed into the driver's seat. I put the key into the ignition, brining the truck to life. "What are you giving away?"

"Just some things I don't need anymore." She smiled at me.

"Do you want to tell me what really happened today? You said that you had a disagreement with your boss?"

"It's not a big deal. I didn't want that job anyway. Like you said, most ad executives don't start out as secretaries. I was approaching the whole thing wrong."

I gripped my hands on the wheel. "What did that asshole do?"

"Mason?" She lightly touched my arm. "Are you okay? You've seemed a little on edge tonight. Are you still not feeling well?"

"I'm fine." I was never sick. I just couldn't face her last night. But when I had made her cry it felt like a part of me was hurt. I never wanted to see her upset. *Then I shouldn't have stolen her idea. Fuck!* I gripped the wheel even tighter.

"I really appreciate you helping me move."

I nodded. Of course I was going to help her move. I'd do anything for her. My grip eased on the wheel a bit. That was it. I'd tell her it was time to make things official. Maybe that would make telling her the truth better? I knew she wanted me to be her boyfriend. Isn't that what every girl wanted? To take the next step? I wanted that too.

"You can turn in here," Bee said and pointed to the Goodwill on the corner.

I hit the turn signal and pulled into the donations drop off section.

"I'll grab it. You can just stay in the car."

"All the boxes are heavy. I'll get it." I turned off the car and hopped out onto the pavement.

I heard Bee's door shut and she appeared next to me as I unlocked the door and lifted it up. I picked up the box marked "donations." It was one of the heaviest ones.

"Really, Mason, I can get that." She put her arms out.

I laughed. "Lead the way."

She pressed her lips together and then turned away from me. We walked together toward the drop off door. She opened it for me. As soon as we were inside she rushed past me and started talking to the person standing there.

"Okay, we just have to look through it to give you a tax credit," the lady said.

"Oh, no need," Bee replied. "It's just a bunch of junk."

The lady made a funny face.

"I mean, not junk. It's nice stuff. CDs, DVDs, and some old clothes. Someone will definitely want to buy it. But it's just stuff. Nothing valuable or anything. Just give me the smallest tax credit possible."

Why was she being so weird? I set the box down. We weren't in any rush.

"Nonsense," the lady said. She walked over to the box and opened up the lid. "Wow," the woman said and pulled out a wedding dress.

Is that why Bee was acting strangely? Did she not want me to see the dress? I knew she was engaged. Maybe a small part of me didn't realize how far she had almost made it down the aisle with that ass of an ex of hers. But it didn't matter. She was mine now. At least for as long as she didn't know about what I had done.

The thought I had earlier returned to me, about making things between us official. Bee was the commitment type. Patrick had been her only other boyfriend. If I told her I wanted to make it official, was I basically asking her to marry me? I thought I'd want to run. But I didn't. Maybe I was just desperately clinging on to anything I could think of. Maybe I was losing my mind. Or maybe that was what I wanted. A white picket fence, two kids, and a smoking hot wife? That didn't sound so bad to me. Actually, it sounded kind of perfect. I peeled my eyes away from the dress and looked at her.

She looked embarrassed. No, she looked sad. And it wrenched my gut. I wanted to make her happy. I'd do anything to make her happy.

"How much did this cost?" the woman said and turned to her.

Bee shrugged.

The woman looked back and forth between us. "Oh, I see. Your husband didn't know you were parting with your dress? That's very sweet. You should resell this, though, not give it away. You can make a pretty penny."

Bee didn't say anything to correct the woman about her assumption between us. "That's okay, it's not about the money."

Husband and wife? Now that someone had said it out loud it didn't sound nearly as appealing. I wasn't ready for that. One day maybe. And maybe it would be with Bee. I wasn't ready yet, though. I couldn't have kids. And I didn't want a picket fence. I loved living in New York.

"If that's what you want." The woman wrote something down and handed the paper to Bee. "Definitely worth more than the smallest tax credit. Someone will get good use out of this."

"I hope so." Bee walked past me and out the door back into the cold.

"She must have looked beautiful in this," the woman said to me.

"Yeah." I quickly followed Bee. She was already getting into the truck.

I didn't say anything as I climbed into the driver's seat and started it back up. I pulled out of the parking lot and back onto the busy streets of the city.

"I'm sorry about that," Bee finally said. "I was just trying to get rid of it."

"It's okay. I get it."

She turned toward me. "Mason?"

"Yeah?" For some reason the way she had said my name made my heart beat faster. Had she already found out what I had done?

"I really like you."

I sighed with relief. "I really like you too." Instead of following the GPS, I continued going straight. I knew exactly what I wanted to do.

"Kendra's place is that way," Bee said.

I ignored her. I felt awful about stealing her idea. But I didn't feel awful about getting the Sword Body Wash account and jump starting my ad agency. It was hard not to tell her about it. I wanted to share my good news with her. But I couldn't. Not yet. The least I could do for now was share that success with her.

"Mason?"

"I think you should move in with me," I blurted out before I could change my mind.

"You want me to move in with you?"

"It feels like you already have." I smiled at her. "I'm not sure when the last time was that we didn't fall asleep together."

"It's still a big step," she said.

"It's one that I want to make with you."

"I don't want you to ask me just because I lost my job and you feel sorry for me."

"I don't feel sorry for you." I pulled up in front of my apartment and cut the engine. I reached over and grabbed her hand. "I like falling asleep with you and waking up next to you. I'm asking you because I'm greedy. I can't get enough of you." I ran my thumb along her knuckles and over the tan line on her ring finger. She nervously touched that spot all the time. Like there was something there that nothing else could fill. She probably didn't even realize she was doing it. But it broke my heart a little every time I saw her do it.

I felt guilty about what I had done. But everything else I said was true too. I wanted to fill that spot on her finger. Not with a ring. Not yet, anyway. I wanted to be enough for her. Just me. Because she was enough for me.

She looked up at me. "I can't get enough of you either."

"So is that a yes?"

"Of course it's a yes!" She unbuckled her seatbelt and moved onto my lap. She grabbed both sides of my face and kissed me.

I thought I had already felt guilty. But the way she was kissing me? I was going straight to hell.

CHAPTER 61
Bee

I love you. Why can't I seem to make the words come out of my mouth? It was a stupid question to ask myself. I knew why. Because I was scared of getting hurt again.

My head was nestled in the crook of his arms and I was tracing my index finger along the contours of his six pack. It was okay to be vulnerable sometimes. Loving him could end in heartbreak, but it could also lead to something wonderful. I didn't want to be a cat lady. I didn't want to be scared to put myself out there just because of what might happen. Mason had asked me to move in with him. Clearly he was just as vulnerable as me. And I wanted him to know how I felt. He needed to know.

"You said you wanted to be the reason why I stayed in New York," I said.

He ran his fingers through my hair. "I remember."

"Well, you are."

He laughed. "I didn't mean I wanted you to lose your job."

"I know." I moved so that my forearm was on his chest. I rested my chin against my arm and looked up into his dark brown eyes. *I love you.* I wondered if he could tell what I was thinking. "Are you going to try to fix things with your parents?" I could feel his chest tense beneath my arm.

"What does it matter?"

"I just don't see how you could not be speaking to them."

"You don't really speak to your Dad," he said.

I swallowed hard and dropped his gaze. "That's not really my choice. It's his."

"I know. I'm sorry." He ran his fingers through my hair again, but his chest remained tense.

"Whatever disagreement you had couldn't be enough to make you lose a relationship with them."

"I told you. We had different ideas of what my future looked like. Which is important to me. And I thought it might be important to you too."

A future with Mason? That's what I wanted. But his broken relationship with his parents was the last thing nagging at me. I wanted a relationship with my dad. But he walked out on me and my mom. He didn't want to be a part of my life. Mason's parents cared so much about him that they wanted him to have a secure, happy life. My dad didn't give a shit about what happened to me. Mason didn't even realize what he was giving up.

I shifted off his chest and sat up. "I want a future with you."

He stared back at me. "But?"

"What was the fight about exactly?"

"My dad wants me to take over the family business. MAC International isn't for me, though. I hate finance. And I told him that. But he doesn't care. He doesn't care about my happiness. I want to be in advertising. He thought I couldn't do it without his money but..." Mason's voice trailed off. He sat up and put his hand on the side of my face. "Advertising makes me happy. *You* make me happy. I don't need them."

"They're your parents, Mason. It's not about needing them. It's about the love that you share. They're your family."

He frowned. "My dad doesn't care about my happiness."

"I'm sure that isn't true. He's probably worried about the company he started. He doesn't want it to fall apart when he retires. And he probably wants to know that you and the company will be secure when he's not there. He's trying to take care of you. And maybe, just maybe, he's as stubborn as you."

Mason sighed. "You don't even know him."

"But I want to."

"You want to meet my parents?"

"We're living together. Isn't that kind of part of the package?"

"Trust me, you don't want to meet them."

I bit my lip. I did want to meet them. "I was thinking about Penny and..."

"Oh." Mason ran his hand through his hair. "This isn't like that, Bee. I'm sure my parents would want to meet you. They'll be thrilled that I have a girlfriend. I mean they want me to end up with some rich snob probably, but they definitely disapproved of the way I have been living. Before I met you, I mean. Like the clubs and stuff. They'll be relieved that you're sweet and beautiful and smart and that I'm not paying you." He pressed his lips together, clearly hoping that I had somehow missed the fact that he had called me his girlfriend.

"Girlfriend?"

"Yeah." He put his hand on the small of my back and pulled me on top of him. "I did tell Carter that you were my girlfriend the other day. It just slipped out. I know we haven't really talked about that, but..."

"I like the sound of that."

"You do?"

"I do." I placed a kiss against his lips.

He grabbed the back of my head, deepening the kiss. It didn't matter what was going on with his parents. He had asked me to move in with him. He had asked me to be his girlfriend. I was on the top of the world. And maybe I'd be able to help him work out his problems with his parents. I wanted him to be happy. Something had been bothering him the past few days. The way he reacted to me bringing his parents up made it seem like that was the problem. He'd given up his nightlife for me. He'd given up his bachelor pad. I wasn't going to nag him about this. They'd work it out. And I'd be there for him if he needed me. I wanted to be his rock. Because somewhere along the past month he had become mine.

His hand drifted to my ass.

I laughed as he rolled on top of me, pinning my hands to the mattress.

"Your way or my way?" he asked.

"Your way." I had given him my heart. Tonight I would surrender my body to him. Not that I didn't want to. I wanted to give him every piece of me. And I loved everything he did to me because I loved him. *I love you,*

Mason Caldwell. Hopefully I'd find the courage to tell him soon.

***

When I woke up the bed was empty beside me. There were small red marks around my wrists where the handcuffs had been. Just thinking about last night made me blush. I quickly climbed out of bed. I didn't have anywhere to go today, but Mason did. And I wanted to make him breakfast. I didn't want him to think I was mooching off of him. I'd start looking for a job this morning too. If I had to find a menial job while looking for the perfect fit I would. I had worked as a waitress during college. I could do that again. But this time I was going to hold out on an advertising job as the next full time position I accepted. No more bullshit stepping stones. And no more bosses like Mr. Ellington.

I opened up the top drawer of Mason's bureau. I hadn't unpacked anything yet, but he had cleared this spot for me awhile ago when I started spending the night so much. I pulled on a clean pair of jeans and a tank top. One of the best things about Mason's apartment, aside from him being in it, was that it wasn't freezing cold. I would have had to wear two hoodies in my apartment to be this warm in the morning.

Today I was going to tell Mason that I loved him. I wasn't going to wuss out like I had last night. I didn't know very much about Mason's dating history. Kendra had said he hadn't had a girlfriend since high school. But that was information she found on Facebook. It wasn't necessarily true. I had only ever told Patrick that I had loved him. And I was nervous that Mason wouldn't say it back. Maybe he had never said it to anyone before. Maybe I'd be his first. I laughed at the phrase. I definitely wasn't Mason's first anything. It would be better if I hoped to be his last.

I walked out into the hallway. I froze when I heard Mason's voice.

"I'll get in touch with my contact on the cheerleading squad today," he said. His office door was open. I knew I shouldn't eavesdrop, but he had gotten my attention. Was he talking about the woman from that club he took me to? The ex cheerleader who had tried to give him a blowjob right in front of me? The memory made my stomach churn. He told me he had given all that up. I thought about how she had touched the belt on his waist. I had never been a jealous person. I guess it had started after Patrick had cheated on me. It was hard for me to trust anyone. But I trusted Mason. For some reason, my feet didn't agree with my mind, because I had inched closer to Mason's office door.

"We won't need a permit for Central Park," Mason said. "The Knicks already have it. Besides, we'll be using cell phone cameras and keeping it really simple. The best part is that no one will ever really know whether it was staged or not."

Silence. My heart was beating fast. *The Knicks cheerleaders?* This wasn't about him hooking up with that girl from that club. He was talking about an ad idea. *My* ad idea. Had I told him about that? I knew I told him I was upset that Jenkins pitch had gotten chosen. But I never told him about my pitch. I definitely hadn't.

"I already have the actor. I'll call you later with an update, John. We should be good for next week, though."

John Landry? From Sword Body Wash? My whole body felt cold. Mr. Ellington had said we lost the account. Had Mason stolen it? With my idea? How the hell did he know my idea? I leaned against the wall. My coworkers had heard it. Mason was friends with Jenkins. Maybe...oh my god. I tiptoed away from his office and into the kitchen. I grabbed my purse off the counter and pulled my notebook out of it. I flipped through it until I came to the torn out page.

Mason had left me a note the morning after he had slept at my place. I ran my finger along the jagged edge of the page. Mason had read through my notebook. He had read through all my marketing ideas. Is that why he had been so persistent after I drove away on our first date? Had he just wanted information about what Kruger was doing? So he could steal clients? For what, Blue Media or maybe even himself?

I felt cheap. And stupid. Of course Mason didn't actually like me. He was just using me. I put my notebook back into my purse. He was Mason Caldwell. And I was just me. He used women for a living. All he knew was paying women for sex.

When Mason turned the corner and walked into the kitchen I just stared at him. He came over to me and leaned down for a kiss.

My knees felt weak. I wanted to grab the back of his neck and pull him down to me. I wanted to kiss him. Because this asshole had tricked me into falling in love with him. So instead of punching his beautiful face, which he deserved, I wanted to rip all his clothes off. This felt worse that Patrick. Worse because I hadn't even guessed what was going on. Mason was right. I was naive.

I put my hand on his chest so that his lips didn't meet mine.

He smiled down at me. "In the mood for more than kissing? I think I have time for that."

"You're disgusting." My voice sounded small. Why did I always sound so pathetic whenever I needed to be strong?

"You didn't think what we did was disgusting last night." He gave me his panty dropping smile.

"I need to go." I nodded, as if encouraging myself that I was making the right decision.

"Wait, what?"

"I made a mistake. This was a mistake. I'm sorry." And why did I always apologize? What on earth was I apologizing for? I turned away from him. I needed to find my coat and my shoes. I needed to get out of his apartment. I slipped on my boots that were next to the door.

"Bee?" He put his hand on my shoulder. "Are you okay?"

I pushed his hand off of me. "Am I okay? Of course I'm not okay." I could feel the tears falling down my cheeks. I was such an idiot. I kept falling for the wrong guys. The worst possible guys.

"What's wrong? Baby..."

I put my hand up so he wouldn't touch me. "You know what's wrong."

"No, I don't. I asked you to move in with me. I asked you to be my girlfriend. I would have guessed we were in a good place."

"Exactly, Mason. You made me fall in love with you."

A smile spread across his face. "You're in love with me?"

"No. I mean yes. I don't know! You tricked me."

"I didn't trick you." He took another step toward me.

"If all you wanted was sex and information, fine. But I asked you not to break my heart. You didn't have to do this. You didn't have to take it this far. You made me fall in love with you."

His eyebrows lowered slightly. "Bee..."

"Don't you dare throw some lame excuse at me. I heard you on the phone."

I watched his Adam's apple rise and fall. "You don't understand."

"Were you or were you not talking to John Landry?"

"I was, but..."

"That was my idea, Mason. You stole my idea. You read my notebook."

"I didn't mean to steal your idea. It just slipped out when I was on the phone with him. It was the first thing that came to my head because it's a really, really good idea. I accidentally saw it in your notebook the other morning. I wasn't snooping, I was just trying to get..."

"Do you think I'm a complete idiot?"

"Of course I don't. You know how I feel about you."

That you really like me? He was so full of shit. "And how did you get John Landry's phone number? Is that why you came to the office that night when I was working late? To steal my contacts?"

"No. It wasn't like that. You know none of this was ever like that."

"Oh, is that where you drew the line? Not stealing phone numbers of clients off my computer?"

"Bee, if you would just give me a second to explain..."

"Is that why you agreed to the blind date in the first place? Because you knew I worked for Kruger? You set me up."

"I didn't know you worked for Kruger. All I knew was that you were a secretary."

"So what, you just randomly decided to try the whole dating thing? You were sick of living your life of sin? What?"

"Bee..."

"What, Mason? Why the hell did you even go on that date in the first place? You can have any girl you want in this stupid city. Why did you go on a date with someone like me?"

"For two Knicks tickets! Jesus." He turned away from me and ran his hand through his hair.

"What?" I didn't know what he was going to say. But I hadn't expected that.

He turned back toward me and ran his hands down his face. "Carter and Marie gave me two Knicks tickets for promising to take you out and show you a good time."

"You're lying. They wouldn't do that. I'm not some charity case."

"I don't think you are. But what do I know, right? I'm just your rebound aren't I? Isn't that why Carter and Marie set you up with me? To get over Patrick?"

"Yeah, but..."

"Well, great. I'm glad I could help." He was pissed now. He had let me yell and scream and berate him. He had remained calm the whole time. But when he mentioned Patrick, something changed in his face. Suddenly it felt like I was in the wrong.

"Mason."

"You were still in love with him when we met. You're probably still in love with him. So what the hell are you doing getting mad at me and saying that you love me? You don't love me. You love him."

Is that why he was so upset? He didn't believe that I loved him?

"And I didn't trick you. I accidentally saw what you wrote in your notebook. I accidentally pitched your idea to John Landry. But you don't want my excuses. So I don't know why I'm bothering. Why don't you just run back to Patrick. Clearly that's where you belong."

"I don't love Patrick. I don't want to be with Patrick."

"Then maybe you should find someone who you deem fit for your time. Because clearly it's not me. I have better things to do than stand here and argue with you."

"What, like cater to your new account? The one you got with my idea?"

"Don't act so innocent, Bee. Like you didn't get everything you wanted from me? Like you weren't using me?" He laughed.

"What are you talking about?"

"You only wanted to be with me because of my money. Well guess what? My dad cut me off. I'm not getting his inheritance. Without the Sword account I'd be as broke as you. I'm not a catch, I'm a fucking mess. You're better off without me."

"I don't care about your money. I didn't even know you had any money when I started falling for you. I just liked you for you. Money doesn't matter to me."

"So you just spread your legs that fast for anyone? You're easy, Bee. You're just like every other girl in this fucking city."

"And you're just like every other arrogant, pretentious bastard."

"Guilty."

"I never should have trusted you," I said.

"Don't give me that shit. I told you I wasn't a nice guy. You had me pegged from the very start. It just made you want me even more. And it was damn fun stringing you along, waiting for you to beg me."

"So this whole thing was a game to you?"

"A game I always win."

"You're such an asshole."

"Speaking of assholes, I need to go tell my boss that I quit. Thanks, sugar, I really owe you one." He walked over to the door.

"I know you weren't pretending, Mason. I know you feel something more than that for me. It wasn't a game. I know you feel it too. Can we please just talk about this for a second?" *He has to feel it too.*

"Fucking is my hobby. You were right from the start. You shouldn't have gotten attached."

"So that's it? You've gotten what you wanted and now you're done with me?"

"Like I said, you were easy."

I should have seen it coming. I had gotten so many warnings. I had seen warning signs myself. But I didn't pay attention to them. He completely blindsided me. It was easy for that to happen when you let yourself be vulnerable. I had fallen in love with another asshole.

"I hope you enjoyed your game, Mason." I grabbed my jacket and ran out the door. This time he didn't call after me. He had gotten what he wanted. He used me and cast me aside like a hooker. Because that's all he knew. He was a sad, pathetic excuse for a man. And I was an idiot for thinking he'd change for me.

Chapter 62
Mason

I was on my fourth drink, but nothing could seem to numb the pain. It had felt amazing to tell Darren that I quit, but it would have been more rewarding if I hadn't just had the worst morning of my life. I still couldn't believe I said all those things to Bee. But how could she say all that to me? I hadn't tricked her into falling in love with me. She didn't love me at all. She was still in love with Patrick. I downed the rest of my drink and waived the bartender over for a refill.

I stared down into my glass when the scotch was filled up to the top again. I couldn't go home. I knew Bee wouldn't be there anymore. And that thought killed me. All her stuff would be gone, but there would be that lingering smell of her. I didn't want to fall asleep in an empty bed. I didn't want to do anything without her. Asking her to move in had been a shot in the dark. I had hoped I could get her to stay. I was a fucking idiot. I tilted my head back and downed half of my next drink.

"Matt told me I could find you here," James said and slid into the bar stool next to mine. "Do you want to talk about it?"

"There's nothing to talk about." I slammed my glass back down on the bar.

"Well, I heard you landed the Sword Body Wash account. And three others. You'll probably get a few more before the week is over."

"Yeah." I stared down into my glass again.

"So shouldn't we be celebrating? This is everything you've ever wanted."

"I thought it was."

"You're getting soft like me, huh?"

"No." I felt like I wanted to cry. *Fuck, I am getting soft.*

"Being in love doesn't make you soft, despite what my brother says."

"I'm not in love." I moved my glass around so that the ice cubes clinked against the glass.

"So she's just some girl? There's plenty more right out that door. I guess you'll forget about her in a few days then."

"I don't want to forget about her." And I couldn't. How could I possibly forget about Bee? She was smart, funny, and that perfect combination of beautiful and sexy.

"Because you love her."

"Maybe." I looked over at James. "She told me she loved me. Not in like a cute way, like in a throwing it in my face because she hates me way." I didn't want to tell him about stealing her idea. I didn't want anyone else to know how big of an idiot I was. "I screwed up."

"So why don't you go talk to her?"

"We're done. There's nothing to talk about."

"If you're this messed up, I'm sure she is too."

"I doubt she is. I'm pretty sure she's just hung up on her ex. I was a filler. She's probably running back to him right now."

"If she is, it's only because you pushed her away."

I put my elbows on the table. I did push her away. I told her she was easy. I told her she was just like every other slut in this city. I was a prick. But she just had this way of making my blood boil.

"You must have seen the way she looked at you. She was already in love with you at the Silver Gala. You've just been too stubborn to see it."

"I can't talk my way out of it this time. She hates me."

"All I know is that it's lonely living in this city by yourself. Not having someone to share the good and the bad with."

"She ran when it got messy. She's not the type of girl that sticks through the bad times." Even as I said it I realized it was a lie. She wanted to stay and talk it out. Even after I stole her idea and landed an account that should have been hers. Because she cared about me. She loved me. And I pushed her away.

"I'm just saying."

"Mason!" Matt burst into the bar with a huge grin on his face. I had texted him earlier about landing the accounts. I wanted to celebrate and drown my sorrows. My brother was the perfect guy to do that with.

James slapped me on the back. "Telling the truth is better than any grand gesture. Talk to her."

"You're not staying to celebrate?"

"It's cold and late. All I want is to go home to the woman I love. I guess that makes me soft. But I've never been happier."

"Just because that works for you..."

"Stop standing still, Mason. You're going to want to have someone to share all this success with. Don't make the same mistakes that I did."

James always seemed calm and collected. But I saw the flash of pain across his eyes. It was gone in a second. I let go of the drink in my hand. He was right. Drowning this feeling with scotch wasn't going to help anything. I didn't want to lose myself the way he had lost himself. And I was sick of standing still. I was sick of the easy women who threw themselves at me. And the even easier ones that I had to pay for. I was lying when I said Bee was easy. She was complicated and perfect and real. She was the only thing in my life that felt real.

"Hey, James," Matt said as he passed by James going toward the door. Matt sat down beside me and clapped me on the back. "Congrats, man."

"Thanks."

"Another round on me?"

I looked back down at my empty glass. I could sit here all night, trying to erase the memory of her from my mind. But what was the point in that? I'd just wake up tomorrow still missing her. I didn't need a glass in my hand. I needed her hand in mine. She fit. She was the perfect fit. "No." I stood up and pulled on my jacket. "I have to go."

"What? I just got here."

"There's something I need to do."

"Mason?" Matt called after me, but I was already running out of the bar. I needed to talk to Bee. I needed her to know how I really felt.

***

I pressed on the call box outside of Kendra's apartment building. I had run all the way there, stopping only to grab a dozen roses at a stand on the corner a few blocks back. I was out of breath and my lungs burned from the cold air.

The doors buzzed. I grabbed the handle and ran inside, skipping the elevator and sprinted up the steps instead. When I got to 307 I pounded on the door with the side of my fist.

Kendra's face fell when she opened the door. "I thought you were Chinese food."

"Is Bee here?" I tilted my head to the side and saw all of Bee's boxes in the small living room area of the apartment. "I just need to talk to her for a second."

"She's not here, Mason."

"I can see her stuff. Come on, it's important."

"She's not here. She dropped all her stuff off and left."

"Did she say anything to you?"

"She didn't have to." Kendra's eyes narrowed. "Do you have any idea how long it took her to get over Patrick? How much that hurt her?"

I didn't need the guilt trip right now. "I mean did she say anything about where she was going?"

"Like I'd tell you? You're lucky I'm not kneeing you in the balls right now. I will take these, though." She grabbed the roses out of my hand.

"Can you tell her I'm looking for her? I already tried calling and she's not answering."

"Maybe you should take the hint, Mason. Just leave her alone."

"I can't leave her alone. I'm in love with her."

Kendra just stared at me. "She didn't grow up here like you and me. She needs a nice, normal, suburban guy."

Like Patrick? You've got to be kidding me. "She does belong here. She belongs with me." I grabbed the roses back out of Kendra's hand. "And you better get used to me, because I'm not going anywhere."

"Well, I do admire your persistence." She folded her arms across her chest.

"So are you going to tell her I was here?"

"I'll think about it."

"Are you going to tell me where she is?"

"I'd tell you if I knew. She just came and dropped her stuff off. She was a mess. And she wouldn't talk to me about it." She lowered her eyebrows slightly. "At least she talked to me about what happened with Patrick. Whatever you did, I think it hurt her even more."

Bee was more upset about our fight than when she broke it off with Patrick? Maybe she was over him. Maybe she really did love me.

Before I could ask any more questions, Kendra slammed the door in my face. I looked down at the roses in my hand. Telling the truth probably was better than some grand gesture. But James didn't know what I had done. A grand gesture might be a better tactic.

Chapter 63
Bee

I stepped off the bus and pulled on my hat and gloves. The city had felt cold because I was alone. That's why I had thought it seemed so much colder than back in Wilmington. I had never been alone at home. I had my mom and my friends. And then I had Patrick. Love somehow created this internal heat so I never noticed the wind biting at my cheeks. But I was cold now, colder than I'd ever been. I pulled my coat tighter around myself.

With each step I had taken away from Mason's apartment earlier, I had to will myself to keep going. All I wanted to do was run back to him and tell him that I was sorry. That I wanted to work through our fight. I knew that he hadn't read through my notebook with the intention of stealing my ideas. He had just been looking for a sheet of paper to leave me a sweet note. He was a good guy, no matter how bad he said he was. But he didn't seem to want to be the man that I saw. He reverted so quickly back to his old ways as soon as things got hard.

My feet crunched in the snow on the sidewalk. I would have followed Mason anywhere. *Just like I had followed Patrick to New York?* I shook the thought away. I fell too hard, too fast. I hadn't learned from my mistakes. I fell for another jerk. And I loved him. I loved him so much.

But the truth was, Mason didn't feel that way about me. I had told him I loved him and he told me I was easy, like every other girl he had ever met. And maybe I was. Mason was only the second person I had ever slept with, but I jumped into bed with him. I didn't hesitate at all. I fell for his smooth talking and dirty mouth. *God his mouth...*

Stop it! I was done. I was done with love. And for the moment I was done with New York. I needed to feel like I could breathe again. I thought coming back would make me feel better. But it was just as cold here as it was in New York. Maybe even colder. Because tonight I felt so alone, like a piece of me was missing.

It wasn't too late to go back. I could still tell Mason that I was sorry for jumping to conclusions and for not hearing him out. I walked up the front steps and stopped outside of the door. But I couldn't swallow my pride this time. Mason didn't want me anymore. I didn't want to give up on what we had, but I didn't see any other option. *He doesn't want you. He never did.* All he had to do was tell me to stay, like he had the other night. But now that made sense too. He was guilty and could barely even face me. That's why it looked like he was worried about losing me. He just wanted a few more nights with me. For my body. Because that's all it ever was.

I knocked on the door and tried to stop the tears from coming.

A minute later my mom opened the door. "Bee? Bee what are you doing here?"

I was never good at controlling my emotions. Just seeing my mom made me feel like I was back in grade school. "Mom," I said, choking through a sob.

"Oh, sweetie." She pulled me into the house. It was warm inside. But I was still cold. Even when she wrapped her arms around me I still shivered.

"I keep making the same mistakes," I said into her shoulder.

My mom laughed. "I'm guessing this is about Mason?" She patted my back and released me from her hug. "Come in and sit. Did you want something to drink?"

That was always my mom's go to thing for house guests. Making sure they weren't parched. I didn't need a cup of hot tea, though. I needed a serving tray full of shots. "I'm okay."

"You don't seem okay," she said as she sat down and gestured for me to sit beside her.

I sat down and pulled off my gloves. "After what happened with Patrick I told myself I needed to take things slow. To take the time to see if a guy was worth my time."

"It doesn't matter how old you get, you still fall just as hard." My mom gave me a sympathetic smile. "It's about the heart not the head."

"But I knew better. Everyone told me he wasn't a good guy. Heck, *he* even told me he wasn't a good guy."

"And is that what you want? A good guy to settle down with?"

I put my face in my hands. My face felt like ice against my palms.

My mom ran her hand up and down my back. "You can't plan everything out, Bee. That's not how life works. So what is it that you really want?"

"Well I should be able to plan a little better than this." I lifted my face out of my hands. "I don't even know what

I want anymore, Mom. I moved to New York because I was in love. And when Patrick and I broke up, I told myself I had to stay to prove to everyone that I had what it took to make it. But I only just realized that it wasn't what I wanted. None of it was what I wanted. I'm just scared of being alone." As soon as I said it, I wished I could take it back. My mom was alone. My father had walked out on us and left her devastated. Just because I was upset didn't mean I had to be inconsiderate.

"You're never alone, Bee." She put her hand on my forearm. Even though I had basically just said I didn't want to turn out like her, here she was taking care of me.

"I know." I swallowed hard. "I got fired."

"From a job you hated."

"Yeah, but it paid the bills."

"Barely. That job wasn't what you wanted. Now tell me what you really want."

"I don't know what I want." I stood up. "Why do you keep asking me that? I don't know, Mom. I don't know."

"You do know. You know and you're scared to say it because you're sick of being hurt. That's not living, Bee. You don't have to admit it to me, but you know what you want. At least tell yourself. What do you want?"

"Him!" I closed my eyes, trying to prevent my tears from spilling over. "I just want him."

"I know how much it terrifies you to say that you want someone instead of some random goal. Because you may end up getting hurt. You might end up alone like me."

"Mom." I sat down next to her. "That's not..."

"No, it's fine. What I never told you growing up was that I never regretted any of my decisions. Your father was my great love. No, it didn't last. But I wouldn't change a second of what we had. And he gave me you, the best possible gift anyone could ask for."

I wanted to cry all over again.

"Don't you ever run away from something great just because you're scared. That's not the girl I raised."

It didn't matter that I had wound up in New York because of my ex or that I stayed there out of spite. I still found what I wanted. "I want to get a real advertising job. I don't want to have to live pay check to pay check anymore. I want to be with Mason."

"There you go. You already knew all of that. So what are you doing here in the middle of the night waking up your mother?"

I laughed. "I missed you."

"I missed you too, sweetie. But I'd rather you be across the world and happy than right beside me and sad."

I sighed. "I know."

"Now let me get you that cup of tea." She patted my knee and stood up.

I knew what I wanted. But I couldn't shake the feeling that Mason didn't want the same thing. It wasn't like I could make him fall in love with me. He had made it perfectly clear where he stood.

Chapter 64
Bee

My phone started buzzing. I yawned and swiped my finger across the screen. "Hello?"

"So now you're answering phone calls?" Marie's voice cut through the line like a knife.

"Hello to you, too, Marie." I had been screening all my calls for the past week. Just because I knew what I wanted didn't mean I had enough confidence to go get it.

"Do you have any idea how worried we've all been?"

"My mom told me you called the house a few days ago and talked to her. You knew where I was."

"Yeah, no thanks to you. Kendra and I have been taking turns calling you a million times a day."

"I've missed you guys too."

Marie laughed. "Does that mean you're coming back?" The edge in her voice was gone. She sounded like her normal, sweet self again.

"Of course I'm coming back."

"Good. You should probably make that this morning. You have an interview at 2 o'clock."

"Wait, what?"

"Kendra said someone called with an ad job opening. You weren't there so she pretended to be you. Your interview is today."

"Really? What agency?"

"I forget the name. Stop moping around and get your butt back to the city, Bee."

I laughed. "I'm on my way."

***

Mason had called a few times the first two days I had skipped town. He never left a message and then his calls had stopped. Normally that would have deterred me. But I wanted to think with my heart for a change. And my heart said that if he really was done with me, he wouldn't have called at all. He had called because he cared too. It didn't matter that his calls had stopped. He probably wanted me to reach out to him. To let him know that I wanted him too. But I couldn't talk to him over the phone. It needed to be face to face. I'd do it tonight. I was determined to win him back. Right after I aced this interview.

I slid my key into the lock and opened up the door. Kendra was sitting on the couch in pajamas. A bowl of popcorn was on her lap and she was watching some daytime soap opera.

"Kendra?"

She jumped, sending a few popcorn kernels onto the floor. "Oh my god, you're back!" She put the bowl down, ran over, and gave me a big hug. "Marie said she talked to you. I don't know why, I just didn't think you'd come back. I mean, I hoped you would. I was worried you wouldn't."

"You know that dumb boys can't scare me away from this city."

She laughed and released me from her hug. "Well I definitely didn't think you'd choose to come back on Valentine's Day of all days."

"Oh." I hadn't even been paying attention to the days. Was it really Valentine's Day? My heart sunk a little. Mason hadn't called me in several days. What if he was spending Valentine's Day with someone else? "Happy Valentine's Day, Kendra," I said as cheerily as possible.

"Well, that didn't sound sincere at all. He comes by every night after work, you know." She pointed over to several vases of flowers sitting on the counter.

He does still care. "What does he say?"

"You need to talk to him for yourself. I'm not getting in the middle of it. He's starting to wear me down though. I like having flowers all over the apartment." She laughed and sat back down, pulling the bowl of popcorn back onto her lap.

"Wait, what are you doing home? It's the middle of the day."

"You didn't hear?"

"Hear what?"

"Kruger went bankrupt. I'm out of a job."

"Wait, what? Kendra, I'm so sorry."

Kendra laughed. "Well, yes and no. Kruger did go bankrupt. They sold their company to some other agency, though. Which wasn't for much since all of Kruger's clients bailed. But whoever bought it gets to keep all of Kruger's employees if they want. So I'm not actually out of a job I hope. But they're redoing the office or something and conducting interviews for all the current employees. My interview isn't until tomorrow."

"So you think you'll be okay?"

"Yeah, I'm fine. Without Jenkins, I'm one of the top performers. Hell, I'll probably get a raise. And I don't mind having the rest of the week off. This is awesome."

"What about Mr. Ellington?"

"Oh, he got fired. The new guy came in and basically threw him out of the office. And there's going to be a lawsuit about sexual harassment too. That asshole had it coming. The whole thing was so much more entertaining than Layla Torrez getting naked on live T.V."

I laughed. "So you've met the new boss? Do you like him? Hopefully he's better than Mr. Ellington."

"Personally, I think he's okay. Some people like him more than others. I'm getting used to him. Actually, I'm excited to see what you think."

"Me?"

"Yeah. That's where you're interviewing."

"At the old office? What's the name of the agency that took it over?"

"I don't think it has a name yet. Maybe there will be a meeting and we'll get to vote or something. Wouldn't that be cool? You should get ready though, you don't want to be late. I don't want to have to work there without you."

"But I don't have any experience. I'll probably just land another job as a secretary."

"Maybe he'll actually appreciate your ideas. He doesn't think of you as a secretary yet, so don't let him. Show him you have what it takes."

I nodded my head. "So this company just called and asked for me to come in for an interview?"

"Yeah, I think they're trying to find fresh talent. They're probably calling people all over the city."

My stomach churned. "Way to boost my confidence."

"But you have experience with the rest of the Kruger employees. You're a shoo-in."

"Okay." I took a deep breath. "I'm going to go change."

"Yeah, get out of here, you're interrupting my show."

"Who's the cat lady now?" I said and lifted off the lid of one of the boxes I had left in the middle of Kendra's living room. Kendra never did anything she didn't want to. Which apparently included leaving boxes in the middle of her living room all week. I grabbed a nice blouse and a skirt and walked behind her couch to change. I'd move the boxes into the spare bedroom tonight.

"Maybe you had it right all along. Comfy pants and a good show? This could be a fun Friday night. I totally see it now."

"Yeah. I guess." But that wasn't wanted what I wanted anymore. Unless I was doing it with Mason.

Kendra turned around. "Geez, Bee, you need to cheer up before your interview. I can literally hear the depression in your voice." She stared at me for a second. "Are you going to hear him out? I don't think he's going to stop trying to talk to you any time soon."

"My plan is to go over to his place tonight and talk to him. I have a lot to say too."

"He's already heard an earful from me. Unbutton the top button of your blouse, Bee."

"What? No." I put my hand in front of my throat.

"Trust me. Everyone uses their assets to land a good position. All the other hires are probably unbuttoning the top two buttons. The new boss is young. Make him drool. Then maybe we can be cubicle buddies."

I laughed. "You don't think I can land the job with my ideas?"

"I didn't say that. Suit yourself." She turned back to the T.V.

I sighed and unbuttoned the top button of my blouse. It couldn't hurt. As long as I made it clear that I was never going to give him sexual favors. I was not going to have another Mr. Ellington situation on my hands. I still couldn't believe someone was suing him. I should probably find out more about it so I could give my statement too. I quickly pulled on a pair of heels.

"How do I look?" I asked and walked in front of the couch.

"Hirable. Oh!" Kendra stood up and ran into her bathroom. She ran back out and tossed me a tube of lipstick. "Do the whole red lip classic thing. Guys dig that too."

"Is this how you landed your first advertising job?" I untwisted the lipstick from the tube and applied it.

"A girl never kisses and tells. Just kidding. Maybe. It's Valentine's Day, though. It wouldn't hurt to be a little flirtatious. Guys get sentimental about this holiday too, you know. He'll probably hire you just for batting your pretty eyelashes at him."

I smacked my lips together. "I'm not doing that. How do I look now?"

"Perfect. Drool worthy. I can't wait to hear how it goes."

"I think I'm going to get it." I made sure my notebook was in my purse before heading to the door. "Wish me luck!"

"You're not going to need luck." She winked at me.

I'm glad she was so confident in me, because I was getting nervous.

Chapter 65
Bee

It was hard focusing on the words written in my notebook. I was distracted by the thought of talking to Mason later. His words had hurt me. But with each day that passed, they stung a little less and I just missed him more and more. He had been partially right about me. I wanted to move on from Patrick when I had met him. I had been a little easy. Maybe a lot easy. I shook my head. I didn't see why any of that mattered, though. It didn't take away from how I felt right now.

I just needed to make him listen to me. I didn't care that he had stolen my idea. I didn't care that he had pushed me away. He was stopping by Kendra's every night waiting for me to show up. Clearly he realized he had made some mistakes too. But maybe tonight wasn't the best time to do that. I didn't want his judgment to be clouded just because it was Valentine's Day. Or maybe that would help my case. A little extra nudge toward romance never hurt anyone? *Says the girl that's been burned.*

I took a deep breath and tried to concentrate on the words in front of me. Getting this job would be great. Having a good salary would be great. But I'd still feel empty if I didn't have him.

I turned to the page I had written about fairytales. Maybe I'd pitch that idea today during my interview. Then I wouldn't have to separate out the thoughts of Mason rolling around in my head. My missing him would just make the pitch even more sincere. And it was appropriate considering the holiday.

The subway came to a stop. Normally it was jam-packed during my morning commute, but in the middle of the afternoon it wasn't crowded. I didn't have to shove through anyone getting off. The past few weeks before running away, I had been sharing a cab to work with Mason. If we could work though things, it was still going to be different. He'd be staying home and I'd be heading to work by myself back on the subway. I loved those cab rides. The way he kept his hand in mine and squeezed it whenever he wanted for me to look over at him. Not that he had to do that very often. I couldn't keep my eyes off of him.

I walked up the steps and lifted my shoulders, bracing myself against the cold wind that rushed toward me. If I did get this job, I wondered if any of my former coworkers would throw me under the bus and tell the new boss I was just a lowly secretary. I'd definitely have to prove myself.

I ducked my head down as I walked past a homeless person sitting on the curb. Today I didn't even have a penny to give him. I grabbed the handle of the door I never thought I'd be going through again. I still couldn't believe Mr. Ellington had been fired. I liked the new boss already.

My heels made that annoying clicking noise as I made my way toward the elevator, but it was better than the sound of my beating heart. I could feel it in my bones. This was the turning point.

When I stepped off the elevator, I was amazed by how different the office already looked. The Kruger Advertising sign was gone, and there were people painting the office a pretty shade of light blue. It already seemed more cheery. A large reception desk had been put at the front of the office and a woman was there organizing some papers behind the desk. I really hoped I wouldn't be working alongside of her. Not that she didn't seem nice. I just couldn't do that again.

I walked up to the woman. "Hi, I'm Bridget Cowan. I'm here for an interview."

"Oh, yes." The woman sifted through the papers. "Bee Cowan? Is that it?"

"Yes." I smiled. Kendra must have told them I preferred to be called Bee. I already felt a little more comfortable. I tried to focus on my breathing so that my pulse would be tricked into slowing down.

"He's expecting you. You can just take a seat right over there and I'll let him know you're here." She gestured to her left and picked up the phone that was on her desk. There were a row of soft looking chairs and a plush couch outside of Mr. Ellington's old office. They were all empty.

"Thank you." I walked over and sat down on the chair farthest away from the office door. My desk that had been right outside Mr. Ellington's office was gone. I vaguely wondered what had happened to the picture I had left behind. Patrick and my smiling faces were probably sitting in a dump right outside of the city. I ran my thumb along the spot where my engagement ring once sat. When Mason had said I should just run back to Patrick, not even a small part of me considered it. There was nothing to run back to. All I'd be doing was running away, and I didn't want to run away from Mason.

I looked down at my hand. For a while there had been a small tan line where my engagement ring used to sit. It was almost gone now, like all the evidence of Patrick and my relationship would soon be gone. And the thought was terrifying. Not because of Patrick, but because of Mason. I didn't want Mason to become a distant memory. I'd regret that for the rest of my life. I had been thinking more and more about what my mom had said. Without a doubt in my mind, Mason was my great love. Was not answering his calls a mistake? Had I already lost him too? Maybe Valentine's Day was getting in my own head.

I needed to focus. I pulled out my notebook and opened up to a random page, but the words didn't seem to make any sense. *Focus.*

The receptionist walked over. "He's ready to see you now." She gave me a small smile.

I'm not ready. Shit. I could feel my heart beating out of my chest.

She opened up the door to Mr. Ellington's old office and gestured for me to enter.

"Thank you," I said over my shoulder as she closed the door behind me. I swallowed hard and turned around. My throat made a small squeaking sound when I saw him.

Mason Caldwell was sitting behind a new desk, where Mr. Ellington's old desk had been, with a smile on his face. No, he was standing and walking toward me.

"Mason." I could feel all the emotions from the other day coming back. But mostly I felt the warmth wafting off of him. His warmth was the only one that could seem to make the cold disappear.

"I wasn't sure you were coming back." He had stopped right in front of me. He didn't reach out for me or try to kiss me.

But I still felt warmer than I had all week. "I meant what I said, Mason."

He scratched the back of his neck. "I know I'm an asshole."

"No. I mean, I love you." There, I said it without sounding like I wanted to rip his head off. That was better right? Would he believe me now?

He lowered his eyebrows slightly. "I need to talk to you."

I bit my lip. "I'm so sorry about everything I said, Mason. The only thing I said the other day that was true was that I loved you. I love you so much."

He closed his eyes for a second as though what I was saying hurt him. When he opened them, he didn't lock his eyes with mine again. "Can you take a seat?"

He still didn't believe me. Or maybe he didn't want to hear it. He still wasn't touching me. I couldn't stand the distance between us. I walked past him and sat down in a chair in front of the desk.

I heard him sigh. Instead of going around to the other side of the desk, he sat down in the chair beside mine and grabbed my hand. *Finally.* I felt the familiar spark ignite through my hand.

"You bought Kruger Advertising?"

"For barely anything, yeah. I'm just going to tell you everything from the start okay? I just need you to listen and not get upset. Promise to let me say everything I need to say?" He ran his thumb across my knuckles.

I nodded.

"This is everything. The good, the bad, the in between. And I bet you'll want to take back what you just said after you..."

"I won't."

He shook his head. "I don't go on blind dates, Bee. Actually, I don't go on any dates at all. I wasn't interested in a connection, in the whole romance thing. Just sex. That's it. That's all I wanted."

"I know."

"Carter and Marie were pretty insistent. I kept saying no. I keep my private life and work separate. All they knew was that I was single and that you were too. I knew you were wondering why the hell they would set you up with me that first night. But it's just because they didn't know me. It had nothing to do with whether you're easy or not, which you aren't. But they offered me Knicks tickets if I agreed. I'd get to go to a game and possibly get lucky? It sounded like a fair deal to me. So I said yes. I never expected someone like you to show up."

"Someone like me?"

"You took my breath away, Bee. But I only have one move. I mean," he shrugged, "plenty of moves to get to an end point. I wanted to fuck you. That was it. That's always the end game for me. And when you drove off in that taxi, it just made me want you even more. I couldn't stop thinking about you. I kept telling myself it was about the sex.

Just getting to have you. It was more than that, I know that now, but I was fighting with myself about that. Instead of accepting that I actually had feelings for you, I made it some sick game in my head. I knew you were damaged. I mean, not damaged, that was the wrong word. But wounded, you know? From what happened with Patrick. So I took things slow for the ultimate prize. You."

"That's why it was so hard for me to read you. You kept changing. You were brash yet kind. You were so confusing. But that doesn't change the way I feel about you now."

He cleared his throat. "Mostly brash actually. I had a friend of mine dig up information on you. That's why I took you to all your favorite restaurants and..."

"You stalked me?"

"I didn't..." He stopped himself and ran his hands through his hair. "Loosely, maybe. And just at first. I don't know what came over me. You just seemed like this goal that I had to achieve. And I didn't care if I had to cheat and play dirty to get you in my bed. But the more time that went by, the more I started caring about you. It wasn't just about sex anymore, it was about you. I liked hanging out with you. And yes, when we finally gave in to that temptation, it was explosive. But it wasn't about that anymore. You've consumed me. And it terrifies me, because I've never felt this way before."

He laughed and ran his hand through his hair again. "I kept getting this weird tightness in my chest ever since we met. I thought I was dying. But I think I was just worried about losing you. I've never been that attached to something before. Someone." He leaned forward and put his hand on the side of my face. "You are not like any other girl in this city. I don't want you to think that I kiss everyone I meet the way that I kiss you. Or that I look at anyone else the way that I look at you. I'm addicted to your laugh and the dimples in your cheeks when you smile. Your warmth and optimism despite everything that's been taken from you. You're beautiful inside and out. And the only thing for sure that I know in this crazy city is how I feel about you."

"And how do you feel about me?"

"I love you, Bee. I love you so much."

"I thought you were done with me?"

"I can't ever quit you." He grabbed my arm and pulled me onto his lap. "I love you so much." He leaned down and kissed me.

I was never going to question his motives or resist one of his advances again. I was always happiest when his arms were around me. I didn't care if he had gotten Knicks tickets or stalked me. I cared about what all that led to. Us. And all of that lead to where we were right now.

He groaned into my mouth as his hands slipped to my ass. "God I missed you."

"I missed you too."

"I was so worried you weren't coming back." He kissed the side of my neck. "I was so worried that I lost you."

I pulled back. "You're not so easy to quit either, Mason Caldwell."

He moved his hands back to the sides of my face. "I'm so sorry that I hurt you. I'm never going to hurt you again."

"I'm sorry too. I just freaked out when I heard you on the phone. But I know you weren't trying to steal my ideas. I know you're a good person."

"I didn't even finish everything I needed to tell you. You're good at distracting me." He didn't make a move to push me off his lap. Instead, he pulled me closer, letting me rest my head against his shoulder. "Seeing your marketing ideas was an accident. I was just trying to leave you a note. But it was hard to look away. Your ideas are good, Bee. Good enough to land the Sword account."

He was fiddling with the ends of my hair. I closed my eyes and just breathed in the familiar scent of him.

"James called me after that Layla's Predictions fiasco. He had a friend on the board that knew the company was losing all their accounts. It was pretty clear that Kruger was going to go bankrupt in a few days. I needed to take that shot. It was just an opportunity I couldn't pass up."

"I'm glad you got it. I'm not mad at you."

"But I knew everyone at Kruger was going to lose their jobs..."

I laughed and lifted my head off his shoulder. "That explains your reaction that night. You knew I wasn't going to get a promotion. Why didn't you just tell me?"

"James made me promise not to tell anyone. His friend could have gotten in a lot of trouble if anyone who had stock in the company suddenly started selling their shares."

"So, you got Knicks tickets to go on a date with me, stalked me, turned our relationship into a game, stole my advertising ideas, let me believe I was getting a promotion when you knew I was getting fired, and then bought the company that fired me? Is that about right?"

"Yeah, but I..."

"What's your end game now?" I tried to raise my eyebrow. I hated that I couldn't give him the same challenging look that he was so easily able to give me.

He smiled down at me. "A good friend of mine told me that until life gives you something right, it's hard to realize how wrong you've been." He pushed a strand of hair out of my face. "I haven't really been living. Not until I met you. You're my end game. Making you happy is my new permanent end game. And," he grabbed my waist and stood up. He set me down on the edge of the desk and leaned into me. "The same friend told me that women prefer the truth over grand gestures. But I'm kind of a fan of grand gestures." He grabbed a business card off his desk and handed it to me.

"Bee Inspired Media Group?" I looked up at him. "You're naming your new company after me?" I felt a flutter in my chest. It wasn't just a symbol of his love. It was the grandest apology I had ever seen.

"No. Well, yes, but there's more." He tapped the side of the card.

I looked back down at it. *Bee Cowan, co-founder of BIMG.* My eyes darted back up to his. "Mason, I can't do this with you. I've never even had an advertising job."

"You landed our first account."

"*Our* first account?" I looked back down at the card.

"For the record, we have seven other accounts that I landed with my own ideas. That was the only one I stole, I swear. We can probably get a few more with some of your other ideas, though."

"You really want me to do this with you?"

"I wouldn't want to do it with anyone else. You have what it takes, Bee. And I always want you by my side."

It was like every dream I had rolled into one. "This is a very elaborate Valentine's Day gift, Mason." I couldn't seem stop looking at the business card. I had never even had my name on a business card before. And now I was the co-founder of a huge company?

"Hmm." He put his index finger under my chin and titled my gaze back to his. "I hate to break it to you, but this isn't your Valentine's Day gift."

"It's not?"

"How about you go back to Kendra's and get changed? I'll pick you up in an hour."

"I came back to New York with the idea that I had to win you back. Not the other way around." I ran my fingers down his silky tie. "I had completely forgotten that it was Valentine's Day. You don't have to do anything else. I don't even know if I can accept this. I didn't get you anything, Mason."

"You came back. That's all I wanted." He leaned down and placed a soft kiss against my lips. "Now go get ready before I throw you on top of this desk and the receptionist gets the wrong idea about my hiring process."

I laughed. "Mason, I was always going to come back. You're home to me." It was the highest compliment I could give someone. Even more than saying I loved him. He was it for me.

"I like the sound of that. Now, go get ready." His hand slipped down my back and he squeezed my ass.

I laughed again and wrapped my arms around him. "I'm so happy."

Chapter 66
Mason

I looked down at the ring on my desk. After talking to Kendra last week I had run to the nearest jewelry store and bought the most expensive ring in the case. Rash and poorly thought out. I was upset and drunk and I was feeling desperate. I just wanted Bee back. It would look perfect on her finger. And when she ran her thumb along the spot, she'd be thinking about me, not him.

I didn't want her to come back to me just because I offered her a ring, though. I wanted her to want me. Really want me, the same way I wanted her. *No, needed her.* When she had left it felt like I was suffocating. It was all consuming and terrifying.

I opened up my new desk drawer, put the ring inside, and closed the drawer again. One day I would propose to her. When the thought didn't make my pulse race. I knew I wanted forever with her. But it was too much too soon. I wanted to take my time with Bee. I wanted to enjoy each and every second of every day.

Which was why naming the company after her and asking her to be my partner was a big step in itself. And that felt right. The timing fit for that. And just seeing her face light up made me smile. She deserved half too. It was her idea that had kick started everything. My goal ever since I graduated from college was to start my own agency. Who knew I just needed to fall in love in order to finally get my priorities straight?

I looked around the large office. I was excited to get another desk in here and to share this office with Bee. Most couples probably felt anxious about being with their significant other every second of every day. But it's all I wanted. Being able to close the blinds and have her whenever I wanted wouldn't be so bad either.

I tightened my tie and stood up, pulling on my suit jacket. Not more lies or games or any of that. From now on, I was going to tell Bee the truth. It wasn't something I was used to doing. But I wasn't going to risk losing her again. I had full confidence that we could grow this business together. I had full confidence that she was my future. But before I could jump in, I needed to hear her say it too. I wasn't going to break her heart. I was terrified that she was going to break mine, though.

***

I knocked on the door and Kendra opened it.

She had a huge smile on her face. "You won her back, huh?"

"It was probably all the flowers."

"Probably."

"Are you having fun preparing for your interview tomorrow?" I asked.

"Psh. I'm pretty sure my best friend is going to hire me. She likes working with me too."

"Thanks for helping me out."

"Of course. We had her totally fooled, right? Was she surprised you were the new boss?"

"I don't think it even crossed her mind."

"You know, you're really not so bad, Mason. I had you all wrong."

"You didn't. But Bee changed me."

"Ugh. I hate Valentine's Day. All of that romantic crap. It makes me want to throw up."

I laughed, but my laughter stopped when Bee stepped out of her bedroom. She really did take my breath away. She was wearing the red dress I had bought her for the Silver Gala. Hopefully tonight would end the way I had planned, unlike the last time she had worn it. She had curled her hair and it draped over her bare shoulders. Her smile seemed to have a direct effect on my groin. I was used to having her a few times a day. It had been way, way too long.

"You look beautiful."

Her cheeks blushed in that way that made my chest feel tight. I welcomed the feeling now. It was the feeling that kept me going now.

"You look very handsome," she said and smiled up at me.

"Vomiting over here!" Kendra yelled from the living room.

I grabbed Bee's jacket and her hand and pulled her out of the apartment. "Come on. There's something we need to do together."

"What is it?"

"A New York City Valentine's Day tradition. Despite what you said before, you do belong here. New York is better off with a girl like you. So I'm going to make sure you become an official New Yorker tonight."

"An official New Yorker?"

"Mhm." We stepped out onto the street. It had started to snow. Bee's fingers tightened around my hand. I loved how her hand fit perfectly in mine.

"Is that for us?" She was staring at the horse drawn carriage in front of us.

"The first thing is a late night carriage ride through Central Park." I grabbed her hand as she stepped up into the carriage. I scooted in next to her and pulled the blanket onto our lap. "Have you ever been in one of these?"

"No."

I put my arm across her shoulders. "It's super touristy, but it's kind of a stepping stone toward being an official New Yorker too."

"Is that so?"

I pulled her in even closer as the horses started to trot forward. "Yeah. And honestly, I've never been on one of these either. I've been posing as a true New Yorker this whole time."

Bee laughed. "So why haven't you been on one before?"

"I've never had anyone I wanted to go on one with." I smiled down at her.

"You have all the right lines, Mason Caldwell."

"Does that mean you want to be my girlfriend again? I'm pretty sure we had the shortest relationship in the history of relationships."

"Yeah, I didn't even get to tell anyone that you were my boyfriend. I like saying that."

"I've been referring to you as my girlfriend for awhile now. I don't know why I didn't just talk to you about it. I've been kind of a mess."

"You've been distracted."

"Maybe." I ran my hand up and down her arm. "Speaking of telling people, I talked to my parents while you were M.I.A."

"You did?" She pulled back slightly. "About your argument, or about us, or what?"

"All of it. They want to meet you. If you still want to meet them."

"Of course I want to meet them. Do you think they'll like me?"

"I think they're going to love you. When I told them I had a girlfriend my mom got so excited. Just say the word and we can meet up with them somewhere for dinner one night. Or you can see where I grew up."

"Do they have embarrassing pictures of you all over the house?"

"No." I laughed.

"Really? Geez there are so many horrible pictures of me at my house."

"Now I kind of want to see that." I squeezed her shoulder.

"You want to meet my mom?"

"I'd love to meet your mom."

"You're just diving head first into this thing now, aren't you?"

"This past week, I've found out what it's like when you're not a part of my life. I hated every second of it. I'm all in, Bee." *Say it back.* I needed to hear her say it. That she wanted to be with me as much as I wanted to be with her. All my cards were on the table. Each second that passed made my heart beat a little faster. *Say it back, baby.*

"I'm all in too." She leaned against my shoulder. "I feel the exact same way."

I couldn't help the sigh that escaped from my mouth. *Okay.* I rested my head on top of hers. Now that I had gotten through the hardest part, we could have some fun. I loved that dress on her, but I probably should have told her to wear pants.

Chapter 67
Bee

I laughed as I started to fall again. Mason grabbed my hips to steady me, but I was already sliding forward on the ice. I ran straight into his chest, making him topple backwards as his skates slid out from underneath of him. I laughed as I fell down on top of his chest.

"Ow," Mason groaned. He was slightly out of breath and his nose was pink from the cold. It was still flurrying and I wished I could capture this moment forever. He looked so handsome and happy. I had been so worried that I wouldn't be enough for him. But he had made all my worries go away with our conversations earlier. He wanted a future with me. Or he wouldn't have asked me to be his business partner.

"Sorry." I smiled down at him.

"I'm pretty sure you broke my ass."

"No! One of my favorite parts of you!"

He laughed and sat up. "How does hot chocolate sound?"

"Perfect." I stumbled onto my feet. It was hard skating in the long dress, but it had still been fun. I reached my hand out to help him up. He grabbed it and pulled me back down on top of him.

"Are you trying to break my ass too?"

"I would never. That is my favorite part of you."

"You're a butt guy? How did I not know that?"

He shrugged. "I'm a Bee guy. Now let's go get some hot chocolate. I'm freezing."

We both got to our feet and skated off the rink, hand in hand. I sat down on the bench and undid my skates as he bought hot chocolate at the refreshment stand. He had said he had done this before with his mom and his brother when he was little. But again, no one special later in his life. The thought of me being his first love made me feel warm. I didn't even need hot chocolate. It did feel good when he put the cup into my hands, but maybe it was more the gesture than the warmth from the cup. He was taking care of me. He was showing me a romantic side of New York that I hadn't experienced. He was trying to tell me I belonged. Maybe even more so with him than in this city. I wasn't sure why he was trying so hard to convince me. I had been convinced a long time ago.

But I had run. I hadn't meant to hurt him. I never wanted to hurt him.

"You okay?" he asked as he put his arm around my shoulders. "I didn't actually break your ass did I?"

I laughed. "No. You didn't. Mason?"

"Yeah?"

"What did your dad say about the fight you had? About wanting to take over his business?"

"You were right. They're proud of me."

The way he said it sounded strange. Like he didn't really believe it. "Is that what they said?"

"Yeah. It was weird. I've spent so many years resenting them. I've been such an idiot. My dad just wanted what was best for me. He thought that was taking over the family business. He didn't know about all my dreams. Because I didn't tell them. I shut them out."

"They didn't know you wanted to start an advertising agency?"

"No. They knew I wanted to work in advertising." He laughed and shook his head. "My dad said I had turned out just like him after all. And he was excited to have another entrepreneur in the family. I didn't think that would be their reaction."

"Why did they cut you off then?"

"They wanted me to come back. Or maybe they just disapproved of my lifestyle. A combination maybe? It was just a misunderstanding. They were really excited to hear about you too. Almost as excited about hearing about the new company."

"Did you tell them about splitting it with me?"

"Splitting it? Who said anything about splitting it?"

"Oh. Sorry. I didn't mean..."

"I'm just kidding. Of course we're splitting it. And I didn't tell them about that. I'll let them meet you first. They'll get it." He smiled down at me.

"You don't have to do it, you know. You could just give me a normal position at the company. With Kendra or something. I don't need to share the business with you. I just want you. I don't want all that."

"I want to do it with you." He squeezed my shoulder. "Besides, I was getting really excited about the idea of sharing an office with you."

"It's too much, Mason."

"It's not like I'm going to let you skate by. You'll have to do half the work. I'm good with my decision. It's what I want. But if it's not what you want, we can talk about it."

"I won't be holding you back?"

"You won't be holding me back."

I smiled and looked up at the snowflakes falling down on us. The sky had an orangey glow to it. "You named your new company after me."

"I find you kind of inspiring, Bee. Now, there's one more part to the night. We can count snowflakes on our tongues on the way to the taxi."

I laughed and stood up. He remembered what I always did with my mom in the snow.

***

"Do I have to keep wearing this?"

"Yes," Mason said as he grabbed my hand, pulling me out of the taxi.

"I can't see anything."

"That's kind of the point, baby." He lightly grazed the side of my cheek with his lips. He had undone his tie and blindfolded me with it in the car.

"If this involves jumping off the Brooklyn Bridge into freezing cold water, I'm not sure I want to be an official New Yorker."

"Nothing that crazy, I promise."

"Have you done this before?"

"Blindfolded a woman and lead her toward the icy waters of the East River? Only a dozen times."

I meant to shove his chest but my hand landed on his abs. God I loved his abs.

"You're getting a little ahead of yourself there. That's the after party."

I laughed, but kept my hand on his abs. It helped me walk forward a little less shakily.

"Whatever it is we're actually doing, have you done it before?"

"I've been here before, yes. Not like this, though."

I heard something ding and then suddenly I wasn't cold anymore. We must have stepped inside a building. "Are we just back at your place?"

"So eager." He lead me farther into the building and then we stopped.

"Ah!" I almost fell over when the floor started moving.

Mason laughed. "It's just an elevator, Bee. You're okay." He had pressed my back against the side of the elevator.

My fingers were gripping his shirt tightly. I tilted my head up even though I couldn't see him.

"You know?" He kissed the side of my neck.

It felt like I could melt onto the elevator floor.

"The last time I had you in this dress, I had pictured doing all sorts of unspeakable things to you." He kissed my neck a little lower.

"Unspeakable?"

"Your favorite." He lightly bit my earlobe.

A small moan escaped from my lips.

"But not yet, baby. Not until you're a real New Yorker."

"You don't want me right now?"

"You should see the way the other people in the elevator are looking at you right now."

"What? Mason!"

He silenced me with a kiss. A kiss that made the tips of my fingers and toes tingle. He pulled away far too soon.

"We're alone." His voice was low. He had missed this too. "But we still have a few things to talk about."

The elevator doors dinged and I felt a blast of cold air hit me. Mason quickly wrapped his arms around me again.

"Where are we?" It was freezing. Way colder than it had been before. The wind whipped through my hair. We had to be up high somewhere.

"Bee." Mason pulled us to a stop and put his hands on either of my shoulders. "I could say all that cliché stuff about you being the other half of me and all that. And it is true in a sense. I'm a better version of myself when you're around. I'm not even sure I like the guy who I am without you in my life. But all of this is new to me. This feeling is new."

Holy shit, is he going to propose? I didn't want him to propose. I wanted to enjoy where we were. I didn't want to rush this feeling. We had our whole lives for that. I did want him in every way possible. But not like this. Not because he was scared I'd walk away again. I wasn't going to do that. "Mason..."

"But it's a little of an understatement to say I have commitment issues. I know you want the whole white dress and a ring thing, but I'm not ready for that. And I'd be lying if I said I was. I know how I feel. And I'm hoping that's enough. I'm never letting go of this feeling. You're all that I think about. But I need more time for all that. I want to take things slowly with you. I like taking things slow."

It was like he had just hit every worry. My tears felt icy as they fell down my cheeks. I wished he would take my blindfold off. I wanted to see him. "I have commitment issues too. I'm terrified of love because I'm terrified of losing it."

"You're not going to lose me."

"I don't want you to make promises you can't keep."

"I'm not going to break any promises I make you. I'm not letting you go. I'm never letting you go." He pulled the blindfold down my face.

The whole city stretched out beneath us, completely lit up in the night, covered in a blanket of freshly fallen snow. It was beautiful.

"Because this is how you make me feel. Like I'm on the top of the world. And when I let you walk away, it felt like I was freefalling from this building. I've never felt so alone before."

"Me too. I mean, not falling, because I've never been up here." I smiled up at him. "I just felt really, really cold. Like your arms were the only thing that could ever warm me again."

"I don't want to be alone anymore, Bee. I want to be with you. Ever since I've met you, I haven't been able to stop thinking about you. And I'm so sick of standing still. I said a lot of things I didn't mean the other day. I think I was just scared to tell you I loved you because of all the stupid shit I had done. Telling you and then you walking out seemed unbearable. So I just said all these terrible things. But it didn't make it any less painful. I still had those feelings even though I didn't tell you."

"It's okay, I think I was kind of easy."

He laughed. "Because I couldn't keep my hands off you. I knew what I was doing, and I knew what I wanted. But you were anything but easy."

I smiled up at him. He had snowflakes in his hair and his nose was still pink from the cold. I wasn't sure I had ever seen him more handsome.

"I know I was a mess when you met me. I'm still a mess. I think part of what took me so long to realize I was in love with you was because I couldn't believe you could possibly love me. You deserve better than me, Bee. You deserve..."

"A great love. You're my great love. You make me feel like this too." I glanced back at the horizon stretched out before us. "Like I'm on top of the world. I've never felt that way before."

"You haven't?"

"Never."

"Well that's good. I already had a moving company pick up all your boxes and bring them back to our apartment."

"So cocky."

He grinned. "Yes...I am." He glanced down at his pants and then back up at me.

"We've had this conversation before, Mason. That is not what cocky means."

"Isn't it though?"

"No. You always make everything dirty."

"Welcome to the city of sin, baby."

I laughed. "Does that mean I'm an official New Yorker?"

"A kiss at the top of the Empire State Building on Valentine's Day seals the deal. Do you think you're ready to hold that title?"

His question was deeper than just about being a New Yorker. It was about being his business partner. It was about being his. I was all in. It was time to start our life together. And I couldn't imagine my life without him. He had given me my dream job, but more importantly he had given me himself. He had opened up to me in a way I didn't even know he was capable of. I had gotten everything that I had ever wanted. "I'm so ready." *Take that, New York.*

He leaned down and kissed me, making my whole body feel warm with the delicious sparks that that only he could give me.

And I knew it didn't matter where we were. Whether we were at the top of the Empire State Building or in the middle of Central Park. Wherever he was, that was home.

Epilogue

Mason

My best friend was finally getting hitched. I still wasn't sure why James hadn't asked me to be his best man though. The best man was supposed to be a best *friend*. Not a little brother. I took another sip of my scotch as we waited for Rob to arrive. Another reason why Rob shouldn't be the best man...he didn't value the functionality of a watch.

"We should already be on the way to James' office," Matt said, checking his Rolex.

See. Matt understood the concept of time. "This is why I should have been the best man."

Matt laughed. "You gotta let that go. James isn't going to change his mind."

I ignored him and took another sip of scotch.

"Look at it this way," Matt said. "When you marry Bee, who are you going to ask to be your best man?" He pointed to his chest.

"But that's different."

He laughed. "How is that different? Rob's my best friend, but I'm still going to ask you to be my best man. You're going to ask me, just like I'm going to ask you. Just like James asked Rob and Rob will ask James. You're just butthurt that you don't get to host the bachelor party at your new club."

"I'm not butthurt." What the hell was he talking about? My ass was fine. "But yeah, I pushed up the opening date so that we could celebrate there. And now not only did Rob finalize the bachelor party plans without me, but he also didn't give me enough notice to cancel the opening night of Club Onyx. I'm going to miss it." I was the king of bachelor parties. *Ask any male on the Upper East Side.* I'd had this party planned to a T, despite James and Bee's concerns. If I wasn't allowed to be the best man, I could at least throw the best damned bachelor party ever. And I thought Rob and I were on the same page...until he finalized the itinerary at the last moment.

"There will be plenty of parties there. No worries."

He didn't get it. Bee Inspired Media Group was doing amazing. But Club Onyx was a fun side project Bee and I were doing together. A top-secret, exclusive club. Not even Matt knew all the particulars. He also didn't know that Bee was involved with the planning. After I called it quits on my underground dealings, we thought it would be fun to start something on the up and up. Together. Just...hushed.

"Will Bee be attending the grand opening without you this weekend?"

I almost spit out my scotch. "What? No. She doesn't..."

"I know that she knows. Obviously she knows. The two of you are glued to the hip."

I opened my mouth and then closed it again. There was no point in lying to him if he already knew. "No, she won't be going without me."

"Are you sure about that? Maybe she's planning Penny's bachelorette party there. I can't even imagine all the crazy stuff they could get into."

I laughed. "No. She definitely wouldn't tell Penny about Club Onyx."

Matt shrugged. "Yeah, probably not. Penny's too innocent for something like that." He looked down at his glass.

Recently Matt had been saying weird shit like that. Smart remarks about Penny and James. He was giving me a lot of shit when it seemed like he was upset about something too. Maybe he was pissed he wasn't James' best man either. Before I could ask him about it, he started talking again.

"So who's holding down the fort for opening weekend if you two aren't attending?"

"Our business partner, Tanner Rhodes."

"Tanner Rhodes?" Rob asked and clapped me on the back.

I glanced at my watch to verify that Rob was over twenty minutes late. *Turd.* Okay, fine. Maybe I was a little jealous that he was the best man.

"I don't trust that guy," Rob said. "He seems...off."

"Tanner?" I shook my head. "You just have to get to know him. He's cool. And I'm pretty sure he has infinite funds, which means he's a great business partner."

"Maybe so. But I swear I saw him wearing elf shaped Crocs the other day outside that new sex club you're starting with Bee."

Rob knows too? How the hell does everyone know Bee's involved in this? "Bee isn't part of..."

Rob pretended to crack a whip and made the accompanying whooshing noise. "Of course she is. You do everything together."

"Whatever, you're both just jealous that I'm in love." After the words fell out of my mouth I instantly regretted them. Not just because they were cheesy as hell, but because Rob chuckled and Matt started laughing hysterically.

"Right," Matt said. "Because being in love is better than..." he scanned the bar for a victim. "Fucking that brunette's brains out."

I didn't even bother turning to see who he was talking about. I had my girl. And these two idiots just weren't getting it. "You'll both see. One day you'll want to settle down and you'll understand."

Instead of laughing, Rob just shrugged. And then he abruptly changed the topic. "Sorry I was late, by the way. I got stuck in traffic. I really need to move back to the city."

That was a weird segue.

"And I'm sorry about the last minute change of plans," Rob said. "I just really needed to get out of the country for a bit. Do you ever find that you kinda get stuck in a rut with your routine? I feel like I need a change. I'm getting restless in Newark."

Matt and I exchanged looks. What was up with Rob tonight? He'd usually be the first to make some crude remark about the brunette in the corner. And he rarely ever tried to start philosophical discussions. Yes, I joked around with Rob about him being immature and annoying. But only because I viewed him like another little brother. We weren't just friends. We were family. Which meant his odd behavior had me a little worried. "You okay?" I asked.

"What?" Rob smiled like he always did. It was rare not to see a smile on his face. Like it was rare not to see his older brother scowling. "Yeah, I'm good. Of course. And I brought everything we need for the kidnapping." He tapped his satchel. "We should probably get going before James leaves for work. I want to make sure we take him by surprise. And our flight leaves in...well, it'll wait I guess." He smiled again.

Luckily we weren't flying commercial, or Rob definitely would have made us miss our flight. But I wasn't really worried about his lack of time management anymore. Something was seriously up with him. He'd seemed fine when he got here. So... *Holy shit*. I stared at him. It was my love comment that made him act weird. Not joking around about the brunette. Feeling like he was restless? I was pretty sure Rob was ready to settle down. But instead of saying anything, I kept my mouth shut. The last thing he needed was for me to joke around about it. Especially if he didn't even realize what he was missing yet.

I closed our tab and followed him and Matt out to the town car. It was only a few minutes before we arrived at James' office building. We all stepped out of the car and grabbed the necessities out of Rob's satchel.

"Let's go scare the shit out of our best friend. The bachelor party starts...now!" I pulled on the black mask in the middle of the busy New York City sidewalk.

Rob laughed and pulled on his mask too. Matt followed suit.

Maybe this weekend officially marked the end of James' being a bachelor. But I had a feeling Rob would be following his lead soon. *You never know.* Maybe he'd find someone at the Blue Parrot Resort this weekend. After all, all the best love stories always begin with a good old-fashioned kidnapping. Or something like that…

I lifted my very-real-looking fake gun. Rob was notoriously good at getting arrested for stupid shit just like this. *Please don't let me end up in prison.* Bee would seriously kill me if she had to bail me out of jail.

"This is a hold up!" Rob yelled as we burst through the doors of the first floor.

A few women who were leaving for the day screamed and ran outside.

Yeah…we were definitely going to get arrested this weekend.

About the Author

Ivy Smoak is a bestselling New Adult Romance author. When she's not writing, you can find her binge watching too many TV shows, taking long walks, playing outside, and generally refusing to act like an adult. She lives with her husband in Delaware.

Twitter: @IvySmoakAuthor
Facebook: IvySmoakAuthor
Goodreads: IvySmoak

Made in the USA
Monee, IL
24 May 2020